GREEN LIGHT TO KILL

GREEN LIGHT TO KILL

A
Richard Leon
Noir Novel

authorHOUSE®

AuthorHouse™
1663 Liberty Drive
Bloomington, IN 47403
www.authorhouse.com
Phone: 1-800-839-8640

Published by AuthorHouse 08/29/2015

ISBN: 978-1-4817-6784-2 (sc)
ISBN: 978-1-4817-6783-5 (e)

Library of Congress Control Number: 2013911407

Print information available on the last page.

This book is printed on acid-free paper.

For Lonnell who loved me when no one else would and on days when I didn't deserve it, thank you for Mercedes and Saladin.

And thanks for that love.

I would like to acknowledge my good friends Aleksandr Garber for believing in me and for his assistance and Jeff Stockstill for his encouragement.

And my daughter Mercedes for making this novel happen.

Prologue

No Jokes

Christmas Eve 2008

New York City; Isla de la Juventud, Cuba

JASPER BOHANNON, AMERICA'S first black elected president along with his wife Carmen, who was heavy with child, sat on the floor in their Upper Westside apartment, where they wrapped Christmas gifts for their two daughters.

She asked him: "Jas do you realize our son will be the first baby born in the White House since John John, President Kennedy's son?" Jasper Bohannon looked up and answered, "I hadn't thought about it, Carmen, but that's incredible, are you sure?"

"You know I've done my research."

"Yes, you're very thorough, a walking encyclopedia."

"I'm just a warehouse of useless information." They laughed and he said: "Have you decided on a name yet?"

"I've narrowed it down to Martin and Randolph. Which do you prefer?"

"Whatever you decide will be perfect, honey, you let me select the girls' names so it's only fair that you name our son."

"I'm leaning toward Randolph, I've always like the sound of Randy."

"It does have a ring to it."

A cold winter rain drummed on the window and she looked out at the cityscape: "It would be delightful if this rain turned to snow the girls would love it!"

"The proverbial white Christmas would be perfect. Let's listen to Bing Crosby's *White Christmas* maybe that'll speed things along."

Carmen smiled: "What an excellent suggestion," stood up, padded across the room, say'n: "If it does maybe we could take the girls to Central Park and let them romp in the snow."

He told her, "The Secret Service would be extremely nervous about that, dear. Moments like that are histories now, Carmen."

"I guess you're right, privacy's in our rearview." She shuffled through a stack of CD's, located Crosby's and inserted it. Bing's rich baritone filled the room. The president elect's Codex 4 went. He rose from the floor, crossed to the credenza where the Codex chirped its unique sound, he noticed the name on the caller ID and said: "It's President Murphy."

Carmen said back, "Maybe he's calling to wish us a Merry Christmas," as she turned Bing down.

"Not on this line," he picked up: "Good evening, Mister President and Merry Christmas." Two-term President James Murphy replied, "Thank you and the same to you and your family." This was the first time they had spoken since he called him on election night to congratulate him on his victory over Republican Senator Jake Carlisle.

President Murphy said: "I wanted to alert you to an operation that's taking place tonight."

"Which operation would that be?" Jasper Bohannon demanded as he motioned for Carmen to leave the room. She slipped past him, dodged around the corner, went into the den and closed the door.

"I'm sending the Eradicators in to Cuba to arrest Dimitar Spasića, a Serbian warlord whose been hiding out an island off the southern coast of Cuba."

"Eradicators?" Jasper Bohannon inquired hearing the name for the first time.

"They're the ultimate secret White House unit that will be at your disposal to do the heavy lifting that the CIA, the SEALs and the Rangers can't handle. Their mission is to do whatever the president deems necessary to protect the internal and external security of the United States."

"Who else knows about them?"

"Only the president, General Sam Falk, he's the head of the unit, the Head of Homeland Security and of course your Chief of Staff will be privy to their existence. No one on the Hill knows about them, they're that secret."

"Who authorized this?"

"They've been operational since the Eisenhower administration. It's been whispered they were the brain child of Allen Dulles himself."

"That long and they've remained a secret, that's hard to do in Washington."

"I agree. They're stationed at an ultra secured area near Quantico. They are an elite Marine Force Recon unit. The most skilled fighting men we have in our quiver. It's takes three to four years of training to be a force recon man. They're tougher than the SEALs and the Rangers combined. They're assassins for the lack of a better term."

"Sounds impressive."

"As my son would say these guys are no jokes." Jasper Bohannon laughed and asked, "What's the purpose of this mission?"

"We have a working agreement with the UN and we loan out the Eradicators when asked by the Secretary General. The UN issued an international arrest warrant for this Spasića character for crimes against humanity. During the Balkans conflict he was a super nasty guy, he ordered the killing of thousands of Croatians and Albanian Muslims. The UN has been trying to find him for fifteen years but to no avail. But the CIA received proof positive info that he's been hiding out on Isla de la Juventud since late last year."

"Is this information reliable?"

"The CIA turned a high Cuban official who told them about his whereabouts. So I ordered the Eradicators to go in and bring him to

Guantanamo where he'll be turned over to the UN," President Murphy told him.

He carried on: "The team will jump into Cuba within the hour. I'll let you know the outcome."

Jasper Bohannon said: "I appreciate you telling me this I want to be as current as possible when I assume the presidency," and the president told him, "Not a problem and one final thing Jasper, you need to be extremely watchful of Jake Carlisle, he's taken his defeat personally and he will be your toughest opposition on the Hill. He's known to be a sore loser and very vicious when he doesn't get his way."

"Thanks for clearing the sky for me on that one, Mister President."

"You're welcome and good evening and try to enjoy your Christmas, it's the last one you'll have that will be private, and after this you belong to the public."

"Understood," Republican James Murphy switched off. Democrat Jasper Bohannon called Carmen back in to finish wrap'n Christmas morning thrills.

AT THAT SAME moment Captain Clark pushed the throttles forward and the C-130 raced down the runway and lifted into the night sky. The Hercules ascended to 10,000 feet and leveled off. The captain spoke over the intercom: "Staff Sergeant McLain you can commence the decompression process." The sergeant came back: "Roger that, sir." The moon shone bright as they cruised west headed toward Isla de la Juventud.

Sergeant McLain, the physiology tech, approached Major Shamus "Skeeter" Macklin say'n: "Sir, it's time to gear up." Skeeter said, "Well be about it," donned his full face mask with microphone and the PT starting checking each man's oxygen equipment to make sure everything operated properly. They in turn put on their masks. Satisfied he spoke to Captain Clark: "Everything's good to go back here, sir." The captain acknowledged: 'Thanks McLain," and pulled back on the controls and the plane rose steadily to 35,000 feet, the launch altitude for the Eradicators' HAHO jump.

The drone of the C-130's turboprops played loud in the cabin and Skeeter Macklin spoke into his microphone above the din: "This mission is a crucial operation ordered by the president, we're to go in and snatch this Spasića bastard and bring him back to Gitmo, alive". He looked at his second in command and his best friend, Captain Mickey Stovall: "Mick this operation won't be as difficult as the one we did in the Libya last year, remember?"

Although they were best friends, Mickey always addressed Skeeter as *sir* in the presence of the men, "Yes sir, that was a real ball buster," which was the understatement of the year. Skeeter Macklin led a team on a snatch and grab mission in the Sahara. They were ordered to seize a notorious Afghan drug trafficker wanted by the US as a major heroin supplier hid'n among a local Bedouin tribe. The mission went south due to faulty Intel the analyses at Langley had guaranteed Omar Khan would be at a site fifty miles south of Benghazi, but the analyses had failed to consider Bedouins are nomadic and frequently move their camps. They disembarked from a sub stationed in the Gulf of Sidra and came ashore via Zodiacs. They set out under the cover of darkness and force marched inland to where the CIA said Khan would be, but unbeknown to the Agency the Bedouins struck camp two hours earlier and headed east farther into the desert. Skeeter Macklin had to decide whether to abort or pursue.

Major Macklin spoke to his twelve man squad: "Men, I've decided to continue the mission; we've come too far to turn back now." He pointed to a corporal, "Finch take five men double back to that farm we passed about two clicks ago and commandeer eleven of the horses in the corral and catch up with us as quickly as possible. If you meet any resistance from the owner give him this chit and tell him we'll return his horses posthaste," he handed the promissory note to him, "and Finch station two men there to make sure no one tries to contact anyone. And disable any means of communicate you may find." Finch took the chit and placed it in his breast pocket and said: "Aye, aye sir." He turned to the others and asked: "Any of you have experience dealing with horses?" Two men raised their hands, Finch said: "OK Smith, Vargas come with me, Michaels and Forte fall in with us." Finch threw up a salute and Skeeter saluted back and the group raced off head'n to the rear.

Skeeter Macklin turned to his remaining men and said, "Alright let's move out on the double." There was a chorus of, "Aye, aye sir." Skeeter took the point and the others fell in behind him in single file follow'n the tracks in the deep, deep sand.

The full moon lit the way as the unit trekked farther into the desert. The four meter high dunes made the going arduous to say the least. After an hour Skeeter ordered the men to halt and to take a ten minute break. They collapsed on the desert floor. They were spent and immediately grabbed their canteens and started gulp'n water.

The officers moved away separating themselves to discuss the situation out of ear shot of the troops. Both men were out of breath and Mickey Stovall took a long swig and said, "Skeeter this sand's a bitch, how far to you think we've come?"

"I'd say about two clicks at best."

"That's all, my calves are burning."

"Drink Mick, drink," Skeeter Macklin told him and then said, "Finch should be at the farm by now, on horseback they should catch up with us in about an hour. Those Arabians are bred for this shit."

"I don't know how these Bedouins can survive in this environment."

"They've been here for eons, it's in their DNA," Skeeter Macklin told him, Mickey Stovall told him back: "I don't know how they can do it without any Bud Light."

Skeeter Macklin cracked a faint smile: "Mick I swear you're a card, one of a kind. Give the men another five minutes and let's get back to it." Mickey shouted over this shoulder, "Men we hit the trail in five," after five minutes had elapsed Mickey Stovall called out: "Alright men fall in and let's move out." They rose to their feet and fell in behind the officers and went on after Omar Khan and his Bedouin protectors.

MEANWHIILE, FINCH AND the others had reached the farm. He started bam'n on the door. It swung open and the old man eyes widened when he saw the heavily armed Finch standing before him. Finch took a stab at the old man understanding English and said, "Good evening, sir, sorry to disturb you but we need to borrow several of your horses."

Surprisingly, the old man understood perfectly, he started to object but thought better of it noticing the others positioned behind Finch with their weapons trained on him, so he nodded his approval.

"Thanks." Finch being as polite as possible said, "Sir, I hope you don't mind if we make a quick search of your home." What could the old man do but comply, so he nodded again and Finch spoke with Forte: "Make a thorough search for any kind of weapons and disable any phones or whatnots, most Ricky tick." Forte responded as ordered, brush aside the old man and made a tour of the four room house. The old man's wife put up a protest in Arabic, calling them swine; the old man said something to her in their tongue and silenced her.

Forte completed his search and reported back to Finch: "No weapons or phones, Corporal."

"Great - Forte, you and Michaels remain here and stay alert."

"Roger that."

Finch led the rest to the corral, opened the gate and they shuffled in among the Arabians. Vargas, raised in New Mexico, had no problem culling out eleven. He and Smith put saddles on them. Finch pulled the chit out of his breast pocket, handed it to the old man, then the four marines swung up into the saddles, put their heels into the horses' flanks and headed out at a gallop with more Arabians strung behind, the old man stared at the chit, looked up and watched his horses fade to black.

An hour or so later they caught up with Major Macklin's group who were most relieved when they saw them approach. Finch reported what happened at the farm and Skeeter told him: "Well done, now let's get after these guys." Skeeter Macklin, Mickey Stovall and the other marines saddled up and rode out after Omar Khan.

It was almost two in the morning when they came over a dune and spotted the camp fires in the distance about a mile away. Skeeter signaled halt. Everyone dismounted. Skeeter told Vargas and Smith, "Remain here with the horses and keep them quiet, and be ready to book as soon as we return with Khan." He led his men on foot toward the Bedouin encampment.

Soon after they reached the top of a tall dune, everyone laid prone Skeeter Macklin flipped his night vision monocular down to his eye and panned the camp below. All was quiet at the oasis. A lone Bedouin moved about as he placed wood on the fires. Skeeter signaled Mickey Stovall to take the team and set up a perimeter around the camp. They fanned out and took up firing positions. Skeeter Macklin crept slowly forward toward the tents and moved past camels squatted on the ground. He heard a tent flap rustle, as luck would have it, Omar Khan in his distinctive Afghan cap came out and made for a stand of trees and started to relieve himself.

Skeeter Macklin crept up behind Omar Khan, stood and placed his arm around his neck and started squeezing, Khan reached up and tried to break Skeeter's hold, and he struggled briefly before he passed out. Skeeter eased him down, placed duct tape over his mouth, secured his hands behind him, hoisted him over his shoulder and moved back though the trees to Mickey Stovall's position and said: "That was painless let's clear out." The marines returned to where the horses waited, he lifted Khan over one; they swung themselves into the saddles and raced back to the farmhouse to pick up Forte and Michaels. The Arabians moved with considerable ease up and over the dunes at a full gallop. They arrive at the farm, collected the men. Skeeter thanked the old man and handed him a wad of hundred dollar bills, the old man's eyes lit up, Skeeter ask him to accompany them back to the Gulf of Sidra so he could bring his horses back to his farm. The old man happily went along and the group galloped to the Mediterranean with Omar Khan. There they were met by sailors from the sub, climbed into the Zodiacs and left Libya with their prize. No harm, no foul, mission accomplished.

THE C-130 SHOOK as the plane flew west through turbulence toward Isla de la Juventud. Skeeter glanced around the cabin to see if any of his men showed signs of oxygen depletion. McLain, the PT moved about checking each man's supplemental oxygen settings, made certain everyone was receiving one hundred percent oxygen as the Hercules approached its 35,000 feet launch altitude.

The radar operator studied the screen as it traversed; he noticed a heavy cloud formation over the Caribbean. He switched on the intercom to address Captain Clark, "Sir, radar indicates there's a strong weather system build up over the Caribbean headed directly toward the LZ."

Captain Clark: "Roger that."

He switched on the cabin intercom and announced to the Eradicators: "Listen up; radar indicates a strong weather system is moving toward the drop zone at fifteen miles per hour, which suggests you'll be jumping into violent weather activity. Major Macklin please pick up the direct line to the cockpit."

Skeeter rose, padded forward and unhooked the mike: "Macklin here."

"Sir, radar informed me there's a severe storm heading directly over your LZ. Do you want to abort?"

"No, continue on course." Skeeter said as a matter of fact.

"Sir, I strongly suggest you reconsider, this is a hazardous situation."

"Duly noted Captain, but proceed as planned."

"Sir..."

Skeeter Macklin rode over him: "Captain it's my call and I take full responsibility."

"Yes sir," the captain conceded, "continuing as ordered. We are ten minutes away from our stand off position, will advice accordingly."

"Very well Captain." Skeeter said and placed the mike back in its holder. He turned and strode back into the cabin. Mickey Stovall looked up and demanded, "Problem sir?"

"The captain was expressing his concern for our well being."

"Just like these sky hops always crying." Mickey Stovall spat out.

"Mick is there anyone who you approve of?"

"If they're not in this man's Crotch hell no. OoRAH!"

Skeeter Macklin bent down and whispered: "Mick you're sick," Mickey Stovall turned to face him: "I know," and flashed his grill. Skeeter rose up and spoke to the men.

"Settle down and listen up," they snapped to, "here's the skinny there's a violent thunderstorm approaching the LZ and we'll reach our stand off position within," he looked at his watch, "nine minutes. By my calculations the storm will pass directly over the LZ as we float in." He paused and looked at his men, reading them, he went on: "This is the most difficult scenario I can image. Even the knuckleheads back at the Pentagon couldn't dream this up. It's going to be one hell of a ride down, so get your game faces on and let's do this. They don't call us the Eradicators for nothing. We're going to come in like Batman but only we're coming in twelve deep." The men laughed, Mickey Stovall sported a wide grin and yelled: "OoRAH!" and the men echoed.

The flight crew heard the hilarity that came from the rear. Captain Clark said to his co pilot, "These guys have guts because they're nuts," the co pilot chuckled: "Spot on, sir," and returned to his duties.

Skeeter Macklin assessed things he knew he was lead'n them into an intense situation. This was going to be tough, not the objective but the jump. Snatch'n Spasića was the easy part. As a group they've done many missions like this before, but now the weather was the foe, nature itself, therein laid the rub.

He let his men shoot the shit keeping them loose and agile and not tight and apprehensive. His Batman joke seemed to have done the trick. Captain Clark's voice came over the intercom: "Approaching standoff position." Skeeter shouted: "Snap to," and the men including Mickey Stovall became battle ready.

THE LIGHT FROM the lamp on the night stand washed over Simona Martinez as she slept, after passing out from too much fun and too much rum. Dimitar Spasića, one of the most wanted men in the world, only Bin Laden and Al Zawahiri outranked him, stood over the bed and stared down at his twenty-three year old plaything and inhaled her beauty. He thought how fortunate he was to have her, this grand villa and all the trappings his stolen Serbian money could buy. Dimitar Spasića had everything but the freedom to come and go as he wished. He understood that could never be; he was confined to this island prison safe from everything but his past.

He climbed into bed next to Simona, kissed her forehead, placed his head on the pillow and quickly fell asleep unaware that someone was com'n to turn out the light, the party's over.

TWO MINUTES UNTIL standoff position," Captain Clark's voice came out over the intercom, "jumpers prepare to exit the plane."

Skeeter Macklin moved through the cabin past his men lined up at the rear ramp. He stopped and said to Mickey Stovall, "Let's get this done without any hiccups. This is my last jump and I don't want to lose anyone on my final mission."

Mickey Stovall's jaw dropped: "What do you mean this is your *final mission*."

"What part of final don't you understand?"

"Well this's a shocking revelation, when we hit the ground I want to hear your reasons."

"It's personal Mick, it's something I have to do."

"What about the team?"

"I'm leaving them in capable hands, yours." Mickey Stovall was about to protest but fell silent as the PT approached and triple checked his supplemental oxygen bottle to make sure as he had the others, that Mickey had no symptoms of hypoxia and decompression sickness. He stepped up to Skeeter, repeated the process. Satisfied everyone was fit to make their jumps he crossed the aisle and stood against the wall.

Captain Clark announced: "Fifteen seconds to stand off..., ten nine..." Skeeter now in front of the team kept his eyes on the red light, "four three..." the light went green, and Skeeter Macklin leaped out into the frigid black. One after another the Eradicators hopped and popped and followed him into the dark, their chutes deployed immediately as they filed in behind Skeeter in a stack formation descend'n to their LZ thirty five miles away.

The star spangled sky glowed white hot. Skeeter Macklin looked up over his shoulder to see if everyone was in proper descent attitude and then he looked at his GPS, the MA2-30 altimeter and his watch verifying they were on course and on time. A sickle moon peeked out from behind a hint of cloud and the wind picked up.

Each man's chute was meticulously apportioned so that all members' weight was identical so they would descend at the same rate of speed. The group maintained their horizontal plane as they floated silently onward to Nueva Gerona; a small village located about two clicks south of Dimitar Spasića's villa. Now fifteen miles from the LZ, Skeeter could see a large cloud formation over the island. He saw flashes of heat lightning briefly illuminate the black. The wind increased and they had to constantly pull on their toggles to maintain their course.

SHAMUS MACKLIN WAS a product of a proud Irish family from South Boston. The Macklins were among the first Irish to settle in America, long before the potato famine. One of his ancestors was killed during the Battle of Bunker Hill. His roots go back to the dawn of American independence.

The Macklin clan became staunch believers in the American concept. They had a literal adherence to the words expressed on the bedrock of Americanism, the Declaration of Independence and the Bill of Rights. The Macklins bled red, white and blue.

Throughout the course of US history, his family was in the forefront of just causes. They were prominent in the Abolition Movement Sean Macklin was a contemporary of Frederick Douglass. Several Macklins fought in the Civil War and marched with the suffragettes. Whenever there was a struggle for justice the Macklins was there doing their part to ensure everyone was afforded the opportunity to experience the length and breadth of democracy. They went against the grain during the busing troubles in South Boston in the 70's. The Macklins are quintessential Americans true practitioners of America the Beautiful, who crowned their good with brotherhood.

Shamus Macklin's parents died in a car accident his senior year in high school, being the only child he didn't have any immediate family so after graduation he enlisted in the Corps, which became his new family.

When he arrived at Parris Island, the skinny kid from Boston stepped off the bus, his head drill instructor, Gunnery Sergeant Winterhawk, a full blood Lakota walked up to Shamus and said: "You skinny little shit you need to suck you some blood, you little mosquito. I'm going name you Skeeter and I'm going to swat your ass every chance I get. Now get yourself over there and fall in with the rest of those maggots." Shamus Macklin did as ordered and fell in with the other recruits one of them snickered and whispered, "*Hey Skeeter*" and the name stuck.

After a brutal fifteen weeks, Skeeter added on thirty-nine pounds of fury and graduated from MCRD with honors. The Corps immediately assigned him to the Second Recon Battalion at Camp Lejeune. There the final honing transformed PFC Shamus Macklin into Skeeter the Mosquito who was out for blood.

THE TEAM NOW five miles from the LZ floated down toward Isla de la Juventud, they rapidly approached a large cumulonimbus cloud, the mature stage of the thunderstorm. Whips of lightning zigzagged across the sky in a freakish display. Loud bangs of thunder stunned the Eradicators within nanoseconds, Skeeter Macklin and his men felt their concussions. *Oh* the clamor. As they descended into the cloud the lightning and thunder intensified, the wind blew harder making it extremely difficult to stay on course. Inside the cloud heavy droplets pelted them, Skeeter was relieved it was rain they were encountering instead of hail, which could severely damage their canopies, possibly causing them to deflate or be punctured and put the team in extreme peril. If this were to happen the Eradicators would fall like stones and they'd have to deploy their reserve chutes and if these were damaged by the hail or failed to open the team would plummet to their deaths.

Now enshrouded in total darkness, only in cloud lightning provided brief moments of illumination, they could feel the heat as they continued downward. The bangs of thunder rocked their world. This was the most harrowing thing Skeeter had every encountered, even more terrify'n than the shock and awe campaign during Operation Iraqi Freedom, that was child's play compared to what he was going through tonight, when Skeeter's recon platoon HALO jumped into Baghdad head of the Coalition Forces. His recon unit performed green ops for the advance marine elements. His team reported Iraqi troop concentrations and movements to the Cobra helicopters, several times the green ops turned black and red hot when they had to engage Fedayeen Saddam irregular troops inside the city. His unit had to evade, fight and evade militia units as they kept HQ up to speed on the situation inside the city.

That was then but now this storm tested his will and he questioned his decision to proceed with this mission, but here he was leading his men through the madness. They finally emerged out of the cloud and continued down toward Dimitar Spasića's hideout. The downpour was intense as they approached five hundred feet, they came closer to the LZ, Skeeter felt his lead bag thud on the ground, and he landed seconds later. He gathered his canopy and saw his men come in behind him; he tried to count them as they landed. They repeated the process, gathered their equipment and Skeeter did a head count, he was relieved that all had survived. Mickey Stovall approached and said, "Sir, that was a horror movie starring us that was some super scary shit," and Skeeter Macklin said, "Mick you have a knack for understating everything, neither Stephen King nor Dean Koontz couldn't pen a story as horrifying as that. That was the most frightening thing I've ever encountered. Check on the men and see what their psychological state is and then form up and let's go get this bastard responsible for us having to endure that." Mickey shifted off to take roll call and then spoke to them individually, he could see the fear dissipate in their eyes, the rain continued to pour, satisfied everyone was okay, he told them: "Alright men that was baby shit you should have been with the major and me on a midnight run into Mosul now that was some serious shit, so get in gear and let's go get this clown," and they set out do just that.

They double timed through the rain toward Dimitar Spasića's villa compound. Lightning continued its electric dance and the thunder bangs masked their approach. Skeeter Macklin raised his arm halt'n the squad, crept up to a tree and peered around it out at the villa. The rain had caused Dimitar Spasića's security guards to seek shelter from the storm this was good, allowing the marines to creep into the compound unnoticed. Skeeter signaled to the group to advance and they crept forward, he motioned for three men to cover the entrance, he and the others scaled the wall and dropped silently to the ground, Skeeter Macklin eyes toured the area, saw two guards huddled under the verandah, a chink of light shone from a bedroom above and he signaled for someone to take care of them. Two jarheads slipped up behind the guards; they were quickly and quietly subdued.

Skeeter Macklin took out a floor plan of the villa, he recognized they were underneath Dimitar Spasića's bedroom where the light shone through the verandah doors. He whispered to Mickey Stovall, "Accompany me inside," Mickey nodded *OK* and they stepped through the front door, entered the foyer, all was quiet, they proceed to the staircase, went the steps arriving at the top they shifted soundlessly to Dimitar Spasića's bedroom door, stopped and listened, no sounds emitted from within Skeeter turned the doorknob, they entered the bedroom and saw him sleeping contently alongside Simona. Skeeter Macklin and Mickey Stovall stepped up, saw Dimitar Spasića's Glock 45 on the night stand, Skeeter took the gun, shoved it in his belt, turned out the light as a bang of thunder exploded above the villa, the noise startled Dimitar Spasića awake he looked up, lightning backlit Skeeter and Mickey, he tried to bring his eyes into focus, he asked, "Whose that?' and Mickey Stovall informed him: "It sure isn't Santa Claus you scumbag but you're a Christmas present for the UN," and shot him with his tranquilizer gun, Dimitar Spasića immediately passed out, Mickey zipper cuffed him and bound his hands behind him. Skeeter Macklin grabbed him, hoisted him over his shoulder and they exited the room, Simona continued to sleep through the storm and the abduction of her lover. They reached the ground floor, formed up with their team and left the compound headed to their rendezvous with a sub that waited for them about ten clicks out in the Caribbean. They started hump'n in that direction with Dimitar Spasića in tow.

DURING OPERATION DESERT Storm Corporal Skeeter Macklin along with the second reconnaissance platoon quick roped down from copters near the enemy lines. They were on high risk String Ray black ops to engage the vaulted Republican Guard and were ordered to direct artillery on the enemy's positions.

Lt. Simon Lewy led the unit toward the Iraqi lines and they came under intense fire from the enemy in trenches fronted by barbed wire, the scene smacked of WWI. The Iraqis opened up as the marines cut through the wire, Lt. Lewy and all of the senior noncoms were killed by RPG's, Skeeter Macklin saw the LT fall, assumed command, assessed the situation and he knew if they were to survive they had to get through the wire, flaming red hot tracers whined overhead. Skeeter aimed his laser on a spot in the wire, ordered everyone to lop grenades at that location the marines threw fifty frags and blew a path through the wire. He then ordered his men to heave smoke grenades far to the left and far to the right of their location to trick the Iraqis into thinking the marines would attack com'n out of the smoke, instead Skeeter shouted: "*ON MY LEAD*," jumped up and stormed through the gap with his men hard on his heels. Once they cleared the wire they spread out in a frontal attack formation and charged the trenches and caught the Iraqis off guard as they fired through the smoke filled area of the battleground. The marines bound over the parapets shoot'n and stabb'n as they went, once inside the trench they fanned out in two directions fight'n their way through the arteries until they secured the entire trench line in their sector. Skeeter grabbed the phone, called in 155mm rounds on the other trenches in the complex. The entire system was decimated by the barrage, when the smoke cleared quiet fell over the battlefield, Skeeter ordered his men to prepare to repel any Republican Guard counterattack, none came and they held their position until they were relieved by elements of the Second Marine Division, the regimental commander after hearing what Skeeter had done, awarded Corporal Shamus Macklin a battlefield commission and recommended him for the Silver Star. 2nd Louie Shamus Macklin earned his commission the old fashion way, he fought for it.

RAIN CONTINUED TO pour as the three Zodiacs laden with the Eradicators, Dimitar Spasića and navy coxswains churned over six foot swells headed to the submarine stationed somewhere off the Cuban coast. The wind blew hard causing the boats to struggle in the chops and helped dampen the sound com'n from the outboards. The boats rose and slammed down onto the waves add'n more water to the mix. Skeeter and his team held on tightly as they proceeded toward the USS *Key West* lying in wait farther out in the Caribbean.

No one spoke, what was the purpose if one couldn't be heard over the din whipped up by wind and sea. Dimitar Spasića bound and gagged with a bag over his head laid on his back as sea water washed in water boarding him, Skeeter Macklin looked down, watched as he struggled and gasped with each ensuing blast that came into the Zodiac. Skeeter cracked a smile as he laid there and endured the torture. He said in silence *this couldn't have happened to a better asshole,* a chuckle slipped past his lips, he was enjoying this oh so much. Off in the distance lightning flashed and thunder boomed. Again lightning briefly lit the dark and back lit an image to port. Skeeter Macklin looked up as lightning sparked once more and the image appeared again about a hundred yards away; Skeeter recognized the outline of a Cuban patrol boat. He signaled the coxswain to cut engine, the others boats followed suit and the Zodiacs came to an abrupt halt in the stormy sea.

The patrol boat's search lights traversed the water, Skeeter Macklin knew the Cubans were look'n for them, someone back at the villa must have freed themselves and realized Dimitar Spasića had been abducted. The Zodiacs bobbed in the hills and valleys of water as the patrol boat crossed their bows fifty yards away. The searchlights passed twenty feet in front of the lead Zodiac and just missed spot'n them and the Cubans went on. They waited a full five minutes before the coxswains ignited the engines and the boats struggle onward toward their rendezvous with the *Key West*.

Skeeter Macklin thought how lucky they were not to have been seen, he was grateful for the storm that he had cursed minutes before the dismal weather prevented the Cubans from spot'n them though the downpour. The boats continued head'n farther into the Caribbean, Skeeter glanced at his watch the hands indicated they were a half hour behind schedule, but he knew the sub would wait.

So in the darkness around four thirty the outline of the *Key West's* cunning tower appeared about a quarter mile away off the starboard bow everyone was glad to see it lying there in the water. The sailor flashed a signal as they approached and received the sub's answer moments later. The small crafts pull alongside the sub sailors secured the lines, everyone disembarked, climbed onto the *Key West*, Skeeter Macklin was relieved that none of his men were lost or injured on this mission. He led the team and the frightened Dimitar Spasića down the ladder into the sub's interior.

The Officer of the Day said, "Welcome aboard Major, it's good to see you," and Skeeter Macklin informed him; "It's good to be seen," and they shook hands.

He addressed the OD: "Have the master at arms escort the prisoner to the brig and no food or water until we reach Gitmo," the young Ensign replied, "Aye aye sir," and said to the master at arms, "Chief Matthews take the prisoner directly to the brig and no provisions until we reach port," the chief said back: "Roger that sir. O'Hara and Curtis transport the prisoner directly to the brig and instruct the guards he's to receive nothing until we dock at Gitmo..."

Skeeter cut in on him: "And Chief leave him bounded and gagged, do not remove the head bag," the chief replied: "Understood sir," and they bustled Dimitar Spasića to the brig.

Skeeter Macklin turned to Mickey Stovall say'n, "Mick tell the men to retire to their quarters." Mickey said: "Yes sir," and then said, "OK men stand down, go shit shave shower and shampoo and hit the rack," There was a chorus of: "*OoRAH*" and the grunts left the forward control room headed aft.

Skeeter spoke with the OD: "Would it be an imposition if someone whipped up some chow for my men?"

"Not at all sir, considered it done," and he turned to a sailor: "Smitty see that these men are fed immediately, they deserve it." Smitty acknowledged him and spoke over the sub's intercom: "Chief Flynn have a cook and three men report to the mess and prepare breakfast for the marines." Skeeter thanked the ensign. Major Macklin and Captain Stovall left the control room and stepped off to the officer's quarters. Over their shoulders they heard the captain bark: "Helmsman set a course for Guantanamo and prepared to dive," the helmsman repeated the order, "Setting course for Guantanamo and preparing to dive, sir," and the USS *Key West* began to slip beneath the waves.

NOT MUCH MORE than a half hour later Mickey Stovall padded out of the rain room and toweled off after his shower, he heard the water being turned on as Skeeter Macklin commenced his. Mickey started reflecting on what Skeeter told him prior to the team's jump from the C-130. He ask himself whether he was jok'n about this mission being his final one, surely his friend was josh'n but then again he never knew him to be a bull shitter, not Mister Serious, kidding wasn't in his DNA. Although his crack about Batman alleviated the tension the men including him experienced it was the perfect tonic that cured everyone's fright. He wondered if Skeeter was afraid of what they were about to face as they prepared to leap into the unknown. Mickey felt an icy cold jolt run down his backside just think'n about them float'n down through the cloud at its most violent time, Mickey Stovall heard himself say: "That was some frantic shit," and he laughed to suppress the memory of the experience.

He returned from his reverie, stood there, looked at himself in the mirror as he brushed his hair and thought how would the Eradicators be without their fearless leader, could he replace his shadow, fill his shoes? Would the men respect his leadership, even though he's been a member of the team for seven years and its XO for the last three he had a pang of doubt that wouldn't go away. Sure he was an A1 jarhead but leadership was never his strong suit. Even when he was the star player on his college basketball team he never was considered the leader of the team, he always deferred to others, even during his All American year at the Naval Academy, he was reluctant to assume command out on the floor although he was the rah rah guy on the bench and in the locker room. Mickey Stovall, believe it or not was a shy kind of guy.

Yeah he was known to crack wise whenever there was an opportunity to insert some mirth into the mix, especially before he went on a mission. It always helped him conquer his own fears.

Captain Mickey Stovall was what they call in the Corps a 'spit and polish gyrene', *Mister Squared Away.* He was known to wear his dress blues whenever he had the notion. Everyone agreed he was a top notch marine, no one doubted that. Only Mickey had reservations about himself, this insecurity was rooted in his childhood by his parents; although he knew they loved him they seemed to dote over their first born and the baby of the family more than they did him, Mickey being the middle child.

Growing up in Harrisburg, PA was your standard childhood affair plenty of fun and all that but something lacked, something he couldn't put his finger on. Even when he starred on his high school team he was reluctant to assert himself verbally. He received tons of adulation but there existed a hole in his life. He was showered with scholarship offers, everyone campaigned hard for him to accept Penn State's but he chose the Naval Academy instead to everyone's dismay; the home town hero rejected the state school for the *Naval Academy.* His mom was deeply disappointed, but his dad, a veteran of Vietnam understood his son's decision and gave his unconditional support. So Mickey Stovall, the black kid from Harrisburg, PA left home to become what they call 'a marine's marine.'

He heard the shower cut off, he turned on his heels crossed the stateroom to his rack and settled down, Skeeter Macklin stepped out of the head in his skivvies rub'n his head with a towel: "There's nothing like a hot shower after a grueling day."

"Ah the pause that refreshes, huh?" Mickey Stovall said.

"I believe that was Coke's slogan back in the day."

"Really?"

"Really."

"We'll never let it be said that Mickey Stovall is a plagiarist."

"Quoting something or someone is not plagiarism, Mick," Mickey Stovall said: "In that case I feel so much better," Skeeter Macklin told him: "Mick there are times when you cease to amaze."

"That's what I do Skeeter keep people astonished," Skeeter Macklin looked down at him, shook his head and replied, "Like I always say Mick you're one of kind."

"I don't think the world could handle two Mickey Stovalls at one time."

"I concur that would be much too much to cope with."

Mickey looked at him and said, "What do you think going to happen to that Spasića fuck?" changing the subject.

"The UN will probably turn him over to the Hague to stand trial, convict him and I hope they fry him or whatever method they use in Europe to rid the world of shit birds like him, he was a nasty bastard even that prick Saddam wasn't as demented as he was."

"These guys are like the Hydra you kill one and two more assholes pop up. You know Skeeter sometimes I think we're fighting a losing battle. Just when you think we've got the upper hand another turd drops out to commit atrocities more horrendous than the turd before did."

"Yeah, I think you could be right, but if that didn't happen we'd be out of business."

This was Mickey Stovall's chance to broach the subject about Skeeter Macklin retiring from the team: "In that vein what's this nonsense about you hanging up your guns?"

"Nonsense is it? This is my life we're talking about here."

"Maybe that was a bad word selection," Mickey Stovall said sheepishly. There was regret in his voice, Skeeter Macklin sensed it and said: "Let's say it doesn't make sense in view of what we've accomplished over the past six seven years, but there comes a time when one has to make tough choices but in this instance it's an easy call for me."

"Thanks for giving me an out, but if I may ask what's going on?" Mickey Stovall inquired; Skeeter Macklin paused for a couple seconds and told him: "Jessy's pregnant."

Mickey jumped up and hugged his friend, "That's fantastic news, congrats man," he release his embrace, stepped back and said: "When is she due?"

"Late April."

Mickey Stovall beamed and asked, "Is it a boy or girl?"

"We want to be surprised, I'm pulling for a girl, there hasn't been a female Macklin born into our clan in the last ten years, we have enough knucklehead boys born over that period to muster a platoon. My cousins are boy making machines." Mickey Stovall said: That's great, a little Skeeter running around in her tutu," Skeeter laughed, took his towel off his shoulder and threw it at him. "In all seriousness my decision is predicated on the fact that it wouldn't be fair to Jessy and the baby to keep them waiting and waiting for me to retire while I'm off doing the wet work and you know General Falk's policy you can't be married if you're member of his beloved Eradicators."

"Mad Sam doesn't know?"

"You're the only one I've told, I'm waiting until we return to Quantico before telling him."

"That's going to be volcanic, Krakatau in proportion."

"Yeah I suspect he'll go nuclear, but it is what it is and I wouldn't be dissuaded by his speech about '*your country needs you*', you know his spiel."

"And how, I remember when I vaguely hinted I was considering retiring and he went ballistic with his patriotic pitch, it was so compelling it brought tears to my eyes. The man knows how to hit you in your red, white and blue heart."

A rap came at the door that interrupted their conversation. Skeeter Macklin said: "Enter," the door swung open, a steward said, "Here's your meal, sirs, complements of the captain," he pushed the cart into the room and laid the table for the officers. Mickey Stovall stepped over, raised the lids and checked the contents, "Filet mignon and all the trimmings a meal fit for kings." The steward smiled and said: "Only the best for the best sir," and exited the room, Mickey Stovall said, "And Dom Perignon, now that's gratitude for you," and they settled down to eat.

LATER OVER CHAMPAGNE Skeeter Macklin asked, "How would you like to be the kid's godfather?" Mickey Stovall almost choked on his Dom Perignon; he righted himself and set the glass down, "Me??"

"No, the guy sitting next to you."

"What about a member of your family, someone among the hundreds of cousins you have?" Skeeter told him, "None of them are closer to me than you, Mick, we're like...like brothers you know that."

"Ditto on that Skeeter, I'd be honored," he outstretched his hand and they shook on it, Mickey Stovall raised his glass: "I wish you, Jessy and my goddaughter the best and you know I'm always there for you."

"Yeah how well do I know that, you've save my bacon several times," and Mickey Stovall came back: "That ain't nothing but a tie Skeeter you've done the same for me."

Skeeter Macklin said: "I'm bushed, I'm hitting the rack."

"You can put me down twice for that," they rose from the table and Skeeter laid down and sleep quickly took him. Mickey looked at his friend and said in silence, *that's one hell of a guy right there*, doused the lights, plopped down into his rack and drifted off just as fast.

1

Free Cheese

January 20, 2009
Stone Mountain, GA; Washington, DC

IT WAS A RAINY night in Georgia when a gold Maybach hustled west on Stone Mountain Highway. The Mercedes' twelve cylinders thrummed as the Benz raced to a secret rendezvous on top of Stone Mountain.

Thomas, the chauffer adjusted the mirror that gave him a clear view of his employer, Robin Calhoun, the Republican junior Senator from South Carolina. Robin Calhoun was a great grandniece of John C. Calhoun six times removed. She grew up in Charleston listening to her elders recite oral histories about the Old South. As a child she'd stand at her mother's knee and marvel at the conversations among the old folks about the glorious past, as they reminiscence and told tall tales about antebellum Charleston.

Ruby, her mother could speak from memory about the by gone days handed down to her by Robin's granny. She filled her ears with tales of valor and chivalry this was a tradition in their family since the end of the Civil War. Southern pride was alive and well in the Calhoun household. Little Robin Calhoun would stand there mesmerized and hung on Ruby's every word. Her imagination would place her in scenes described in the wondrous stories her mother spoke about. She could see herself danc'n with dash'n suitors' vy'n to be her beau. She was so enchanted that CC kiddingly called her 'Scarlett' after the character in '*Gone with the Wind*'. Little Robin Calhoun considered herself a twenty century southern belle.

She found the stories far more informative and entertaining than the lies she was forced to endure in school. Her father, Cody Calhoun, called CC by friend and foe alike would rail that the victors wrote the history in their favor, slanting the truth and varnishing over the facts. CC would spouse the southern view point which painted a picture of the grand life of Old Charleston. Cody Calhoun was also the Grand Cyclops of the local Ku Klux Klan den, where he and his fellow travelers would exalt distorted laments of a lost cause.

Robin Calhoun glanced out the window as the car followed the road that led to the park. Now she could see through the rain the floodlights illuminating the images of Robert E. Lee, Stonewall Jackson and Jefferson Davis astride their warhorses carved into the granite. This was her first visit to the monument since her parents brought her here as a three year old in 61, the carvings were incomplete at the time, she had to catch her breath as she gawked at the iconic images of her heroes. Robin Calhoun felt a tangling wash over her as the car drew closer and her heroes grew larger.

Thomas took the off ramp to Stone Mountain Park. The Maybach came to a stop at the entrance gate, the driver's window slid down, Thomas said to the guard: "Reverend Blount is expecting us," and he waved him on. The Mercedes went through the park on the road to the top of the mountain. The car pulled into the parking lot Thomas cut the engine, got out, walked around and swung the door open for the senator. He put up an umbrella, handed her out and they stepped toward a man who stood in the rain.

Robin Calhoun said to him: "Hell of night to meet," there was a hint of acid in her voice and Reverend Blount told her: "It's good to see you too Robin and how's the good senator feeling on this historic evening?" She shot back, "Cut the crap Moses, is everyone here?" as she looked around.

Reverend Moses Blount, head pastor of the White Salvation Church told her: "Everyone but Max Bedford, he was late getting into Atlanta

International rain delays and all that, he called and said he'd be here within the next ten minutes."

Robin Calhoun rolled her eyes, "It's always something with that one can't that bastard ever be on time? This makes the fourth time he has been late to a meeting and tonight's meet is the most important one we will have again as a group and this guy is tardy. I will not stand for any screw ups it is too late in the game, Moses."

"Robin please control your temper and be tentative to others," she was known to be ill tempered and uncompromising. She came back: "Tentative my ass everyone should pay attention to what I am saying not the other way around," she carried on, "you seem to have forgotten that I am the head of the SOS..." Moses Blount broke in, "How can we forget you make a point to let us know every opportunity you get."

She ignored that and said to her chauffeur, "Thomas bring me my briefcase from the backseat," he handed her the umbrella, walked to car and returned with her briefcase she handed the umbrella back to Thomas, he stood there and held it over her as she opened the briefcase, reached inside, came out with a flask, unscrewed the top, knocked back a shot of Jack Daniel's and placed the flask back inside.

Reverend Blount conveyed: "Go easy with that Robin, you need to be razor shape tonight and there's no time for any of your alcoholic rants."

She snapped: "When I need your advice I will ask for it - now lead me to Cole Harper," they started walk'n toward a large group of men who stood off to themselves. They looked up and saw them approach, "Here's the senator now," Cole Harper told them, somebody said: "I hope she's not under the influence," someone else added, "She has a serious problem." They went silent as she and Moses Blount stepped up.

"Good evening Senator," that was Cole Harper speaking, he was an SOS mole who worked at the Department of Transportation in Washington.

"Hello Cole, we have to wait for this Max Bedford who has a knack for being late too everything that is important. I will not tolerate anymore of his bullshit, time is tight and everything has to happen on schedule if we are to achieve our objectives."

Cole Harper and Robin Calhoun were ex-lovers, so he took the liberty to say: "What did you do take a shitty pill this evening Robin?" She looked him hard in the eyes: "I am going to overlook that for the time being, now let us get things started I cannot wait for this Bedford to join us."

Just then headlamps from a taxi appeared, it pulled into the parking lot, and Max Bedford got out, paid the driver off, put up his collar and ran toward Robin Calhoun and the others. She put up a brow. She was visibly pissed. Everyone sensed it. Max Bedford, out of breath said: "I'm sorry, but the plane was delayed for an hour circling the airport waiting for an opportunity to land," with his hand outstretched he made the rounds and greeted everyone: "This is a historical occasion and I'm so excited to be here," he came to Senator Calhoun holding out his hand, she refused his offer and said point blank, "What is it about you Bedford that you cannot seem to be punctual this is getting to be perpetual habit with you..." Max Bedford tried to speak, "My sincere..." Robin Calhoun rolled over him: "I do not want to hear any of your lame apologies, this is getting tiresome and I refuse to tolerate it anymore, one more instance of this and you will be excommunicated from the organization, understood?"

Max Bedford tried to reason with her: "Yes, but sometime things are beyond my control Senator but I will make a serious effort to be on time in the future you know I'm dedicated to the cause." Bedford was a nationally syndicated right wing radio talk show host who was a critical component of the SOS's agenda.

"Be that as it may, this is your final warning no more of this or you will be replaced with someone who is competent, we need souls who are committed and focused. What we are about to undertake is crucial. Tonight will be the first salvo in our gaining the South's independent from those stinking Yankee bastards. If you all..." she looked around at the group as they listened to her tirade, "...are not committed to this struggle I advise you to vacate at once, I only want those who are dedicated to establishing the independence of the South.

"Our soldiers are ready to launch the opening volley tonight, this is our Fort Sumter..." she stopped to let that sink in as she read their faces everyone was enthralled, so she went on, "...and make no mistake about it we will win this time. Our guerrilla operations will bring the fight to the North where we will create chaos and confusion in their cities, panic is our ally in this fight. At last the *SOUTH HAS RISEN AGAIN*." And everyone let out the rebel yell that filled the valley below with celebration.

Robin Calhoun let them holler for a full minute. She stood there and basked in the outpour'n of southern pride. She let them glad hand and back slap before she continued. They finally fell silent and stood there. She savored the moment then she told them: "As we stand here above our iconic leaders of the past we shall resume the war they so gallantly started over one hundred and forty eight years ago, but I guarantee you the outcome will be different this time," as the words left her lips, there were murmurs of consent and heads bobbed in agreement.

"The tactics we will employ will keep the enemy off guard and on their heels. As they celebrate at this so called President Bohannon's inauguration party we have a surprise in store for them. Our soldiers are ready to unleash terror on Washington that will shock the world and crash his party," they relished very syllable in her speech.

Robin Calhoun raised her arm, waved it in a wide arc: "Soon all you see before you from the Atlantic to Texas, from the Gulf to Kentucky and up the Mississippi to Missouri will be free of the tyrannical control of those damn Yankees. This is our time, we shall not fail, we did not lose the Civil War, we lost our will to continue, well now we have regained the means and desire to resume the fight and we shall prevail. The so called end of the Civil War was just half time now let us go win the *game*."

There was an explosion of cheers. Ripples of conversation broke out.

Robin Calhoun stood there taking it all in, several of the men's eyes started to well up and tears began leak'n down the contours of their faces. The senator was just hit'n her stride. Finally she spoke: "Make no mistake this is our time to resurrect the South and restore all her past glory." Again the men went nuts. They grabbed and hugged each other and whooped it up. She had them right where she wanted them they were so gassed up they would have jumped off the side of the mountain if she told them to. Robin Calhoun knew she had power over men, but never to this extend. She raised her hand a hush fell over the scene. She let the moment hang for a beat or two and then said: "The second phase of the war will start at ten o'clock tonight. The hour of the rebirth of the Confederate States of America is at hand and long may she reign," that did it, now she had them in the palms of her hands.

Robin Calhoun sensed it was time to seal the deal. "Are you ready to fight and perhaps die for our cause?" She asked, with an air of bravo and total confidence.

"*YES,*" they yelled as one.

"Have you the dedication to see this through?"

Again a chorus of: "*YES.*"

"Then I am prepared to lead you..." she pointed at Reverend Blount, "...excuse me Moses - lead you to the promised land," chuckles broke out all around.

She waved her hands, silence returned and the rain ceased. It was miraculous.

"Are you willing to follow me in this struggle?"

"*YES.*"

"Do you accept me as your leader?"

Again *YES.*

She announced: "If you are willing to follow then I am able to *LEAD.*"

Her words hung in the air.

Then the mountain top erupted with enthusiasm.

They raced up and surrounded Robin Calhoun, she had their total devotion.

A full ten minutes later Robin told them she had a pressing schedule and that she had to leave. "I want you all to go to your hotel rooms, turn on Fox and you will hear reports of our surprise soon after ten, Reverend Blount would you accompany me to my car?"

"Why of course."

"Thank you," she told him and said to the group: "All of you present here at this momentous time shall go down in southern lore as the original SOS, the *Saviors of the South.*" Happiness prevailed. The only thing absent was the *I Wish I Was in Dixie* soundtrack.

It was over Robin Calhoun a daughter of the Confederacy had won the hearts and minds of its sons. She turned on her heels and bi pedaled to the Maybach with Reverend Blount and Thomas drafting in her wake.

Thomas opened the trunk, took out a plastic bag and a box that contained a pair of Ferragamo shoes, closed the trunk and Robin took the box as she removed her rain soaked flats. She gave them to him, he put them in the plastic bag and said: "I'll have them cleaned for you ma'am."

"No, dispose of them," she told him and he said, "As you wish," and handed her into the backseat, she pressed a button, lowered the window and said to Reverend Blount: "Moses, three million dollars will be wired into the Sumter Fund's account in the morning from our cousins in Belize. I will call tomorrow evening with instructions as how it will be disbursed."

"Understood. Senator that was a magnificent performance you did John C. Calhoun proud."

"I guess it's in the genes, Moses," he smiled, shook her hand, turned and stepped to his car. She watched him walk away and noticed Cole Harper pass'n by, she called out, "Cole could I speak with you?" He spun around, strode up to the door, Robin outstretched her hand grabbed his crotch and squeezed. He winched in obvious pain. She told him: "My shitty pill just kicked in. Cole do not ever again speak to me in the manner you did tonight," she tightened her grip on his nuts and yanked on them, Cole Harper howled, she released her grip and he fell over head first onto the pavement. Robin Calhoun said: "Let us go now Thomas," he put the Maybach in gear and they drew away. She opened her briefcase, took out her flask, stared at it and then said: "Well Jack it looks like we did it," and knocked back a shot.

Around twenty minutes later her smartphone went. "Yes."

A voice said: "Everything is set, by your command," she said back, "Very well you know what to do," and thumbed off.

WHAT'D SHE SAY?" asked Charlie Best as he steered a non-descript eighteen wheeled Peterbilt on congested eye 95 outside Washington, DC.

"She said it's a go," Roger Smith told him. They were SOS operatives assigned to launch their first attack on the United States of America. Roger Smith and Charlie Best were ex-cons and members of the Aryan Brotherhood. Both were devoted hate mongers. Their hatred was seasoned after serv'n significant time in various penitentiaries. Smith was a former Green Beret who received an undesirable discharge from the army after the general court martial failed to convict him of killing an entire Iraqi family in Ramadi during the Second Gulf War. The army couldn't prove their case because Roger Smith intimidated the army's witnesses. He got word to the three soldiers who were scheduled to testify against him threaten'n to have their families killed back in the States if they choose to tell the court they witnessed Sergeant Smith woefully machine gun the Iraqis in their home. After the case was lost the army decided Roger Smith was a psychopath who was unfit to serve in the US Army.

Charlie Best was your garden variety racist who loathed anyone who wasn't a WASP. His hatred was rooted in the dogma he was forced to listen to by his uncle who reared him after his parents abandoned him in rural Alabama. Charlie acted out his uncle's fantasies to kill blacks and Jews. One night in 97 he along with three others kidnapped a local rabbi, tied him up, poured gasoline over him and set him on fire. The police arrested him after his accomplices rolled over and told them Charlie Best was the mastermind. After the prosecution proved the state's case, the jury convicted him of manslaughter instead of first degree murder the conviction the prosecutor sought. He was sentenced to ten years, but he gained parole after he served only six.

Charlie Best sat at the wheel as he read the overhead sign that told him the 395 on ramp was a quarter mile ahead, he eased the semi over to the right lane and said to Roger Smith, "Have you heard from the commander?" he referred to Billy Bob Broussard the leader of the SOS strike forces.

"He just texted me about ten minutes ago confirming the Chief's..." Robin Calhoun, "... orders."

"What'd he say?"

"You know Billy Bob he was amped up, bit'n at the bit rar'n to go."

"Yeah that's what I'm talk'n about." Charlie Best yelped.

"Everyone's geared up. How long have we been waiting and training?"

"Five years that I know of. They say this whole rebellion thing was planned way back in the sixties." Charlie Best told him, and Roger Smith said: "I heard talk it's the brain child of the Chief's father, too bad the old boy's not here to see his dream come true."

Charlie Best asked, "What do you think our chances are of making the big old US government cave into her demands?"

"I don't have a clue, I'm just a soldier, but I'm sure she has something big up her sleeve. Plus she's paying us some serious *jack*.

"It's just about the money with you, isn't it?' Charlie Best looked over at him, Roger Smith turned to face him and said, "Don't get me wrong I'm down for the cause, but ideology don't pay the bills, know what I'm say'n?" Charlie turned back and looked out at the road and said: "Shit it ain't do'n too bad keep'n that radio dude Max Bedford in the chips. He's mak'n millions chat'n on the radio. He's one shit talk'n dude, man."

Roger Smith said, "Every time I listen to his show I'm ready to start off'n folks left and right. That guy knows how to hit my nigger hating buttons." They laughed and fist bumped.

Charlie Best told him: "Here's the on ramp to 395, DC straight ahead," and Roger Smith said: "This is going to be oh so good when we drop our surprises in on these bastards."

"Everything still set for ten?"

"Yeah, yeah," Roger Smith looked at his watch, "a few minutes from now."

"Are the boys ready back there?"

"Each one I handpicked myself. Those guys are just as committed and cold blooded as we are Charlie. Trust me no one's gonna choke."

Just then Roger's cell sounded, he answered: "Yes".

"Standby to commence firing sequence in five minutes," this was Billy Bob Broussard on the line.

Roger Smith said, "Will do."

"Are the men ready," Billy Bob asked.

"Rip roaring ready, everyone's anxious to get this party started."

"And shut down another one," Charlie Best said off to the side," Roger Smith looked over at him and gave him a thumbs up.

Billy Bob: "Tell Charlie I heard that and too stay focused.

Roger: "Will do."

Billy Bob: "Have your men commence on my mark."

Roger: "Copy that."

Billy Bob: "Stand by."

Roger: "Standing by as ordered," Billy Bob placed him on hold. He looked at the GPS and he saw the semi was near their Rubicon. This was reached a minute or so later; Charlie Best crossed the 14th bridge and exited onto 395 headed into DC proper.

Now Roger Smith picked up his two-way and said: "Gray Ghost Two this is Gray Ghost One, do you copy?"

"Gray Ghost One this is Gray Ghost Two copy loud and clear."

"Stand by to commence fire mission, over," Roger Smith said, "Copy that, over," came the reply.

What the trailer tractor towed into the heart of Washington was a specially rigged one. It had been modified at considerable expense into a moving weapons platform. Gray Ghost Two was the call sign for a three man crew manning an 81mm mortar inside the trailer along with this crew were two others: Gray Ghost Three and Four. These call signs were chosen in honor of confederate Colonel John S. Mosby, known as the *Gray Ghost* who led guerrilla raids deep behind Union lines during the war.

The trailer had been converted into a self propelled indirect fire weapon using the 81's as the delivery system. The trailer was Billy Bob's creation. He and his identical twin brother Billy Ray were born in the bayou country of southern Louisiana they were the sons of a Cajun couple who had seven other children. Their father was a poor shrimp boat operator working out of Iberia.

When the twins were born, their parents struggled to support the older children so they sent them as infants to be raised by their mother's brother and his wife in Shreveport. Uncle Pierre's wife was barren so they happily raised the boys as their own. They were exceptionally bright and mechanically inclined, they'd tinker with all sorts of gadgets taking them apart and reassembling them. They had an innate talent for repairing, anything that had a motor or a moving mechanism.

The Broussard twins excelled in high school, graduated with honors. They enrolled together at Louisiana Tech where they joined the ROTC program, upon graduation were commissioned into the US Army. The brothers served their entire hitch at Fort Lewis in Washington here they were seduced by the white supremacy teachings of the charismatic leader of the Aryan Nations. Even though they were born and raised in Louisiana, they weren't brought up in a bigoted environment. Their aunt and uncle were middle of the roaders; in fact the Broussard twins had many black friends growing up in progressive Shreveport. But their constant exposure to the racist and antigovernment rhetoric of the Aryan Nations' leader turned them into die hard bigots.

They were recruited into the SOS by Max Bedford, who openly attended the militia compounds. He noticed the twins, took a shine to them and convinced them to join up. Max Bedford only recruited southerners; this was Robin Calhoun's policy, she didn't trust nor want anyone who wasn't born and raised in the south in her organization.

Once committed to the SOS the brothers rose fast to positions of authority and were given direct command of all of the SOS guerrilla units. They used their contacts and SOS funds to bribe soldiers stationed at Fort Lewis to let them slip on base and steal weapons from the armories, significant dollars were paid to acquire the mortars and the ammo. The twins used their mechanical skills to design the hydraulics to lift the platform that elevated the mortars to a firing height enabling the weapons to be adjusted to make sure the rounds would fly through the openings in the trailer's roof, three sections had been cut of out and replaced with doors that automatically collapsed inward, then they'd rotate back swing'n up folding themselves out of the way.

Charlie Best, Roger Smith and their crew tested the system and weapons at night travelling through Utah, firing practice rounds into the desert, everything functioned perfectly. The Broussard twins had designed an ingenious terror apparatus.

AT THE WATERGATE hotel President Bohannon's inaugural party was in full swing. The ballroom roiled with levity, joy permeated the air, and everybody was upbeat. They had reason to be, this was an historical occasion. Stories would be told with few embellishments by those in attendance, well into the future. They will tell anyone who bothered to listen that they were at the mother of all parties and sub characters in a story played out across the American stage. If someone took a snap shot of this moment in history they would be in the picture, the night American pride was on display.

Top Democrats glad handed and made the circuit and congratulated one another on this impressive victory for the Democrat Party. Now they controlled both Houses of the Congress, the White House was back in their charge. What could be better?

Newly appointed Chief of Staff, Taylor Jackson stood among a group of high powered mucks and their wives, Taylor raised his glass and said to them: "Ladies and gentlemen here's to a brighter day, a new dawn has arisen over this great land of ours. Change was on the wind we saddled up and rode it to victory." Everyone glowed, raised their glasses to salute Taylor Jackson the president's friend and campaign manager, the energy that propelled Jasper Bohannon to the Oval Office. Everyone jockeyed for position to take the lead to win over the man who had the president's ear. New Mexico Governor Raul Nunez chooses to make his move in the lull as everyone stood there reflective on Taylor's inspirational words. He broke the silence: "Taylor could I speak with you for a moment privately?" Taylor Jackson looked at him: "Why of course Governor without the great state of New Mexico's electoral votes we wouldn't be here, we'd be somewhere licking our wounds like Jake Carlisle is doing at this very moment," laughs overlapped the moment.

Taylor Jackson said to the group, "Ladies and gentlemen please excuse me, like that great American Douglas MacArthur said on many occasion, '*I shall return*'," he grabbed Governor Nunez by the elbow and they stepped off. Folks saw them com'n, recognizing Taylor Jackson they gangway parting like the Red Sea, all eyes were on him, grins shone brightly on their faces as the pair flowed to the bar, Taylor summoned the bartender, he sauntered over and said: "What'll you have sirs?" Taylor looked at the governor, "You call it and I'll buy it," the governor laughed, before he could reply, the bartender interjected, "No money required, what would the gentlemen prefer?" Taylor Jackson told him: "Why you don't decide for us, that way we can't go wrong," the bartender enjoyed that, turned away feel'n warm and started mix'n their drinks.

Governor Nunez asked: "How did you become so smooth, Taylor?"

Taylor Jackson answered, "I practice Governor you can't win the championship if you don't practice." The governor slapped him on the back and said: "I love that, you will be quoted," Taylor Jackson said in his best W.C. Fields voice: "I got a million of 'em." Again the governor cracked up at Taylor's wit.

"Raul what do you want to speak with me about?"

"Well Taylor, can I be direct"

"Why by all means."

The governor cleared his throat and said, "To perfectly blunt Taylor to paraphrase you, without my states' electoral votes we wouldn't be standing here, and that's a fact."

Taylor Jackson's brows went up, "Did I say that?"

"Yes moments ago," Nunez said unsure of his footing and just how to proceed.

Taylor Jackson let him off the hook, "Yes it's all coming back to me, what it is you want governor, precisely?"

"Well there's an old Russian proverb, 'The only free cheese is in a mouse trap.'"

"Well said, I'll add that to my things to say, now that we've exchanged witticisms, what's on your mind?"

"Immigration," the governor told him.

"That's a sensitive subject these days you know how adamant the Republicans are about that."

"The Republicans aren't in power. The president campaigned hard on it out west promising to place it high on his to do list. Now that we have the momentum, we need to seize the opportunity pass immigration reform before the euphoria dissipates and the Republicans right themselves and dig in their heels against it. Now is the time to take full advantage of that euphoria and get it done."

"That's very persuasive, but what about the jobs issue, you know we are in the middle of a recession, creating jobs is priority number one, our foremost concern and close on the heels of that, the president wants to tackle the health care issue and we have to strike while the iron's hot."

"I understand the immediate priorities the administration is facing. The president has my full support on those topics the overall concerns of the country must come first, I get that, but once they've been accomplished, he should focus on regional matters and what concerns us out west is immigration. We need a reform bill that is fair and balanced..." Taylor Jackson broke in: "I didn't know you watched Fox News Governor," and grinned, Governor Nunez said: "Contrary to popular belief Taylor, Fox doesn't have a monopoly on words, even their tag line is open to question."

"Governor, I like you."

"As the kids say, back at ya," just then the bartender returned with their drinks, he sat them on the bar Taylor reached for his glass, worked it and beamed. He said to the bartender: "That my new best friend is a masterpiece, wouldn't you agree Governor?"

Nunez had just finished tasting his, he said to the bartender: "You must have brought out a ladder to reach this, this is top shelf." Taylor Jackson turned to the governor: "You're good Raul I think I've finally met my match," he reached in his pocket, come out with his roll, peeled off two twenties handed them to the bartender who gladly accepted. Taylor said to him, "Well done, young man well done," the bartender stepped away feel'n like Taylor Jackson had just made his day.

They stood there nurs'n their drinks finally Taylor spoke into the silence, "Raul here's what I'll do for you, just as soon as we get those priority issues put to bed, immigration will be the next in line. We'll give it a hard push and we will not stop until we push it across the finish line, how's that?"

Raul Nunez was delighted: "Perfect," and they shook on it. At that moment the band stopped play'n a Tito Puente mambo tune and broke into '*Hail to the Chief*' as President Bohannon and his visibly pregnant wife, Carman stepped into the ballroom with his Secret Service entourage hard on their heels. Taylor Jackson said: "As we live and breathe here's the man himself," he placed his glass on the bar, Nunez did the same, and Taylor grabbed the governor by the elbow and the pair bi pedaled through the knot headed for the president.

INSIDE THE TRAILER nine men scurried and readied the 81s for firing. Three men were assigned to each mortar: the gunner and two ammo bearers, the walls were stacked to the ceiling with cases of high explosive and white phosphorus rounds, the crates were strapped to the walls to insure they wouldn't topple over causing a horrific disaster.

The mortars stood silent on the platform as the men ran a complete check of the weapons. Harry Reynolds, the squad leader, double checked everything to make sure all the components were ready for the work ahead. He meticulously examined the blast attenuator, site unit, mount and the cannon making sure they were operable. Reynolds paid special attention to the base plate, the section that stabilized the mortar. He looked carefully to see if it was anchored securely to the platform, he examined each bolt that locked the base plate in position. Any loose bolts could cause the 81's to slip off and possibly tip over. Satisfied, he walked over to the console in front of the trailer, looked at the computer screen displaying a map of metro DC. His fingers danced across the keys as he selected his primary targets. A map showed key government buildings each colored in red. Next, range finding software calculated the distance from 395 to the target zone. The maximum range of the 81s was three and a half miles, the seat of American power laid well within this. Now the computer calculate the maximum rate of fire of thirty rounds per minute times three for a sustained five minutes, they could rain four hundred and fifty rounds of pure hell on an unsuspecting Washington.

Harry Reynolds factored in the semi's speed of sixty miles per hour; he knew they would reap havoc over a wide swath of the metro area. The primary target zone encompassed the Pentagon, Ronald Regan Airport, Fort McNair, the Capital and the White House itself. Of course accuracy would be diminished by the movement of the semi, but this was okay, even near misses would have the same psychological impact as a direct hit. Each round would be a winner.

Billy Bob had issued a fire mission for five minutes in duration and then the attack would cease. Five minutes was more than enough time to shake up the world. An attack at the heart of American democracy would vibrate around the world at the speed of light. The morning's news and conversations would be solely devoted to what was about to happen. Robin Calhoun was right this event would get everyone's immediate and undivided attention.

Harry Reynolds' two-way spoke, it was Roger Smith: "Gray Ghost squad leader this is Gray Ghost One prepare to fire for effect." Reynolds said: ""All weapons prepared to fire on your command."

"Roger that, stand-by."

"Copy that."

Roger Smith clicked off and said into his cell, "All weapons manned and ready," Billy Bob replied: "On my mark in one minute." Roger Smith relayed the order.

"Copy that," Harry Reynolds said, he turned to the crews: "Commence firing..." he looked at the clock on the forward wall, "...in thirty seconds." He pressed a button and the roof opened, the platform carrying the crews and mortars rose to the firing position.

Inside the cab, Roger Smith held his cell at his ear, the two way poised at his lips. Charlie Best steered the semi through the curve, head'n east on 395, he could see the lights of the Pentagon to his left; the semi crossed the bridge spanning the Potomac now they were at the point of no return. They reached fail safe.

Billy Bob followed behind in a blocking car along with two others, no one was armed if by chance after the attack they were pulled over by the police they wouldn't find any incriminating evidence such as guns and so no one would do something silly and get into a shootout with the cops.

Now the semi traveled parallel to DC proper, traffic flowed at a steady sixty two, Charlie Best held the Peterbilt slightly under sixty. He looked to his left, the city was lit up. He said in silence, *what a sight,* he had tinge of apprehension but he quickly moved past it, refocused his attention on his role in this affair. Roger Smith rid'n shotgun sat there as they waited for the green light to start the fireworks.

Charlie Best's palms were sweating he rubbed them on his pant leg, gripped the wheel and said, "How much longer?" Roger Smith told him, "Relax and remain steady."

"I'm about to piss my pants over here, the waiting is fuck'n with me."

"Same here, but once the firing starts you'll feel so much better."

"I hope so, this suspense is killing me."

"Well don't die behind the wheel you got me in here," Roger Smith said trying to break the tension, Charlie Best forced a grin and said: "I'll try to postpone my death until this is over, how's that?" Roger Smith retorted, "Fine by me."

Back in the trailer the platform was locked in place, Harry Reynolds stood on the deck directing the angle of fire for each mortar. Gray Ghost Two was positioned facing due north; three and four faced northwest and west respectfully.

He stood behind the mortar teams where he could supervise the firing of the 81's, the gunners stood to the left side of the mortars where they could manipulate the sights, elevating and traversing wheels. They laid the mortars for deflection and elevation. The first ammo bearers stood to the right of the weapons preparing the ammo waiting to pass it to the gunners. The second ammunition bearers stood to the right rear of the 81's behind the first ammo bearers, their job was to maintain the rounds for firing.

Stacks of HE and WP rounds were positioned to the left of the second ammo bearers where they could feed them to the first ammo bearers who'd hand them to the gunners to drop into the tubes stand'n by to do their dirty work. Everything was set.

Following behind in the blocking car Billy Bob stared at his digital watch, counted the final seconds, his mouth went dry, his heart thumped like a kettle drum. He held his mobile to his lips, his watch told him it was ten o'clock, with no hesitation he said: "Fire at will," inside the Peterbilt's cab Roger Smith heard the command, immediately spoke into his two way and repeated the order, back in the trailer Harry Reynolds dropped his hand as he shouted: "*Fire*."

The three gunners released their cartridges down the cannons base end first, the primer caps struck the firing pins explod'n the ignition charges and the expanding gas forced the cartridges from the mortars. Even though the trailer's walls were lined with sound absorbing materials the clamor was deafening. The rounds flew out into the night sky. In quick succession the gunners dropped alternating HE and WP rounds down the tubes within ten seconds fifteen were on their way into Washington, DC.

2

Red Glare

Washington, DC; Toledo, Belize

AT THE SAME time against the background of pending doom the streets were clogged with festive Washingtonians and out-of-towners that crisscrossed the streets and avenues as they honked their way around the city. Revelers padded the sidewalks in celebration of the transition of power. Everyone had their happy clothes and their happy faces on; all was well in their hearts and minds.

And then it happened.

All hell broke loose.

Whispering death silently drop from the sky without a sound, the whining noise associated with incoming mortar rounds was pure Hollywood. The salvo from Gray Ghost Two slammed into Northeast Washington pepper'n Massachusetts Avenue between Third and Sixth Streets. HE exploded on the roof of the National Museum of American Art, several near misses occurred just south of Ford's Theater on E Street. The area had come under a barrage of mortar shells. Hot pieces of shrapnel flew in every direction. Cars crashed into each other overturning some, others careened into pedestrians who padded the sidewalks. People stampeded en mass as more explosions could be heard com'n from other parts of the city.

Shell after shell rained on the panicked throngs, people screamed and shoved one another out of the way like wildebeest crossing the Mara to evaded the crocs, everyone was out for themselves. Pandemonium fails to describe what was happening all over Washington. People reverted to their base instincts; survival at all cost. To fall meant one's demise there was no chance of get'n to your feet. Those who did fall or were shoved to the ground were trampled to death. Folks dove into doorways, under parked cars seek'n shelter and protection from the steel rain. Explosion after explosion rocked the city. Terror was the order to the hour. Bedlam, mayhem and carnage sent those who moments ago were party'n up and down the avenues into full panic mode as they tried to take cover wherever they could, finding a place to seek refuge from the deluge. Still the rounds kept drop'n, nowhere was safe. The shells fell in a high angle arc and they plunged down with tremendous speed all over the target zone.

Gray Ghost Three's shells smacked into downtown and caused major damage. Windows were blown out adding shards of glass to the mix. The National Aquarium was set ablaze by WP shells. The FBI and Justice Department buildings weren't spared they absorbed several direct hits. The chaos that happened near and around Massachusetts Avenue was duplicated here. All along Constitution Avenue traffic came to a halt, riders sat terrified in their cars look'n out at the breakdown of order as it unfolded before them. And the shells kept com'n.

Gray Ghost Four's rounds created mass hysteria between Pennsylvania and Constitution Avenues. Foggy Bottom, the State Department and the Federal Reserve sustained massive damage. Multiple fires broke out from WP and their toxic fumes drifted on the wind. Unfortunate souls were splattered with white hot phosphorous and all types of shrapnel. Nowhere seemed safe from the incom'n mail, flashes from exploded shells could be seen everywhere.

Several rounds from Gray Ghost Three flew directly over the White House rock'n Lafayette Square, one exploded in front of the Decatur House. WHOOMP, WHOOMP, WHOOMP, sounded all around DC. The shell'n was especially heavy along K Street where it inflected horrific destruction. An undetonated round lodged into the roof of the World

Bank. The entire corridor between K Street and Constitution Avenue was inundated. East of Constitution was the only area of center city that was spared. Capitol Hill and everywhere east and south went unscathed by the madness.

The first rounds landed at one minute after ten they kept com'n until six after. Various buildings were hit by incoming shells many were set alit by WP's. The attack did what Robin Calhoun intended it caused chaos and confusion, now she had her Fort Sumter.

Finally it was over, the explosions ceased, sirens filled the void.

BILLY BOB RASIED his night vision goggles looked out the back window and surveyed the damage, many fires glowed in the distance, smoke drifted over the city, he said in silence: *How's that for the rocket's red glare?* The blocking car followed closely on the semi's tail Billy Bob lowered his goggles, turned around and said to no one in particular: "Now that's a sight to behold, those pompous bastards have a major clean up job on their hands," the pair in the front said nothing to that, he picked up his cell: "Proceed to check point Zulu," he clicked off. Inside the cab Roger Smith told Charlie Best: "Head to Alexandria," "*ALRIGHT*." Charlie yelped. Check point Zulu was a truck stop outside of Alexandria. Charlie and Roger followed 395 to the 295 south to double back into Virginia, leaving a traumatized Washington DC in their wake.

PRESIDENT BOHANNON WAS engaged in a conversation with Governor Nunez and his Chief of Staff. Taylor Jackson said to the president, "Sir I agree with you the immigration question is sensitive and we have to proceed astutely, once we've addressed the jobs issue, we'll have enough clout with the body politic to ram through an immigration bill that will be amenable to all parties concerned," Nunez tried to suppress his smile, the president said: "You think we should leap frog immigration over health care?"

It was Taylor Jackson who said, "Sir, that's going to be your toughest battle, so save it until last. You have to spend your political capital judiciously. Wait until you have two wins under your belt before you step in the ring for that fight."

The president chewed on it for several seconds then said, "Perhaps your right," he turned to face the governor: "Raul you can rest assured that my administration will throw its full weight behind the immigration issue. Jot down your thoughts, send them to Taylor and I will pass them along to Speaker Bonacci, she'll do her fullest to make it happen."

Raul Nunez could no longer withhold his excitement, this slipped past his lips: "That would be fan-fucking-tactic excuse my French Mister President," who said, "Your pardon is accepted, although it sounds very much like something Taylor here would say, you know how eloquent he can be." Taylor Jackson and the governor threw their heads back and laughed. The president outstretched his hand and they shook on it. Nunez said: "Mister President as Bogey said to Claude Rains: 'I think this is the beginning of a beautiful relationship'," the president asked, "Who's Bogey, you or I?" before the governor could reply the door of the Watergate ballroom flew open as Secret Service agents scrambled though the crowd, they rushed up, one of them said, "Mister President, you have to leave at once," they surrounded him and bustled him out of the room, Carmen Bohannon was gathered up and agents ushered her out hot on her husband heels.

Taylor Jackson left the governor stand'n there and took off after them while toss'n this over his shoulder, "Raul, call me," and raced after the president. Nunez watched them depart wondering, *what's going on?* The partiers continued enjoy'n themselves totally unaware of what just took place.

On his way to his limo the president was informed about the brazen attack on the capital of the United States of America. Taylor Jackson listened in on the briefing, his jaw dropped: "Mister President this is a dastardly deed it's a tragedy of epic proportions who could behind this, al-Qaeda?" he looked at him and he saw ugly anger in his eyes, what the president said belied what was in those eyes and without a trace of emotion he said calmly: "Taylor contact the Vice President, the National Security team, Oscar Valdez at Homeland Security, the Secretaries of State and Defense and the Joint Chiefs have them meet us at the White House within forty minutes. I assume the streets are jammed, have Marine One land in front of the JFK Center and pick us up." Taylor Jackson pulled his cell out called Andrews as ordered, the president went on: "Also tell them to send Marine Two to fetch and ferry all pertinent members of the Security Council to the White House, select a location that's immediately accessible for all, get it done."

Taylor Jackson said, "Right away Mister President." The president looked out the window he saw the plumes of black smoke boiled into the night sky and said in silence, *Jasper what a way to start your first day on the job.*

The president's wife had sat there and listened in finally she said, "Jas do you think it's wise to return to the White House at this time? There could be another attack, I heard Agent Johnson say several rounds just missed the White House."

The president looked at her, "Carmen I will not be intimidated by these terrorists, that's the reaction they would want and I can't let whoever's responsible for this think and believe they can interrupt the normal flow of business of governing the country. No I shall go to the White House, get started on finding out who's behind this and bring them swiftly to justice."

AS IT DREW closer to eleven o'clock in the Oval Office President Bohannon stood looking out at the smoke plumes that drifted over his nation's capital. The view was excruciating, he knew every heart in the country ached and there would be uproar for revenge. This was one of the worst scenarios someone could conceive. Why the attack was planned and executed this night of all nights and with such precision and timing? This question vexed him. It was obvious to him this was a deep seated hatred event. An emphatic statement was delivered to the front door of America, right at her heart. He said in silence: *Whoever is behind this is totally ruthless and unforgiving. The perpetrators of this crime are cold blooded calculators; only someone with a warped thought process could have ordered this up, one capable and willing to conjure something more horrific in the future. This unknown adversary is capable of and perhaps intends to execute more heinous acts. This could be the opening round in something far more sinister.*

The president felt a knot in his gut something didn't feel right about this. The apparent consideration would be to look toward America's current enemies and assume they were the culprits.

He anticipated a consensus of uproar from those he was about to meet with in the Situation Room. Voices would clamor for immediate retaliation in greater magnitude than was inflicted on Washington. All fingers would be pointed at al-Qaeda, the obvious suspect. He had to somehow rein in the hawks that would campaign hard for a tactical nuclear strike on any country or countries that had even loose ties with the terrorist organization. Yemen? Somalia? Sudan? Even Pakistan was a possibility to reap American revenge. Someone has to pay, quickly and dearly. It would take all of his considerable skills to keep the hawks in check. He faced a difficult task ahead moments from now. Reason had to prevail over emotion. He couldn't permit the hardliners on his Security Council to maneuver him into running off halfcocked, doing something rash propelled by blind emotion. Something he was responsible for and regrets later if it turned out he ordered the use of American nuclear options and an innocent country was vaporized because the hawks craved blood.

This weighed heavy on the president, he had to control his own emotions as he gazed at the glowing skyline of this proud city. He could hear the cries from Washington to Florida, Maine to California and in the outer states. The country was in pain once again the second time this decade. He looked at his watch, two minutes to show time when he had to step on stage and deliver the command performance.

There it was again, that something that didn't feel right he couldn't put his finger on it. A fleeting thought quick stepped across the back corridors of his mind. A thought he couldn't corral and bring to the fore, a thought mov'n too fast to lock in on.

President Bohannon and the country needed each other: he needed the nation to believe in his judgment the country needed him to comfort and to protect them in this hour of sorrow and in the days ahead. *Give me strength and wisdom, give me strength and wisdom* was his mantra, he chanted it as he watched news helicopters hover'n over different parts of the city, he could hear F15s' roar overhead as they patrolled the sky above Washington. Come sunrise he'd make a complete inspection of the city landing Marine One wherever possible to get a ground's eye view, letting the people see their president was out front taking the point because they elected and expected him to lead. He had to be visible to the populace, the Mourner in Chief and not just a talking head on TV.

They needed him to be accessible out among the citizens sharing their pain, grieving with them show'n them he truly, truly cared.

Jasper Bohannon could feel the weight of the nation on his shoulders, the people elected him to carry it and that's what he must do.

There it was again.

Something wasn't quite right about this entire episode. This affair had a smell about it, all was not as it seemed. He didn't hear the raps at the door that intruded on his worry, so Chief of Staff Taylor Jackson came into the Oval Office: "Sir the National Security Team is fully assembled in the Situation Room," Jasper Bohannon remained at the window in deep thought, "Mister President?"

The president failed to respond to Taylor but spoke aloud to himself: "Something stinks in Denmark", Taylor Jackson asked, "Demark? You think the Danes are behind this?" The president turned from the window and said: "Of course not, I was merely paraphrasing Shakespeare," and said in silence: *This waves like a false flag, there's a wider purpose here* and then said: "Let's be about the nation's business", and he padded out the door headed to the Situation Room with his Chief of Staff stepping behind.

NOT MUCH MORE than a half hour later Jake Carlisle's phone chimed on a table by the window, he turned down Fox News, rose from his sofa, crossed the room and picked up. "Jake have you heard what happened in Washington??" this was Robin Calhoun on the line. "Yes, I was just watching the news, what a horrible situation, from the reports coming in the city sustained tremendous damage and there's a high body count," he told her. Robin Calhoun smiled and her eyes shone with triumph.

"How awful," she said, "who do you think is behind this, al-Qaeda?"

"So it would appear, there's been talk they were planning another major attack here in the States, seems they may have struck again."

"Those Islamic bastards, we have to respond in kind immediately, this cannot go unchallenged," she told him, he replied, "I'm sure the Joint Chiefs have things in motion as we speak."

Robin Calhoun was in her hotel room in Atlanta reclined on the bed where she nursed Jack Daniel's on the rocks; she was in a stupor and celebrated her master stroke visited upon Washington.

She was playing the role trying to shift the spotlight on al-Qaeda instead of her SOS. She told him, "You know Jake this would not if happened if you had won the election," she had to smother a laugh.

"I don't know if that's accurate, Robin."

"Of course it is they would not have the balls to do something as bold as this if you were at the helm. They choose to do this to test this weak ass boy the country elected..." he cut in: "Careful Robin your bigotry is coming through." She drove right past that telling him now: "al-Qaeda would not dare to do this if you were in the White House instead of Bohannon, that spineless bastard does not have the stones to do anything," she said trying to stroke his ego.

"I don't think that's a fair statement, Robin it wouldn't matter who was in the White House if they could do the country harm they would," she won't let it go, "Not if the White House was occupied by a strong person like yourself. You remember how weak kneed that boy was in the Senate,"... Jake Carlisle shook his head, "...he caved in on more than one occasion whenever we put up mild opposition to his Senate proposals," she was enjoy'n her charade to the fullest, she worked her Jack, swallowed and continued her act: "I am cutting my holiday short. I will return to Washington in the morning to make demands on the Senate floor that we retaliate immediately against those Islamic fascist sons of bitches."

The senior Senator from Virginia replied, "Let's not get over heated, we have to wait on the CIA's assessment..." she charged in: "Wait for what, anyone with half a brain knows this was al-Qaeda at work here, believe me their finger prints are over this," she grinned, she was enjoying her deception oh so much.

"You're probably right..." she stepped in again: "Probably? You know in your heart this was an al-Qaeda operation," trying to plant that seed in Jake Carlisle's head.

"My assumptions have no bearing on the situation," he countered, "let's wait until the facts and evidence are placed on the table."

"Again, wait for what, for those bastards to escape like we did after nine eleven? Vacillation allowed Bin Laden and his cohorts to get away because we delayed our response. I say nuke those sand niggers and turn all that worthless sand into glass."

"Robin have you been drinking?"

"What does that have to do with anything?" She was super sensitive about her problem.

Trying to be delicate as possible Jake Carlisle said: "It's just sometimes when you've had a little too much you're not at your rational best," Robin Calhoun had to control her temper and she backed off a tad, "I appreciated your concern love, I will ease up a bit, you are correct we all must be on our A game at this point in time."

"That would be wise." Robin Calhoun changed the subject when she said, "When are you returning to the Hill?"

"I'll leave McLean early in the morning, go to Dulles and hire a helicopter to ferry me into the city," he said, she asked, "Why a helicopter?"

"According to the cable channels all of the streets in and around the Capital Building are clogged with debris, wrecked cars and such, the copter can put down somewhere close."

"That makes perfect sense."

"I suspect Bohannon will address a joint session of Congress sometime tomorrow night," over on her phone Robin Calhoun said: "That is going to be interesting hearing that slick bastard talk around this."

"I take it you'll be present?"

"I would not miss it for the world, I am due to leave Atlanta International at eight forty-five arriving at Regan around nine fifty," she informed him, he said, "I'll have the same helicopter service there to meet you and bring you into the city."

"Thank you, love. I really want to watch him squirm delivering his address to the nation."

"Robin must you always be the cynic? Give the guy a chance to do his job, after all he's only been president for twelve hours or so."

"That is twelve hours too long," she laughed and then said: "Okay I will give him the benefit of the doubt for a day or two, but if he does not do something to avenge this horrible deed, I'll start yelling at the top of my voice demanding the House start impeachment proceedings," she was playing her concerned senator role to the max.

"Impeachment, that's way over the top even for you, Robin," he told her and she threw back: "I will give that boy a week at the outside, not a day longer before I start calling for his head," Jake Carlisle shook his own head, he knew she was well into her binge after their three year affair he knew her well.

Choosing to change the topic, he switched gears: "Will you be available for dinner say late tomorrow evening?" He asked.

"Why Jake, is my love feeling horny?"

"Well I would like to spend some quality time with you," he told her, she came back: "Quality time is it? That is rather a quaint way of saying you want to get laid, rather charming actually."

"Well?"

"Of course you want quality and I need quantity," she laughed at her own joke.

"Your place or mine?"

"That depends."

"On what?"

"Whether you tell me what I need to hear," Jake Carlisle knew what she meant so he said: "You know very well that I love you Robin."

"*Bingo.* We have a winner. Be at my place at eleven o'clock on the dot and you shall have your quality time."

"I'm counting the hours."

"Me too love," she said with a coo in her voice.

"Until then."

"Goodnight Jake," that had a strong dose of Marilyn Monroe sprinkled all over it, in fact she couldn't have cooed it better.

"Goodnight Robin."

Robin Calhoun returned the receiver to its base and said, "Men are such fools," then she raised her bottle and said, "Jack you are the only man I can count on," and poured herself another shot.

BACK AT THE White House President Bohannon concluded his meet with his National Security Team, he told them, "I expect detailed reports and damage assessments for all pertinent departments along with all possible military scenarios on my desk by eight this morning. Director Matthews I need you to accompany the Attorney General and me on an inspection tour of the entire impact area at first light," Matthews was the Director of the FBI, the president went on: "Oscar..." Oscar Valdez the head of Homeland Security, "...ride along with the Vice President in Marine Two and evaluate the situation in sector B."

"Yes Mister President," the Director answered and Oscar Valdez echoed.

"General Higgins I want you to notify the commanders of the Virginia and Maryland National Guard that I'm federalizing their units immediately, executive orders will be conveyed to them within the hour. I want them on scene by ten AM today. They're to assist the Metro police and first responders in distributing provisions to those in need, maintain order, prevent acts of looting and if necessary suppress any instances of civil disobedience."

"Yes sir," the general said. The president turned to his left and faced the head of FEMA: "Bill I want temporary housing trucked in for those who need a place to stay. Find open spaces in the Virginia and Maryland for these trailers to be set up. We will allow them to stay in these accommodations until they are able to find alternative living arrangements or until their residences have been repaired at our expense of course. And Bill they will not be charged any rent or required to pay for any utilities this will be free gratis a courtesy of their government. Adequate food and water is to been given out to all in need. I will not accept any hiccups, glitches, snafus or excuses that were associated with the Katrina debacle that occurred in New Orleans, understood"

William Cummings, FEMA director said: "Perfectly sir," all eyes were riveted on him as he ended the meet on this note: "I think that covers matters for the moment, ladies and gentlemen I expect results posthaste," with that President Bohannon stood and said to the room, "I want the perpetrators of this crime found, tried, convicted and executed with the quickness, understood?" There was a chorus of "Yes Mister President", and he turned and exited the Situation Room with his Chief of Staff at his shoulder.

On their way back to the Oval Office, he said to Taylor Jackson, "Have the press secretary notify all networks I wish to speak to the nation at eight o'clock..." Taylor wrote this on his notepad. "...the speech will be followed by a Q&A with the media and make certain the reporter from Fox is seated down front and I will field the first question from that person." Taylor Jackson looked at him, "Do you think that's wise, sir."

"Taylor you're a movie buff aren't you?"

"Yes sir."

"Well you should remember that you keep your friends close and your enemies closer, I want to be able to shut them down from the very beginning."

"I like it," Taylor grinned understanding the president's motive clearly.

Taylor Jackson said: "Mister President you handled that meeting with aplomb, you plucked the hawks' feathers," and flashed his grill again.

"Taylor all that was accomplished was I gained us a little breathing room for the moment, soon they'll be in full flight squawking their heads off, we've to get the bottom of this as soon as possible or those birds of prey will thrust their talons in to me in no time flat feeding me to their chicks, the neo cons and the right wingers who are blogging and tweeting away as we speak."

"Sir, as soon as we gathered the info from the CIA, NSA and the military intelligence agencies we'll know who's behind this, I'm certain of it."

President Bohannon looked at him as they passed the Secret Service agent who swung the Oval Office door open and the POTUS told his Chief of Staff: "Taylor my friend information is not knowledge and knowledge is not wisdom", they shifted inside and the door closed behind them.

IT WAS A quiet evening in the Toledo District of Belize where Dr. Karl K. Kussman was holding court with his underlings, he sat behind an enormous desk flanked by tall bookcases that contained scores of scientific and medical journals, a slight breeze drove through the windows. The room was quite large festooned with all manner of Nazi paraphernalia, SS flags stood in front of the windows fluttering. An oversized portrait of Adolph Hitler hung on the wall across the room directly opposite Kussman's desk, the Fuhrer was bracketed by paintings of infamous Third Reich bigwigs: Goring, Goebbels, Bormann, Mengele and a host of others including his all-time favorite, Heinrich Himmler, all hanging there look'n smug with their eyes transfixed look'n down at the assemblage with sneers permanently etched on their faces. In between each painting were swastikas that completed this Nazi wall of shame.

Karl K. Kussman looked out over the room where his men stood at attention waiting for him to speak. German martial music played low, it provided a soundtrack to the scene. Kussman rose from his chair, placed his hands on the desk, leaned over and said, "Tonight is the night of all nights our southern cousins in America launched a withering attack on Washington DC. Our agents there have informed me within the last hour the city was bombarded by mortars rounds. This is a mild payback for what they did to our beloved Germany. This attack is the prelude of an all war on American soil. They will experience the horror they visited upon our cities during the Second World War; we have provided the monies that funded this insurrection by our southern cousins."

He searched each man's eyes, found total dedication to the cause and complete obedience to him there. He went on: "We will give them all the financial assistance they will need to sustain the conflict but we will not conduct any military operations, we are passive investors in this affair.

Let the Americans, north versus south, Democrats versus Republicans, conservatives versus progressives, right versus left, blue versus red go at each other until they destroy themselves from within. This fight will tear America apart at the seams," he walked out from behind the desk fully clad in the notorious black SS uniform, circa 1932. His black ensemble was quite intimidating from his high shiny black boots, flared pant legs, brown shirt and black tie covered by a black tailored jacket bound at the waist by a black belt with a buckle that featured the motto *Meine Ehre heißt Treue* (My Honor is Loyalty) on it, to his patches, epaulettes denoting his rank and the requisite blood red armband, this was topped off with a peaked cap completing the composition of a madman. Was there a hint of rouge on his cheeks? He stood there ooz'n with authority and commanding fear and respect. His men were identically outfitted but they were of lesser ranks. Karl K. Kussman wore a set of pinch glasses and sported a knock off Hitler mustache he was the evil Reichfuhrer incarnate.

Karl K. Kussman born in the Toledo District was the son of a woman whose ancestors were ex-Confederates who immigrated to British Honduras soon after the Civil War and Kiel Kussman a former SS officer and personal body guard for Heinrich Himmler himself.

After the war Kiel fled Germany using the Odessa ratline eventually making it to Mexico in 58, there he integrated himself into a small German Mennonite community. Many SS soldiers joined up with him in Mexico and they went with the Mennonites to British Honduras in 60, where he met Karl's mother Harriet daughter of a wealthy sugar plantation owner. Kiel become a successful exporter of produce, made a fortune ship'n his products to England and Germany. He poured his earnings into prime real estate in Toledo becoming the largest landowner in the district and one of the richest men in the country. He added to his immense wealth harvesting hardwoods and exporting lumber to Europe.

Kiel Kussman sent his son, when he was twelve to live with a former SS officer who was hiding out in Ohio. Karl was an exceptional student, he eventually graduated from MIT, earned his doctorate in biochemistry, returned to his home now known as Belize. Kiel had indoctrinated his son early to the Nazi idealism and Karl K. Kussman became a rabid practitioner who worshipped at the altar of fascism.

Karl K. Kussman stood before his men, all sons and grandsons of those former SS soldiers said in perfect German, "We are the chosen ones the elite SS and the seeds of the new Fourth Reich which will be established in the so called United States of America. After the SOS have caused the total collapse of the American society, I like our glorious Fuhrer who looks down on us now will step in the vacuum restoring order in their ravaged land. They will readily accept the Nazi solutions to the turmoil and strife that will be the ultimate outcome of the conflict. Be happy in your hearts redemption is nigh," he paused stared out at his automatons frozen in place like the terracotta army. The doctor looked up, pointed at Hitler and plunged on; "Our Fuhrer is smiling down us from Valhalla, please that we have continued the fight, the SS never capitulated. Yes we experienced a major setback sixty odd years ago to the traitors in Wehrmacht, but the Waffen SS were the supreme soldiers who did their duty without question. They took a blood oath to die for the Fuhrer. Tonight I compel you to reaffirm that oath to live and possibly die for the vision our leader saw," he let them absorb that and went on telling them now: "It is your obligation to resume the fight, to bring to fruition that vision for a world under the domination of the *National Socialist Party.* Raise your left hands with your thumb, index and middle fingers splayed and repeat after me."

They did as ordered, Kussman's eyes widened, a resident insanity dwelled in them. He spoke in a commanding voice: "I swear by God this sacred oath that to the Leader of the German state and people, Adolf Hitler, supreme commander of the armed forces, I shall render unconditional obedience and that as a brave soldier I shall at all times be prepared to give my life for this oath."

The men repeated the pledge verbatim when finished Karl K. Kussman raised his arm in the traditional Nazi salute and shouted, "*Seig Heil.*" They echoed, again, "*Seig Heil.*" They chorused. This went on for a full thirty seconds, the room resonated with the voices of the committed.

Karl K. Kussman stood still, held his arm aloft and said to them: "Now I believe you believe, you are truly at one with the cause," with that said he lowered his arm, they did likewise and it was over.

Satisfied he spoke to his second in command, "Obergruppenfuhrer Schell you may dismiss your men."

"At your command Reichfuhrer," he did an about face and told the troops: "Return to your quarters, dismissed," the entire platoon made a right face and smartly marched out. Karl K. Kussman watched them depart and said to Schell, “Your men looked splendid, the discipline you have instilled in them was on full display. I am extremely pleased.”

“Thank you Reichfuhrer.”

“You are most welcome, give them a three day respite and then resume your training regime,” Kussman told him.

“As you command, sir.”

“Take leave and go to Ambergris Cay, stay at my villa and enjoy yourself, you have earned it.”

“Thank you Reichfuhrer, I try,” he said, Kussman told him: “It is very apparent, now be on your way.”

“As you wish Reichfuhrer,’ Schell replied, brought his heels together and gave Kussman the Nazi salute: “*Seig Heil.*” Karl K. Kussman returned his and with that Obergruppenfuhrer Schell turned and left.

Kussman watched him go, smiled and said in silence: *Herr Himmler could not be prouder than I at this moment. The fate of our glorious cause is in good hands, my men are equal to any who came before them, long live the National Socialist dream.*

He walked behind his desk, removed his cap, unbuckled his belt, climbed out of his jacket, and settled down. Kussman glanced at his watch, it was one thirty CST, and he lit the computer and logged on. His fingers skated across the keys and brought up Skype. He saw the icon that told him his expected party waited. He clicked on. There she was.

“Ah Senator Calhoun how good to see you, you look especially divine this morning, however do you do it?”

“Flattery will get you everywhere, Doctor,” she said.

“Beauty demands acknowledgement,” he was aware of her sweet spot she was a sucker for compliments.

“Doctor you do have a way with words,” she told him, he told her: “Gazing upon you, one can only be inspired.”

"What can I say to that?" she asked, "Thank you will suffice". Robin laughed.

For a moment there was a hole in the conversation finally Kussman spoke; "Enough banter," on cue she said, "I assume you heard the good news?"

"Your assumption is accurate I was informed close to two hours ago, congratulations on the success of your mission, I understand your people made quite the statement."

"Yes I am pleased with the outcome," Robin Calhoun said from her hotel room in Atlanta, she had sobered up somewhat.

"What is next on your agenda?"

"I would rather not disclose that at this time, but I assure you Doctor you will be impressed," Karl K. Kussman took that in and replied, "I enjoy surprises ever so much my dear."

"And surprised you shall be."

"Well as they say success begets success, you have my unwavering support."

"Speaking of support, I have alerted my colleague Reverend Blount to expect the cash infusion today, is that still forthcoming?"

Kussman loosened his tie and said, "I am head of you on that front, the transfer was executed upon hearing of your master stroke, immediately, I must say with much relish, took care of the matter." She told him, "Wonderful, it will be put to use expeditiously, I have a lot of mouths to feed and palms to grease."

"An endeavor such as you're undertaking will not come cheaply."

"How well I know."

"After your next surprise an additional five million will be conveyed into your Nevis account that was wise of you to select a country which has not complied with the provisions of the Patriot Act."

"Yes the Patriot Act rendered most safe havens like Switzerland, the Caymans and Nassau useless as secret places to secret one's money," she said and he said back, "That is very accurate they have even intimidated our government here in Belize to submit to their tyranny."

Robin Calhoun told him, "The long arm of the US government is far reaching, come soon that arm will be severed."

"I wish you well in that regard, Senator. You have my utmost admiration and I will render whatever financial assistance you may require in the future."

"Thank you."

"Now I must bid you adieu for the moment I have much to attend to here, my research beckons me," she knew it was time to terminate, "Again thank you Doctor, and I will be in touch."

"I wait that occasion with baited breath, Senator."

"Goodbye," Robin Calhoun said and Karl K. Kussman said back: "Take care and stay safe," the screen went dark. He rose and left the room, stepped toward his laboratory he had pressing research to conduct.

3

Misplaced Manners

1865: Charlotte, NC; Washington, GA

THE DAY WAS bleak as heavy clouds draped over Charlotte, North Carolina it was just after two o'clock the afternoon of April 18, 1865 when Jefferson Davis on horseback rode into town at the head of a contingent of one thousand rebel cavalrymen.

After fleeing Danville, Virginia together with the remittance of his cabinet, Davis boarded a Richmond and Danville Railroad car and headed farther south leaving war torn Virginia behind. They were hotly pursued by elements of General Sherman's army.

Jefferson Davis rode up to the home of Lewis Bates look'n haggard and distraught, he dismounted, an aide took the reins steady'n his horse as the Confederate President strode up to the house and found the door locked, turned around looking visibly disappointed. At that moment a neighbor, Colonel William Johnson raced up and grabbed his hand saying, "Welcome to Charlotte Mister President, this is truly an honor, suh." Jefferson Davis accepted his offering: "Thank you Colonel, I desire that this meeting was under more favorable circumstances..." he was heartbroken those within earshot could hear the stress in his voice... "I fear suh our cause is dire, General Lee surrendered the Army of Northern Virginia to Grant two weeks past," the colonel looked shocked, Davis told him: "I received General Lee's letter to that effect last week."

"Will we continue the fight suh?"

"There is a remote possibility we can further the war if these troops can link up with General Kirby Smith's Trans Mississippi Army, he is in command of thirty thousand battle hardened veterans," he turned, looked at his broke down, hungry and ragged cavalrymen astride their warhorses. His eyes welled up, he carried on, "These men are still prepared to resist and fight the invaders if I command them to do so, they are the cream of our valiant troops, but I am most reluctant to ask this of them, but if I do they will react with the vigor and tenacity which has always been the hallmark of our gallant fighting men. Traits they have always faithfully exhibited throughout the war. Their courage has been on full display over the course of the last four years."

The colonel could hear profound doubt in his voice, but he offered this: "Mister President we can provide you additional troops to carry the fight to the Yankees, I can muster two to four thousand men from right here in Charlotte who are most willing to join up with you suh."

Jefferson Davis told him, "That would be outstanding Colonel, have those men report to my aide de camp Captain Oliver and he will tend to their integration into our ranks."

He turned to face him: "Your country deeply and most profoundly appreciates that, perhaps we can continue the effort and stave off the Yankees until we can marshal enough troops to prosecute the war further and reach an accord in our favor," he said but his heart wasn't in it, his words lacked the conviction of the past.

Colonel Johnson said, "Mister President please allow me the honor of providing you and your cabinet food and shelter while you await the return of Mister Bates, I shall send a niggra to collect him promptly suh."

"Your invite is severely needed. Is it within your province to arrange provisions for these men? They are exhausted and could use a good feeding."

"Of course suh, I will attend to it once you are settled in, the grateful citizens of our fair town will gladly supply food and such for these noble warriors. They can bivouac on the outskirts of town and I am positive the grand ladies of Charlotte will prepare them a meal to remember us by." With that said Confederate President Jefferson Davis and Colonel Johnson crossed the mud caked road to his home with Davis' cabinet members bringing up the rear.

Jefferson Davis and his entourage remained in Charlotte, which served as the last capital of the Confederacy for another week before they had to flee with the Yankees hot on their asses.

The group arrived in Washington, Georgia the morning of May 5. That afternoon Jefferson Davis held his final meeting with his fourteen member cabinet at the Georgia Branch Bank Building. He addressed the small assemblage, told them in an abbreviated speech that their cause was truly lost several members campaigned to continue the war employing guerrilla tactics to harass the Federals, an idea Davis had championed, but under the advice of Robert E. Lee he abandoned the notion viewing it as futile.

But he harbored other plans for the future.

After officially capitulating Jefferson Davis adjourned thanking them for their tireless efforts during the past four years. He wished them well, left the gathering and headed to his temporary quarters where he summoned Major Raphael Moses, General James Longstreet's chief commissary officer. Major Moses hasten to Davis' residence, knocked on the door, it was opened by a Davis aide: "This way Major the president is waiting to receive you in the parlor."

Major Moses stepped in and was led to the parlor where Jefferson Davis sat in a wingback chair bracketed by two Confederate soldiers at his shoulders.

Davis pushed himself up, outstretched his hand, "Welcome Major, I have heard good things about you, your sterling reputation precedes you. General Longstreet has nothing but glowing comments about you and your dedicated service to our cause," Raphael Moses took his hand shook it vigorously and bowed his head ever so slightly. He obviously was shaken in the presence of his president, he said: “It is indeed a great honor to finally meet you suh.”

Davis gestured for him to be seated in a chair opposite him both men sat down facing each other, sunlight filtered in and dust motes danced in the rays. Jefferson Davis said, “Major as you well know we have lost the war, we gave it our all but it availed us nothing,” there was tremendous pain in his words, he paused, gathered himself and carried on: “I summoned you here today because I have one final task for you to execute.”

“I'm at your beckon call Mister President.”

Jefferson Davis blinked back the tears that gathered in his eyes and said to him, “When we were forced to evacuate Richmond, we brought the Confederate Treasury with us, our last supply of gold and silver bullion is here with us. This is my final order as your president...” Moses anxiously waited to hear what he was going to be instructed to do, “...I want you to disburse five million dollars of these assets among the troops who have fought gallantly and without compensation for the last two years.”

Raphael Moses said, “Yes suh, Mister President.”

“These men are hungry, sick, exhausted and many are homeless they could use and very well deserve a stipend from a grateful nation for all the sacrifices they given to the Confederacy.”

“I understand suh.”

“Although five million dollars will not recompense every deserving soldier it might assist in helping them to get back on their feet once they have returned home such as it is. Each soldier should receive fifty dollars to help them get through the difficult times ahead.”

“Rest assured Mister President I swear before you every cent will be allocated per your orders.”

“I have complete confidence in your ability to deliver on that pledge.”

For a sustained moment there was silence in the room, finally Jefferson Davis said: “Major Moses upon leaving these premises head directly to my Secretary of the Treasury and he will give you the bullion and provide the necessary armed escorts to insure that your task is accomplished." With that he stood up, Raphael Moses did the same, Jefferson Davis embraced him, stepped back, and shook his hand, "God speed Major, now be off to do your final duty for the nation."

Raphael Moses reluctantly released his grip on his president's hand: "Suh, your instructions will be executed to the fullest."

"I know Major I have total faith in your abilities to do so."

And that was the last official act Jefferson Davis did as President of the Confederate States of America. Major Raphael Moses turned on his heels, walked out of the room and Jefferson Davis' life to do what he was ordered.

Jefferson Davis sat down, called his aide in he appeared within moments, "Yes Mister President."

"Send someone to fetch my nephews they are currently at the White Horse Tavern and have them brought here immediately."

He said, "At once Mister President," and started to leave, Jefferson Davis stopped him: "And Brooks have someone locate Senator Norris and tell him I wish to meet with him..." he took out his watch, flipped the cover up and said, "...at forty five past the hour."

"As you say suh," said Brooks and set out to fetch his nephews and William Hutchinson Norris.

Five minutes later Beau and Tyler Davis entered the parlor, it was Beau who said,

"You requested our presence Uncle Jefferson?"

"Yes, yes, please be seated," they both sat down, Beau to his right and Tyler opposite him.

They sat there, patiently waited for their uncle to speak, finally Jefferson Davis cleared his throat and spoke: "My dear nephews I have an assignment of major import to discuss with you," his nephews said as one, "Yes suh?"

Before he revealed his request he said, "How old are you boys now?" It was Beau the oldest who said: "I'll be twenty six come July and Tyler just turned twenty four last month."

"My sincere apologies, you no longer can be referred to as boys." They both smiled.

"That said, I have a very, very crucial assignment for you men..." again they beamed, "...it will be the most important decision you all will make in your young lives. As you are quite aware, the war for all intent and purpose has ended and much to my anxiety not in our favor."

They sat there.

"I want you to listen intently to my reasoning before you make up your minds whether or not to accept my proposition."

They remained silent.

"I just authorized Major Moses to extract from our remaining treasury five million dollars in gold and silver bullion to be given to our soldiers as a small token of the nation's gratitude for their service. There remains two hundred thousand dollars' worth of gold left in the treasury and I am going to give you each one hundred thousand dollars' worth of gold if you decide to accept my proposal."

"And what would that be Uncle?" asked Tyler.

"I will get to that directly, but first I wish to convey to you all the reasoning behind my forthcoming request, there is talk that several thousand southern patriots have decided to vacate the country and they intend to migrate to South America and British Honduras..." Beau interjected: "Where on God's green earth is British Honduras?" Before Jefferson Davis could reply Tyler hit his brother on the thigh and said: "It's in Central America you dolt." Beau looked sheepish knowing his younger brother had to educate him in front of their uncle; Jefferson Davis rescued him when he said. "Do not be embarrassed Beau, I just learned of its existence last week," letting his older nephew feel better about himself. He stood up put his hands on his lapels, "Being that neither of you are married nor will things be conducive for the losers of this war for a while to come, I want each of you to go to one of these countries to start a new life for yourselves and to prepare for the future of our country."

"The future suh?" this was Beau speaking.

"Yes there will come a time in the distance future, perhaps seventy five, one hundred or one hundred and fifty years from now when an opportunity will arise here in this country to resume the war against the United States."

Their brows went up and their jaws slackened, it was Tyler who asked: "Uncle Jefferson with all due respect suh, you do not envision us living that long, do you?" Beau laughed and Jefferson Davis smiled, "Now Tyler, although longevity is in our lineage I highly doubt either of you will live to be one hundred and seventy five," his nephews chuckled.

"But I do expect the plan to live on long after we have expired."

"Exactly what is your plan, Uncle?" asked Beau, he told him, "I want you men..." again his nephews enjoyed that men reference, "...to choose which country you will go to, to implement the plan, if you accept go to these countries set up plantations and start raising cotton, sugar and coffee there is a fortune to be made growing these crops. Once you have established your plantations, I want you to set aside twenty five percent of your profits into perpetuity, placed it in a special bank account with Lloyd's of London."

"Why Lloyd's of London, Uncle," asked Tyler, Jefferson Davis told him, "Because that is the most renowned bank in the world and the British were very sympathetic to our cause. If certain events had played out in our favor, the British would have interceded militarily on our behalf, so I believe it would be prudent to reciprocate our British cousins with our funds, of course only you and my closest confidants here would be privy to the existence of this account."

"Who might that be, suh?" asked Tyler, Jefferson Davis told him: "The Blounts and the Calhouns of South Carolina. Those families are the only ones I can trust outside of you two to be entrusted with the money that will be accumulated over the years. The Blounts and the Calhouns are die hard Southerners loyal to the bone."

He paused to allow his nephews to chew on it for a minute or two and then asked, “Could you bear being apart, thousands of miles for long periods of time?”

The brothers looked at each other and back to their uncle, it was Beau who said, “I suppose we could bear the separation if that’s what you wish Uncle.”

“It is my wish but it is your decision Beau, you and Tyler here must make the difficult choice, I cannot and would not order you to do this that will be your calls solely.”

They sat there contemplating Jefferson Davis watched them and finally said: “I want you to discuss the matter amongst yourselves and I will return shortly to hear your decision,” he placed his hands on their shoulders and said, “Pray on it together,” and shifted out of the parlor.

Ten minutes later he returned and found Tyler pacing the floor, Beau at the window with his hands clasped behind his back, they heard him enter and he asked, “Have you decided?”

From over by the window Beau said, “Yes.”

“Well do you intend to share it with me?” Beau smiled, turned and said, “We will do it Uncle, as you well know we have always been the adventurous sorts.”

Jefferson Davis looked at Tyler, “Is this a consensus?”

Tyler told him: “We are in total agreement Uncle, we flipped a coin, I won so Beau will go to Brazil and I to British Honduras because I know where it is and I do not want my brother wandering the seven seas looking for it.” Jefferson Davis uncharacteristically exploded with laughter. His nephews stood there they knew they’d pleased their uncle he finished laughing, held his arms out wide, they walked up, he hugged them and said, “Thank you lads, you have pleased your uncle to no end, your mother and father, God rest their souls, are rejoicing in heaven.”

He released his embrace, stepped back and beamed at his nephews, his pride was evident, and they stood there and knew they had pleased him. They hadn’t seen him this happy in years since the beginning of the war.

The three Davis' enjoyed the moment when Brooks knock on the door, Jefferson Davis said, "Yes," and his nephews watch the smile on his face retreat and was replaced with the somber look they had grown accustom too. Brooks slid the double doors to the side and said, "Senator Norris is here, Mister President."

"Ah yes, show him in."

"Yes suh," they could hear Brooks say: "The president will receive you now Senator."

Senator William Hutchinson Norris stepped into the parlor with his top hat in his hand.

"Good afternoon, Mister President," Norris said.

"I have had better, but your greeting is well intended."

"I understand fully suh, we have had better times."

"Yes we have, but I have no time to allot for reminiscence, there is an urgent matter I wish to declare."

"What might that be?"

"A thousand pardons Senator, I have misplaced my manners, allow me to introduce my nephews, my late brother's sons," he pointed at each in turn, "This scrappy young man is Beau and the blue eyed one is his brother Tyler."

Senator Norris said, "It is an extreme pleasure to meet you fine young southern gentlemen," outstretched his hand, it was Beau who said: "It is truly a deep pleasure to make your acquaintance suh," as he shook the senator's hand, in turn Tyler said, "I share my brother's sentiments, suh," and clasped his hand.

Senator Norris looked at Jefferson Davis: "The Davis stock keeps on growing these two are the flower of southern chivalry."

The brothers glowed.

"Yes I am quite proud of them they like others are the future of the South."

"I concur suh."

"Senator let us get down to brass tacks, shall we? Time is limited for pleasantries, there is a proposal I wish to convey to you."

"I await your thoughts, Mister President." Senator Norris said.

"I understand you are leading a contingent of our disgruntled citizens on an expedition to South America is that an accurate statement?"

"Yes, I have verbal understandings with nine thousand to make the journey, suh."

"That many?"

"I anticipate more will be forthcoming once we have established a permanent and vibrate presence there."

"In that vein, I humbly request that you allow my nephew Beau here to accompany you to Brazil."

"I would consider it an honor to comply with your wishes Mister President, we could use every bright and able young man to assist us in this journey into the unknown, and we shall be the new pilgrims venturing into that unknown."

"Well said Senator, Beau will be a most valuable asset, he is wise beyond his years and will assist you in matters as required."

"I readily welcome him and his esteemed abilities, Mister President."

Jefferson Davis asked: "When are you scheduled to embark?"

"I have passage booked in November of this year my son Robert will be accompanying me. We are due to arrive in Rio de Janerio in December the vessel is appropriately named *South America*."

"How fitting," Jefferson Davis said.

"My dear Beau, Robert is around your age, so I see compatibility on several fronts with the two of you." Beau replied: "I look forward to making his acquaintance and to assist in any manner needed suh."

Senator Norris asked looking at Tyler, "And what is to be done with this one here, Mister President, won't he be sharing passage with his brother?"

Jefferson Davis told him: "No Tyler will be journeying to British Honduras along with another group of our people who have decided to leave also. The British have expressed their willingness to allow them to emigrate because they crave our agriculture expertise. I have been informed the country is amenable for cotton and sugar cultivation that will be Tyler's endeavor and the same with Beau in Brazil."

"Excellent." Jefferson Davis said to the group, "Well gentlemen I guess that concludes that issue, I have pressing matters to attend too, so Senator I wish you a fond farewell, safe passage and much success in your undertakings in Brazil."

"Thank you Mister President and let me extend my deepest and sincerest gratitude for all you have done for our nation. We could not have had a more capable captain at the helm of the Ship of State," he extended his hand and made the rounds shak'n the Davis' hands and said to Beau, "I shall see you in Mobile on the twenty first of November," and he spoke to Tyler, "Good fortune in British Honduras, I have a feeling you will fare well there."

"Thank you suh," Tyler replied.

Jefferson Davis said: "God speed Senator."

"Thank you again Mister President," with that he turned, stepped out of the parlor leaving the Davis' there looking at his back and over his shoulders he heard Jefferson Davis say, "There walks an upright Southerner."

Over the nine days that followed that meeting, Jefferson Davis was continuously on the move, pursued by federal troops who finally caught up with him May 10, in Irwinville, Georgia. Jefferson Davis tried to escape by draping his wife's overcoat over his shoulders, but was quickly apprehended. He was transported to Fort Monroe, Virginia where he was placed in irons for three days, charged with treason and was held there for two years, the charges were eventually dropped, he was released and quietly faded into the mist of history.

During the waning years of his life he received numerous letters from Beau and Tyler that informed him how they fared in Brazil and British Honduras.

Beau along with William Hutchinson Norris arrived in Rio de Janerio on December 27, 1865. Norris and Beau were received by Emperor Dom Pedro ll, who sold them sizeable acreage in the state of Sao Paulo, where Norris started the settlement of Americana. The immigrants thrived and called themselves the Confederados.

Beau Davis developed a large tract and became a very successful growing coffee, cotton and sugar cane using black slaves. Slavery wasn't abolished in Brazil until 1888.

True to his promise, Beau Davis deposited twenty five percent of his profits with Lloyd's of London. The Calhouns and the Blounts of South Carolina used the money to establish the Sumter Fund, named after Fort Sumter, the starting point of the American Civil War.

Tyler made it safely to British Honduras, purchased land in Toledo and became very wealthy growing sugar cane. He also kept his promise and sent his commitment to London. He married a girl from Alabama, a member of the ex-Confederates who immigrated to British Honduras, their great, great granddaughter, Harriet Davis married Kiel Kussman.

4

Mad Moment

2009: Metro DC
1968: Quant Tri, Vietnam

THEY MADE THE trip from Washington to Alexandria less than forty minutes after the attack. Charlie Best took the off ramp lead'n to Eddy's Truck Stop and steered the Peterbilt between two eighteen wheelers. There were at least twenty other semis parked. Eddy's was a major stopover for long haulers trip'n up and down eye 95, here the Peterbilt could be hidden, unnoticed by anyone who might scour the freeway in search of them which wasn't the case at the moment.

Charlie Best said, "We made it! He was ecstatic and pounded his palms on the steering wheel. Roger Smith looked over at him, "Yeah man that was some intense shit getting out of DC," he picked up the two-way: "Gray Ghost Two come in, over".

"Gray Ghost Two here, copy?" Harry Reynolds said inside the trailer.

Roger: "Copy, prepare to disembark."

Harry: "The men will exit in two minute intervals."

Roger: “Copy that, have them group up at Check Point Lima, the commander is there with their payments.”

Harry: “Understood.”

Roger Smith put down the two-way and said to Charlie, “I’ll meet you inside in five.”

“Right on,” Charlie Best said, extracted the keys, opened the door, stepped down, and closed the door and strode to the restaurant. Roger Smith picked up his cell, punched some digits, Billy Bob said, “Yes”.

“We’ve arrived without incident the men are starting to exit.”

“Very well, I’m waiting at the rendezvous, stay put for an hour and then move to Check Point Hilo, I’ll meet you there soon after.”

“Will do,” Roger Smith said, clicked off, opened the door, got out and stepped off to get something to eat.

Inside the trailer, Harry Reynolds opened a trap door in the trailer and the first mortar man slipped down through the opening, remained in a crouch, surveyed the landscape under the trucks to see if anyone stood around or approached their semis from any direction, satisfied he crawled out, stood up and walked to one of three cars they had left at Eddy’s prior to entering the trailer the same way.

All disembarked within twenty minutes, Harry Reynolds was last, he reached up, locked the trap door, reconnoitered, and repeat what the others had done. They all loaded up in the cars and drove off to hook up with Billy Bob to receive their fifty thousand dollar bonuses.

Sometime later Charlie Best and Roger Smith walked out of the restaurant, climbed into the cab and drew away to the SOS safe house to get the Peterbilt off the streets.

AS IT DREW closer to nine o’clock at the White House, Taylor Jackson hurried into the Oval Office where he found the president at his desk busy going over the assessments he requested from his National Security Team. He looked up, his Chief of Staff wore a solemn look on his face, the president said: "Yes Taylor," he replied, "Sir this just came into the communications room." Jasper Bohannon noticed the sheet of paper he was holding.

"What's that in our hand?" Taylor Jackson told him, "I'm afraid it's our worst nightmare come true," he offered it to him; the president took the sheet of paper and quickly read its contents. He reared back in his chair, "This is a blessing and a curse," and reread the dispatch.

"Meaning sir?" What they discussed was a dispatch from the SOS, it stated:

To the president of the United States as of 10pm, January 20, 2009, a state of war has existed between the United States and the New Confederate States of America. Hostilities will not cease until the government of the United States grants complete independence to the original thirteen members states of the Old Confederacy. Coming events will magnify in intensity, there will be repetitious attacks on your cities in the North. A new form of attack will be executed once a week until the aforementioned demand is conceded. There will be no negotiations our demands are emphatic and unyielding. The SOS strongly advises mister so called president that you comply. We demand complete autonomy and sovereignty over our own affairs, a complete and separate entity not subject to the laws of the United States. You will receive further instructions soon, The SOS.

Before the president could clarify what he meant, Taylor said, "This must be a joke, sir." Jasper Bohannon looked up: "Taylor take a glance outside the window and tell me if you see anyone laughing, open the window and find out whether you can hear any laughter." Taylor Jackson looked pained, the president carried on: "This is the most severe crises in our history this SOS mob is deadly serious although they may be new age clowns, but they're definitely not joking."

"I'm sorry Mister President I wasn't thinking properly, sir."

"No harm, no foul Taylor, let's move on."

"Yes sir."

"Contact Oscar Valdez over at Homeland Security, the Vice President, the Attorney General and the Director of the FBI and have them come to the White House immediately." Taylor Jackson had been writing this down, he looked up and said; "No CIA, sir?"

"No this is purely an internal matter we'll keep them looking for outside threats, Taylor this could be America's most vulnerable time in its history, if our enemies old and new see we are engaged in a struggle for the very soul of the nation, believe me they will take full advantage. No let's keep the CIA vigilant, they are our sentinels watching the outside world while we quash this problem with the utmost urgency."

"I understand fully now, sir, I minored in world history, all of the great civilizations imploded from within, they didn't succumb to external forces their own people were their undoing."

"There you go," said the president, "and we cannot allow that to happen, not on my watch, we come to far as a nation and as a people to revert back to the past, we have to keep moving forward and I will not allow the SOS, whatever that is, to destroy our country because of regression. Believe me when I tell you this it's not happening."

"Well understood sir, those are my sentiments exactly."

"I'll alert Admiral Higgins to bring our armed forces to DEFCON Three."

"DEFCON Three, Mister President?" asked Taylor Jackson.

Jasper Bohannon told him: "Yes we can't be caught napping, already the world knows we have a crisis and once it's known that this was a domestic terrorist event, someone might try to make moves, even our old enemies who are our new best friends will take full advantage, maybe not militarily at first, but definitely politically and economically. Taylor this is our toughest hour."

"At the moment we have no friends it's just us, Mister President."

"That my friend sums it up - by the way, have General Sam Falk come here this afternoon around two thirty, clear my calendar until four o'clock."

"General Falk, may I ask why him?"

"You read the Eradicator file, did you not? Asked the president, "Yes sir, but they are a sordid bunch of fanatics," Taylor Jackson objected.

"Yes they are, but they're my fanatics and I need them."

"From their file these guys are unrestrictedly ruthless; I believe the apropos term is, psychopathic."

"That's a might harsh, but if that's what it takes, that's what I'm down for."

Still not happy with it, Taylor Jackson said: "Will all due respect Mister President, I think you should reconsider, these guys will create more damage than they will prevent."

"Under different circumstances that would be funny, but this is a death match and I need my best killers."

Taylor Jackson looked at the president, this was the first time he'd seen this side of him and he was momentarily frightened, he moved past that and came back to it say'n: "Once you uncork these guys you might not be able to put them back in the bottle."

"That's clever Taylor, but no further debate please, and I want General Falk in front of me at the aforementioned time. I need my top dogs." Taylor Jackson looked at the president totally puzzled, he said: "We're talking dogs here?" Jasper Bohannon looked over his shoulder at the city still belch'n smoke from last night's attack, he turned around, "Sidney Bechet, was a great jazz musician who once offered to bet another musician that his dog could out dog his dog, and that's what I'm counting on, I'm going to sic the Eradicators on the SOS and I'm supremely confident my dog will win." What could Taylor Jackson say? Nothing. So that's what he did and just stood there and reeled that in.

Seeing he was totally blown away, the president spoke into the silence: "Taylor, we played a lot of big games together in college, to win those games Coach Miles had to play his first string players and I need our varsity to win this game, so be about getting General Falk here." That put a period on it.

IT WAS TEN fifteen at General Falk's bungalow located in a highly secured area near Quantico. He sat in an overstuffed chair, sipped at his third cup of coffee read'n the morning papers. He read both the Post and the Examiner giving him a conservative and progressive take on last night's event. He always read the local papers to get a total understanding of the thought processes of America from the center outward. General Sam Falk was apolitical, his allegiance was to the Constitution, Old Glory and the Corps in that order; he didn't involve himself in the petty bicker'n of the left and the right. The nation as a whole came first and last in his book nothing else mattered or concerned him, just the continuation of the American way of life.

He put his cup down, lowered his paper, peered over the top at his two English bulldogs camped over by the fireplace nap'n contently. He looked at his constant companions, smiled and went back to his morning read. Mad Sam Falk was a no nonsense guy, very rough around the edges, something he didn't apology for, he knew who he was and he was proud of it. General Falk was one hundred percent American, red, white and blue through and through. He was a career marine, a proven combat commander admired and respected by all who knew him, they accepted his idiosyncrasies, if anyone could be truly called Captain America it was Mad Sam Falk, an authentic American hero.

His Codex 4 sounded, he pushed up from his chair, place the Post on the seat sauntered over to his computer station and picked up his Codex on its third chime, "Falk here."

"General Falk this is Taylor Jackson, White House Chief..." the general rode over him: "I know who you are, get to it," the way he said it was almost an order, his voice commanded such authority even when he spoke of trivial matters, which wasn't often, people would instantly hop to.

Taylor Jackson was taken aback by the general's directness, so he said: "My mistake General, the president requests your presence in his office this afternoon at two thirty."

"Am I to assume this is in regards to last night's cowardly attack on our nation's capital?"

"Yes General, precisely."

"Inform the president I shall there as ordered along with Smedley Butler and Chesty Puller my personal bodyguards...," *This guy needs bodyguards?* "...alert the Secret Service and have passes ready for us when we arrive."

"Of course General, that will be attended too."

"Goodbye Mr. Jackson."

"Goodbye General," Taylor Jackson said, he was happy to get off the phone, he felt an eerie feel'n wash over him, like someone just trekked across his grave.

TWO MINUTES LATER Taylor Jackson came into the Oval Office, stepped up to the president who stood at the window where he looked out at the city, the SOS dispatch in his hand, he said without turning around: "Yes Taylor, what news do you bring?"

"Everyone is on their way, they should arrive shortly."

"Very good. What of General Falk?"

"I just finished speaking with him he'll be here at the appointed time."

"Great, anything else?" the president asked.

"General Falk strikes me as being creepy," he said, he shivered ever so slightly, that feel'n briefly haunted him.

"I thought we've been over this Taylor?"

"I was just commenting sir, no harm intended," the president let it go and said: "Taylor what's the status of tonight's press conference?" Taylor Jackson told him, "All of the broadcast stations and cable channels are on board sir."

"Good. Taylor we have to keep a lid on this SOS matter until I say it should be made public by me alone. No damn leaks."

"Understood."

"Tell the communications director to personally stand by for the next dispatch from this group of murderers and I want it brought to me express, no one's eyes are to read it until I have, understand?"

"To the letter sir." Taylor Jackson replied, the president said to him, "Now leave me with my thoughts. I have much to do and I need to prepare my address to the nation."

"I'll tend to matters Mister President, I'm available should you need me," Taylor Jackson said, turned and took his leave.

AT THE SAME time, General Falk hung up his Codex, went into the bathroom, he had just spoken to Mickey Stovall, he told him to stand by for action and to prepare his team to move out at a moment's notice, Mickey said back: "Will do sir," and Mad Sam informed him: "I'll be in touch after I've met with the president."

The general stepped into the rain room, turned on the water, placed his palms on the wall, lowered his head and let the water cascade over him as he stood there and thought about the things to come.

ON JULY 15, 1968 it was a typical hot and humid day in Vietnam. Captain Sam Falk was leading his force recon company after a successful green ops deep penetration mission somewhere in the Quang Tri Province, back to the regimental HQ. His unit had been in the bush for the past five six days, now they were en route to their fire base with vital Intel that detailed enemy concentrations and movements.

The captain walked with his XO and his radio operator in front of the column, Lance Corporal Billups was on point about fifty meters out. All was quiet as they moved through the brush save the birds twitter'n high in the canopy voic'n love notes to one another. Here and there bugs harassed the marines as they trudged through the overgrowth headed to the safe confines of Fire Base Bravo.

Captain Falk said to his XO Lieutenant Belmont, "Well Vince so far so good," they were no more than four clicks from their HQ, the XO said back, "Yes sir only about an hour and half from a lukewarm shower, some hot chow, a few cold brewskis and then it's to the rack to cop some Z's." Captain Falk turned to face him and said: "There you go again looking into my head," his XO laughed: "Just anticipating your thoughts sir," the captain came back: "Yeah mine and every swinging dick in the company," the lieutenant grinned, "These grunts have been hump'n steady for days now, they could use a fiesta and a siesta," the captain said nothing to that and the XO demanded: "Should we send someone to relieve Billups on point?"

"Yeah he's been hump'n out front for a bit; send someone to relieve him."

"At once sir," the lieutenant said and hollered over his shoulder, "Dunn go and relieve Billups on point." PFC Dunn ran past on the double: "Aye, aye sir," on his way to carry out the order.

A few minutes later Billups hustled back to the column, the captain saw him thread through the trees, he stopped and told him, "Everything looks good up a head sir, though there's a clearing com'n up about a half a click further out." Captain Falk said: "Mighty fine, fall in."

Billups waited for the column to pass, fell in and brought up the rear.

They reached the clearing soon after and Captain Falk raised his arm, the company halted, he looked out over the meadow, it was about two hundred meters across to the tree line on the other side the wood. He said to the XO: "Have the men formed an echelon formation pass the word." The lieutenant repeated the order and it was past back through the ranks to the rear where it eventually reached Billups. They came out of the cover of the thick brush and trees headed to the other side of the meadow, they could see Dunn halfway across out in the open.

The company set out, when they approached the half way point, Dunn was near the far tree line. At that moment mortar rounds dropped from the sky, WHOOMP, WHOOMP, WHOOMP. The familiar clack'n of AK47s came from the undergrowth.

The NVA had waited until the marines were fully exposed before they opened up.

They used Dunn as bait and lured the company into their trap.

Instead of killing him they let him continue to approach their position, a Regular had him in his sights the entire time, when the first volley of mortars exploded, the soldier squeezed the trigger on his AK and PFC Dunn dropped from a bullet that hit him between the eyes.

Captain Falk shouted: “Hit the deck and return fire!” Most of his men already laid prone firing into the trees, the WHOOMP’N and CLACK’N intensified. The captain saw his XO take four rounds to the chest and he fell over, the captain knew Vincent Belmont was dead.

Gunfire did its death dance and raked the clearing; marines were hit from all directions. The causalities mounted up. Mortar rounds kept exploding they created small depressions, where some marines sought shelter from the withering fire. The NVA had the meadow zeroed in and the 82mm rounds continued to come down on the trapped jarheads.

The marines looked for avenues of escape there were none they had stepped into a horseshoe ambush, the NVA now had them hemmed in on three sides. They were pinned down out in the open it was a hundred meters to the tree line from which they came.

The mortars ceased, now the NVA accurately targeted their RPG’s on their position. Several dozen streaks of light and bursts of white hot energy exploded across the battlefield. The RPG’s streaked in slightly at first and more and more slammed into the marines’ position.

Several jarheads looked at each other and one yelled; “FUCK THIS SHIT,” jumped up and stormed toward the tree line, twenty others followed; they fired and zigzagged their way across the open space into the teeth of the AKs.

They were cut down in a heroic charge.

Within minutes Captain Falk saw at least forty dead marines on the battleground, they were being mauled. Bodies were stacked up all over the meadow. The men tried to fight their way out of the ambush, but they were repelled time after time, overwhelmed by NVA gunfire.

Suddenly the RPG's ceased.

There was silence.

Then the Regulars rose up and charged out from the stand of trees bent on the total annihilation of the marines.

From the number of soldiers charging forward it appeared the unit was of battalion strength. The marines fired relentlessly into the horde.

The NVA assault was non-stop they kept com'n and com'n.

Captain Falk laid semi hidden in a depression created by a mortar, from his vantage point he could see the NVA everywhere inside their perimeter. Rounds sizzled and popped all around his location, bullets struck inches from his head, he was alive but moments from death.

The Regulars and the Marines were locked in a death struggle engaged in close quarters combat; hand to hand fight'n and dy'n occurred everywhere he looked. He and his company were overrun.

It was decision time.

His radio operator was hit early in the fight by shrapnel and laid dead about thirty five feet away from Captain Falk, he emerged out of the hole and slithered toward the radio.

His unit was in dire straits.

Hope was abandoned.

He had to make the hard decision, this wasn't going to be a Custer moment and if he and his men were to die then everyone engaged in the battle would suffer the same fate.

There wouldn't be any winners just dead warriors.

What seemed like a lifetime but only a minute later he finally reached the phone, he took out his map and quickly read it, recognized their location, pressed the button and shouted: "Fire Base Bravo this is Captain Sam Falk, we are...," a Regular had him in his sights, he squeezed the trigger, but his magazine was empty so he rushed Sam Falk with his bayonet ready to thrust it into the captain laying there on his back, Sam Falk slid to his left just as the soldier stabbed, he shot him in the heart and chest with his 45…, "under heavy attack from the NVA…," the Regulars kept com'n, he kept firing, they continued to drop in front of him…,"here's your fire mission range nine zero, bearing steady at three five zero, fire for *effect*," his 45 emptied, he rolled over and grabbed the dead radio operator's 45 from his holster, charged it and fired, each round punched a Regular's ticket. Twelve stacked up in front of him. Having spent the rounds from the second 45 he reached for a fallen NVA's AK and started in again; he used the dead soldiers for cover.

He spoke into the receiver and told the 155 battery commander to relay the coordinates to the navy destroyers off shore five miles away, he dropped the phone and rejoined the fight.

The fighting was ferocious he slammed and slammed magazines into the AK and leaned on the trigger rip'n off rounds. Thirty seconds after his desperate call the first of the 155 rounds slammed into the clearing. Explosion after explosion could be heard and felt. Concussions from the 155's sent bodies flying in all directions, shrapnel whizzed everywhere, the Regulars were cut down like blades of grass. Everything around him turned red hot, thick smoke filled his lungs, his eyes burned.

Soon the eight inch shells from the destroyers arrived on scene add'n more weight to the carnage. The heavy metal cocktail of artillery and naval gunfire pulverized the meadow, craters were bored into the ground, men and body parts filled them up.

The bombardment from the 155's and eight inch combo last a full ten minutes and suddenly it fell silent, the noise ceased but the silence was louder than the bomb'n that end moments ago now smoke hung like a shroud over the battlefield.

Many fires burned. Groans and moans in English and Vietnamese started their plaintiff wails from NVA Regulars and US Marines.

The mad moment was over.

Captain Sam Falk was knocked unconscious by the concussion from an eight inch shell, he regained consciousness, a panorama of death and destruction met his every glance, he had been hit twice in his left thigh by an AK and he had a piece of shrapnel lodged in his back, the wings of death had brushed him several times, but he was alive in fact he was the only one left alive, everyone else American and Vietnamese were dead or dying on the battlefield.

Captain Sam Falk had survived the “mad moment’.

Soon after helicopters with reinforcements from Fire Base Bravo arrived they were greeted by a horrific sea of carnage.

The sweet stench of death drifted over the scene.

He was load into a copter and flown to a hospital ship lying off shore, where surgery was performed and he recovered from his wounds.

Captain Sam Falk was awarded the Medal of Honor from a grateful nation. He had survived the ‘mad moment’ which was only the second time in Marine Corps’ history someone was awarded the moniker “The Mad Moment’ and since that battle on a hot humid afternoon somewhere in the Quang Tri Province he’s been called Mad Sam Falk.

5

Smedley & Chesty

Washington

IT WAS LATER that morning at eleven o'clock in the Oval Office where the president and his Chief of Staff awaited the arrival of the VP, the FBI Director, the Attorney General and Oscar Valdez, head of Homeland Security.

Taylor Jackson said into his cell, "I'll inform the president, thanks Kenny," he flipped it shut and said to the Jasper Bohannon, "That was the head of White House Security he said everyone has arrived except the VP who's leaving Blair House as we speak, it shouldn't take more than a few minutes for him to stroll over."

The president sat at his desk, pushed up his sleeve, looked at his watch, "Excellent, I want to get them up to speed concerning these SOS criminals."

"I agree sir, we have to get on top of this ASAP, and we can't let these A-holes..., he was always careful not to use profanity in the presence of the president..., "think they can get away with this heinous crime." The president nodded and said, "Has the communications director received any further notes from these people, I'm being kind when I say that, as of yet."

"I spoke with her moments ago before I came in she said nothing has arrived thus far from these weasels."

"That might be an insult to the entire weasel family."

"You're right sir, I apologize to all the weasels of the world," Jasper Bohannon said, "I believe your earlier expression was most fitting in describing these folks, but in that vein we will ferret out these criminals and bring them to justice."

"Speaking of dispatches, earlier you made a comment about it being a blessing and a curse, what did you mean sir?"

"Ah that," the president stood up, adjusted his tie, walked from behind his desk, stepped up to Taylor placed his hands on his shoulders, looked him in the eyes and said, "The blessing is it will quell the hawk's lust to launch a nuclear strike against an innocent country which was my most dreaded scenario in this madness. Now we know this was a domestic terrorist event that fortunately alleviates the pressure from the right to do the unthinkable."

"Most astute sir and the curse?"

The president took his hands down, stepped to the Resolute Desk, leaned back on the front of it, folded his arms, as Taylor stood there waiting for his answer, the president said: "Now that the culprits of this unscrupulous act have identified themselves, I have a difficult decision to make."

"Meaning sir?"

"Even though we have a group of psychopathic citizens who've staged what could be the most notorious crime in American history, the burning question is how do we go to war with our own people, we went down that road in the past and it fractured the country like no other event in our history. Its repercussions are still felt to this day. Obviously whoever is behind the SOS organization desires to revisit the ugliness of that affair Taylor therein lays the curse."

The Chief of Staff made no reply and stood there awestruck his admiration for his Commander in Chief and personal friend deepened, finally he said: “I see it clearly now sir, we’re not playing tiddlywinks here, you’re correct we need to sic our dogs on these A-holes ASAP.”

“I see you’ve come around to my way of thinking on how best to tackle this problem.”

“Yes I have sir, these scoundrels must be eradicated,” just then his smartphone went. It was the Head of White House Security telling him all of the expected guests were present and waited in the outer lobby, he told the president this and he said, “Have them shown in,” as he climbed into his jacket and buttoned it. Through the door came the quartet of the most powerful individuals in his administration.

IT WAS APPROACHING one forty five in the afternoon when General Falk finished putting his uniform on, he had chosen to wear his winter greens instead of civvies to meet the new president. He looked most impressive as he stood there with rows of fruit salad on his chest, scrambled eggs on the brim of his barrack cover and a French Fourragere draped over and under his left armpit. He truly looked the part of a Baby G in the USMC, the personification of all the Corps stood for, a frontline warrior in the flesh. General Falk was no myth he was the real deal anyone could see that once the gazed upon him. He smiled pleased with the image he saw in the mirror. He had aged well over the years, his rugged look reminded folks of the Marlboro man, although he didn’t smoke, never had.

Mad Sam was ready to get after these cruds that dared attack his beloved America and its capital no less, he fumed inside he was ready for war. A no holds battle with those loathsome characters was about to be waged, he intended to loose the full fury of his Eradicators.

This was a no bullshit moment.

He stepped to his computer station picked up his smartphone and called his driver First Sergeant Cooper, “Top bring the car around we’ll be outside momentarily,” he said and heard the first sergeant say, “Right away sir.”

The general pick up his swagger stick tucked in under his arm and said, "Smedley and Chesty fall in on me," his bulldogs rose from their personal sofas, raced up to him, sat back on their haunches and looked up, he said, "Stand by for inspection," the dogs ears twitched, they waited for the next command, the general said: "*TENT HUT*, "they instantly stood up and stood there stiff legged and waited. He walk up to Smedley looked him up and down, he had his scarlet Marine Corps band blouse on, the general said: "Present arms," the dog raised its front paws one after another and the general examined each one, satisfied he said, "Mighty fine, now open your breech," Smedley opened his mouth, his long tongue dropped out, Mad Sam bent down and sniffed; "Smedley you've been hitting the gee dunk again, shame on you," he rubbed his head: "You have your good cookie medal on properly, very squared away." He turned smartly, stepped up in front of the second bulldog and repeated the routine, "Chesty, I swear you look superb in your dress blues, well done lads, you're two are AJ squared away gyrenes," the dogs visibly grinned.

Smedley Butler and Chesty Puller understood multiple commands, the general had trained them well, he put them through puppy boot camp the day he brought them home to the Barn, six years ago.

Satisfied all three of them looked razor sharp, Mad Sam put their leashes on and said: "Right face, *HOA*," the dogs faced right, "*FORWARRRD HOA*," and they marched off.

Outside Top Cooper held the door open, the dogs leaped in, General Falk followed, they settled on the back seat and he said: "Now lads I want you be on your best behavior, we're off to see the boss and Chesty no begging, understood?" he acknowledged with a bark. Top entered the car, Mad Sam said: "Take us to the White House," and they drew away from the curb headed to 1600 Pennsylvania Avenue.

BACK AT THE White House President Bohannon wrapped up his meet, everyone had offered an opinion, after they had their say, Jasper Bohannon said: "Ladies and gentlemen, now that we've finalized our strategies to prevent the next attack and to totally eliminate this terrorist organization by concentrating our efforts on finding out who are the demented ones responsible, any questions?"

One after another they said: "No sir, Mister President," and he said back, "Good, I'll keep you in the loop as events unfold and one more thing this is crucial, no leaks, this must remain under wraps until I think it's right to reveal what we know to the public, understand?"

There was a chorus of yeses.

"Well folks, I believe that concludes things for now, thanks for your attendance," with that they rose, shook the president's hand and made for the door to do their parts to get to the bottom of the situation. When the door closed, Taylor Jackson said: "Once again you handled things with equanimity sir." Jasper Bohannon said: "Why the bouquets? Save the praise until we have accomplished what we've set out to do, prior to that it's just misplaced adulation, leave the pom poms at home."

Taylor Jackson was somewhat hurt, he meant well, but he knew, the president was right, now was not the time for taking bows, nothing had happened to warrant such premature cheers.

The president glanced at the clock over the fireplace it was two fifteen, "General Falk is due within fifteen minutes is he not?"

"That's correct sir, from what I've been told he's one punctual dude, sir," the president quirked a brow at that and went back to the stack of files in front of him.

DURING THE FORTY minute ride to the White House General Falk sat in the rear, looked out the window and reflected on his conversation with Skeeter Macklin back in December.

When Skeeter returned from the Dimitar Spasića operation he went straight to the Barn to inform the general that he wanted to submit his resignation. The general sat there behind his desk as Skeeter explained his reason for leaving the Corps, the reaction he received was one eighty from what he expected. The eruption Mickey Stovall and he forecasted aboard the *USS Key West* wasn't forthcoming.

Mad Sam sat there taking it all in, when Skeeter finished he merely said: 'Major Macklin your country appreciates your service and the Corps your unwavering professionalism and dedication, the Crotch is losing one of its finest marines, I wish you and the bride the best. By the way have you chosen your best man yet?" Skeeter told him he hadn't, General Falk said: "Well in that case I humbly ask that you consider me for that distinct honor Major." Skeeter was stunned, he'd never known the general to be sentimental and was delighted, he said, "Of course, General the honor would be all mine, sir." General Falk said: "Mighty fine," and then asked, "When's the wedding?"

"January sixteenth sir."

"Did you know that's my birthday?"

Surprised Skeeter Macklin said: "No sir I didn't."

"Well it is and your wedding will be the best birthday present I've ever received," they smiled, the general stood up, outstretched his hand and they shook on it.

On January 16, 2009, four days before the attack on Washington, DC Skeeter and Jessy were wed it was a beautiful ceremony all the Eradicators were in attendance along with her family and many members of the Macklin clan, and yes Smedley Butler and Chesty Puller were present also. The bride and groom flew from Dulles International to enjoy the vanilla beaches and pistachio waters of San Andres for a week of sun and fun on their honeymoon.

Top Cooper drove through DC proper he avoided the congested streets that led to the White House, General Falk saw the pall that hung over the Capital, he snapped out of his reverie and anger replace the tender memories of the wedding. The car stopped at the security gate, the window slid down and Top said: "General Falk to see the president," and was passed on. They pulled up to the entrance, Top got out, raced around, opened the back door, Mad Sam, Smedley Butler and Chesty Puller stepped into the White House to meet the new President of the United States of America.

Inside the Oval Office, Taylor Jackson received word that the general had arrived and was on his way there. He told Jasper Bohannon, "They've arrived sir."

The president looked up from his stack of files: "They?"

"Yes sir the general and his two bodyguards some guys named Smedley Butler and Chesty Puller."

"Bodyguards? Those names sound vaguely familiar, have we met them?"

"Not that I know of sir."

"Well have them shown in."

The interior of the White House was a hive of activity, but everyone paused as they watched the trio flow past headed down the hallways to the Oval Office. The Secret Service Agent swung the door open and they entered.

The president was seated behind the Resolute Desk with his Chief of Staff stationed in front slightly to his right, he looked up his jaw dropped for a moment he collected himself, smiled and said, "General Falk welcome the Oval Office," stood up, came from behind the desk and stepped up to the general with his hand outstretched say'n, "It's a deep pleasure to meet you. Who have we here?" the president looked down at the bulldogs, General Falk said: "The pleasure is all mine, Mister President," as they shook hands, "These two rogues are my Devil Dogs, the one in the red band blouse in Smedley Butler and in the dress blues is Chesty Puller."

The president bent down offered his hand in turn the dogs sniffed it and he was accepted as a friend. Jasper Bohannon said: "Good representations of the breed, General they look very smart in their uniforms. Where have I heard those names before?"

"Thank you Mister President, I'm quite fond of these lads, they're named after two of the Corps toughest and feistiest generals sir."

"Ah yes, now it comes back to me they certainly look the part I might add. Those two men are legends in the Corps from what I recall."

"Your recollection is correct sir, they were some tough SOB's and these lads here can live up to their names."

"I bet they can - General Falk I'd like you to meet my Chief of Staff Taylor Jackson," the general replied, "We've spoke on the horn earlier it is a pleasure to match the face with the voice, how do you do?" Taylor Jackson shifted over, "I'm well sir thank you." Just then the bulldogs viciously growled at him, General Falk snapped: "Belay that," the growling ceased. "I beg pardon Mister Taylor my lads have lost their etiquette."

Taylor Jackson had taken a step back when he heard the warnings and looked very concerned, "That's quite alright General, I have that effect on dogs when we first meet, I'm sure they'll adjust."

The general said: "As I," and spoke to his Devil Dogs: "Go over by the fireplace and parade rest," they obediently went the Oval Office's fireplace, settled on their haunches and kept their eyes on Taylor Jackson.

The president said, "Very interesting encounter - would you be seated here on the sofa General, and let's get down to the business at hand." General Falk said, "Yes Mister President we have much to discuss concerning this hideous crime perpetrated on our country," he followed him across the oval rug, placed his cover and swagger stick on the table beside the sofa and waited for the president to seat himself, then he settled on the sofa and crossed his legs: "I'm all ears, Mister President."

Jasper Bohannon picked up the SOS dispatch from the coffee table that separated them, reached over and handed it to the general: "This came into the communications center earlier this morning please peruse it before we start." General Falk took it as his eyes moved over the words, the president sat there watching him, from the expression on his face he could see the general was super pissed. When he finished he looked up and Jasper Bohannon could see the intense pain and hatred that dwelled in those eyes.

The general put ice in his voice, "This is an abomination, sir."

"I share your sentiments General, I hear your outcry and it's well placed."

Falk: "SOS?" What is this, a sick cry for help? Shit on the shingle? Does anyone know what this acronym stands for?"

Bohannon: "The intelligence agencies, civilian and military are trying to decipher it as we speak, checking back Intel to see whether it's been used in the past."

Falk: "Whatever it stands for, these are..., can I be me sir?"

Bohannon: "By all means, General."

Falk: "Thank you Mister President, these are a bunch of sick fucks."

Taylor Jackson stood beside the Resolute Desk far from Smedley Butler and Chesty Puller who still had their eyes locked on him; he cringed at the general's salty language, something the president didn't tolerate within his earshot.

This was new.

"Under the circumstances that's well said and I agree with your word selection completely."

Taylor Jackson looked aghast.

Falk: "Well every puzzle has a solution, this will be figured out in due time, but that's cold comfort in view of what these bastards have done to our great nation, sir," he paused for a brief moment and carried on: "Mister President I swear on the Constitution, I will do whatever is necessary to hunt these sons of bitches down...," Taylor had a mental fit hear'n the general express himself in such terms..., "and put a permanent end to this secession bullshit. This is bullshit ala mode. Why it's championship *bullshit*."

Taylor Jackson couldn't bear it any longer even though he possessed a potty mouth he was embarrassed by what was heard but the president seemed okay with it. Between what he listened to and the bulldogs' eyes on him, Taylor Jackson had to invent something to get him out of the Oval Office so he broke in: "Excuse me Mister President and General Falk I just received a text from the communications director, if you all would excuse me I'll head out to see what it is she wants."

The president said, "Yes it might be something urgent." Taylor Jackson took to his heels, mak'n it for the door, Smedley Butler and Chesty Puller tracked him all the way, the door opened and Taylor Jackson was gone. The general studied them as they watched him and said in silence: *That's rather odd of my lads.* He had his suspicions but he didn't give them voice. He spoke to Smedley and Chesty, "Hit the rack," they lay down and closed their eyes. The president laughed and asked: "Do you only speak to them in military terms?"

"Yes, but mostly in Corps jargon sir."

"I see - you were saying General."

"Can I speak candidly, sir?"

"I thought you were."

Mad Sam smiled at the president and Jasper Bohannon smiled back, the general carried on: "Sir, I was born in Texas, a geographical occurrence that was beyond my control, I had to listen to that confederacy foolishness all my young life, I thought it was bullshit then and I know it's bullshit now," the president sat and hung on his every word.

The general told him: "That issue was settled a hundred and forty odd years ago and these SOS bastards have the gall to want to revisit that insanity is a direct affront to what this country has accomplished. All the hardship and grief we have suffered together as a people and now these assholes want to tear it apart this cannot and will not happen," he was steamed up above two twelve boil'n over with anger.

The president rather enjoyed the general's earthiness; he was tell'n it like it is.

Mad Sam: "Sir if we don't stop them and nip this in the bud it could blossom into something quite ugly."

Jasper Bohannon: "What's the expression? You've got to fight fire with fire," he answered his own question.

Mad Sam: "That's exactly what I intend to do, sir, I'm guided by experience."

Jasper Bohannon: "I not only agree with you, I'm with you."

Mad Sam: "Mister President if we don't get on top of this immediately you'll be receiving flak from all corners of the political landscape."

Jasper Bohannon: “This is above and beyond politics, to the world in general and to Americans in particular it’s the story of the nation’s worse perversion.”

Mad Sam: “If there is hell on earth it is Washington, DC today.”

The president reached for a large file on the coffee table opened it and said, “I’ve read the Eradicators file, I must ask you why your men take such unnecessary chances? I read Major Macklin’s report about the Cuban mission.”

General Falk told him, “Boldness is the hallmark of the Corps sir and the Eradicators are the epitome of that creed and that shall not be compromised by timidity.”

Jasper Bohannon chewed on that for a moment and said: “I understand the UN paid a substantial reward for the capture of the Serbian warlord.”

“Yes they did, the money was donated to various charities sir, that’s always been our policy.”

“I’m aware of that General, your integrity is beyond reproach.”

“Thank you, sir.”

“Back to your Eradicators, I read the file on your current team leader Captain Stovall.”

“Yes sir,” the general waited to hear what the president had to say about Mickey.

“From what I’m able to discern, he had questions raised about his psychological profile and his tactics have been questioned by several psychoanalysis’ he has a propensity to go off the reservation it seems.”

Mad Sam informed the president: “With all due respect sir, Mickey is no mouse, pun intended.” The president laughed and said: “I guess you told me.”

“I meant no harm sir,” and Jasper Bohannon said, “None felt General, in fact I rather enjoy your condor, I find it refreshing, someone who speaks truth to power," and the general said to him: "An ass kisser I'm not sir."

"General Falk, I have entirely too many of those within the confines of the White House as it is."

"Well sir, that's never been my strong suit." Again the president laughed.

"Sir the Marine Corps is your private army, that's well known and has been a staple of the presidency since the dawn of the republic, but the Eradicators are your hit squad that's what we do and we do it well."

"That's exactly what the country needs at this moment in time."

"Not a problem sir, but I must qualify things." The president looked at him and demanded: "What might that be?"

The general paused to assemble his thoughts then he said, "I will only deploy my men when the situation is just, we will not engage in any illegal undertakings. I can't and will not ask my men to commit crimes in the name of anything that is unjust."

The POTUS: "I'm glad to hear you say that, it's a position that I share."

The general: "A lot of let's say unsavory things have been done in the name of the red, white and blue, but all they've done, who shall remain nameless, is stained our flag and Constitution. And I will not nor will my men be a party to anything like that sir."

The POTUS: "General Falk you probably already know this, but I want to let you know that I'm aware of it also."

The general: "What might that be sir?"

The POTUS: "A true American is one who speaks up when his or her country is wrong and is willing to die for their country when she's right."

The general: "Mister President I've never hear it said so concisely, so precisely and so eloquently. My respect meter just overloaded."

The POTUS: "Thank you General, I have my moments." Mad Sam roared with laughter, Chesty Puller and Smedley Butler opened their eyes, sensed all was well and went back their canine dreams.

President Jasper Bohannon told General Sam Falk: "You can rest assured this president will never order you to do anything woeful that will darken the sunshine of America."

"Well said sir, I see you are a man of principle," and Jasper Bohannon told him: "That's makes two men of principle and integrity sitting in this room, space I proudly share with you."

"Ditto sir." The president looked at the general and said: "I see you're wearing your Medal of Honor."

"Yes sir, I always don it when I'm in uniform."

"My I inquire as to the circumstance under which it was earned?"

"It's a long story sir," Mad Sam said, he was obviously reluctant to speak on it, but this hesitancy was put aside by the comfortably he felt with the man who sat across from him.

The president said: "I have time to listen if you wish to share your story with me."

"You really want to hear it sir?" and Jasper Bohannon told him: "Here I await General, please tell me."

So he did.

When the telling was done the president said: "Absolutely amazing General, utterly astonishing."

"Yes sir, in a word it was harrowing," and the president told him: "I can't possibly image what it must have been like; you have an incredible story to tell." Mad Sam said: "Only God know my story sir, I'm just living it line by line, page by page, chapter by chapter working my way to the end."

"Aren't we all General," the president said and Mad Sam replied, "Yes but most of us are unaware of it." The president looked at the clock it told him he had another twenty minutes to devote to the general, so he said: "Back to the issue at hand."

"Yes sir?" Mad Sam waited.

Jasper Bohannon asked the hard question: "General Falk in your learned opinion where do you think the SOS will strike next?"

"Well sir, there are thousands of soft targets in America where they could do their dirty work and cause major damage, generating massive hysteria among the populace, like shopping centers, theaters, sporting events, subways and other places that are low risk to them but could yield high rewards in the sense these events could have the desired effect of creating chaos and confusion throughout the country."

He carried on: "Terror is their objective, and terror employed properly can induce a frightened society, which is the main objective of any terrorist organization."

"That bad, huh?" asked the president and the general told him this: "Terror can breed chaos and chaos can beget anarchy and that's the catalyst for the complete breakdown in societal stability, if that happens it could mean the end of the United States as we know it today."

Jasper Bohannon said, "That's a frightening scenario General," and Sam Falk said: "It's a distinct possibility if we don't root out these rats that are occupying our house."

The president placed his left hand on his forehead as if what he just heard gave him a headache, he shook his head and said: "Wow."

Mad Sam said" "I hate to be a prognosticator, but we have a larger picture to cast our eyes on, that's even more frightening," the president told him: "Spare me nothing General, spill it."

The general paused and then spoke the unspeakable: "There's always the possibility of biological or chemical airborne agents that can be disbursed in our cities and then you have the multiple of one hundred thousand of what could happen."

Jasper Bohannon: "Very bleak General."

Mad Sam: "Yes indeed sir, and then there's the mother of all possibilities."

Jasper Bohannon: "Let's hear it."

"The dirty bomb," that in itself was a bomb dropped into the president's lap.

Jasper Bohannon rose up from the sofa stepped over to the window, there he stood with his hands clasped behind his back and gazed out at the Rose Garden. He contemplated what General Falk had told him. *A dirty bomb that would be the ultimate disaster, a device that could, no would devastate the nation's psyche not to mention the destruction it would cause to the target city or cities. Over the past thirty years the country looked outward on guard from radical groups, thinking that's where the fear lay, but now that fear could come true originating from within executed by a homegrown terror group. What did Taylor say about great civilizations imploding from within?*

This was the nightmare that stared the new president in the face.

He couldn't ignore the general's dire scenarios; he had to anticipate the worst, *is this objective of the SOS?* He had to assume it was and work out from there.

The president said over his shoulder, "General Falk," Mad Sam responded, "Yes Mister President?"

"I've processed your keen observations and have arrived at a conclusion."

"Yes sir."

"We have to get out in front of this situation, not react to...," he hesitated before he completed his thought, Mad Sam sensed it and waited for the president to continue. He struggled to say what was obvious, calling the SOS exactly who they were, it finally slipped by past his lips..., "these traitors, but we have to anticipate their next move and make sure we do everything in our power to thwart whatever they plan to do."

"I agree Mister President, this call for action not reaction."

"We are in accord, General in their note they stated another attack would be forthcoming within seven days from yesterday."

The general scanned the dispatch and said: "That's correct sir," the president told him: "We have six days to prevent them from duplicating the scene outside this window. I assume, correct me if I'm wrong, the success of last night's attack would tend to embolden the SOS to repeat it again by attacking another major northern city using the same tactic - what's your professional opinion?"

"Sir if the enemy has had success using a particular tactic they continue to deploy it until it fails. Success breeds success, it also builds arrogance and over confidence, we will use that against them."

"My thoughts exactly," President Bohannon said, General Falk told him: "We can't be passive but proactive and take the fight to the enemy once they've indentified themselves."

"Getting them to show their faces is the chore we face."

"I agree, trust me they will raise their heads and we will cut their damn heads off."

"To your point about arrogance, only someone with a massive ego could conceive an event such as this, their thinking is my enemy is stronger than I but I am smarter than he is, that's their Achilles heel, their ego."

The president turned around, "Therefore...," he crossed to the sofa and settled down, he went on, "...we have to go on the offensive."

"You're absolutely correct sir, there's an old Marine Corps adage, 'the best defense in a good offensive' it was coined eons ago and it will be the doctrine of the Corps forever."

The president sat back placed his arm along the top of the sofa, crossed his legs, his posture stated he had supreme confidence in the man who sat opposite, he said: "You are to have unbridled access to Intel from any agency you may require, I will sign an order to that effect immediately."

"Well understood sir."

"Of course this falls under the umbrella of Homeland Security so run everything past Oscar Valdez."

"By all means sir."

"We want to stay within the perimeters of the law."

"Perfect, Mister President."

"But you will have total autonomy in executing your operations the only oversight will be mine. Keep me appraised on a daily basis I want to be current, I don't need to know the particulars, my concern is results. I'm interested in the baby, not the process."

"And results you shall have sir."

"That General is a foregone conclusion I have total faith in your abilities and those of your men to deliver the desired result to this crises."

"Which is if I'm hearing correctly sir, is total eradication," Mad Sam said and the president told him: "With extreme prejudice and no remorse."

The general nodded and said, "It shall happen per our orders sir."

"Very well General Falk."

"Mad Sam."

"Excuse me?"

"Those I consider as my friends and kindred spirit call me Mad Sam sir."

"I like that General, Mad Sam it is."

"Mighty fine sir."

The POTUS: "Mad Sam you have the green light to kill."

"And it shall be done sir. Forgive my colorful language when I first arrived I was so furious I was beside myself."

"Your language was most appropriate it characterized the situation and conditions perfectly, I enjoyed you being yourself, it quite refreshing to hear real talk that's truthful and forthright, no need to feel uneasy, I can sense you're at your best when you are Mad Sam himself."

General Falk smiled he like that a lot. "Mister President may I offer a word of advice"

"Of course, your insight is most welcome, speak freely Mad Sam, what advice do you have to convey?"

"Mister President that advice is trust no one...," Jasper Bohannon broke in: "Not even you?" and the general said: "Sir I trust no one but myself and only some of the time, that way I know I won't be betrayed. If things go askew, I have no one to blame but myself. One can be too giving of their trust only to be disappointed and deeply hurt by those we've trusted."

"Very profound, it shall be applied in all caps, underscored and italicized."

Mad Sam smiled: "I like that Mister President I like it a lot."

At that very moment Taylor Jackson scrambled in and closed the door, he held the second SOS dispatch in his hand, Smedley and Chesty opened their eyes at the sudden change in atmosphere and locked in on Taylor Jackson, he said "Sorry to interrupt sir, but this just arrived," he outstretched out the envelope to the president.

Jasper Bohannon took it, Mad Sam glanced at his dogs as the president opened the sealed top secret flimsy, and he sensed the bulldogs were tense and zeroed in on Taylor Jackson, once again he said in silence: *My lads are behaving rather oddly, what is it about this guy they don't like?*

Just then the president spoke: "Gentlemen what I have here is the second dispatch from the SOS," he handed it across the coffee table to the general, he took it and it read:

To the so called president of the United States you must address the Congress and introduce a bill allowing the southern states to secede legally or there will be multiple attacks like what was inflicted on Washington. These attacks will not cease until the US government capitulates to our demands. Major causalities will accrue and massive destruction will be the outcome if you don't comply.

We are the Saviors of the South, the SOS; we shall not cease hostilities until our demands are met. Each week you delay another of your major cities will be attacked and each ensuing act will be more damaging that the last.

Time is ticking you have six days to react to the above in the affirmative, The SOS.

Mad Sam studied it then looked up, once again with that look in his eyes, Taylor Jackson saw it, he was frightened; he swore he could see the fires of hell burn'n in them.

The general said: "This is utter insanity Mister President, these maniacs actually believe in this bullshit and that's where the danger lies, what we have here are insane zealots."

Jasper Bohannon told him, "We have five days to stop these zealots...," Taylor Jackson stepped in: "Six, sir..." the president looked at him: "Six what?" he went on, "The note said six days sir."

"True that, but I wanted it done in five not six," he looked at General Falk and back at Taylor Jackson: "How did you know the note says six days?" He turned to Mad Sam, "I believe the general and I are the only ones who've read it, and neither of us mentioned anything about time constraints." Jasper Bohannon and Mad Sam looked at him and waited.

Taylor Jackson said, "Just a guess sir, I recalled the first note stated a week and I did some quick math sir, I happened to be correct, that's all," which sounded fair enough, the president said, "General we have us a prognosticator," and winked, Mad Sam understood the joke and smiled, Taylor Jackson relaxed and glanced at the dogs, yep they watched him.

He shuddered.

General Falk had an *'aha'* moment, he held the dispatch aloft and waved it, "Sir they just raised their heads, telling us who they are, the Saviors of the South, how stupid of them." Jasper Bohannon looked at him: "Explain further General," and he said: "Sir now that they've identified themselves, it's no longer a mystery, they just lost their edge," the president said: "Go on."

"They made their first mistake which will lead to others. In any successful terrorist or guerilla organization anonymity is the key to their survival. Remaining X the unknown allows them to move about freely undetected and unsuspected, but once they've shed the cloak of X the unknown that's when they lose the fight sir."

"Understand fully and thanks for clearing the sky on that for me."

"We'll just shot a back azimuth and it will lead us straight to the core eventually, things have started to unravel as we speak sir."

"I see, they couldn't keep their egos in check, they had to let us know what SOS meant. You're absolutely correct General, that's our starting point, work backwards from there," the president said and the general replied: "You got it sir, I'll have Captain Wong, our computer genius begin a search, somewhere these clowns have left a trail that will lead us to their doorsteps, we've going to kick in every door and kill everyone inside, this calls for no prisoners, none of these cruds will live to tell the tale, not to the courts nor to the publishers."

"To quote an esteemed friend of mine," the president said: "I like it, I like it a lot."

Mad Sam said, "Sir, you're good, very good," and Jasper Bohannon told him: "Seems I had another moment." They laughed. Taylor Jackson was totally mystified about what had transpired between the president and the general while he was absent.

The president said: "General we have a lot to do so let's be about doing our jobs. I've a nation to console and govern so make this go away quick, fast and in a hurry."

General Falk said: "Consider it a bad memory with a good ending."

"I love happy endings, Mad Sam," Taylor Jackson's eyes blinked, did he miss something? *Mad Sam?*

"Well sir if you'll excuse us me and my lads we'll be off, so by your leave Mister President."

"General it's been a severe pleasure. I look forward to seeing you again soon and reading your daily reports, as soon as we put this affair in its death bed, let's do lunch here at the White House."

"I await that sir with a whet appetite; I've heard the dining here is superb, a seven diamond fare, so the faster we get finished, the quicker we eat."

The president laughed: "Mad Sam you're old school," Taylor Jackson's forehead wrinkled, the general said: "It's been said I'm the principle, the principle with the paddle in hand, Mister President I'm off to spank some ass."

"Mad Sam you're a scary guy." Jasper Bohannon said as he stood up, the general did the same, pulled his blouse down tight, picked up his cover, his swagger stick and said: "That I am sir, but I'm your scary guy, who's going to say boo to some folks, I'm not Casper, I'm Spooky."

The POTUS laughed again.

He had grown fond of General Sam Falk in the brief ninety minutes they spent one on one, he felt he was in the presence of someone as devoted to the country as he was. He was confident at this moment all would end well.

Jasper Bohannon and Sam Falk stepped toward the door, the general said over this shoulder: "Smedley and Chesty fall in on me," the bulldogs rose, waddled over and stood there, Taylor Jackson tried not to look afraid, but something about these dogs intimidated him.

They were at the Oval Office door, the president said: "Well Mad Sam until the next time," he offered his hand, the general said: "Mister President I can tell you've been a man everywhere you've been, the country's in good hands," and shook his hand. Taylor Jackson swung the door open.

The president said: “Thank you Mad Sam, I’ll try to live up to that.”

“Sir you already have,” said the general, he shifted out into the corridor and strode off with Smedley Butler and Chesty Puller padding at his side.

The president turned, stepped behind the desk and started looking over his speech. Taylor Jackson held the door open and watched them recede down the hallway, a couple of times the Devil Dogs shot glances over their shoulders at Taylor Jackson.

Mad Sam, Smedley Butler and Chesty Puller turned the corner and they were gone.

6

Constipated People

Stone Mountain, GA, 1961; Metro DC

IN THE EARLY morning hours of April 12, 1961, one hundred years to the day of the start of the Civil War, Cody Calhoun stood on top of Stone Mountain clad in his KKK klown suit, there was a moon but half full and in its light a huge cross stood surrounded by a large contingent of Klansmen and Klanswomen. Here a hint of cloud drifted over the scene still the conical hats, masks and white robes could be seen clearly. A large bonfire was ablaze, cinders popped continuously here and there. Above the crackle the voice of Robert Sheldon using a microphone could be heard loud and forceful. He was the Grand Wizard of the Mississippi White Knights of the Ku Klux Klan. He stood atop an erected platform elevated high above the white clad knot his black satin getup reflected the tongues of fire that leapt from the stack of burn'n wood.

The scene was quite comical but deadly serious there wasn't a hint of humor in what was being said. Behind the Grand Wizard sat rows of local Klan leaders from surrounding states, a cabal of shadowy white supremacy thinkers. The gathering was assembled in celebration of past glory and they were here to glorify the third rebirth of the Ku Klux Klan America's original terrorist group.

The organization had two prominent eras in its violent history and now the next wave of this insanity was prepared to wash upon the nation's shores like a red tide sting'n everyone with their tentacles of hate. The seeds of violence were sown this morning that would be the bane of the South during the 60's. Here at this occasion was the last gasp of a terrorist group comprised of thugs, misfits, malcontents, ethno centrists and a host of corn pone bigots, a backward look'n mob that longed for the images of the Old South they saw in their rearview mirrors. They were present to witness the lighting of the cross. Several Klansmen roamed the perimeter with loaded rifles at the ready, ready to shot anyone stupid enough to want to come see what was going on. Even out here in the open this was a secret event. The state of Georgia in cahoots with the Klan had given them permission to conduct their rally on Stone Mountain. A permit to pour their poison over one another reinforcing their hatred with a warped concoction of racism, sexism, anti-Semitism, nativism and every form of isms that suited their hate agenda; the resurrection of a sick way of life.

Three year old Robin Calhoun stood between CC and Ruby in her little klown getup. Her parents had brought the child to Stone Mountain on this particular morning in remembrance of start of the Civil War in their beloved Charleston. They were situated in the front rank that formed a semi-circle around the platform, the bonfire and the cross. Little Robin Calhoun looked out through the holes in her mask as the krowd went through a moon phase, complete lunacy.

This was her initiation to the racist ideology she would adhere to throughout her life. She was infected with the hand me down dogma that would poison her young impressionable mind, being twisted by flawed rhetoric from the charismatic manipulator who spooked the crowd. Although she was too young to comprehend what was said, she was infatuated with the pomp and circumstance.

Her parents along with everyone in the krowd were mesmerized by the intoxicat'n speech which would motivate them to acts of extreme violence. Blinded by misplaced devotion, accepting falsehoods as truth, they were vulnerable to the wishes of others, their ignorance was overwhelming. Not allowing themselves any thoughts other than those being espoused from the platform, cajoling them to dive into the waters of violent crime. This inability to think for self was a perfect example of how far out the cult mind can be manipulated lead'n them down the garden path of destruction.

Several hooded men stuck their gasoline soaked rag poles into the fire igniting them they held the torches high and waited for the command to light the cross. It approached four twenty seven the exact time the first shots were fired on Fort Sumter. CC picked up Robin, positioned her on his hip and said, "Your daddy wants you to remember this moment for the rest of your life, understand?" Little Robin Calhoun said: "Yes daddy," he smiled and kissed her cheek through her mask. At that precise moment, the Klansmen threw their torches at the base of the cross it came alive as an inferno that symbolized hatred and intolerance.

Little Robin Calhoun who watched in awe, eagerly clap'n her hands, CC looked at his daughter; he knew she was the future of the South and he also knew she would do her daddy proud.

Cheers erupted from the press and echoed throughout the hills below Stone Mountain. The Klansmen and Klanswomen jumped up and down and shouted lust'n for blood; they were born again bigots, just constipated people with constipated minds.

LATE IN AFTERNOON at Barn, General Falk sat at his desk fronted by Captains Andrew Wong and Mickey Stovall, they were the general's Mister Inside and Mister Outside. They sat in their chairs ramrod straight as the general brought them up to scratch about what took place in the White House and what were the president's orders.

"Men we're up against the clock on this one, it has a short fuse and we have to prevent it from going bang," Mad Sam told them, they sat there, he went on: "The president has given us total latitude to complete this assignment...," he paused, he had their undivided attention, "...Captain Wong I want an immediate search and find evidence of where Saviors of the South may have been mentioned in any media format."

"Yes sir." Andrew Wong said.

"This is key gentlemen, once we know the identity of just one of these rats we're going to immediately seize that person and apply measures which will convince him to name names." The general looked at Mickey: "Captain Stovall when we have this person in custody I want you to apply your unique approaches to extract the Intel we need, save the Q&A take him straight to the rack."

"Yes sir," Mickey Stovall said. They waited for further comments from the general.

Mad Sam picked up his cup, worked his coffee and then said: "Men we have no time for any forms of niceties, this is the ultimate showdown, the future of this country hangs in the balance, understood?"

There was a duet of: "Yes sir."

"A first responder found an unexploded round lodged in the World Bank roof, they disarmed it, this is the ordnance serial number they found on it," he handed Mickey Stovall a slip of paper with the info written on it, Mad Sam carried on: "Captain Wong run the serial number and find out where it originated, it's standard military issue so that shouldn't be difficult finding out where it was shipped to contact the Joint Munitions Command at the Rock Island Arsenal they're responsible for munitions production and storage depots in sixteen states. Once you have gotten that info give it to Captain Stovall and Mickey get all over it."

"Yes sir," the captains spoke as one.

"What we have now is two valuable pieces of Intel, one the name of this traitorous clique and the means to find their supply source. To obtain military ordnance they had to have coerced same armory personal somewhere here in the US on one of our bases, we find that base it was issued to, we snare our first rat, understood?"

The captains nodded in the affirmative.

"Andrew I want results on those issues by...," he pushed up his sleeve, looked at his watch,"...by twenty two hundred. Beat the bushes, shake the trees, stir up the dust, and find out what we need to know."

Andrew Wong said: "As you say, sir," he then said: "I may have to step on some toes to get that ordnance info some individuals might not want to delve into things after the sun goes down." Mad Sam was visibly agitated and full throated he sharpened his definition, "Fuck the bullshit, I don't care who gets upset they can do whatever they want on their time, they can go hump a tree I don't give a fuck, but when I say jump I want them to start bouncing up and down like a pogo stick getting us that info we need."

"Sir some of those guys are high ranking..." Mad Sam rolled over him: "I don't care what their ranks are no one is ranked higher than the president and as his lead dog I will not tolerate any foot dragging. End of story."

Andrew Wong said: "Understood sir, if you'll excuse me, I'll tend to it straight away."

"Very well Captain, you're dismissed," with that Andrew Wong stood up, did an about face and moved off to the Barn's computer center.

General Falk watched him leave and turned to face Mickey Stovall: "Captain, the president had a mild concern about your tactics."

"Really sir?"

"Yes he momentarily did until I explained the rules of the road to him and how effective and persuasive your methods are, President Bohannon is completely on board, so do not restrain yourself," Mickey Stovall smiled and said: "Aye, aye sir." Mad Sam: "Captain you are to do whatever, I repeat whatever is necessary to secure the names of these SOS bastards ASAP. Time is not our friend."

"I totally understand sir."

"Falcon E1 will be at your constant disposal, its fueled and standing by at Andrews, as soon as Captain Wong gives you the base location take five of your team and fly there with unfettered delay." Mickey could see the thunderheads gathering in his eyes.

"Yes sir."

"Now I have to prepare for evening colors, so off you go and good hunting."

Captain Stovall took his leave, as General Falk looked through a stack of papers piled on his desk, he said: "Smedley and Chesty get ready to strike the colors." The bulldogs wagged their tails and grinned.

A LITTLE WHILE later Mad Sam, Smedley Butler and Chesty Puller stood at attention, they waited for the sun to slip under the western horizon. First Sergeant Cooper along with two other marines lowed the Stars and Stripes from it half-mast position, the president had order all American flags across the country to be flown at half-staff in respect for the attack on the Capital.

General Falk saluted and taps played in the background, the trumpet's plaintiff wail provided somber notes as the ensign slowly came down. The color guard uncoupled the standard and proceeded to fold it up, finished Top stepped up to the general saluted, Mad Sam returned his, took the Stars and Stripes and smartly did an about face and strode off into the Barn with Smedley Bulter and Chesty Puller hurry'n at his heels.

ROBIN CALHOUN CAME awake about five fifteen that afternoon, she made it from Atlanta to Dulles where the copter scheduled by Jake Carlisle whisked her away to Georgetown.

She had returned to the scene of her crime, very upbeat, as she flew into DC she had a bird's eye view of the destruction she caused. She looked down at the devastation inflicted on Center City. She smiled in her mind, Robin Calhoun had done it and she gloated: *This is just the beginning we will have our independence or there will be no America, North or South.*

Robin Calhoun knew her gambit was risky. If the US government didn't cave to the SOS's demands and they continued their guerrilla activity the chaos and confusion could get out of hand and spread to all corners. This gamble had a short shelf life; the clock ticked, their objective had to be achieved within two weeks or what she had unleashed would never be placed back on the chain. The dogs of war could be set loose and in their wake lay total anarchy. Other hate groups, militias, urban gangs and average American citizens would take up their own agendas, releasing their hate, fears and frustrations onto the streets of America causing the threads of chaos to unspool.

And then what?

Marital law??

And then what???

The copter deposited her on a helipad she took the lift down, stepped out, strode through the lobby, waved down a taxi and sat in the back she looked quite pleased at what she saw. The cab drew away taking her home. Inside, Robin Calhoun had that familiar pain in her head; too much Jack Daniel's over the last twenty four hours. Her celebration had tak'n a wrong turn; she couldn't stop turn'n up the bottle and tak'n hits from Jack.

She rose up on her elbow, glanced around, sat up and swung her feet on the carpet. She sat there for a moment, then stood and crossed to the bathroom suite. She reached in the rain room and turned on the shower stepped back loosened the belt around her robe, then her phone sounded, "Damn," she hustled into the bedroom and picked up, a voice said: "Welcome back Senator, I hope you're pleased and I assume my back account has swollen considerably."

"Your concerns are satisfied."

"Excellent," the voice said.

"I need to know exactly what's being planned by the opposition," she was being careful not to speak specifics so innuendo would suffice in case someone might be listening in, the voice understood and spoke innocuously.

"I'll see what's available for purchase you know these items are pricey."

Robin Calhoun: "I'll pay what is required I need more items to complete my collection," meaning she needed info about what the administration was up to and what Jasper Bohannon was planning and she'd pay the price for this knowledge.

The voice: "I'd say we're talking in the neighborhood of let's say a half million."

Robin Calhoun: "Expensive neighborhood," she flipped the phone the bird.

The voice: "But you need it, what was it you said, 'to complete my collection'?"

Robin Calhoun: "Alright, alright" she knew the voice was right without knowing what the president was considering or had ordered she couldn't make the proper moves on the chessboard. The voice could obtain what she needed to stay two three moves ahead in this dangerous game she played. When she fired the starter's pistol the race was on and Robin Calhoun had to cross the finish line first.

The voice: "Very good, I expect the deposit."

Robin Calhoun: "Done."

"I shall have something for your ears shortly," and the voice was gone.

Robin Calhoun knew she needed the voice to keep her a step ahead. She had recruited several high level bureaucrats and turned them into her moles elbow lengths away from top administration bigwigs. They were well placed and would provide her with the info she would need to execute the main event in Boston. The mortar attack and the pending attacks on other cities were feigns to keep the United States look'n in the wrong direction, while the SOS positioned themselves to deliver a blow that would devastated the birthplace of American democracy.

Robin Calhoun hung up the phone and said: "That damn Tennessee hillbilly, trying to bleed me to death, fucking asshole," she was highly pissed; Robin felt she was paying too much, but she was trapped by the circumstance she had created. The voice had Robin Calhoun over the barrel.

AT ROUGHLY THE same time Skeeter Macklin sat at the kitchen table where he watched his new bride prepare dinner, Jessy busied herself stirring a pot and looked over at him, "So honey, what are your plans now that you've retired?"

Skeeter said: "I haven't given it much thought, Jessy," she turned to face him, wiped her hands on a towel and asked, "Why not?" Skeeter Macklin looked up, "Jessy the city's hurting and the country's in pain and I hadn't had time for selfish thoughts."

Jessy knew he was quietly grieving as she was, when the news of the attack reached them in San Andres they immediately suspended their honeymoon and flew back to the States. During the flight she studied Skeeter she could see he was consumed with rage. They hardly spoke on the trip back to Washington she also knew that was not the time for excessive conversation.

"I'm just as grief stricken as you honey, I know you're burning up inside and want to get back into the fight, but that's not your reality anymore. Don't regret the past and don't fret about the future."

"I know, my emotions are running amuck but that's..." he pushed himself up, walked over, stood behind her and wrapped his arms around her waist, "...in the past I made my choice, the right choice for us," he rubbed her baby bump, "It's about the future, yours, mine and that little one in the oven."

She laughed, turned her head and they kissed, "I love you Shamus Macklin."

"That love is requited," she smiled and returned to her cook'n, Skeeter walk to the fridge swung the door open, reached in and came out with a can of Bud Light, popped the top, took a short swig and said: "I think I'll volunteer."

Jessy stop toss'n salad and looked very fretful, "*Volunteer*. Volunteering for what?" Skeeter Macklin had sat down, took another swig and replied: "I've only volunteered one other time that was when I raised my hand to join the Crotch. So I'm raising my hand again..." which he did, "...and I volunteer to be house dad."

She laughed: "That's what I love about you always with the jokes. House dad is it? That's your plan?"

Skeeter said, "You thought that funny? Like Joe Pesci asked, 'You think I'm funny? I'm here to amuse you'."

"Yes like in ha ha."

"Touché my love."

"You're serious aren't you?"

"I certainly am ma'am. What could be better than watching after the little one and operating a business from the confines of home? I call that the best of all worlds."

"How sweet, honey," she said as she laid the table, "What type of business."

"Classic car restoration."

She shot him a curious glance, reached in the fridge and came out with a bottle of wine, "Restore cars here? Where in the backyard? That'll work. I can hear the neighbors freaking out now," and she settled down opposite her husband.

They said grace.

And then Skeeter answered her question, "No I'm going to have the cars restored elsewhere, I have couple of friends, you know Joe Quinn and Sammy Sweet..." she cut in: "Is that his real name or something he thinks impresses the women?"

"No, his given name is Samuel B. Sweet."

"You made that up," she said around a mouth full of salad.

Skeeter Macklin confessed: "The B part, but Samuel Sweet is his name, enough of that, anyway they operate a small restoration shop and I'll give them my business and everyone prospers."

She looked over the rim of her wine glass, "So they do the work and house dad grows fat counting the money?"

"You're on top of your game this evening."

"What game might that be, may I ask?"

"Of course you may," Skeeter Macklin told her.

"Well?"

"You're cooking game has never been better and your comedy routine is at its best."

Jessy laughed. "Here's how it goes, ready?" Skeeter asked.

"As I'll ever be."

"You know what I did with the Sting Ray right?" and Jessy said: "Yes."

"Well after totally restoring it from the ground up, I started surfing the Internet to see what a cherry sixty three split window Vette would sell for you know what I found out?"

"I bet you're going to tell me."

"Over one hundred and seventy five large," he said releasing his punch line that got her attention she looked up from her plate. Skeeter Macklin plunged on: "Counting the money and time that's a hundred grand profits. How'd you like that number?"

"Quite enumerating."

"You're a funny lady, a very funny lady," he said and she told him: "So you like my routine, if that gassed you, wait until you see the standup portion of the show."

Skeeter smiled and went on: "Look in all seriousness..." she stepped in: "I thought I was," and took another sip of wine.

"Well you ease up a bit, I'm busting up over here." Jessy went silent.

"I can sink say a quarter of mil into it buying and restoring four old classics, I know a guy in Des Moines, who has a fifty three Packard Caribbean, a fifty six Lincoln Mark II, a fifty seven convertible El Dorado Biarritz and here's the kicker a fifty three Buick convertible Skylark."

"All this means what?"

"It means once I drop a hundred G's to buy the cars, they're in sad condition, that's why I can pick them up cheap," he told her and she asked him: "One hundred thousand dollars is suddenly cheap? Did I miss the news on that?"

"Between you and Mickey I just can't win."

"Please tell me more."

So he did.

"Now I put the cars up for sale on EBay, opening bids at one hundred twenty a piece, let's say..." she told him: "You're saying I'm listening."

Again he smiled, he loved her wit and he tried to act annoyed: "Well anyway, those bidders will go nuts and drive the purchasing price up around two hundred and fifty G's maybe more, so I'd net a cool three quarters of a million for a year's worth of work."

"So it's I now, I like it better when it was let's do this."

"Oh so now, I've got your attention?" Skeeter asked her and Jessy told him, "You had it along, I just wanted to see if you could convince yourself and I can hear you've done your homework, I think it's a great idea, very lucrative."

"Yes it can be, I'll just restore four or five cars a year and it's a million dollar year business, how's that for enumeration?"

Jessy stood up and cleared the table, finally she told him: "I think you should get started right away, jump into to it now, if you have too much down time, you might become melancholy and long to get into the fight."

"Oh no, I'm out of the hurt business, General Falk and his Eradicators will handle the situation quite well without Shamus Macklin, I turned the page on that chapter of my life, that's in the past I'm looking toward the future..." he paused rose from his chair crossed over to Jessy and looked down at her baby bump, "...and I can see my future in you." Jessy reached up, placed her arms around his neck and kissed him deeply. She released her arms, stepped back and said: "You know how to take care of your homework." Skeeter Macklin beamed and just then the phone rang, Jessy was annoyed at this interruption of a tender moment, "Who knows we're back, it's probably Mom," she picked up the wall phone, "Hello," it wasn't her mother it was her boss Horace Hackett, he said: "Good evening Jessy, sorry to disturb you at home, newlyweds and all that."

"Not a problem there Horace, what can I do you for?"

Her boss said: "Are you still up for that trip to Brazil?" Horace Hackett was the editor for the Washington Sentinel an Internet blog.

"Well I thought I'd put in for maternity leave, and return after the baby's about four months old."

"That is your right, but I'll make a deal with you."

"What kind of deal?" her brows went up, Skeeter Macklin looked at her puzzled.

"I'll pay you for your maternity leave and pay you double if you agree to fly down and cover this story for me."

Jessy wanted to go, it was her story she had been mining it for six months and she didn't want it assigned to someone else, so she said, "Could you hold for a minute, I'd like to discuss it with my husband."

"By all means."

"Thanks," she placed the phone against her chest and said to Skeeter: "You want to resume our honeymoon in Brazil?" Skeeter Macklin looked at her and asked: "Rio? Are you sure you want to take me to Rio?" She slapped his shoulder with her free hand, "I've got a decision to make here and Horace is waiting. We can fly down stay five six days and be back here within a week, plus you know your way around a camera so you can take the video..." Skeeter stepped in: "What story is this?" she told him: "There's group of descendants of ex-Confederates that move to Brazil after the Civil War and no one has ever written a follow up story about what happened to them, it could mean an Internet Pulitzer for me."

"Please don't let me stand in the way of your Pulitzer, I'm in."

"Thanks honey," she told him and removed the phone from her chest and spoke into it: "Okay Horace I'll go, but my husband will accompany me as my camera tech, with pay and you'll pick up all the expenses, how's that?" She winked at Skeeter.

"You drive a hard bargain Jessy, if you weren't my best investigative reporter, I'd say no, but being you are, I'll bite the bullet."

"Excellent. When do you want us to leave?"

"I have passage booked for two, this Tuesday."

"Two?"

"I knew you wouldn't go without your new husband so I planned ahead."

"You sly dog you."

"The tickets await you at Dulles, Avianca Airlines, and you'll fly into Sao Paulo and hop over to Americana."

She looked at Skeeter, "No Rio?" and smiled, Horace Hackett said, "That's the long way there."

"Okay Horace you've got yourself a super reporting duo. Shamus will get film credits, yes?"

"Don't push it Jessy."

"Stop while I'm ahead?"

"Exactly."

"Good evening, Horace and thanks," she told him and he told her: "See you when you return, stay safe," and switched off.

"Well honey looks like our love adventure continues, it's onto Brazil."

"Where exactly?"

"Americana, that's the city started by the ex-Confederates, they call themselves the Confederados." Jessy said and Skeeter replied: "Americana? Confederados? This is going to be good."

BACK AT 1600 Pennsylvania Avenue Jasper Bohannon sat behind the Resolute Desk where he put the final touches on his speech. He had only been on the job for a day and a half and here he prepared to address a grief stricken nation suffer'n from shock and disbelief, what words could be chosen that would sooth the pain his fellow Americans felt at this hour and in the many days to follow.

He had wrestled with this problem the last twelve hours, starting and stopping many times trying to find the proper tone and tenor. It had to be consoling and reassuring to the people that last night's attack wasn't going to interrupt the flow of governmental business and he as their Commander in Chief would do everything in his power to protect them and bring the criminals to justice. His speech had to be pitch perfect, a perfect balance of anger, comfort and reassurance, voic'n their outrage; eliminating their fears and let'n them know he will lead the nation through this period with strength and wisdom.

ALL ACROSS THE country eyes glued to TV sets awaited the president's address from the Oval Office, the setting fit the moment. The press room wasn't the backdrop that matched the circumstance; the press conference was cancelled and rescheduled for six days hence.

Jasper Bohannon sat behind the Resolute Desk, he wore a dark blue suit, white shirt with a red tie and an American flag clasped in his lapel. He waited for the countdown to air time. At precisely eight o'clock the POTUS spoke to the people.

"Good evening my fellow citizens tonight I come to you with a fractured heart..."

IT WAS TWO and half hours afterwards that Robin Calhoun heard the doorbell sound, she knew who it was so she sauntered over in her flam'n red negligee, the light from the fireplace shone through the garment it silhouetted her well-proportioned body, a body that Venus de Milo would have died for, Robin Calhoun had the gear and she knew how to use it. To totally enrapture anyone she let gaze upon it. That someone tonight waited just beyond the door. The door swung open, it was Jake Carlisle standing there with an eager smile in his eyes.

Robin Calhoun leaned on the edge of the door and said, "Why it's the Top Cat come to see his kitten and to get his quality time." Jake Carlisle said: "Good evening, may I enter?" and she told him back: "You may enter anywhere you like," that could mean multiple things, a many fold entendre.

The Senator from Virginia stepped inside she closed the door and inserted her tongue in his mouth, probed deeply, the kissed lasted a full thirty seconds, and she stopped, stepped back and said, "So how have you been?" Jake Carlisle tried to recover from her passionate hello, he told her, "I've been doing a lot of things mainly I've been thinking about you," she smiled, "That I know," and kissed his cheek, shifted to the couch with the Senator from Virginia in passionate pursuit.

Robin Calhoun seated herself, reared back: "Would you like to join me here on the settee?" she was in her southern belle mode. Jake Carlisle settled down beside her and looked deep into her eyes what he saw was two orbs beckoning him to begin the fun and games. Try'n not to seem too rambunctious about it he said: "You're in a playful mood tonight in view of what's happened."

"Oh that, of course I'm appalled and deeply saddened at this horrific attack, those al Qaeda bastards," she played the role to its fullest, she had to present a façade of being an concerned citizen and a pissed off United States Senator, her thespian ship was in Oscar form. Jake Carlisle asked her, "Did you hear the president's address?" and she told him: "Yes I did, it was alright he really didn't say anything it was your standard presidential pep talk, nothing special," coldly.

"I beg to differ with you I thought it was on point, very uplifting and comforting. I thought president displayed tremendous strength that's what the country needs in moments like this."

Robin Calhoun didn't like any of this, she said: "It is just words; words are wind Jake, a lot of flowery bullshit. What I did not hear was why he has not issued the order to strike those Islamofascist bastards who did it instead of spouting generalities I wanted to hear specifics about how we are going to avenge this atrocity."

Jake Carlisle looked at her: "He can't reveal that kind of info, yes he can issue threats and warnings but until the culprits have been properly ID by the CIA and others, I'm positive he will make the proper decision based on the Intel."

"That sounded like some Senate floor double talk," he looked viably pained by that, it contained certain acidity in it, and she could sense it: "Do not be so thin skinned, you know me, I can be a callous bitch at times, not tonight, I want to forget about what is outside that door and see what is inside your pants, do you want to play with my kitty or what?" That was very direct and straight to the point it might take the sting out of what she had said, it seemed to work, "When you put it like that, I guess my grief can wait," he told her and then said: "Here kitty, kitty," Robin Calhoun fell back and laughed uncontrollably, finally she caught her breath and told him: "Oh so you do have priorities?" she cooed and asked, "Want a drink?," actually she was say'n she craved one, Jake Carlisle knew he had to go with the flow so he said, "I thought you'd never ask," Robin Calhoun was pleased and it showed, she stood up, shifted to the bar and started mix'n his drink, he liked margaritas for some reason unbeknown to her, it didn't make sense, it was Jack Daniel's for her, straight and all of the time.

She said, "Of course I feel the same pain as everyone else," she was back in character, "but I do not have any faith in that boy doing the right thing, you know how they are, they cannot handle responsibility and pressure that is a proven fact." Her racism was never far from the surface, everyone in Washington knew where Robin Calhoun stood on the social front, especially the racial issues. She was considered the point of the spear of racial intolerance, but she kept getting reelected, obviously there were many others who shared her sentiments, because of those loyal constituents Robin Calhoun was most confident she didn't have to be the tolerant moderate she was hard boiled right wing and proud of it.

Jake Carlisle sat there he didn't want to respond to that, any comment to the contrary would only exacerbate the situation, inflaming her to spill more venom and he didn't come here tonight for her haranguing so he said: "Let's wait and see what happens before we cast judgment, here come sit beside me," that seemed to work, she let it go for now, sipped at her drink on the way back and handed him his sissy one, "Here you go my love, your favorite," Jake Carlisle tasted it and said: "Perfect." Robin Calhoun settled in next to him: "Well Top Cat what is really on your mind tonight? I sure is not politics could it be my kitty tricks?" Jake Carlisle liked that, her sexual connotations he found quite simulating, there was no tease in this woman, when it came to get'n it on Robin Calhoun knew just what to do. She sat her drink down, poured another shot, looked at him and said, "I'm planning a trip," changing the subject for the moment.

"A trip where?"

"Americana, Brazil."

He looked at her totally bewildered he expected something more exotic like Rio, Bahia or Recife places he had visited, but this was new to him, "Where's that?"

"It is about two hundred miles west of Sao Paulo."

"What in the hell is there other than jungle and shit like that."

"That is where you are so wrong my love, there is a thriving city established by former members of our Confederate family," he looked at her: "Confederate what?"

"Don't you know anything about the Confederacy," she said playfully, he told her: "Of course, it's just I've never heard of this Americana place you referred to."

"Well do you want to know, I'll keep it short," she said and he told her: "Okay educate me."

So she did.

When she concluded he said, "That's a feel good story," catering to her emotions, he could see while she was telling him, that she was completely lost in the world she described.

"So when is this trip you're taking?" he demanded.

"I'm leaving Wednesday the annual Confederado Fiesta takes place next weekend it is going to be fabulous, you want to come?"

That caught him off guard, he wasn't prepare for it so he said, "I wish you'd have told me sooner I would love to accompany you, but I have a big budget hearing to oversee Thursday and it wouldn't be politically healthy if I was gallivanting somewhere in South America instead of tending to the government's financial woes, now would it?" he found a convenient out, he wasn't into the Confederacy nostalgia, even though he was the senior Senator from Virginia a super conservative, he wasn't a bigot and didn't buy into the desire to dwell in the past. His political concerns were government spending, military strength and big business, to him folks were folks. He adored Calvin Coolidge whom he often quoted; his favorite Coolidge witticism was "the business of America is business" and Senator Jake Carlisle made it his creed. In fact he liked it so much he adopted it as his presidential campaign slogan and it was also the main reason he lost the election the voters found it too direct and to the point.

Robin Calhoun had downed three quick shots of Jack and she was ready to let the fun begin so she said: "Are you ready for the boudoir games?"

Jake Carlisle said: "Boudoir games?"

"The bedroom Olympics where you can go for the gold," she stood up slipped out of her negligee and grabbed his hand pull'n him up: "You better hurry or we are going be left standing in the blocks," and she led Jake Carlisle by the hand into the bedroom and closed the door.

Robin Calhoun was a closet cougar she subscribed to a national dating service that supplied her with young men she'd entertain at her secret playpen over in Virginia. Jake Carlisle's and her relationship was pure politics, she knew he loved her but she loved the power she had over him. Robin Calhoun was able to extract a promise from him if he won the presidency she would be appointed to a high cabinet position possibly Secretary of State or Defense. Her involvement with Jake Carlisle was business he was but a mere rung to her climb to the top of Washington politics. Her pleasure came from being serviced by younger men.

At her playpen she was Scarlett O'Whora she was what they call a sexoholic. In the halls of power she was viewed as a prude, but when the real Robin Calhoun stood up it was bacchanal time, she'd give any porn star a run for the money. She was the consummate hypocrite, chat'n one way and behav'n another.

AT THE FALK headquarters late that night, the general sat by the fireplace with Smedley and Chesty at his feet, he was going over other operations at the behest of the UN. With the retirement of Major Macklin he consolidated his men into larger units. He had to promote a captain to major to fill Skeeter's position, Mickey Stovall of course was his first choice, and he'd have to wait until the SOS matter was resolved. He would let it rest for the time being and see how things unfolded.

Mad Sam extended his legs, crossed his ankles, interlocked his fingers behind his head and closed his eyes, he let the past day's events flow past his mind's eye, he had to access things internally to gage what was tangible versus speculation to put things in prospective.

Andrew Wong reported back to the general, he had ran the serial number and the ordnance was stolen in 08 from an armory at Fort Lewis, now they had a starting point on that issue. Mad Sam phoned the Commanding Officer and told him to shut the entire base down not allowing any military personnel to leave. Major General Barry Wallace was irked to say the least, he demanded: "Under whose authority?" his tone was hostile.

Mad Sam said: "The President of the United States."

"President Bohannon?"

"That one," Mad Sam said, even though the man on the other end of the line outranked him by a star, General Falk had the full authority to dictate orders to him.

The two stars immediately lost his edge: "Understood, I was taken aback somewhat, may I ask the reason behind this order?"

"General Wallace this is a need to know situation."

That stopped all further questions about specifics from the two stars in their tracks.

Two Stars: "What's the duration of the order?"

Mad Sam: "Until I been satisfied with my investigation."

Two Stars: "Investigating what?"

Mad Sam: "Once again General that is classified information privy only to the president and me," the two stars waited.

Mad Sam: "Captain Mickey Stovall will arrive at oh three hundred, ..." when Captain Wong gave the info to him he phone Mickey standing by at Andrews and General Falk told him to rush to Washington State, the Falcon E1 went wheels up, and was winging its way there as Mad Sam told the two stars, "...upon his arrival he's to have total access to personnel files, duty rosters and anything he requires that's necessary to aid this investigation. In addition unrestricted entrée to anywhere on the base he deems fit. Furthermore Captain Stovall has full authority to question any personnel regardless of rank including yourself."

Two Stars: "This is serious."

Mad Sam: "Very much so, be advised General no one is to know of Captain Stovall and his team's arrival."

Two Stars: "Of course."

General Falk told General Wallace, "Cancel all pending furloughs and recall everyone that's currently on leave, I want all base personnel present and accounted for by eighteen hundred tomorrow, no exceptions, no excuses, senior grade officers down to lowly privates."

General Wallace: "That might be a tall order to have everyone back on post by the requested time."

General Falk felt his cheeks heat up: "I understand, but it's an absolute must that everyone reports back by the prescribed time, I don't care if they're at the bottom of the Marianas Trench, climbing Mount Everest, stranded in the jungle or orbiting the planet."

The two stars knew it was futile to question further so he complied: "Anything else General?" Mad Sam said: "That should cover things for the moment, if any additional requirements are necessary they will be forthcoming for this end. Expect a signed order from the president within the hour."

"I'll stand by for said order, General."

"Very good, there is one final thing General Wallace whatever Captain Stovall does in the course of this investigation is sanctioned by the president himself. Captain Stovall is not to be interfered with in any shape, form or fashion. He has total autonomy to do his job."

Two Stars: "The president's orders will be followed to the letter."

Mad Sam: "Mighty fine, General once we concluded this investigation if the president chooses you'll be brought up to snuff."

Two Stars: "Very good General Falk."

Mad Sam: "Thanks General," and they switched off.

Mad Sam opened his eyes he was satisfied with the progress they've made since his meet with the president early that afternoon. He reached down, stroked the bulldog's heads, rubbed their bellies and stopped briefly to play with his lads. He stood up, stretched, crossed to the window and looked out at the countryside. The Barn was hidden in the deep wood bounded by high security electrified fences and was under constant electronic surveillance, every inch of the compound could be seen at any time by Andrew Wong in the communications and computer center.

Mad Sam watched the clouds silhouette past the moon as he went on thinking about the SOS matter. Andrew Wong's computer search had two hits that referenced the use of the term Saviors of the South.

The first one was from a speech given by a local politician in South Carolina who mentioned the term encouraging his voter base to get out and vote. On the surface this was rather a clever way to motivate his audience into voting for him, perhaps a harmless choice of words, nothing more.

But the other usage of the phrase held significant import it was spoken by the nationally known and highly controversial Max Bedford. This was good, very good; Max Bedford was well known for his extreme views and a host of subjects particularly what he thought were the injustices inflicted on the South after the Civil War. He was an avid racist and states rights' advocate who championed anything that smacked of being anti US government.

The trail suddenly grew very hot this was a solid piece of information that could escalate matters in their favor.

He turned around, stepped up to his desk and pick up his Codex 4 and President Bohannon said: "Yes, Mad Sam."

"Sir I believe we've found the first thread that starts to unwind this problem."

"Meaning?"

General Falk told the Commander in Chief what he had learned and brought him up to snuff quickly. Jasper Bohannon said: "Very good."

"Yes sir, while they're doing whatever they're doing at this moment, they are unaware that we are sneaking up on them like the Viet Cong, ever so quietly and ever so deadly."

Jasper Bohannon: "I like your analogy very poignant."

Mad Sam: "I feel confident by sunrise on day three we'll have stitched together a quilt that will give us a much better picture of what's what and who's who."

Over on his Codex the president said: "My confidence level just went off the charts, this is very good news, well done General keep me posted as you learn more."

"An absolute must sir."

"I think I'll shut it down for a few hours, what about you Mad Sam, I'm sure you could use a pit stop."

The general laughed and told Jasper Bohannon: "Sir I'm an eagle and an owl I fly day and night."

The president laughed: "Mad Sam you're an American original in league with Will Rogers himself."

"That's high praise, sir, one of my favorite people."

"Well General I look forward to hearing your update tomorrow evening, if you want a face to face notify my Chief of Staff..." Mad Sam hadn't thought about Taylor Jackson and his curious encounter with Smedley Butler and Chesty Puller, if only his lads could explain things, this was now a crawl in his throat. "...and he'll make sure you will be accommodated." Mad Sam said; "Mighty fine sir, by the way your speech was superb, only someone with gifted communication skills could have delivered what the nation needed to hear, it was aces."

"Thank you for your kind and most welcomed words, good night Mad Sam."

"Good night Mister President."

7

Sick Like That

Washington; Fort Lewis, WA; Metro DC

SNOW DROVE IN across the Potomac where it found Jasper Bohannon busy at his desk when Taylor Jackson came into the Oval Office at seven o'clock, he was upbeat and said, "Good morning Mister President, the overnights are in, your speech went over big with the public."

"And to you Taylor," the president looked up: "That's a good thing, but words are like an ointment they can only sooth the pain for so long, the longer we wait for things to materialize, words become meaningless without the action that illustrates the words."

Taylor Jackson stood there for a moment processing that and said, "Of course you're right Mister President..." Jasper Bohannon broke in: "It's not a matter of being right, we all know what's right, the chore is bringing right to fruition. What are the poll numbers?"

Taylor looked at the overnights and said, "Ninety percent approval that's a very high number." Taylor Jackson looked at the president, happy to be the bearer of good news.

"That tells us what?"

"It indicates your speech was received with much agreement by the vast majority of the nation, sir."

"That's all well and good; it's the missing ten percent that concerns me most at the moment."

"You lost me, sir." Taylor Jackson said with a vexed look on his face.

The president told him: "Well Taylor try and get back on the trail and follow along. That ten percent are the dangerous ones, if they unite behind what has occurred indicates they're not with the rest of the country and never will be. Each one is a potential weapon wielding anti American nut job that could be infected with this SOS germ and that contamination could spread to other groups giving them the impetus to launch copy cat activities at this point in time the ten percent F-ups is where the danger lies."

Taylor Jackson stood there and waited.

The president carried on, "We have to crush this now before other crackpots get ideas and start their own little wars. That's why I didn't mention the SOS by name or indicate that this was executed by our fellow citizens that would have been too traumatic causing who knows what to erupt in the streets.

"Americans against Americans is the ultimate catastrophe. If you think its winter now it could be the winter of America, that I can't let happen, so we have to sniff out and snuff out these criminals before they contaminate others."

Now Taylor Jackson understood the gravity of the situation: "If I'm hearing you correctly sir, we have a situation that could get way out of hand if it's not dealt with swiftly."

"That's exactly right," the president shifted gears: "Have you had your morning coffee yet?"

"No sir, I came straight here when I arrived about five minutes ago, I could use a cup, would you like one too?"

"Yes please," Taylor Jackson said: "I'll be right back, sir," Jasper Bohannon said: "Thanks," Taylor turned and went out the door, the president put down his pen, sat back, pinched the bridge of his nose and thought about what he told Taylor.

This was day three on the job and he could feel the weight the other men who occupied the office he now sat in, on his shoulders. He peeled away the onion of American history and felt the immense pressure they had to endure it was evident. They too faced crises that caused them much anxiety.

Now it was his turn to deal with the awesome responsibility of being President of the United States of America, the key word being united, he had to do everything in his power to maintain that union established so long ago, it could not be allowed to be fractured by a group of maniacal terrorists not now, not ever.

General Falk's phone call was encouraging especially the Max Bedford angle that was a good starting point, follow the wordsmith and he could lead them to the author of this horror story, the one who penned this episode. The scribbler would be found and her pen silenced.

Taylor Jackson returned, handed the president his cup of Joe and settled down opposite Jasper Bohannon and asked: "Any news from Mad Sam?" the president shot him a hard stare and held it: "Did General Falk give you permission to call him Mad Sam?"

He looked confused: "No sir, I heard you call him that so I assumed it was alright."

"Well you assumed wrong. Point one you can't do what I do. General Falk only allows certain folk the right to call him Mad Sam, that's an earned privilege." Taylor Jackson shifted in his chair and waited, the president went on: "Point two General Falk gave me permission to call him that until such time he extends that privilege to you, you will refrain from calling him Mad Sam."

"Yes sir, I just thought it was okay."

"Well it isn't."

"Understood sir, may I ask a question?"

"What might that be?"

"Why did you tolerate his salty language here in the Oval Office no less?"

The president sat back, worked his coffee, waited a beat or two and then said: "Did you happen to notice the Medal of Honor hung around his neck?"

"Yes sir." The president said: "That medal allows him to speak anyway he chooses, he earned the right to talk in any fashion necessary to get his point across."

Taylor Jackson felt completely admonished, "I do apologize Mister President, and I will never take that liberty again."

"Fine, now I need to speak with the Director of the FBI, get him on the horn, I need to speak with him about a critical development."

"Right away sir, I'll have your personal secretary tend to it now."

"Very good," Taylor Jackson rose and moved for the door to the president's private secretary's office, Jasper Bohannon heard him say: "Ms. Crawford, the president needs to speak with the Director of the FBI immediately," and the door closed.

WITHIN MOMENTS OF the door closing the president heard the voice of his private secretary coming out over the speaker, "Mister President the Director is on line one sir," Jasper Bohannon answered: "Thanks Ginny," and picked up: "Good morning Director."

"And a good morning to you sir, wonderful speech last night, very inspiring," the president appreciated the accolade, but that wasn't the purpose of his request to speak with the head of the FBI: "Thank you," he left it at that and moved on to the topic at hand: "We have a very promising lead as to who might be involved with Tuesday's attack."

"What do you have sir?"

"The name Max Bedford has surfaced he has on several occasions used the phase Saviors of the South in his on the air tirades."

"That kook spouts his venom on a daily bases, I can see him involved with something like this, maybe not at the center of things, but certainly on the periphery sir."

"Agreed. He's shown a vitriol distain for the Constitution on a lot of levels, some of his comments are on verge of being treasonous."

"Mister President, you're quite accurate in your assessment, his rhetoric boarders on sedition."

Jasper Bohannon: "I think his swill and activities warrants closer scrutiny."

The Director: "What is your instructions sir?"

Jasper Bohannon: "I want his phones tapped and put him under surveillance 24/7 until further notice."

The Director: "Will do, I'll have the SAC in Boston implement the surveillance posthaste and all of his calls will be monitored and recorded within the hour."

"Very good, this could be the snake that leads us to this nest of vipers, ride him hard."

The Director: "With pleasure, if he's involved we'll know for certain within a day sir."

Jasper Bohannon: "Give this your highest priority time is not on our side. Their second communiqué threatened to stage another attack similar to the last or something worse could be in the works within five days from now and I want them stopped in their tracks as soon as possible."

The Director: "Understood Mister President, I'll assign a thousand agents to cover this and I'm confident I'll have a positive outcome to report within that time frame."

Jasper Bohannon: "Actually Director, I want this resolved within three days, four days is playing it too close."

The Director: "Three it is, if we're fortunate we could have it accomplished within two, sir."

Jasper Bohannon: "Love that."

The Director: "Well sir if you'll release me, I'll set the wheels in motion and I guarantee if there's a there, there, we'll find it."

Jasper Bohannon: "The country needs this resolved quickly."

The Director: "And so it shall be Mister President."

Jasper Bohannon: "Alright, I expect an update later this evening, good day."

THUNDER RUMBLED ON the horizon and rain drove against the windows. General Barry Wallace paced the floor behind his desk Captain Stovall tracked him as he strode back and forth, finally he stopped, faced Mickey who stood at ease: "Captain you're positive the mortar round was sent to this base?" he knew the answer was yes, but he was hoping against disbelief. Mickey Stovall looked him straight in the eyes: "Absolutely General there's no doubt, records show it was part of a shipment of rounds delivered here five July oh seven, sir."

The general shook his head, turned and looked out the window at the base, it was eerily quiet. All personnel were confined to their quarters or barracks per General Falk's orders. General Wallace said over his shoulder, "This is a scandal of unimaginable portions Captain," the theft occurred under his command and he saw his career circling the drain go'n down in disgrace.

Mickey Stovall sensed his torment and spoke into the silence, "Sir this is not a reflection on your stewardship..." General Wallace stepped in: "Captain Stovall you're too kind, we both are aware of the consequences concerning this ordeal, heads will roll starting with mine the guillotine is being hoisted as we speak."

The captain smothered a smile at the general's inference, he spoke gently: "Sir I can assure you there will be no blow back..." again the general interrupted him: "Assurances? Nothing is guaranteed, not even your next breath," he walked back to his desk and sat down: "Please be seated Captain," Mickey Stovall did as he was told.

General Wallace steeple his fingers and said: "I didn't mean to be flip Captain, but I know the runnings of this Army. Someone other than the thieves will get mangled in this horrid affair."

Mickey Stovall told him, "General Falk will do everything in his power to make sure you are not held responsible for the theft and the event that followed sir, from what I've been able to ascertain he holds some sway with the president and I'm sure you will be insulated from any repercussions."

"Your words are comforting but I know the mechanics of this man's Army. Someone big will have to take the hit, that's just how it is. Congress will be howling for a senior officer to be the fall guy and unfortunately that guy is me."

"We'll see sir." Mickey Stovall said.

"Enough about my plight what's the plan?"

"I've went over the duty roster and Sergeant Roland Hollis was the duty NCO the night of the theft, I'll start with him, I'm positive after questioning him he will tell me what I need to know, sir."

The general recalled Mad Sam's words about the captain's abilities to delivery on his promise to get the info he sought, "What are your orders Captain?" Mickey Stovall told him: "I need Sergeant Hollis escorted to the mess hall and I'll take it from there sir."

The general nodded, picked up the phone and informed the Provost Marshal to have the sergeant brought to the chow hall under MP escort. He said to Mickey Stovall: "He'll be at the chow hall within ten minutes Captain, do whatever's necessary to get to the bottom of this."

"Oh I will sir, you can bank on that. If you'll excuse me I'll be about it." General Wallace said: "Of course Captain," and with that Mickey Stovall took his leave and left the general with his thoughts.

TEN MINUTES LATER Mickey Stovall strode into the chow hall, the massive room was deserted; the brigade was on deployment to Afghanistan. Staff Sergeant Roland Hollis sat in a chair bracketed by two MP's. Mickey stepped up and said, "You two can go now, we'll take full custody of the prisoner..." Roland Hollis said: "Prisoner, what is this?" Mickey Stovall ignored him and shook his head to the right signaling the MP's to leave, they looked at each other and proceeded to walk out, and Mickey Stovall turned and faced the sergeant: "Now I'm here to get information from you concerning the theft of government property..." Roland Hollis barged in: "I don't know what you're talking about, sir."

Mickey Stovall said: "I believe - no I know you do."

The sergeant was defiant: "That is ridiculous, I've never stolen any government property not even a tooth pick," Mickey said looking around at his men, "Oh we have us a smart ass here, I'll see how cute he'll be..." he glanced at his watch..., "in about twenty minutes from now."

Roland Hollis smirked and said: "You can't prove anything you're saying."

"Perhaps not, but you'll provide all the proof I'll need momentarily."

"What do you intend to do to me?" He demanded.

"That's a good question, the answer is I don't know, I'm going to turn my imagination loose and see where it takes us."

Roland Hollis eyes widened.

"I'm only going to ask you once, are you ready?"

"Ready for what," the sergeant said with a trace of arrogance in his voice.

"To give me the answer to my question," the sergeant asked: "What question is that?"

"Who's all involved with you in this theft of military ordnance?"

"Again Captain I don't know what you're talking about."

"Heard that already and it's the wrong answer. Corporals escort this piece of shit to the freezer area." The marines grabbed him, lifted him from the chair, Roland Hollis put up a struggle and Corporal Wyatt smacked him over the head with a blackjack, he howled and went limp with pain, they drug him across the chow hall, through the kitchen with his toes scrap'n the floor as they went. They arrived at the bank of freezers. Mickey Stovall looked at the thermometer it read minus fifteen below zero. He said: "This'll do just fine," Roland Hollis was hoisted to his feet and started to frail but was quickly subdued by the marines.

Mickey Stovall: "Take your uniform off you don't deserve to wear it."

Roland Hollis: "You can't do this, I have my rights!"

"You had the right to answer my question and you choose not to, so get busy undressing or these men will tear that uniform off of you."

Roland Hollis hesitated; Mickey Stovall drew his SIG 9, charged it: "Take that uniform off now..." he placed the gun against his kneecap..., "or I'll put you on wheels."

The sergeant looked terrified and started undress'n; finished he stood there in his birthday suit with his hands over his genitals.

Mickey told him: "Hiding you Johnson, you prick that's the least of your worries," Hollis was visibly frightened: "Captain I swear I don't know anything about any *theft*."

"Oh yes you do," the captain said to one of his men: "Fetch a large pail of cold water and bring it here," the enlisted man left and went into the kitchen area.

"Now what's going to happen is this, I'm going to place you in this freezer, naked and you're going to immediately develop the symptoms of hypothermia which will begin slowly, your ability to think and move will become cloudy impairing your thought process. Then frostbite will set in."

Roland Hollis couldn't believe what he heard.

Mickey Stovall went on: "You'll start to shiver uncontrollably, your body temperature will start dropping, you'll become weak, lose your coordination, your skin will go pale and here's the part I like, you'll start turning blue," Mickey Stovall grinned: "After that you'll become lethargic, perhaps suffer cardiac arrest, go into shock from there into a coma and the ultimate prize death. I think that about covers it."

Roland Hollis stammered: "*Captain, please don't do this sir.*"

"Oh but I am, you had your opportunity to come clean, but you didn't so in you go," he pulled on the freezer door, it swung open, the cold air gushed out into the hallway. Hollis now knew the captain wasn't jok'n: "Alright I'll tell you what you want to *know.*"

"I already know that, but I want to see you suffer, you little shit before you tell me, I'm sick like that," and shoved Roland Hollis in, he stopped just inside, Mickey Stovall kicked him in his ass, he stumbled into Antarctica and fell to the floor, Mickey pick up the bucket and heaved the water over him, "This will accelerate matters" and closed the door.

Roland Hollis felt the water hit him in the back, his fingers, stomach, knees and toes start to freeze in place, he pushed himself up and shivered like the captain forecasted. He stood up folded his arms, embraced himself. Mickey Stovall looked through the window; Hollis tucked his hands under his armpits and shook violently. He turned around and saw Mickey Stovall at the window he lifted his feet from the floor and left a portion of skin in place; he hopped over to the window and yelled.

Mickey Stovall couldn't hear him but he read his lips, "*LET ME OUT OF HERE.* I'll tell you what you want to *KNOW,*" Roland Hollis pleaded over and over. Mickey had a shit eat'n grin on his face, stared into his eyes and winked at him. He oh so enjoyed the scene on the other side of the window.

Roland Hollis started turn'n blue, the water had started to crystallize, and small icicles hung from his ears and another draped off the tip of his nose. He was near the predicted heart attack. Mickey looked at his watch, he had been inside for about twelve minutes, severe frostbite had sit in, and he looked to be in obvious pain.

Another three minutes elapsed and Roland Hollis was near death, finally Mickey Stovall said, "Bring that shit bird out," his men swung the door open, went inside and rescued Roland Hollis, they brought him out into the hall where he shook uncontrollably, his knees clashed together and his back was coated with a thin layer of ice.

Mickey Stovall said: "That wasn't so bad now was it?"

Roland Hollis' frost covered face seemed to crack, his lips were purple, he was in dire pain. Mickey stepped up: "Did you say something? I couldn't hear you."

He opened his mouth, this tumbled out, "I'll...I'll...tell...tell..you... every...thing," he stopped and stood there and shook. Mickey Stovall said, "Let's wait until you've thawed out some more." The ice started to melt. Roland Hollis stood in a puddle of water and said: "Captain...what do... you...want to know?"

"Simply everything, if you don't give me names, back in you go, this time to stay think I'm bullshit'n lie to me and you'll be an ice statue within thirty minutes," he looked down at the bucket, Roland Hollis saw this and clearly understood the captain's intent. He said: "I'll cooperate sir, honest I will." Mickey Stovall: "You know what I kind of believe you, now thoroughly convince me. From the top, who else was a part of this? Tell me now and tell me all or back in you go."

So he told him.

When the story was finished Mickey Stovall had all of the names and how it went down, he said: "Nicely done, you piece of shit, now put your skivvies on and leave the uniform where it is," Roland Hollis climbed into his underwear and Mickey said to his men: "Cuff this bastard and turn him over to the MP's outside and have them take him to the stockade." They did as ordered and led Roland Hollis away Mickey Stovall thumbed his smartphone and made a call.

GENERAL FALK WAS enjoying lunch he had just returned from his daily walk through the wood, every day him and his lads went for a mid-morning stroll regardless of the weather. Today was brutally cold, but it mattered not, Mad Sam was a creature of habit. He was set in his ways nothing deterred him from his routines.

Smedley Butler and Chesty Puller were curled up in their sofas when the general's Codex went. It was Captain Stovall on the line, "General I'm delight to report we struck gold," Mad Sam said: "Tell me all," and Mickey Stovall brought him up to scratch.

"Well done Captain. How many people are involved?"

"Ten in all sir four officers and six noncoms."

"Where are they now?"

"They're all being held in the stockade sir."

"What's your next move?"

"I've questioned all parties and they folded like tents once Hollis put the finger on them."

"Excellent. Anything else?"

"Sir, here's the kicker the ring leaders are two former Army officers, twin brothers named Billy Ray and Billy Bob Broussard."

"Genuine red necks."

"So it would appear sir."

"Their whereabouts?" the general asked.

Mickey Stovall told him: "From what I was able to gather, they're based somewhere in metro DC possibly in Virginia someplace sir."

"What was the reason for this betrayal, politics?"

"No sir, money."

Mad Sam exploded: "These sons of bitches sold their country out for *money*."

"Money thumps ideology every time sir."

"Incredibly well said Captain, anything else I should know?"

"Yes sir, I checked past troop movement records, it seems this was pulled off while the entire division was deployed in Afghanistan."

"That makes sense they were able to bring it off while the base was basically dormant."

"Yes sir, there's a reason I brought that to your attention."

"Go on."

"General Wallace sir, he was very concerned about this being laid at his doorstep, if he was leading his troops in combat that should exonerate him, shouldn't it sir?"

"Very keen of you Captain, I'll make certain the president is aware of all the circumstances. I'm confident the general will be deemed fault free. Fine officer that one. Pass the word to General Wallace and tell him not to fret there will be no blow back in his direction."

"Well do sir."

"Alright tidy things up and get back here most Rickey tick I need you here to start the hunt for these Broussard bastards."

"On the double, sir."

"Captain?"

"Yes General?"

"Mighty fine work, you did good."

"Thanks sir, just doing my job."

"And that you did, see you when you return."

"Understood sir," Mad Sam switched off, smiled and called the president.

WASHINGTON MIDDAY BRUTAL January weather seasoned with heavy snow had paralyzed every mode of transportation except the DC subway system. Billy Ray Broussard stood on the platform concealed in the press. He cased the subway as a potential target. The SOS had several pinpointed as the next great shock to the American psyche. They were thinking out of the box, the government would never guess nor suspect the SOS might attack Washington again. They'd be concentrating their efforts elsewhere in the country thinking his group wouldn't consider a repeat attack on the Capital.

The SOS had scouted other cities as its next possible target: New York, Madison Square Garden would make a statement, perhaps Chicago or Philadelphia they were ripe for a soft target attack. Wherever they choose to strike next would be a diversion, the main objective was Boston.

Billy Ray moved through the knot, checked out the lie of the land: security physical and electronic, avenues of escape, best times to inflict maximum damage all were factored into his reconnaissance. Every aspect had to be perfect before they would decide where to strike next. As with any guerrilla campaign hit'n the enemy where they were most comfortable was the sweet spot, comfort breeds apathy. The SOS probed deep for the right opportunities that were to their advantage.

Billy Ray hung around the area for thirty five minutes or so, and then boarded a train and headed back to Virginia to report his observations.

AT THAT PRECISE moment in the Barn, Andrew Wong stepped about the communications center looking at his computer bank as he held the Army records of the Broussard twins in his hand. The Pentagon had rushed the files over at the behest of Mad Sam. After his conversation with Mickey Stovall, the general called the president and got him up to date. Jasper Bohannon received the Intel with opened arms, this was good, very good, and they were now out in front of the SOS, where they'd wait around the bend to spring their surprise.

Now knowing the identity of the Fort Lewis heist organizers would lead the Eradicators to the mastermind, the evil genius, the lever puller. Andrew Wong stepped up to each computer displaying images from every surveillance cameras in metro DC search'n for the Broussard twins. Wherever there were cameras positioned their feeds were routed to the Barn, multiple cameras searched the crowds look'n for Billy Bob and Billy Ray Broussard.

Andrew Wong scanned their photos and if they raised their heads the computers would find them, pinpointing their whereabouts which would enable him to track the twins and their movements throughout the metro area. The Barn was equipped with the latest intelligence grade 3D face recognition software that allowed Andrew Wong to capture a subject's distinctive features using super resolution face enhancers. The three dimensional sensors could identify face contours, nose and chin from a wide range of viewing angles magnify skin texture searching for unique patterns and spots obvious in the subject's skin.

He entered the twin's photos into a facial data base and extracted features from the image of their faces, analyzed position, size and shape of the eyes, nose, cheekbones and jaw and compressed the data that was unique for face detection.

Andrew Wong had been at it without much sleep catch'n a nap here and there. He operated on adrenaline. The mission was too important to take timeouts. The captain was on post watch'n and listen'n for the enemy, his computers forward observers. Billy Ray made a pivotal mistake he had looked directly into a platform camera and the computer found him. His image was frozen and the 3D software positively ID him. Andrew Wong pick up the phone: "General we just made one of the Broussard brothers boarding the Blue Line at L'Enfant Plaza," General Falk said: "I'm on my way." Moments later he strode in: "Show me what you have," the captain complied and the general said, "Mighty fine, can you track his movements? What does the time signature tell us?"

"Yes sir, we can check all embark and disembark points along the entire route. The time clock states he entered the train at thirteen thirty."

"Find out where he disembarked."

Andrew Wong fingers slid across the keys and the computer displayed Billy Ray Broussard as he exited the train at the end of the line in Springfield, Virginia. Mad Sam said: "Aha, all roads lead to Virginia, Captain Stovall's hunch was correct. How do we know its Billy Ray and not Billy Bob?" Andrew Wong told him: "Billy Ray has a small scar along his left eye, see?" he pointed at the photo and then at the 3D image, the scar was evident, Mad Sam said: "With today's technology it doesn't pay to be an outlaw." Andrew Wong said nothing to that, the general asked: "Can you backtrack a few days to see if there are video of him riding the system?"

"Yes sir, it'll take a few minutes," the general said: "Good. Let me know the moment you know."

"Will do sir."

"And also tie into the parking lot's security cameras and see if our luck still holds."

"On it sir," the captain said, Mad Sam turned and left him to do his work.

Andrew Wong leaned over the console pressed a key and the Springfield subway parking lot camera came on line. He watched Billy Ray walk down the ramp, stopped, lit a cigarette and shifted off to his car, a sleek red Beamer, he reached in his coat pocket and came out with his keys, unlocked the door, slid into the seat, he adjusted the mirror looked at himself and smiled. He ignited the engine, backed out and moved off.

Andrew Wong hit another key, reversing the image, froze it and zoomed in; he tapped another key, sharpened the image of the license plate, the numbers were clearly visibly, He wrote down the number, picked up the phone and called the Virginia DMV. He waited finally a voice asked, "How may I assist you?" The captain identified himself and asked the woman for the name and address of the registered owner, he waited again she came back and gave him the requested info he thanked her and call the general.

Mad Sam rushed in: "What do you have?" Andrew Wong smiled and handed the general the info: "This is excellent now we know where this bastard lives; we're going to drop in on him tonight as soon as Captain Stovall returns, good work Andrew."

"Thanks sir." Mad Sam was happy and it showed as he headed back to his office.

THIS IS WELCOMED news General," Jasper Bohannon said he'd just returned from the Situation Room with Taylor Jackson, they entered the Oval Office the president removed his jacket and sat down, "What's your plan?" Taylor Jackson took a seat on the sofa and listened in.

"We're going to move on this bayou clown tonight, I'm waiting for Captain Stovall to arrive which should be any moment now sir."

The president loosened his tie, sat back and asked: "Do you anticipate any violence?" Mad Sam told him: "We go in prepared for action sir, that's our MO." Jasper Bohannon said: "Do what's necessary try to capture him alive if possible."

"Yes sir that's our aim but if my men are met with any armed resistance we will take him out along with whoever happens to be there."

The president chewed on it for a moment and said: "Do what you have to do."

"I'll let you know the outcome sir."

Jasper Bohannon said: "Very good."

Mad Sam said: "I'm confident we are getting close to the end sir."

"I like the sound of that."

"Me too Mister President, I'll keep you posted as close to real time as possible," the general told him, Jasper Bohannon said: "Good hunting General," Mad Sam replied, "It's the only kind I like sir." The president smiled, he truly enjoyed talk'n with the general he looked forward to lunch'n with him, "Good afternoon General."

"I anticipate a good night also Mister President," and he rang off.

WHAT'S YOUR READ on the subway system? You think it's a good opportunity for us?" this was Billy Bob speaking to his brother, Billy Ray said: "I've checked out every route and believe me it can be done. These northern bastards are lax at several locations."

"Well I say it's a go, I'll notify the Chief and let her know we'll hit Monday morning during rush hour that'll fuck 'em up good."

They were at their home outside Alexandria in the Virginia countryside, a two story colonial that sat on a twenty acre spread in the middle of the wood. The estate also contained several barns one was used to house the Peterbilt.

Billy Bob lifted a can of beer, knock back a swallow and said: "We'll hit them simultaneously that'll really fuck with their skulls not to mention all the havoc we'll cause, Monday is going to be a high body count day," and laughed. His brother smiled: "Yeah, yeah, keeping them off balance is the key," he was lean'n back against the sink, he straightened up and assumed a boxer's pose, "You know bob and weave, stick and move, float like a butterfly, sting like bee Muhammad Ali ain't got shit on me," he said as he danced around the kitchen, Billy Bob chuckled: "That's right set 'em up for the knockout punch."

Billy Ray stopped his mimick'n and sat down at the table, reached into the twenty four pack, pulled out a brewski popped the top, took a hit, belched and asked, "What time does your team arrive?"

Billy Bob looked at the kitchen clock, "They're due here in about a half hour." Billy Ray put his feet up on the table, crossed his ankles and leaned back, "How long will it take to get to Denver?"

"We'll leave tonight around seven thirty, take our time, make a few stops along the way we should arrive early Monday morning and do the do."

"Why'd you select Denver?" asked Billy Ray.

"That's the city that was designated as the second capital of the United States if anything were to happen to DC back in the fifties during the cold war," he told him.

"I like it, hit both capitals at once that'll spin their heads."

"Glad you approve little brother," Billy Bob said being the oldest by five minutes.

"Are you ever going to stop calling me little brother, bro?"

"Never, that's a permanent fact, we can't change history."

"Yeah, yeah, but we sure as hell can make some," they cracked up.

Billy Bob stood up, stepped over to the fridge, swung the door open, reached in and came out with items to make a sandwich, he asked, "Are you comfortable with that biological shit that Kussman dude concocted? That's some mighty dangerous shit, one whiff and its lights out."

"Think I don't know that, I've read his instructions over and over, he weaponized it into an aerosol with a time release mechanism device. I'll be long gone before it's released," Billy Ray told Billy Bob.

"That guy is one sick fuck. I went down to Belize last year and met with him, all that Nazi bullshit, the guy is one creepy son of bitch." Billy Bob told Billy Ray.

"Yeah, yeah, that may be, but he shares the same hatred for the United States as we do and he's one wicked motherfucker."

IN 1979 KIEL Kussman took his son on a trip to Brazil to meet the infamous 'Angel of Death', Doctor Josef Mengele, the notorious Nazi who oversaw the killing of thousands of Jews at Auschwitz. Kiel took Karl there to meet Mengele to impress his son and he told the doctor that Karl was going to be a doctor too. Mengele took a liking for the boy and said he could be the next great Nazi leader. They stayed at his ranch for two weeks, when they left Mengele gave Kiel all of his research papers and told him in the future his son would discover ways to make biological weapons if he followed his lead. Which Karl K. Kussman did after he graduated from MIT, he had now developed a formula that followed Mengele's schematics. The bio agent Billy Ray intended to release in the subway system was a result of that gift.

The Kussmans returned to Toledo and Josef Mengele drowned off the coast of Sao Paulo two weeks later.

BILLY BOB SAID, "Well just the same you be extremely careful with that shit you know Murphy's Law don't you?" and Billy Ray told him: "Yeah, yeah, I know if something can go wrong it will, don't worry I got this covered, it's going to be a piece of cake, a walk in the park."

"Over confidence has gotten a lot of people killed Billy Ray, I'm just saying be on your toes, I'd hate to lose you because of some miscalculation."

"I appreciate your concern and I'll be careful. Is the semi gassed up and ready to go?" Billy Bob said, "Everything's cool."

"Well I believe you, mister thorough."

"That I am little brother."

"Again with the little brother shit," Billy Ray said and crushed the can on the table and threw it playfully at his brother, they laughed. Billy Ray stood up, retrieved it and placed it in the trash. Billy Bob finished build'n his snack and started in. Billy Ray said: "We're going to give these bastards a double whammy it's going to be oh so good."

"Yeah, a two for one sale."

"You got it," just then Billy Bob's cell beckoned, it was Roger Smith tell'n him the crew would arrive shortly.

"That was Roger, he and Charlie Best are about two minutes out."

Billy Ray stood up walked over to his brother and hugged him: "Take care, man, I'll see you when you get back," Billy Bob said: "I will and you do the same."

Little did they know this would be the last time they'd see each other.

NOT MUCH MORE than a half hour later Robin Calhoun's disposal cell twittered, she reached over, picked it up off the coffee table. She always used a throw away whenever she talked with her field troops, she said, "Yes," Billy Bob told her: "We're ready to roll everyone's present and anxious to get underway."

Robin Calhoun said: "Very good, I expect results come Monday."

"Without a doubt," Billy Bob said.

She ran her hand through her hair, "There is a major bonus waiting for you and your men if it goes exceeding well."

"How's this for a bonus? My brother intends to do his thing Monday also."

"I am listening."

"We've decided to deploy the mad doctor's little toy in the DC subway system which will add more pain to the mix."

"Splendid, the more pain we can give, the more it will strengthen our position. I wholeheartedly approve. A double dose of suffering will do them good; the more the merrier," she pick up her glass and sipped at it, Billy Bob said: "Glad you like it ma'am."

"I love initiative, it shows you sincerely care," she told him, Billy Bob said: "That's a given, I hate these SOB's almost as much as you do." Robin Calhoun said back: "I am glad you qualified that, no one loathes them more than I, that would be virtually impossible," her ego wouldn't have it any other way. Robin Calhoun prided herself on being the number one anti American alive, the chief hater.

Billy Bob knew it was time to terminate so he said: "I don't have a problem with playing second fiddle in the orchestra maestro," she laughed, he went on: "Well it's time to roll, I call you from Louisville," Robin Calhoun said: "Fine, talk to you later."

THE MOMENT ROBIN Calhoun put down the throw away, the kitchen phone at the Macklin residence rang, Jessy was home alone, and Skeeter Macklin was out meeting with his new partners to discuss their plans to start up the restoration business. She expected him home around eight o'clock, maybe it was Skeeter calling, she wiped her hands, picked up on the third ring, "Hello?" it was Fred Harris instead, "Hi Jessy, how's married life?"

"Wonderful, how've you been Fred? The family's okay?" Fred Harris said: "Everyone's fine, when are you expecting?" he asked, she told him, "Come soon, I can't wait to be a mom," Fred said: "I've heard that the epitome of being a woman is giving birth and becoming a mother," she glowed: "Why, what a lovely thing to say Fred."

"Sometimes I have something to say that matters," he told her, Jessy said: "Don't sell yourself short, you have a lot of pearls of wisdom to share."

"Thank you, I've got a hot story you might want to hear?" he told her, "Love a good story, whatcha got?" asked Jessy, she sat down, rubbed her baby bump and waited.

Fred Harris worked part time with Jessy at the Washington Sentinel he also ran his own blog called ICE, Inner City Experience. He asked her: "In your investigative wanderings have you ever come across something called the SOS?"

"I can't say I have Fred." He said, "Neither had I until about ten twelve years ago, I first came across the name when a high profile black entertainer's son was killed by a sniper while he was riding his bike. Near the scene was a card that said 'Courtesy of the SOS', the police thought nothing of it..." Jessy cut in: "It could have been dropped innocuously and had nothing to do with the killing."

"That's what the police thought, but an identical card was found at the scene of a car accident that killed a famous black singer," he told her, Jessy said: "Interesting," she stood up, tucked the phone between her chin and shoulder and busied herself fix'n dinner, Fred Harris went on: "There's more, during the nineties there was a period, every six months something horrific happened to prominent blacks, entertainers, athletes, politicians and other notables. There seemed to be a pattern so I start snooping around and came up with a definite connection to this secret group."

"Now you've whet my appetite, speaking of appetite, I'm in the middle of preparing dinner and my husband's due soon, could we resume this conversation say the week after next? We're taking a trip to South America."

"I'm sorry, I didn't mean to impose, say I have an idea, what if I emailed you the file I've compiled on these incidents, and some of these go back to the early sixties." She said, "That works for me, send it and I'll look it over while I'm on my working vacation," Fred Harris said back, "Great, have a pleasant trip, bye." Jessy: "Good bye Fred, see you when I return," they switched off; Jessy said in silence, *I love a good conspiracy.*

IT WAS JUST after eight o'clock when Charlie Best drove the Peterbilt out of its hid'n place at the Broussard estate and turned left and headed toward eye 95, Billy Bob sat in the rear section of the lead car, the caravan set out for Denver. The five vehicle motorcade travelled down the country road with the Peterbilt bracketed by two cars in front and two behind, they came to a stop at the crossroad that led to the freeway on ramp. They made the left turn and were met by four military Humvees approach'n from the opposite direction. As the last one passed Billy Bob thought that was odd although military vehicles often travelled the back roads, but never at night, maybe it was noth'n, he thought about it a moment, then thumbed on his smartphone and called Billy Ray.

"What's up bro?" Billy Bob said: "Maybe nothing, we just reached the junction and four military Humvees past us headed that way," Billy Ray replied: "So what, they often trip around out here, it's no big thing," Billy Ray was in the den watch'n ESPN highlights, Billy Bob said, "You're probably right, just stay alert, okay?" Annoyed his brother said: "Yeah, yeah, I'll call when you get further down the road," Billy Bob said back: "Okay," and thumbed off.

Billy Ray flipped the cell shut threw it on the sofa it fell in between the seat cushion and the back of the sofa. He grabbed the remote, surfed for a moment, had a thought, got up and went up the stairs, entered a front bedroom to get a better view of the road that ran past the estate. He stood at the window and looked in the direction they would come. Nothing. He stayed there for a minute or so, and then he saw headlights approach about a quarter mile away. He continued to look in that direction wait'n for the vehicles to pass by. Suddenly the headlamps went dark as they approached the driveway they turned into the Broussard property, Billy Ray's heart jumped in his throat he couldn't believe it as the Humvees barreled up the driveway com'n straight toward him.

Billy Ray turned from the window ran out of the bedroom, went down the first flight of steps, stumbled up against the wall on the landing and continued down the stairs as he held onto the banister and took two steps at a time. He reached the bottom, raced to a closet where they stored their weapons, turned the knob and flung the door open, grabbed a M16, several bandoliers of magazines, ran through the lower floor dous'n out the lights and bounded up the steps, turning out the lights as he went into the front bedroom. He hit the light switch the room went black; he stood with his back against the wall and peered around through the window. He saw the four vehicles screech to a halt, the doors flew open at least twelve heavily armed marines sprung out about fifty yards away, they fanned out and high stepped it through the snow.

8

Strange Algebra

Metro DC; Boston; Metro DC; Rural Virginia

YOU HAVE A major problem on your hands," the voice told Robin Calhoun, she asked: "What are you referring too?" there was a trace of arrogance there. The voice said, "No time for haughtiness missy, there's a team of marines headed as we speak to your men's hideout in Virginia." Robin Calhoun dropped her shot glass it clanked on the coffee table crack'n the glass top and tumbled over spill'n her precious Jack onto the carpet, "Shit!" she said, the voice told her: "No time for that either, you better warn your people."

"How do you know this?" she asked, and look down at the coffee table, the voice said: "You don't have time for Q&A," and the voice was gone. Robin Calhoun was stunned, she quickly gathered herself, grabbed a disposal cell and called the Broussard estate. Billy Ray's cell chimed, but the ring'n was muffled by its position wedged between the cushion and the sofa. She let it ring for a minute or so, no answer, she thumbed Billy Bob's number and got an immediate response, "Yes," Billy Bob said, Robin screamed: *"I just received a call marines are heading to your home right now."*

Robin Calhoun's disposal went dark, she stood up and paced the living room *how did this happen*, things were going so well, now her main base was being assaulted by the government's forces. This was bad. She needed answers, *how did they find out?* A myriad of questions sped through her mind, she had to get a grip, settle her nerves and think this through. Like Nero fiddled away as Rome burned Robin Calhoun dither sip'n Jack Daniel's.

AT THE SAME time Billy Bob told Roger Smith on his cell: "I forgot something back at the house...," the caravan was about five miles away..., "proceed on," he didn't want to alarm his men and have panic spread through the ranks, he had to keep them focused on the Denver mission, Roger Smith said: "Okay we'll travel around fifty and you can catch up with us somewhere near Charlottesville."

Billy Bob tried to remain calm, but he fretted about his brother, he said: "I'll have the men with me pile into the other cars and I'll return alone."

Roger Smith told him, "There's an off ramp about two miles ahead...," add'n more time and distance between Billy Bob and Billy Ray..., "you can make the switch there, Charlie and I will continue on." Billy Bob was not happy about further delays but he conceded, "Good enough." They went on until the off ramp came up and they made the transfer. Billy Bob drew away made the loop and headed back to his little brother.

AND THAT WAS only the beginning of Billy Bob's concerns, ten minutes earlier his brother looked out the window as the marines in their winter whites trek through the snow. Billy Ray was trapped. What to do? Surrender was out of the question, he choose to make a stand. Billy Ray waited until they were about thirty yards away then he stepped in front of the window and his 16 spoke.

Glass shattered and window framing splintered, hot bullets peppered the cold snow as he sprayed left and right with his 16. Mickey Stovall yelled: "Return fire and advance at will," his men went tactical, some sought cover behind several trees and went to work and laid down suppressing fire, others advanced two at a time like chess pieces mov'n down the board.

They shot out all of the upstairs windows, where Billy Ray first appeared, but he vacated the room, raced to another upstairs bedroom and waited for a marine to enter his sight picture.

The firing continued as the Eradicators crept closer, one approached from the left, Billy Ray sighted in squeezed the trigger loosed the round and hit the target in the throat, before he hit the ground Billy Ray left that position, bound down the steps and crawled up to the dining room window raised his head and waited.

Mickey Stovall saw his man fall, shouted, "He's on the move fire at all of the windows, keep the bastard's head down," the men concentrated their fire on all of the upper and lower windows, Mickey Stovall ran straight at the front door. Billy Ray crawled along the floor, he stood up, popped off a magazine and hit another marine kill'n him. He dropped down and hugged the floor as he inched his way toward the front door, he knew they'd come charg'n through it at any moment.

Mickey Stovall raised his M4, squeezed off four rounds and blasted the door off its hinges; on the run he tossed the shotgun to Finch. Instead of rush'n through the door he dove through the dining room window, rolled over and came up firing with his MP5 and sprayed the foyer. Billy Ray tried to turn around and fire when he heard Mickey crash through the window but he wasn't quick enough, five rounds from the submachine gun slammed into his lower torso and threw him up against the stair railing, he bounced out of it, fell over on his stomach and gasped, Mickey Stovall shouted: "Cease fire and advance," he stood up, walked over to Billy Ray, kicked the 16 out of reach and then turned him over and said, "Where's Billy Bob, Billy Ray?"

He looked up at him and whispered, "Fuck yourself you... you black bastard," and coughed up blood, Mickey Stovall said: "You're half right I am black but you just insulted my loving parents," and shot Billy Ray in his right ankle with his SIG 9, "Again where's your brother?" Billy Ray grimaced in pain and couldn't say anything, seven Eradicators bound through the door, Mickey Stovall said: "Turn on the lights, search the entire property inside and out for evidence, weapons and valuable Intel."

His men set out as ordered, Mickey Stovall looked down at Billy Ray, "Where were we - oh yes I asked you the whereabouts of Billy Bob and you cracked wise about my birth status," and shot him in his other ankle, "That's one for my mom and one for my dad, now where's your brother?"

Billy Ray was in too much pain to say anything, Mickey Stovall rose up stepped into the dining room, pick up a chair, returned to the foyer and sat down, leaned over with the SIG hang'n between his legs and said: "Oh by the way did I mention you're dying?" and smiled, just then Billy Ray's cell chirped, Mickey Stovall looked into the den were the muted sound came from, he rose and said, "I'll get it, you seem to be busy dying down there. I'll be right back," and shifted into the den, reached in between the seat cushion and the sofa, grabbed the cell and thumbed on, the phone asked: "Billy Ray??"

Mickey Stovall said: "No."

Billy Bob: "Who's this?"

Mickey Stovall said: "Is this Billy Bob? I'm the guy who just shot your brother he's a bit busy dying over by the stairs. Where are you? Why don't you come and join Billy Ray, you two can go out the same way you came in, together."

Billy Bob: "*Fuck you.*"

Mickey Stovall: "No thank you and I wish you'd suppress your homosexual thoughts. Where are you?" Billy Bob had just turned off the freeway and was headed to the estate, he pulled over to the side of the road, and there was nothing he could do, because of his policy of never carrying arms in the cars while on a mission none were available to him. He heard the phone ask: "Are you still there?"

"Yeah I'm still here asshole."

Mickey Stovall said; "Are you coming to join your brother or what? You're not gonna to let him leave here without you, are you?" You traitorous son of a bitch," tormenting Billy Bob.

"I'll get you, you..., Mickey Stovall rode over him: "It's been said before, be original you bayou motherfucker and that's probably an accurate statement."

Billy Bob was hurt'n and furious at the same time he flowed from one emotion to the other that vied for dominance pain versus anger.

"Well if you're not going to show up, I've got to go and finish off Billy Ray, he waiting to die, I think I'll help him along, I'm a merciful guy you want to hear?" Mickey asked him as he shifted into the foyer. Billy Bob went silent, he heard Mickey Stovall say to him: "You want to say goodbye to your brother before I put a bullet through his head?"

Billy Bob: "You bastard."

Mickey Stovall: "I've been over that already with Billy Ray; do you want to say goodbye or what?"

Billy Bob: "I swear I'm going to get you."

Mickey Stovall: "That sounds like you don't have anything to say to your brother, so here goes, listen to this," he put the cell next to the barrel of the SIG 9 and fired and shot Billy Ray between the eyes. Billy Bob Broussard pound on the steer'n wheel with his fist and screamed, Mickey held the phone to his ear, listened to him sob and said in a sing song voice, "Oh Billy Bob, Billy Ray's on his way to hell, where are you Billy Bob?"

"Fuck you find me."

"I will and when I do it isn't going to be pretty," Mickey Stovall told him, Billy Bob said: "I hope you like Boston baked beans, you sadistic fuck," and switched off. Mickey Stovall said in silence, *Boston baked beans? What does that mean?* He bended down and rummage through Billy Ray's pockets for evidence and clues.

His brother sat by the road, his heart broke down and he cried, his brother was gone, for the first time in his thirty two years he felt alone. Memories dashed through his mind, now there would be no more future ones, just the past. He gathered himself, ignited the engine, he heard sirens approach, looked into the rearview and saw the flash'n lights blink on the ambulances as they raced toward him, he waited for them to pass, there were five in all.

Billy Bob Broussard hung a one eighty, headed off to catch up with his crew with animosity in his heart.

IN BOSTON AT that precise moment SAC Dennis McMorris sat in his car along with SA Adam Segal outside radio station WBMA. The SAC received instructions from the Director of the FBI earlier this morning to implement immediate and constant surveillance of Max Bedford. His four hour show was over at ten o'clock. Dennis McMorris looked at his watch in five minutes he'd bound out the door.

Dennis McMorris said to Adam Segal, "We've been ordered to tail this guy around the clock, listen to his calls and get photos of everyone he makes contact with. Did you bring all of the proper eavesdropping equipment?" Adam Segal said back, "Yes sir," the SAC told him, "The Director wants to us to get all the data on his guy possible and as soon as possible," he unscrewed the top off his thermos filled his cup, "You need a refill?" he asked his subordinate, "Yes sir, mine could be heated up a bit," he extended his cup and his boss topped it off.

"How does this guy rate?" asked the SA, Dennis McMorris looked over at him: "The Director believes he might be involved with the attack on Washington."

"*Whoa.*" I was wondering sir, why you'd be in the field on a cold night like this," he smiled at his superior who said: "Segal if you want to advance in the Bureau you have to be hands on."

The SA asked, "That's the prescription for success?" and the SAC told him, "In the Bureau it's always has been and always will be. This could mean a king size feather in your cap if we can get the goods on this fellow."

The SA sipped at his coffee, "Have you ever listened to this guy's rants? The things he says would make Hitler blush."

The SAC told him, "He's one sick puppy. He's hard wired with that hate shit."

"You know I wonder about these right wing nuts, if they really believe their crap or is it just a show," Adam Segal said, Dennis McMorris told him: "Most of these clowns are in it for the money; hate pays well, that's the strange algebra of bigotry."

"I read somewhere this character makes over thirty million a year slinging hate over the airways."

"I rest my case, it's an age old game, buyers are liars and sellers are thieves feed the poor hope and the rich fear will get you paid well - hey here's our guy's limo now."

They were parked a block away from the station, they looked out the window and saw a black limo pull up and double parked outside the entrance, two minutes later Max Bedford bound out the door, he climbed in the rear, the driver closed the door, ran around, got in and they moved off.

"Showtime," Dennis McMorris said, turned the key, drew away from the curb out into the traffic and followed Max Bedford.

INSIDE THE LIMO he said to his driver, "Head to the Renaissance Waterfront Hotel," he was due to meet with Reverend Blount at the 606 Congress Restaurant and was running behind schedule. Max Bedford looked out at the Boston skyline and said in silence, *what a glorious view, too bad it will be toast soon. But that's the nature of war there has to be causalities and destruction.* He reached in his liquor cabinet and poured a drink to fortify him, Moses Blount was Robin Calhoun's right hand man and the director of the Sumter Fund so he had to be careful when he dealt with him. Any slip ups he'd surely report them to back to her. And she could be a bitch at the drop of a hat, but she was dedicated to the cause, so he tolerated her once this was over he'd square her ass away, he was tired of her condescending attitude, *who did she think she was dress'n me down in front of everyone* on Stone Mountain? She must have heard him think'n about her because his smartphone went and it was Robin Calhoun on the air.

For a moment it startled him, he thumped on, hit speaker, "Good evening," he said affably, she snapped: "I wish it was."

"You seem upset, so what's the issue now?" he asked.

"We have a major one that's what. The government raided our base in Virginia."

"*What.*"

"You heard, somehow they found out about it and have complete control of the facility."

"This is not good," he said, she said back: "Very astute, of course it's not good it's a disaster you moron." He bit his tongue and said, "There's no need for name calling."

Her tongue a whip, she lashed him with it. "Well don't make stupid comments and you will not be called corresponding names, okay?" Robin Calhoun was super pissed and she had to take out her anxieties on someone and that someone was Max Bedford.

SAC McMorris said to Special Agent Segal, "Are you getting this? This is gold."

"Yes sir I'm recording everything as they speak, who's the female?" he asked, Dennis McMorris said: "I don't know he hasn't called her by name, hopefully he will." They were using a laser eavesdropping device to listen to the conversation. Adam Segal held the laser out the window, the beam was aimed on the back window of the limo and it picked up everything loud and clear.

Robin Calhoun said, "Well this stops nothing we are still going ahead with our plans, we have come too far to abort now."

Max Bedford chewed on it for a moment and then said, "Of course you're right there would be some setbacks but we must continue on, I'm heading to meet Reverend Blount now to formulate the final plans."

"Well that's good, he will call me after your meet," and she switched off.

Dennis McMorris said, "Damn he didn't say her name, but that's okay we are seriously on to something here, we need to cover this guy like a blanket I'm sure he'll lead us to everything we need to know about this group and when he does we'll nail his ass."

Max Bedford sat in the back of the limo and thought; *this has taken an unexpected turn.* If the government was this close they'd have to be extremely careful for now on, no room for any errors, the attack on Boston would have to be moved up perhaps, he'd see how things played out with Billy Bob's next move and plan out from there. The limo arrive at his destination, the valet swung the door open, Max Bedford left the interior and handed him a ten spot, strode into the hotel, padded through the lobby and went into the restaurant, the maître de said, "Good evening Mister Bedford your party has already arrived I'll show you to your table." Max Bedford followed him, Moses Blount noticed them thread through the tables, stood up and waited, they stepped up and he outstretched his hand, "Good to see you Max you look well," the maître de put in, "Your waiter will be here presently enjoy your meal," turned on his heels and returned to his station.

"I wish it was a good occasion, Reverend..., they settled down and Max Bedford leaned over, "I just spoke to the boss and she said there's been a major setback."

"What kind of setback?" Moses Blount asked.

When the limo arrived at the hotel entrance Dennis McMorris told Adam Segal, "Hang loose, I'll go inside to see who this Blount person is and call, be ready to move, hopefully they've taken a seat by a window so we can continue listening. I'll take some photos of them and see who this other player is." He pushed the door open and Adam Segal slid over behind the wheel. He watched the SAC enter the building he waited per his instructions. Dennis McMorris came into the restaurant looked across the room and saw they were indeed seated at a window; he stepped over to the bar while the maître de was busy and ordered juice. He phoned Adam Segal: "Luck's with us, they're seated by a window, drive around to the south side of the hotel, park and lock in on them," Adam Segal said, "I'm on my way." Dennis McMorris turned casually around and position himself to take photos of them with his in button micro camera.

"From what she said the Virginia headquarters was overran by government forces. The reverend's eyes widened, "Not good, not good at all," Max Bedford agreed, "You're so right, this could be earthshaking, we might have to step up our timetable."

"Agreed. Is everything in place?" he asked.

Just then the waiter appeared they went silent, "Are you ready to order?" Moses Blount said, "Bring us tea for now we haven't looked over the menu as of yet, hopefully by the time you've return we'll have decided," the waiter smiled and said: "Very well sir, take your time," and moved off.

Max Bedford said, "The only thing absent is the schedule, once we have that, things will be put in motion based on that information."

"When do you anticipate having it?"

"It's been promised by midweek, but I wish we could get it sooner, but that's not under our control, we'll just have to remain calm and wait."

"How reliable is your contact?"

"He's very well placed, and has immediate access to the information we need, he's always delivered in the past the information always check out right on schedule and right on time, so I see no problem with him being consistent." Moses Blount said: "Not to mention he's being paid very handsomely, but I'm not complaining mind you it's a necessary expenditure."

Dennis McMorris downed his juice, paid the barkeep off, strode toward their table, he quietly snapped photos as he approached and purposely past them on his way to the restroom. While inside he hit Adam Segal on his cell, "Are you getting everything?"

"Yes sir, good stuff enough to pinch them," he was amped to make a collar.

"Rein up your pony cowboy; we'll let the Director decide when we snatch them up. You'll have your fifteen minutes so cool your jets, okay?" Adam Segal said weakly, "Yes sir."

"Now I'm going to get a few more shots of this Blount character and I'll be right out." Dennis McMorris walked out of the restroom and past their table click'n his camera all along the way. He was certain he had enough photos and left the restaurant.

They had ordered their meals and began to eat then Moses Blount looked up from his plate and said: "Well hopefully Billy Bob will be able to do his thing out west come Monday; the boss said he's going to rain some hell on some unfortunate souls."

Max Bedford said, "Pray for him Reverend and us too." Moses Blount said, "Praying and having them answered are two different things my friend." Max Bedford said, "Amen to that." They eat their meal and talk about nothing of any import, finished Max Bedford said, "Reverend I have to run, I've have a late meet with some local party people I'm trying to wring some money out of them, speaking of money my guy will need a considerable payment for the info he's going to provide." Moses Blount told him: "Not to worry the Sumter Fund has plenty of cash we just received a major infusion from our cousins in Belize, so money is not a problem, okay," he said confidently. Max Bedford picked the bill up looked at it, and went in his pocket, exposed his roll peeled off two fifties put them on the tray stood up and said: "How long will you be in our fair city," the reverend said, "My flight leaves for Charleston at one forty five in the morning, I'll be glad to get back down below the Mason Dixon Line it's too cold up here for these old bones." Max Bedford laughed and said, "Have a safe flight and I'll talk with you later," they shook hands, he spun on his heels and left.

Outside the FBI agents drove around to the front and waited, Max Bedford came out, climbed in, the limo drew away, and Dennis McMorris and Adam Segal wedged their way into traffic four cars behind.

MAD SAM WAS at his desk going over the info Mickey Stovall texted him, the outcome at the Broussard estate was fruitful, the FBI arrived, combed the property and discovered a treasure trove of evidence that implicated the twins as major culprits in the January 20th attack.

They found empty mortar round cases, an operational mortar, numerous weapons of all descriptions and they hit the mother lode when they came across the biological canisters. The FBI called the hazardous materials unit to have them analyzed. The general was quite pleased at the success of Mickey Stovall's raid. The downside was they lost two marines and three others sustained wounds none of them life threatening. His heart was heavy he'd write their relatives immediately and recommend each of the fallen for the Bronze Star and Navy & Marine Corps Medal.

The investigators came across the semi's tire tracks now they knew how the mortars were being transported and deployed. Andrew Wong contacted the U.S. National Photographic Interpretation Center which constantly photographed the metro DC area. He analyzed their photos and found pictures of the Peterbilt when it left the Broussard estate and got on the Capital Beltway. He ordered the NSA to reposition its new speed cameras which could use their satellites to measure average speeds over long distances, the cameras combined number plate reading technology with a GPS receiver. With this techno-ammo Andrew Wong could find, and track the semi, have it intercepted and neutralized.

Now the game was on.

LATE THAT NIGHT at the White House Jasper Bohannon wound down his day reading to his daughters, Carmen had fallen asleep and he put in time just being dad. His Codex went he put the book down, kissed his girls and told them to say their prayers and padded out of the room. He picked up: "Good evening General." Mad Sam said, "It's both a good and depressing evening sir." The president went tense, "Give the worst first."

Mad Sam told him the worse, Jasper Bohannon sighed, "That's very unfortunate General, it always hurts when we lose any of our fine fighting men and women."

"That is so, but frontline soldiers kill and die sir, that's nature of the business we're in," he said philosophically. The president said: "I'll pen letters to their love ones immediately," Mad Sam said, "That's most appreciated sir, if you don't mind I'd like my letters to accompany yours."

"Of course General, that's an excellent gesture letting the families know that their sons and brothers are sincerely missed by their government and that we as a nation will never forget the sacrifice they made, and how they gave their last full measure, defending their country."

"I agreed sir," there was a pause in the conversation finally the general said, "Now on to the upside sir." Jasper Bohannon said, "Yes General please enlighten me."

Mad Sam told him what happened in great detail and where the situation stood at the moment.

The president: "What's the next move?"

Mad Sam: "With Captain Wong's findings I'm confident we can run these folks down soon sir."

The president: "That's good to hear, seems we are ahead of schedule on our self-imposed deadline, which is a good thing. Stopping the bio attack was stupendous work General your men are to be commended."

Mad Sam: "Thanks sir, but I believe there's something else afoot."

The president: "Your concern?"

Mad Sam: "Captain Stovall said Billy Bob Broussard said something strange at the end of their conversation."

The president: "Exactly what was said?"

Mad Sam: "He told the Captain, 'I hope you like Boston baked beans'."

The president: "Very curious indeed, what's your read?"

Mad Sam: "My gut tells me the attack three days past and the planned attack on the subways and their pending mortar attack are ruses and the real target is Boston."

The president: "Why there?"

Mad Sam: "I can't put my finger on it but it doesn't feel right to make a comment like that, and not have it mean something crucial, I think I'll concentrate my focus on Boston after we've corralled this group and their terror platform."

The president thought about that and said, "Play to your gut General and divert whatever you need to the Boston area, it may mean nothing but we have to take all threats seriously."

Mad Sam: "I share your opinion sir."

The president: "It's been both a productive and tragic day hopefully the upcoming days will be more of the former General."

Mad Sam told him, "We'll do everything is our power to bring about that result sir."

"Once again, General, I have full faith in you and your men to deliver on that exertion."

"That's what we aim, no intend to do, sir, if you don't mind I'll return to matters," Jasper Bohannon said, "Of course, don't let me detain you, good night Mad Sam."

BUT THE NIGHT was not over for the president, he had just hung up and the Codex sounded its familiar chime again, this time it was the Director of the FBI. Jasper Bohannon knew his nights were not his alone he belonged to the people and picked up, "Yes Mister Director what have you got, great news I presume?"

"Your supposition is most acute sir," the Director said, the president smiled: "My ears are yours," and the Director walked him through the night's events in Boston.

The president had stepped into the Yellow Oval Office and stood at the window behind the Truman Balcony where he looked out at the Washington Monument as the Director brought to a close his assessment of things, Jasper Bohannon said, "Most productive, any idea who this mystery woman is?"

"Not at this time sir, we run a voice analysis. Our voice identification experts and linguists detected a faint accent they believe its origin is from the southeastern part of the country, possibly South Carolina or Georgia."

The president said: "That narrows it down considerably each one of our southern states has its own distinct accent, but that still encompasses millions of people."

"That's true Mister President but not many of them would be in position to bring something like this off and that person whoever she must be highly influential and has to be extremely wealthy or have access to considerable funds to finance an endeavor such as this."

"I believe you're right on the money, no pun intended," the president said, he had a hint of chuckle in his voice.

The Director caught it and replied: "Speaking of money I think we should follow up on this Belize angle, from the conversation we recorded this Reverend Blount said they received a significant amount of funds from there. I'll assign an agent or two to follow that lead and see where it takes us. In addition we'll find out what this Sumter Fund is all about, again the South Carolina inference."

"Excellent. What do we know about this Blount person?" Jasper Bohannon said as he turned from the window, stepped to the sofa and settled down.

"We ran a check on him and he's the head of the White Salvation Church in Charleston and preaches an extreme brand of white supremacy. From what we've been able to ascertain he has a large following of likeminded individuals, I'll alert our Charleston office to monitor his activities and see what else he will reveal about himself and his so called church."

"Hmm, all roads are leading to South Carolina? Where is this Max Bedford from originally, I don't think he's a Bostonian do you?" The president asked. The Director told him: "He's from Tennessee sir, we ran an extensive genealogy check on him and it seems he's, get this, a distant relative of Nathan Bedford Forrest of KKK infamy."

"Yes, that makes sense he too was an avid racist, I guess as they say it's in the DNA." Jasper Bohannon stood up, and returned to his bedroom sat on the edge of the bed, he was fatigued but continued the conversation: "What are you intentions on apprehending these two?" The Director said, "I told the SAC in Boston to hang back and keep the light on Bedford, I think it might be best to let him continue his activities, he will eventually leads us to the big fish and the other players in this scenario and that goes for Blount also."

"Good thinking Director, if we were to snatch them up that might cause the others to go to ground and we don't want that. Eventually the mice will lead us directly to the head rat and we'll put a period on this entire affair."

"You're right sir, we have them in our constant sights they're not going anywhere, we can cuffed them whenever we're ready, let's see what unfolds."

"Alright, thanks for the update, keep at it, I have a heavy schedule tomorrow so I am going to retire for a few hours, we'll continue tomorrow."

"Fine by me sir, good night Mister President."

AT ROBIN CALHON'S townhouse the following morning she woke up with a severe hangover and deep, deep troubles on the war front. Last night's debacle was disheartening, she spoke with Moses Blount after his meet with Max Bedford and the conversation encouraged her not. He told her they had to accelerate their timetable last night's event dictated so.

She headed for the rain room, when finished Robin Calhoun dressed, called for her car, she had an important vote to cast in the Senate and rolls would be taken within the hour. She had to maintain all appearances of being the dedicated junior Senator from the great state of South Carolina, even though she was the architect of trying to destroy the United States. Robin Calhoun was confident she was two three steps ahead of the president whom she considered not to be her equal in intellect and certainly not on par with her in cunningness. No one in her estimation was as sly as she. Robin Calhoun was the ultimate megalomaniac she thought she was Miss Invincible, the untouchable one, but she overestimated herself and underestimated her adversary. That would be her downfall; ego like the president said, was her Achilles heel.

THE MORNING DAWN caught Andrew Wong at his computer bank where he monitored the NSA's speed cameras they were positioned to track Highway 81 west of Charlottesville. He hadn't slept for twenty four hours the situation called for his undivided attention, they were closing in on the SOS he was confident they'd have them located within the next hour or so. Mad Sam told him they had to pick up the tempo time was tight. Billy Bob Broussard had to be stopped, with the death of his brother the general knew he was irrational and would be very vindictive, his instability could cause him to go on a violent rampage and use his terror weapon to wreak havoc throughout the countryside of Virginia and possibly into Tennessee.

Mad Sam entered and said: "Any progress Captain?" as he looked over his shoulder, Andrew Wong said, "According to the cameras we narrowed their route down to within fifty miles, they should be located soon sir."

"Good, I want these bastards found and eliminated soon as possible, Captain Stovall is standing by with his team at Quantico, they'll board an

Osprey and be airborne when you've pinpointed the whereabouts of these criminals," the general told him, Adam Wong said, "I'm on top of it sir, if they're on the road I'll find them without a doubt and something else is peculiar sir," Mad Sam asked: "What's that Captain?"

"The photos show the semi was being trailed by two cars and perhaps others in front the truck is being escorted sir."

"This means the mortar crews are travelling in those cars, which is good the weapons wouldn't be manned when we attack."

"Yes sir."

"Well I'll leave things in your capable hands Captain it's time for morning colors, my lads and I will be there as usual." Andrew Wong said: "Aye, aye sir."

LATER THAT MORNING on Capitol Hill there was big buzz about the impending vote on a critical spending bill due to the crisis on Wall Street. Congressional members were deciding whether to pass legislation to bail out the banks and financial institutions. The press was in full attendance and the Senate was packed with its members.

Robin Calhoun had just arrived she made the circuit, greeted her fellow Republicans and campaigned for their yes vote. She came upon Senator Carlisle and said, "Good morning Jake, how have you been?" This was for anyone within earshot's benefit. Jake Carlisle played the role to perfection, "Why it's good to see Senator, how was your trip home? Everything's okay in South Carolina?"

"Wonderful thanks for asking." She said, looking around the Senate Chamber siz'n up things, "How do you intend to vote?" Jake Carlisle said: "Now Senator no fair peeking before the test." She smiled and said, "Ever the clever one, Senator, I guess we will have to wait and see which way you come down on this bill, I am all for it, we have to intercede, this recession thing could deepen and we cannot allow that for the sake of the country." She sounded very convincing and sincere. He told her, "Still fishing Robin, nice try, I'll keep you and everyone else in suspense until its voting time."

Staff members bustled about and Senators made sure they'd looked good for the CSPAN cameras; everyone was jittery about the upcoming vote.

Robin Calhoun said, "Well your turn will come up immediately after mine so I will not have to wait so very long to find out which you will go on this issue." Jake Carlisle looked around the room and up at the gallery which was packed to see if he recognized anyone up there he scanned the crowd and saw a familiar face it was Sierra Montgomery an ex-lover who was still bitter about their breakup. Sierra Montgomery was a DC socialite, local gossip and Congressional groupie, she had had relationships with ten of the senators down on floor, and she was look'n directly at them when Jake Carlisle looked up. Their affair ended on a sour note, she had grown attached to him especially when the polls indicated he'd win the election but was upset by a small margin of electoral votes, the election was decided by New Mexico falling into Jasper Bohannon's column. He had broken off the relationship about three months ago but Sierra Montgomery was reluctant to accept it, she was sore loser and was play'n the jilted lover card to the hilt. Unbeknown to Jake Carlisle she had been stalk'n him and knew of his relationship with Robin Calhoun; in fact she had tailed him to Robin Calhoun's townhouse the night before and took photos of him as he entered her residence and caught Robin as she leaned against the door in her flaming red negligee. Sierra Montgomery was plot'n her revenge for being spurned by Jake Carlisle. She was itch'n to reveal what she knew to the tabloids and blogs.

Jake Carlisle said, "Well you know shortly where I'll land on this issue," as he eyes slid away from Sierra Montgomery and back to Robin Calhoun, she looked around and made sure no one would hear her when she whispered: "Can you hear my kitty purring? Why don't you stop by tonight and stroke it," she cooed and left him stand'n there blush'n. Sierra Montgomery caught this, she knew him well and she burned. Jake Carlisle collected himself and headed for his seat as the Vice President graveled the Senate to order. Everyone took their seats and the voting began.

MEANWHILE ON HIGHWAY 81 Billy Bob Broussard sat in the back seat and looked out at the Virginia countryside as it flew by think'n about last night. He had to withhold his emotions and not let his men know he grieved about how life would be without his brother, he had to accept it, and life had to go on.

Billy Bob the lone twin, now focused on the mission ahead, he pledged to avenge Billy Ray's death by raising hell in the United States of America and do whatever it took to make it the Untied States of America. Billy Bob was now suicidal about it, he didn't care if he lived or died, and he'd take as many as possible with him. They had been travel'n steadily from some hours now and as it got closer to eleven he ordered the caravan to halt from lunch and restroom breaks.

ABOUT FIFTY MINUTES later everyone had eaten and relieved themselves except Harry Reynolds, who became ill and it felt like his stomach would never settled down he had been in the restroom hurl'n for about fifteen minutes, they lost valuable time so Billy Bob decided to let the Peterbilt and the others continue on while he remained at the restaurant. He said to Roger Smith: "Rog you and Charlie start out with the others, I'll hang back with Harry and we'll catch up when he's through puking his guts up," Roger Smith told him, "Okay, we'll keep it around fifty five you shouldn't have a problem catching us."

Billy Bob said: "I'm cool with that, you know how sensitive Harry's tummy is," and laughed, he put up a good show for his men, and said: "I'll pick up the taps you guys hit the road." Roger Smith, Charlie Best and others filed out climbed in the vehicles and pulled out onto Highway 81, leav'n Billy Bob and Harry Reynolds behind.

CLOSE TO HIGH noon Harry Reynolds finally emerged from the restroom he looked peaked, Billy Bob said, "I hope you feel better than you look; you look like shit," Harry Reynolds said back, "Thanks for the pep talk coach now put me back in the game." They laughed. Billy Bob paid their bills they left the restaurant climbed in the car with Billy Bob behind the wheel and moved off. They rode in silence, Harry Reynolds was still a bit queasy and Billy Bob was thinking about his brother, this couldn't be, but it was, *that bastard who killed him is gonna get it*, even though he didn't know who he was, it didn't matter someone, *a lot of people* were going to pay and pay dearly, this he promised Billy Ray.

Billy Bob kept the speedometer on seventy five try'n to run down the others, the car came over a hill and he could see them about four miles away headed up another, "There they are, it won't be long before we can fall in," this was Billy Bob speaking, he looked at Harry Reynolds: "You okay?," Harry said, "I'm fine," and Billy Bob told him: "You need to see a doctor about that ulcer," Harry Reynolds said, "Okay mom, I'll eat my veggies, now keep your eyes on the road."

Billy Bob smirked and said, "Always with the smart shit, huh?"

"You know how I am, being a wise ass runs in the family, I can't help myself."

Billy Bob looked out the window saw the last car go over the hill, he heard a loud sound overhead turned and noticed a V22 Osprey fly'n about a thousand feet above, his heart jumped in his throat, he knew this was bad, very bad. He said to Harry Reynolds: "I think we have a problem, be casual and look to my left," he did and said back, "What the fuck are they doing way out here is there a base near here?"

"Afraid not, my friend this is major and us with no weapons."

"I told you we should be pack'n, you think they're look'n for us?" he asked and Billy Bob said, "We'll know real soon," and backed off the gas, slowed down to fifty five and kept his eyes on the Osprey as it flew past.

On board Mickey Stovall held his Zeiss glasses and looked off in the distance, spied the Peterbilt ascending a hill and said, "There she blows," and grinned, "Got you, you sons of bitches." He lowered the binoculars and said to his men, "Prepare for battle, Corporal Finch man the Ma Deuce if they try to make a run for it light 'em up." Finch went to the back ramp, assume the position, racked the bolt, the Osprey caught up with the semi, flew past, started to descend and hovered over the highway about a half mile in front of the lead cars.

Inside the Peterbilt Charlie Best said, "*What the fuck*," and Roger Smith woke up looked out the window, "*Shit*." Charlie Best yelled, "What should I do?" And Roger Smith told him: "Whatever you do don't stop, keep roll'n," he picked up his two-way to speak to the other drivers in the cars he hollered: "*Don't stop keep go'n*." He heard the three drivers said in concert, "*Okay*," there was panic in their voices; but the driver of the trailing car started to back off and watched the Peterbilt fade into the distance.

Mickey Stovall said, "Looks like these clowns are going to try to make a run for it, good, Finch pepper the highway with a warning burst, crank off about a hun." Finch unleashed the 50 cal and huge rounds marched up the highway tear'n up concrete as they headed toward the cars. Charlie Best said, "*They're firing at us man*," Roger Smith said back, "No shit Sherlock and keep this son of a bitch mov'n straight at 'em!"

Mickey Stovall said, "I love fools, Finch no more fuck'n around show them what you can do," Finch like that, elevated the 50 and shot holes through the fairing just for fun. The Osprey rose up fifty feet above the highway, hovered and let the semi pass underneath Finch peppered the top as it went by, big bullets ripped into the trailer, Charlie Best tried his best to keep the Peterbilt on the highway he was sweat'n bullets as real ones chewed up the trailer, ricocheting around inside.

Roger Smith saw the lead cars speed off in the distance, they were doing over a hundred, they approached another hill that slowed the semi, he was hold'n on for dear life, he looked at Charlie Best as he struggle with the wheel, who said, "Did you see that gun underneath the plane?" Roger Smith said, "If they turn that loose we're fucked."

They referred to the remotely operated weapon turret for the GAU17 mini gun, a nasty piece of work. The car behind raced past the semi, Captain Stovall told Corporal Finch, "Take that car out," the Osprey rose higher and kept pace, Finch shot out the tires and it careened off the highway flipped over several times, exploded, car parts became shrapnel and whizzed in every direction.

Billy Bob and Harry Reynolds crested the hill and began to coast down, just over another hill about a mile away they saw what happened, Billy Bob slowed down further, looked at the smoke waft upwards and said, "I'm make'n a U turn," swerved across the meridian, took off in the opposite direction and removed themselves from the battle in the rearview. Billy Bob was hav'n *'A Bad Day at Black Rock'*.

The co pilot rotated the mini gun fired at the lead cars; they were hit by hundreds of rounds and crashed, repeating what happened to the first one. Now only the semi was left, the mini-gun swung back and started in on the Peterbilt, the windshield was disintegrated rounds filled the cab, Charlie Best and Roger Smith were laced with hot lead, Charlie Best slumped over the steering wheel, it spun to the left, the semi skidded and jack knifed. It twisted down the highway and tipped over, slid'n on its side as sparks flew everywhere and finally it stop and straddled the highway block'n it to all traffic.

It was over.

The Osprey came down vertically in a field alongside the road, the squad of Eradicators ran down the ramp toward the Peterbilt, spilled fuel ignited, they halted and raced back into the craft, it rose as the semi exploded and mortar rounds ignited inside the trailer and blew it apart. The Osprey engines rotated and flew higher as Mickey Stovall, his men and the aircrew watched the fireworks below.

9

Hope's a Drug

Metro DC; Belize; Metro DC

IT WAS IN the middle of the afternoon when General Falk received a detailed report from Captain Stovall who sat in front of the general's desk. When he finished the general said his patent phase, "Mighty fine, Captain, mighty fine." He was obviously pleased and carried on, "The president will hear of it shortly," and spoke to Andrew Wong seated next to Mickey Stovall, "Captain Wong you did yeomen work on this, without your diligence we'd still be hunting for those kooks and they would have created mayhem somewhere in the country. Outstanding show both of you gentlemen will receive the appropriate commendations I'm talking Distinguished Service Cross and Silver Star here, nothing less."

The captains glowed.

Mad Sam looked at Mickey Stovall, "Do we know whether this Billy Bob Broussard bastard was among the dead?" Mickey said, "Not as of yet sir, most of the bodies were fried to a crisp, the FBI will try to identify them through dental forensics, I don't think fingerprinting an option, but you never know those guys can do wonders these days." The general reared back in his chair ran his hand over his high and tight and chew on it while his subordinates waited. Mad Sam leaned forward, "Until that's proven we will operate under the assumption that he's still alive. He may not have been with these other SOS bastards, I can't shake that comment he made to you, what was it Captain?"

Mickey told him: "Hope you like Boston baked beans, sir," the general said, "Yes that's it, a rather queer comment to make during the heat of battle wouldn't you agree Captain?" Mickey Stovall said, "Whole heartily sir, he said it with such relish and scorn, like he was secretly informing me about an impending doom, that's my take on it sir."

"Aha. Captain Wong what's your read?" Andrew Wong considered it for a moment, "Sir it would appear to imply that Boston is going to be cooked in some form or fashion, that's only thing I can glean from it."

"Cooked huh, very interesting, Captain would that suggest nuclear or some sort of dirty bomb?" Before he could answer the general went on: "During my visit with the president we discussed that exact scenario, he was very rueful about it. Let that be our hypothesis until proven otherwise, I believe that's the correct avenue of approach, agreed?"

The captains nodded in unison and chorused, "Yes sir."

The general stood up, "Well gentlemen keep after it, and Captain Stovall maintain your search for this Billy Bob turd until the forensics is concluded. And Captain Wong you explore all dirty bomb feasibilities."

Again they said yes sir as one.

"Gentlemen you have your tasks and I have mine it's time for my lads and I to take our daily constitutional into the wood. Keep me updated on all progress or setbacks," Mad Sam said as he rose and shifted to the window.

They stood up took their leave and left Mad Sam at the window where he thought about the past two days developments, he was content that things were happening in their favor, but the baked beans was troublesome, he'd tend to it upon his return and call the president, he said over his shoulder: "Smedley and Chesty what time is it?" The bulldogs woke up at the sound of their names ran to get their leashes, trotted up and wagged their tails, the general bend down, attached them to their collars, "Ever the eager beavers, let's head out," he swung the door open and Generals Mad Sam Falk, Smedley Butler and Chesty Puller moved off to commence their trek through the wood.

AS SOON AS they got back inside the Barn Mad Sam phoned the White House, he spoke to the president and brought him up scratch. Jasper Bohannon was elated at the news, but the general dampened that enthusiasm when he told him they hadn't confirmed the demise of Billy Bob Broussard. The general told the president they would continue to hunt for him and Captain Wong was busy running different mass casualties' scenarios as it related to the comment he expressed to Captain Stovall.

Jasper Bohannon said: "I'm quite pleased with the progress your men have made and action they took in hunting down those terrorists. Continue your efforts we especially need to find out the SOS's true intentions." General Falk replied, "We will not cease until that's determined and all of them are apprehended or killed sir."

The POTUS: "General are medals appropriate for the men involved in this affair?"

The general: "I'm glad you asked sir, I firmly belief the officers are due special considerations and the enlisted men also, if you don't mind I will send you my official recommendations to that effect sir."

The POTUS: "What about yourself General?"

The general: "Sir I appreciate your inquiry but these men are putting their lives on the line, I'm just merely sitting on the sidelines calling the plays, having been a frontline warrior, I think they deserve the honor, not I, beside where would I put them? My chest is top heavy as it is."

Jasper Bohannon laughed: "Your modesty is quite refreshing General especially here in Washington where everyone is trying to take bows at every turn, I understand your logic and will respect your wishes."

Mad Sam said, "Thanks sir, now I believe it's time to return to my duties, I'll keep you informed as situations unfold Mister President."

“Very well as always it’s a sincere sensation speaking with you General.”

“Why thank you sir,” the general said and Jasper Bohannon told him: “I await your further updates, good afternoon,” and switched off.

IT WAS TEN thirty when a sharp knock came at the door. And another. Robin Calhoun sat on the sofa with the ever present glass of Jack in hand; she wasn’t expect’n anyone, especially not someone to drop by unannounced. Maybe it was Jake Carlisle tak’n her up on her invite, she smiled, rose, crossed the room, looked at herself as she passed the mirror hold’n that smile as she swung open the door and found Billy Bob and Harry Reynolds stand’n there. Her jaw went slack: “What the...,” Billy Bob brushed past her, and shifted into the foyer with Harry Reynolds hard on his heels. Robin Calhoun was shocked to say the least, she closed the door and said, “What in hell are you doing here and coming to my home no less?”

“There’s been a serious disaster...,” she broke in: “What are you saying?” Billy Bob looked at Harry and back at her and said, “Disaster as in disaster. We were attack by airborne forces south of Charlottesville this afternoon.” Robin Calhoun in obvious disbelief said: “That cannot be...,” Billy Bob cut in: “Believe it why else would we be here?”

“Yes, yes,” she tried to regain her composure, “Come into the den and tell me what happened.” They bi pedaled into the den where they sat Billy Bob and Harry Reynolds on the sofa, and Robin on the loveseat and Billy Bob filled her in on what happened.

After he made the U turn and sped away, put’n as much distance between them and the carnage as possible, he drove like a mad man to Charlottesville, dumped the car in a shop’n center park’n lot, waved down a cab, and rode to the bus station where they bought tickets to Washington and now here they were. When he finished she said, “How in the hell did they locate you, better still how did they know about you?” He told her, “I don’t have a clue, unless there’s leak somewhere.”

“Impossible,” she objected.

Billy Bob looked at Harry Reynolds and back at Robin Calhoun, "Something is going on, last night they raided the farm and killed my brother." Harry spoke for the first time, "*WHAT.* You didn't tell me that." Billy Bob said, "I kept it to myself I didn't want to spook the guys." Harry Reynolds: "That's bullshit, you knew these bastards were on to us and didn't say anything that's some foul shit Billy Bob."

Robin Calhoun: "I tried to call your house but no one picked up the phone I was trying to warn him they were coming. How do you know he is dead?" Billy Bob fought back his emotions, "Because the bastard that killed him made me listen when he shot my brother, that's how."

The room went quite. After a minute or so it was Robin Calhoun who spoke into the silence: "I am very sorry to hear that Billy Bob I know how close you two were, I know words are not comforting at this time and perhaps never will be, I am truly sorry." She was actually being sincere.

Harry Reynolds was pissed, "You had no right to withhold that information, and we lost eleven good men this afternoon, because you thought it might spook the men, well now they are spooks." Robin looked at Billy Bob and tried to break the tension between them, "I can understand your reason but perhaps you should have told them."

"Well I didn't and its water under the bridge now, I plan to continue and see this through. Harry you can book if you want but I'm in for the long haul."

Harry Reynolds said, "Did you hear me say anything like that, I'm just piss that you withheld something as crucial as that, especially from me. We could have figured out something and perhaps those guys would be alive now. That's all I'm saying, don't read anything else into it, okay?"

Robin Calhoun spoke again: "I own a condo here in Georgetown that's vacant at the moment you can stay there until I return and then we will figure out what to do about finding new people to execute the main move." Harry Reynolds asked, "Is there something else I don't know about?" Billy Bob said, "Harry relax will you, you know how it goes, need to know, right now you don't need to know what's up, I'll tell you soon enough okay?" He reluctantly agreed, "Alright, but you should have let me know about last night," Billy Bob: "Let it go man - Chief we should be on our way to this hideaway of yours, clear our minds and get ready for the final operation. Where are you going and how long will you be gone?"

"To Brazil, I will be gone about five days. I am leaving Monday afternoon. Come let me give you the keys to the condo, I will call a taxi, and have it pick you up on the corner." They rose from their seats, left the den; the men made for the door and stood in the foyer while Robin Calhoun made the call. When she finished she said: "The taxi will be there within ten minutes. Here is the address, I will contact you when I return, and Billy Bob do not came here again understand?" Billy Bob started to say something but thought better of it he knew how violate she can be, so he kept quiet about that and said: "Understood," she swung the door open and they stepped out into the frigid night.

Robin Calhoun closed the door leaned back against it and said, "Things are not going well, right now I need a drink," she padded over to the bar, picked up the bottle looked at her glass and said: "Fuck it," and turned the fifth up and hit Jack hard.

LATER MUCH LATER in Toledo, Karl K. Kussman was busy in his lab where he worked on new a biological weapon and was not having much success, but he was proud of the one he'd designed for the SOS to use in the United States, that was a masterpiece. He was clad in the requisite garb when dealing with hazardous materials. The red light flashed, he knew there was something urgent to attend to. He stepped out of the lab, removed his mask and answered the wall phone it was Obergruppenfuher Schell, "Pardon the interruption Reichfuhrer but you have someone waiting on Skype." The doctor said, "I'm on my way," and rang off.

He strolled across the compound, entered his office, went to his desk, sat down clicked on and there was Robin Calhoun wait'n with a distraught look on her face, "Ah it's you my dear what a welcomed surprise, how are things?" he asked and she told him: "Not very well Doctor we have had several setbacks as of late." Kussman said, "From the beginning," and she quickly brought him up to snuff. The doctor said, "Quite disturbing my dear quite, you are positive the bio weapons were seized?"

She said, "Yes it would seem so, they raided my main operative's headquarters and I am sure they seized everything that pertained to our operations. We intended to deploy the canisters Monday in the subway system but now that has been neutralized by these Yankee bastards."

The doctor said, “I see, this is indeed a major reversal of fortune, your timetable has been severely disturbed, what is your next consideration?”

She was reluctant to expose her hand but she was pressed for help so she told him: “Well we intend to completely decimate downtown Boston and the harbor area.”

Kussman knotted his fingers and placed his hands on his ample stomach, “Now you have whet my appetite, in fact I'm having a hard time from allowing myself to drool over it,” he said maliciously, and went on: “What do you require of me in this instance? I am quite certain there is another reason for this conversation other than to enlighten me about the recent bad occurrences you've been unfortunately experiencing. Am I not right?” He asked anticipating her response. She paused before she said, “I need your help Doctor.” He said back, “In what fashion my dear?”

Her hesitancy was evident and she waited a moment before she submitted her request, “I need manpower to execute the mission in Boston,” she finally told him. The doctor sat there, now he knew he was in the driver's seat so he replied, “You know it's my policy not to become physically involved in your matters up there, that is beyond my province.” He played with her emotions to extract the most out of the situation. Robin Calhoun was compelled to plead: “Doctor I realize this is a request that goes against our prior agreement but circumstances have altered that considerably I am desperate, as you can see the situation hangs in the balance I need assistance here and right away if we are to succeed in this war.”

The doctor said, “Well my dear you must reveal your intent in that regard before I can begin to contemplate your appeal, there shouldn't be any secrets between us it's too late in the game for that, don't you think?” Robin Calhoun knew he had the leg up on her, “You are absolutely correct, Doctor,” so she relinquished and told him what the Boston mission entailed. When finished he said, “Absolutely exquisite my dear, simply delicious.” Karl K. Kussman admired daring and chicanery. “Well done, your wiliness is to be commended I'm impressed to an enormous extent.”

Robin Calhoun smiled she felt she'd won him over, “I am glad you approve Doctor, it is well thought out something I have been planning for a while now, and I have a deep mole in the government that will supply us with the necessary info to bring this off.” The doctor was indeed aroused and not just spouting word noise, "I'm willing to supply you with the necessary manpower to assist you, how many men do you required to realize your plan which I must say is sheer genius, I envy your fertile mind."

She was gladdened to the imp degree. Robin Calhoun told the doctor: "I think four or five will be sufficient." Now the doctor knew he had the upper hand and said: "Well that could be arranged, but what's the benefit for me in this affair?" She was anticipating that: "What do you want as compensation?" Karl K. Kussman rubbed his chin as if in deep thought and finally told Robin Calhoun: "If you succeed in your war and have achieved your objective of independence for the South I think a high cabinet position would be in order, or say Vice President of the New Confederate States of America, it has a definite ring to it wouldn't you agree?" Robin Calhoun was taken aback by this she wasn't expecting that, not the Vice Presidency that was reserved for someone special in her life, but she had to go with the flow and agree to this extortion, she said with much enthusiasm, "What a splendid idea, I think it's perfect with me as president and you as my VP, we would make an excellent governing team." She didn't really mean it but it sound good.

Karl K. Kussman was no fool by any stretch, he had other designs in mind but presented the facade of being swayed by her spiel, he had his own agenda and it didn't included Robin Calhoun she was just a means to an end. He believed he was the hand behind the puppet. The cross was on, they both had other motivates in mind, two double dealers at work here. They had their knives sharpened to thrust into each other's backs, devious characters play'n a serious game of one upmanship.

He said, "My dear you have completely convinced me to go against my better judgment but the thought of not participating and should you be successful without my assistance would be too much to bear, especially when I do so covet the position discussed, you have my full support. I will assign my best men to assist you in your Boston, shall we say tea party, and it will be oh so scrumptious, yum, yum."

She asked him: "When will you be able to send them?" He asked her: "When is their presence required?" and she told him: "Next week, but I will confirm that shortly I am due to hear from my source soon about certain details that need firming up. I will let you know later today, hopefully." The doctor replied, "Good so I can make preparations for their departure, I will send you my best soldiers, believe me they are die hard warriors ready to participate in a glorious cause, superb fighters who are totally committed and dedicated to the downfall of the United States of America, you will be pleased."

Robin Calhoun said, "Thank you so much Doctor, I feel abundantly better now, you will not regret your decision." The doctor smiled and said: "I have no doubt about that my dear, now if you'll release me I'll start the ball rolling as they said up there, immediately." Satisfied things had gone well, she said, "Of course Doctor I have to make preparations after I have returned from my short trip to Brazil." Curious the doctor inquired: "What may I ask is the occasion for such a jaunt, my dear Robin?" She told him: "I am attending the annual Confederado Festival in Americana," he said, "Ah yes our South American cousins' celebration of our Confederate heritage, what a grand spectacle that is, I had the occasion to attend it once when I went to Brazil with my father long ago, wonderful experience for me. Do enjoy yourself and we will speak again upon your return. Oh by the way whom should my soldiers' link up with once they arrived in the States?" Robin Calhoun told him: "Our main operative in Boston is Max Bedford and he will instruct them and they will be under the command of Billy Bob Broussard." Kussman said: "Good, I met him when he came down here, superb patriot."

"Very much so," and Karl K. Kussman said, "Well my dear I'll set things in motion on my end have a safe and enjoyable trip, good night," and he was gone. Robin Calhoun sat in front of her computer satisfied that things were back on track. Now all she needed was a lover for the night, she reached for the phone and dialed the escort service.

THE NEXT DAY at the Barn inside the communications center Andrew Wong received a call from the Charlottesville Police Department informing him they came across a car left overnight in a park'n lot ran the plate number and it came back that the registered owner was one Billy Bob Broussard. The owners of a restaurant where it was parked in front of said the car had been there since around two yesterday afternoon. Andrew Wong asked: "Have you towed it away?" The officer on the phone said "Not yet, it's due to be removed shortly though." The captain asked: "Are you on scene as we speak?" He was told yes, the captain then asked the officer if he was equipped with a fingerprinting kit, he was a shift commander and replied: "Just so happens I do have one with me," the captain was encouraged by that and said, "Wipe the car completely and rush the results to me ASAP."

"Understood sir, I'll have them processed and emailed to you within fifteen minutes," Andrew Wong said, "Very good, I'm standing by."

SOON AFTER HIS computer peeped alerting him there was an urgent message in his in box; he opened it, clicked on the icon, found what he waited for, printed it out and struck out for the general's office. Whom he found busy working through a stack of papers on his desk, Mad Sam looked up and said, "You look like the cat that just swallowed the canary, extremely happy, what you have discovered Captain?"

Andrew Wong handed the general the printout, Mad Sam read the results and exclaimed: "Superb work Captain this confirms that bastard is still with us and as a bonus we now know the identity of one of his terrorists' cronies, one Harry Reynolds, this is a good, very good. As always Mister Inside you have scored another touchdown, mighty fine Captain you cease to amaze," the general told him with a wide grin on his face. Adam Wong glowed know'n he had made Mad Sam happy; a happy Mad Sam was a good thing.

He told Andrew Wong: "I'll relay this to Captain Stovall he can intensify his hunt for these shit birds and clip their wings for once and all. And of course the president will be as pleased as I am." Andrew Wong felt warm from the praise the general bestowed on him. Mad Sam asked: "Any progress on the dirty bomb front?"

Andrew Wong said: "I've ran all possible scenarios sir, and tapped into the Pentagon, CIA and every other intelligence agency's war games probabilities and contingencies and came up with the usual results nothing we haven't known possible for years sir, but maybe one of these is the means in which they will do their dirty work, but I don't suspect so sir." Mad Sam said: "Keep at it - say have you slept recently? You looked tired." Andrew Wong said: "I'm fine sir," and the general said, "Well don't pushed it too hard, the body as well as the mind need to be reenergized often, so take a break and get back to it after you've rested, that's an order Captain," the general said emphatically. With that Andrew Wong went to his quarters to cop some well deserved Zs. Mad Sam used his Codex and phoned Jasper Bohannon.

IT WAS JUST after ten o'clock when Jessy's smartphone went her and Skeeter rode in his 63 split window Vette they were do'n some last minute shop'n for their trip to Americana. She looked at the caller ID, "Oh Lord, it's the town gossip Sierra Montgomery," Skeeter Macklin looked over at her, "She's got something juicy to tell, the local snitch is a busy little bee always with the scuttlebutt that one," Jessy: "Not to mention the Congressional slut," Skeeter: "Now, now, be nice," and Jessy informed him: "A rose's a rose and ho's a ho, if I'm refereeing a fight a left hook is a left hook you have to called 'em like you see 'em," Skeeter laughed and she thumbed on hit the speaker, "Hi Sierra it's been awhile," the smartphone said, "Yes it has, how's things with the new hubby?" Jessy told her, "Just peachy and how's *your* love life?"

"You know me I'm making the rounds," Sierra Montgomery said with no shame at all she was quite proud of her rep as the DC depository. Jessy said, "What's the occasion Sierra?" As if she didn't know she was about to drop some morsel of political high jinks and she was right, "Guess who's doing who?" Sierra Montgomery asked, Jessy told her: "I give up I lose my psychic powers yesterday," and Sierra had to tell her: "Well I have it from a most reliable source...," Jessy cut in: "Who might that be?" Sierra Montgomery: "Why me of course, who else?" Jessy looked at Skeeter shook her head and said, "Well what is it that you have that so pressing?"

Sierra: "Senators Robin Calhoun and Jake Carlisle are an item, how's that for a scoop."

Jessy: "Not that prude."

Sierra: "I beg to differ she's more active than I am, if that's possible."

Jessy: "I think you're making this up, Sierra," prodding her to reveal more, Jessy was enjoying this oh so much.

Sierra: "I'm not one to make up things whenever I tell you something you can take to the bank, its gold. Yeah, yeah, she projects the image of being a goody two shoes but I know she has both feet in the freak zone on the down low, the hush, hush as it were."

Jessy: "Far being it from me to dispute you Sierra, you would know everything there's to know on that front." Skeeter was listen'n and was muffling his laughs with his left hand while he steered the Vette through the traffic with his right, and it was difficult to shift gears.

Sierra: "All true so help me God."

Jessy: "Do you have your right hand raised?" Skeeter was dy'n off to her left.

Sierra: "Funny, funny, Jessy." She was annoyed that Jessy wasn't tak'n her seriously.

Jessy: "The question is why are you telling me this??"

Sierra: "I thought you might want to post it on your blog."

Jessy: "Well you thought wrong, you have the *Washington Sentinel* confused with the scandal rags, that's not our forte, Sierra, maybe you should contact the *DC Tattle Tale* that's right in their wheelhouse."

Sierra sang: "I have photos."

Jessy: "Thanks but no thanks, Sierra," she was growing tired of the banter and was ready to close the conversation: "Look Sierra, my husband and I are out and about doing some shopping so I have to let you go, okay?"

Sierra Montgomery was reluctant to let it go and said: "Are sure you don't want to break this story?" Jessy told her: "I'm positive as always Sierra it's been a gas, but I have to run now, okay?" Sierra was extremely disappointed she wanted to do some serious damage to Jake Carlisle and Jessy wasn't play'n along with her, "Maybe I'll take your advice...," Jessy cut her off: "It wasn't advice dear it was merely a suggestion, I really have to go we'll talk went I get back, bye" and hung up on her. Skeeter said, "Now that was one wild conversation," and Jessy told him: "It's always a workout whenever I'm forced to talk with her," Skeeter looked over at her, "Well, why don't you just not answer when she calls?" Jessy looked him in the eyes and came back: "Honey, there's no fun in that." Skeeter Macklin gave up and pulled into Nordstrom's park'n lot killed the engine; they got out and strode hand in hand toward the store.

AT NINE O'CLOCK that evening at the White House the POTUS and his Chief of Staff went over the Stimulus Bill that passed in both Houses of Congress, it was a designed to bail out Wall Street and to prevent the banks from imploding, sending the economy into a further spiral and a possible depression, Taylor Jackson said: "This is a great accomplishment sir, you've saved the country tremendous financial anxiety and it will jump started the economy once the money kicks in," they sat in the Oval Office settled on sofas opposite each other, the fireplace was lit, Jasper Bohannon looked over at him: "I believe you're right, I wanted more money allocated but the opposition dug their heels in, I think we're about three hundred billion shy of what the Budget Office recommended, but we'll have to live with it and make sure every penny is put into the system." Taylor Jackson said: "The hope is to insure the banks and big business will turn the spigots on thereby creating jobs that's the key sir."

The president told him: "I understand your intent Taylor my friend, but hope is a drug that can get you strung out. A hope fiend is worse than a dope fiend. Everyone's always yearning for this or that, the thing is we must will it so, and have faith that things will improve not to wish they'll happen." Taylor Jackson said: "Mister President your logic is one of a kind, never have I heard someone shoot down hope with such accuracy, you have to know things instead of keeping one's fingers crossed and knocking on wood, that's a fool's paradise, we tend to build castles in the air, thirsting for things to fall in our favor which only increases that anxiety if I'm hearing you correctly sir." The president said, "Well you took the long way there, but you're correct, hankering does us no good, we've got to make it happen."

Taylor Jackson once again was duly impressed with the president he knew he'd back the right horse when Jasper Bohannon declared he was mak'n a run for the White House eighteen months ago. Even though they've been friends since college, Taylor always prided himself with bet'n on a sure thing and he had won big. Their relationship developed at a small school in Kentucky, where Taylor was the quarterback and Jasper Bohannon a wide receiver, the country boy from Knoxville and a city kid from New York. They were also roommates and that's where their lifelong friendship started.

Taylor Jackson said, "Do you think Senators Calhoun and Carlisle will attend the bill signing ceremony, Monday sir." The president replied: "It would be a good thing to have all hands on deck to show the country there's solidarity on this issue, but who knows about those two, even though they both voted for it, but you know politics or is it politricks? The opposition didn't want to fall down on the wrong side of history on this one. So they might show up, if not so be it."

"Well we know Senator Carlisle never met a camera he didn't like and any photo op that furthers his ambitions he'll take, the guy loves the spotlight."

"We all crave attention to some degree, even myself, the fans love it when you win, remember how it was in college after we'd won a game, the crowd went nuts, same thing in this game too, everyone wants to be included in the picture with the winner."

Taylor Jackson laughed. Just then the president's Codex 4 chimed, he said, 'Who might this be?" as he stood up and crossed to his desk, Taylor took a stab at it: "Probably General Falk sir," the president said, "Wrong," and picked up, "Good evening Director how's your day been?" The Director of the FBI told the POTUS: "It's been your usual crime fighting day sir, staying after the bad guys making sure we keep the pressure on them no matter what their status is small time or big time, they will not escape the long arm of the law," Jasper Bohannon smiled and replied: "Speaking of bad guys anything happening on the SOS front?"

The Director: "Nothing of significance to report on the Boston situation, the subject hasn't led us to anything that's earth shaking, we have him under constant surveillance, we're monitoring his calls and radio show, he's spouting his usual poison nothing of any importance has been said, just phone calls to some friends and girlies that's about it on that front sir?"

The POTUS: "Well keep at it he'll slip up, they always do, over confidence has been the bane of many a fool."

The Director: "You're so right Mister President, our jails and prisons are crammed with over confident individuals, who thought they were keener than the rest of us. All we're waiting on is for him to name that female and then we'll slam the cell door shut on him."

The POTUS: "Like that old game show back in the fifties, 'Will the mystery woman please sign in', huh?"

The Director: "Exactly sir, that's well put. Eventually he'll make that one mistake that'll lead us to the evil mastermind they always do Mister President without fail."

The POTUS: "Okay Director, keep at it and enjoy the remainder of your weekend if you can."

The Director: "The same too you sir, it's been one hell of a week to say the least."

The POTUS: "That it has, that it has Director, and we'll speak again Monday afternoon unless something breaks on your end. Good night."

The Director: "If and when something happens that significant you will hear of it, good night sir."

Taylor Jackson asked: "Anything encouraging sir?" The president said, "Yes and no, the FBI is on watch for a slip up which hasn't happen yet, but it will, just as sure as the sun will come up in the morning."

"Sir may I say something on the personal note." Jasper Bohannon looked at him on his way back to the sofa, settled down and said" "Yes, of course what is it."

Taylor Jackson hesitated, the president waited, he noticed his preoccupied expression: "What's wrong?" still he wasn't forthcoming so Jasper Bohannon said, "Okay out with it, what's the problem?" He said, "It's not really a problem it's just I keep having this dream..." he was slow to reveal what dream was about, the president waited, and finally Taylor spoke: "I hope you don't think this is silly, but ever since General Falk brought his bulldogs here in the Oval Office I've been having this reoccurring nightmare that they're attacking me. Frankly sir, I'm scared to death of them." Jasper Bohannon suppressed his urge to laugh he knew the man was serious so he said: "What do you attributed that too?"

"Well sir, when they were here they won't take their eyes off me, you remember when they first saw me they growled so viciously I think they meant to do me harm, every since I have been having nightmares about them mauling me to death. I'm totally frightened, sir, to put it bluntly."

The president said, "I'm sure it's just a bad dream Taylor nothing more, although I do recall them taking a dislike to you, do you have a bad relationship with dogs? They can sense whether someone is afraid or hostile that's a proven fact, dogs are canny like that." Taylor Jackson was visibly distraught over this and it showed prominently on his face, in fact he was start'n to sweat, the president asked: "Are you alright? You seem to be shaken just talking about it?"

"Last night I woke myself up from the screams I was making, my wife freaked out, it's really bothering me, I request that if the general returns with them that I be excused sir, I just don't want to be in the same room with them called it paranoia or whatever but I'm really disturbed by this." Jasper Bohannon said soothingly: "I can see and hear you're concerned...," Taylor Jackson cut in: "I beg our pardon Mister President I'm extremely worried about it."

"Well let's not split hairs here, Taylor, maybe you should see someone about your anxiety, I think that might help you get over this fear you have." He hated to see his friend so bummed out, he was certain it was purely psychological and nothing else, Taylor's mind was just mess'n with him, nothing more.

"Maybe you're right sir, Sally said the same thing, I think I'll see somebody about it and thanks Mister President for not laughing at me."

"I would never do that Taylor if something is bothering you, it affects me also," just then the Codex went again, which brought the conversation to a close. The president stood up, and stepped to his desk to answer it.

TWO DAYS LATER Robin Calhoun left for Brazil she was upbeat about attending the festival in Americana this was where she could live out her antebellum fantasies, assume her Scarlett O'Hara persona and get lost in Confederacy nostalgia, she intended to savior every moment. She was momentarily leaving the woes about the war she started behind, she just want to take in the ambiance of the Confederados, Americana and bask in the memories of a bygone era, something she has longed for, to actually live the life of a genuine southern belle, even if it was only temporary she'd be experiencing it for herself and vicariously for her mother, Ruby.

MEANWHILE AT THE Macklin residence Jessy and Skeeter finished pack'n and looked forward to resume their honeymoon and cover the story about the Confederados; they too were excited about their trip to Americana.

10

Cat That Counts

Americana, Brazil; Washington

FORTY EIGHT HOURS later Jessy and Skeeter toured the city, they flew into Sao Paulo, then boarded a local bus to Americana, spend the night rest'n, now they were out and about tak'n in the sights. They had anticipated a small town but what they encountered was a thriving city that teemed with activity.

"I wasn't expecting this, I thought it would be some backwater settlement but I'm impressed." Skeeter Macklin said as they padded down Praca dos Americanos the main thoroughfare doing what tourists do. Jessy said, "I told you it would be exciting, maybe not your coveted Rio, but it's still quite enjoyable, so far the people have been very pleasant, not what you would encounter in Rio or Sao Paulo."

"Maybe we should rent a car, make the rounds, checkout the rainforest," he said, Jessy told him: "Settle down, let's not get carried away here Marco Polo, the rainforest is definitely out of the question or anywhere else there are things that can eat you. I didn't come here to be lunch for some animal I can't even pronounce the name of." Skeeter

Macklin looked at wife and said: "Jessy you're too much, that's why I love you so - speaking of lunch, hungry?"

"Well kind of, you know I'm eating for two," she said rub'n her baby bump, "the one in the oven needs nourishment too."

"Are you feeling okay?" She said: "I feel great - hey let's check out the vendor across the street," Skeeter came back: "This from the one who doesn't want to be eaten by something she can't pronounce but she's willing to eat it?" Jessy chewed on that and said, "Well maybe I can wait until there's a more traditional restaurant around, I'm sure there's one up ahead, monkey or other exotic critters are not on my menu today."

They continued on, went in and out of shops, purchased souvenirs and whatnots, pressed on until they spotted a typical Brazilian style restaurant and strode in.

JUST THEN ROBIN Calhoun padded out of the Royal Palm Plaza Resort a five star fare about twenty miles from Americana. No matter where she went Robin Calhoun had to go first class nothing less would do, she had rented a convertible Gran Turismo to tool around in, the valet opened the door, she sized him up, smiled, handed him a ten spot, held onto his hand a bit longer than necessary, climbed into the sports car and moved off to Thomas Norris' villa for lunch and discussions about the upcoming festival three days hence.

She had the top down and her Gianfranco Ferre sunglasses on. She was step'n out to be seen by everyone with a pair of eyes; Robin Calhoun was a comely woman by anyone standards and she loved to flaunt her looks, but a pretty face doesn't make a pretty mind.

The sleek ride raced down the highway at a good clip she loved the warm sun bearing down on her and the wind blew her hair about. Robin Calhoun was in a happy zone, she anticipated four wonderful days here in South America away from the cold and the politics of Washington. Here she could lose herself in the moment, pretend to be someone else and put her problems on hold. Fantasy would do her good, her reality up north was not quite what she had planned, things had taken a wrong turn, she believed they would make a course correction once the event went down in Boston, that would be the defining moment to the entire affair, she was extremely confident it would make the United States government give in to her and the SOS's demands.

Robin Calhoun noticed the sign that indicated she was about a mile from the entrance to the Norris' ranch, she arrived about a minute later turned into the long driveway, stop at the security gate and said: "Scarlett O'Hara to see Thomas Norris, I believe he is expecting me," the guard scanned the guest list, nodded and waved her on. The gate swung open and Robin Calhoun drove on toward the villa that sat atop a hill about three miles away.

Thomas Norris was the great grandson five times removed of William Hutchison Norris, the family had fared quite well since their arrival after the Civil War, and on the way to the house she looked out at the pastures and saw thousands of cattle stand'n on the land. Robin sensed the Norris' were very, very well off, she smiled, took in a deep whiff, "Smells like money," as the Maserati swoop the curved driveway that led to the villa, an exact replica of an antebellum home in the old South.

She saw two men stand'n under the portico, she stopped and was met by a manservant who opened the door, handed her out and said: "Good afternoon Miss O'Hara, Mister Thomas waits on the veranda out by the pool, this gentleman will escort you there," Robin Calhoun said in perfect pitch, "Why thank you suh, what a lovely outfit you've adorned, so debonair," and zipped off to meet Thomas Norris.

They round the corner, Thomas Norris saw them approach, he rose from his chaise lounge, went to meet Robin with his hand outstretched: "Welcome to my humble abode, Miss O'Hara," he knew her name but everyone was play'n the role, getting into character for the big fiesta. At least twenty men and women lounged around the veranda and pool area.

Robin said, "My what a lovely plantation you have suh, reminds me of South Carolina in so many ways, simply divine," her accent was straight out of the eighteen hundreds, Thomas Norris led her by the hand to a chair, she curtsied and settled down, "Why thank you Mister Norris, it's so good to be in the presence of such a fine gentleman," he smiled and said, "Perhaps the lady would desire a refreshment, it's quite warm today, what would be your pleasure ma'am, if I could be so bold, my man here...," who was stand'n at the ready, ..."makes a superb mint julep," Robin Calhoun said, "That would be simply perfect," he asked her, "Would you prefer boahbahn, rum or brandy ma'am?" She told him: "Boahbahn of course suh, anything else would be sacrilegious, an absolute affront to the all the great mint juleps that when before it."

Thomas Norris said: "Then boahbahn it is," to her and to his servant he said, "Dudley please attend to that for the lady, only your best will do for such a fair lady as she." He turned and left them alone Thomas Norris said, "How do you like Americana thus far, ma'am?" Robin Calhoun: "Quite charming, the scenery is reminiscent of Georgia suh, the trees and all, a wonderful setting, I truly enjoyed the scenic drive over I found it to be very handsome country." She was really in character. He told her, "Well I am pleased to hear your wonderful assessment of our city and look forward to hearing more, but if you'll pardon me I must attend to other matters, please make yourself at home, Dudley shall return shortly with your drink."

"Suh your hospitality at the moment is beyond measure, I'm sure I will be please to no end, Mister Norris." Thomas Norris bowed and said: "Excuse me I shall leave you now, but I pine to return to your presence," with that he turned and left. Robin scanned the area and noticed there were several young men eye'n her; she dropped her eyes, moved her head slightly to the right, then looked back at one in particular and smiled.

A tall young man about thirty or so rose from this chair and sauntered over, Robin pretended not to be interested and turned away, he stepped up and said: "May I sit down and join you ma'am?" she removed her glasses, looked up: "A bit forward aren't you suh?" He knew it was all a game and played along: "'Tis indeed an awkward moment, shall I vacate or stand here and look the fool for assuming I'd be welcomed?"

"You can do whatever you wish suh, it matters me not, if you leave or stand there like a statue, but beware of pigeons," he told her: "You must be clairvoyant, pigeons, and I get along famously," and froze in place. Just then Dudley arrived with her mint julep and said, "Here's your drink ma'am, I hope you'll enjoy it, if it's not to your liking I will discontinue my craft at once," and waited, Robin Calhoun took a sip through the straw and sighed: "What a delight, your career is safe suh, I shall require another shortly." He said: "At your beckoned call ma'am," and spoke to the man fixed in place: "What you like another iced tea Mister Thomas Junior sir?" He told Dudley, "Presently I'm busy trying to attract pigeons," Dudley looked puzzled and left them, she sip'n her mint julep, him stiff as a board and Robin Calhoun asked, "Are you Mister Norris' son?" And he told her: "I been accused of that," Robin was embarrassed, "Oh my

Lord how crass of me, I'm so sorry, pardoned my ignorance, do accept my apology and please be seated." He told her: "Aha, so now I'm welcomed, it's takes a certain pedigree to be accepted by the lady so it would seem," and smiled.

Robin Calhoun laughed and patted the seat next to her indicating for to him sit down, he hesitated, mak'n her waited and then complied. "Tell me your life story, I have my entire lifetime to listen," Robin Calhoun said, "My aren't we the suave one." Thomas Junior told her, "It came with instructions, how to win a lady's heart in twenty five words or less," she threw her head back and giggled, "I think I might be in over my head, you could drown me with your wit suh." He said, "My intent precisely, then I can dive in to save you, isn't that the way it's done in the movies?"

Robin Calhoun liked this guy, she liked him a lot, and he'd be in her bed this night. He asked, "And you are?" She said, "Why Scarlett O'Hara of course." He said back, "Well frankly my dear I *give* a damn." She lit up: "You quite the smooth one suh, careful you could win my affections...," which wouldn't take much, "...you've caught me at a vulnerable moment and my knees are beginning to grow weak." Thomas Junior said, "That's another of my intentions, ma'am making your entire body weak after we get to know one another better."

Robin Calhoun said to herself: *Little do you know you're in for the ride of your life,* she said to him: "Should I call you Rhett or Ashley?" fluttering her eyelashes. He told her, "If I remember my literature correctly, Scarlett loved Ashley but Rhett was the one who bedded her, am I not right?" Robin was impressed and said: "Am I to assume suh that is your intent?" He told her, "Only if it's your desire ma'am."

They looked up and saw his father approach with a woman at his side, Thomas Junior stood up, his father said to Robin, "I see you've met my son, careful Scarlett he's quite the rogue in these parts," and she said, "Why suh, he was just demonstrating his knowledge of southern literature, I must admit I'm dazzled by his grasp of the subject."

The elder Norris said: "Perhaps the money I've forked out for his education is finally bearing fruits," he smiled at his son and went on: "Please allow me to introduce Dame McKnight, she's our event coordinator she will fill you in on all the details for the festival." Robin outstretched her hand daintily and said: "It's a severe pleasure ma'am," Dame McKnight took it and said: "What lovely specimen, you'll look fabulous in costume, come let me explain the order of business to you," she held on to her hand, Robin Calhoun rose up and said to Thomas Junior, "It was a sincere delight talking with you suh, perhaps we can share a dance at the cotillion?" He told her: "That is a foregone conclusion ma'am; we shall dance until the cows come home." She smiled and the women left them stand'n there. Senior Norris said, "Careful with that one son, she's a tiger I can tell."

Junior: "You're dating yourself Father, the term is cougar, now." Senior: "Be that as it may, the cat that counts is her kitty."

IT'S BEEN A wonderful day honey, I'm totally exhausted, I think I'll lay down for awhile and get rejuvenated," Jessy told Skeeter. They just returned from their tour of the city, having been on the move for five six hours, she was spent. Skeeter Macklin put his arm around her waist, escorted her in the bedroom, helped her lie down, removed her shoes and said: "You and the little one get some Z's and I'll check the equipment to make sure everything's working for the shoot, okay? Jessy said, "Okay honey," and sleep took her. Skeeter covered her up and thought how lucky he was to have survived the wars and to have this woman as his wife and the mother of his child.

FOUR DAYS LATER at the Royal Palm Plaza Resort Robin Calhoun emerged from the rain room with a towel wrapped around her head, she just had taken a shower and stopped at the edge of the bed, looked down at Thomas Norris Junior, a ghost of a smile flitted over her lips; it had been three days of bliss. She knew she'd rock his world and he was totally infatuated. Weren't they all she thought as she stepped away, reached in the closet, came out with a robe and climbed into, this cavort was com'n to an end.

It had been a plus to her vacation.

The Confederado Fiesta was today, Saturday and the festivities began at ten o'clock, five hours from now and she had to get ready to become the belle of her dreams, Scarlett O'Hara in the flesh, her alter ego would come to life. Robin Calhoun had selected with the help of Dame McKnight a gorgeous yellow hoop skirt to wear she had to get to the hotel hair dresser to have her hair coiffure into the sausage ringlets just like Vivien Leigh wore. She wanted to be as authentic as possible so she chose a large straw bonnet with huge ribbons to tie under her chin. She couldn't decide whether carry a fan or a parasol. Well that would be determined later, now she had to rouse her beau and have him leave, so she could begin her conversion something she had been wait'n for since her daddy, CC first called her Scarlett.

Robin Calhoun shifted over to the bed, bend down and blew into Junior's ear and woke him with a start and laughed: "Time to raise and shine lover, we have to get ready for the cotillion," he reached up and tried to grab her, she avoid his attempt, "Now, now there is no time for that, maybe later if you are a good boy, so gather your things and be underway." Thomas Norris Junior was smitten and it showed his eyes burned with love and he hated to leave, but her persistence forced him to collect his clothes, dress and when finished he asked: "Must you return so soon? We've only just begun to live...," she broke in: "Now we are quoting the Carpenters?" he said, "Who?" she told him: "Never mind I will explain later now off you go," as she stepped to the door and held it open, he reluctantly walked up, kissed her, then said: "What if I accompany you back to the States?" She thought *what! This is bad, why do they always want to hang on?* She told him: "Maybe later you can fly up and visit, I have a very busy schedule, things I must attend to upon my return, after you can come and stay awhile," she was willing to tell him anything to get him out the door. That seemed to do the trick and it made him glow he told her: "Fantastic," and padded out happier than an exaltation of larks.

She closed the door and said aloud, "You have created a monster Doctor Frankenstein, Robin, you have to stop working your magic on these poor fools."

And she started to dress to make her hair appointment.

BY TEN O'CLOCK the festival grounds were alive with activity, three thousand people from all over Brazil were here to watch or participate in the fiesta. It was set in the middle of huge cane field, with the customary stalls sell'n food, art objects and such, it was part country fair and part bazaar, there was a stage where young girls performed the cancan and a band played lively songs as they kick their legs up. There were an assortment of contests and speakers ranted on about the Old South. A girl squealed when her name was announced as Miss Festa Confederada 2009.

Skeeter Macklin moved through the press shooting video, Jessy provided the voice over, she conducted interviews with the locals, occasionally appeared in shots, she had told him to make sure not to shoot her below the chest line, she didn't want her baby bump to distract from the story. Skeeter put up a slight fuss, saying he wanted to be able to show the baby later how its mother was carrying it around on the job.

Two events were scheduled, the public fare and the private invitation only gala at the Norris ranch. Jessy's boss Horace Hackett had campaigned hard to get an invite to cover the Norris soiree, finally Dame McKnight relented and gave him the okay to send a news team to cover the event.

After spending time in the cane field they decided they had enough footage and drove in their rental to the Norris ranch. Jessy and Skeeter were allowed to enter the premises where they saw numerous vintage horse drawn carriages transport'n guests to the villa; they proceeded at a slow pace trapped between two hacks. Skeeter Macklin behind the wheel looked out the window and said, "Quite the show, these folks take their nostalgia seriously," Jessy told him: "Some people can't let go of the past, they love to dwell in the memories of what was, some are in permanent denial about the way things are, longing for yesterday."

"Well I'm an advocate of the here and now, the past is for those who can't face the present and are afraid of the future," Jessy looked over at her husband, "So you've become a philosopher in your retirement years, is that it? Don't you long for the excitement and danger of your past life?"

"Not in the least, my world is bound in what's ahead for us as a family and not traveling down memory lane, my past life is just that, past." Jessy smiled, leaned over and kissed him on the cheek, "Shamus Macklin, I do love you so."

He pat her on her baby bump and said, "I can tell," she laughed as the car wound through the driveway and pulled into a park'n space. "Wow, this is positively overwhelming," she said look'n at the villa. Skeeter told her: "Yeah some guys have it all, but I wouldn't trade any of this for you and that baby you're carrying, you two are the most precious things in the world to me."

"That's so sweet, honey," she said and opened the door, "I think we have some great footage of the public show it was very entertaining, it should go over well on the blog, letting folks see what became of the people who left after the civil war, maybe it will closed the door on that chapter of the country's history, closure as it were," She reached in, grabbed her laptop and closed the door.

Skeeter had gotten out, opened the trunk, was gathering the camera equipment when a tenant approached and said, "Ms. Macklin I presume?" She said, 'Yes" and waited, he handed her their press passes and said: "Dame McKnight left these for you and said you will have unrestricted access to the grounds and she looks forward to seeing you later." Jessy took them, "Thanks so much, we'll try to be as unobtrusive as possible."

He smiled and took his leave, Skeeter closed the trunk, picked up the equipment, they walked around to the veranda, stopped, took in the scene, and the entire area was transformed into Hollywood. Confederate flags and bunting flew everywhere. Everyone was outfitted in mid nineteen century garb, the ladies in their magnificent hoop skirts and the men in their dash'n Confederate uniforms, reminded one of antebellum Atlanta or it could be the back lot of MGM circa 1938, it had an authentic feel, the ambiance was perfect, a show of southern bliss staring none other than Robin Calhoun as Scarlett O'Hara.

There was a twelve piece string band that featured fiddles, banjoes, mandolins and dulcimers, guitar, tambourine, bones and drum positioned on a specially constructed bandstand, a wood floor was laid across a wide swath of the lawn for danc'n, the smell of fried chicken and bar b q hung in the air. It was down home to the max. A large canopy covered the set protecting the ladies from the hot Brazilian sun. Skeeter set up the tripod, attached the camera and trawled. On cue the band broke into '*My Old Kentucky Home*', couples made for the dance floor and waltzed around it.

Robin Calhoun sat with a group of women, some sat under parasols, others fanned away, all sip'n mint juleps; she had brought a flask of Jack to fill in the gaps. She had her hair in sausage ringlets dyed ebony and wore pale green contact lenses, she hired a make up artist to give her the complete redo she was Scarlett O'Hara personified. She had her white gloves on, the last accessory she adorned after having a hard time pull'n her bright spring yellow dress over the hoop, she was bona fide from her hoop skirt down to her drawers, the corset was fit'n kind of tightly, but that was okay if it made her uncomfortable it was worth it, this was her dream come true.

A woman said to no one in particular: "I been livin' here darn nears my whole life, and I've nevva seen such a spectacle like this, isn't it just divine all these handsome beaux?" She said to Robin: "Look at the sweet one sittin' at the table fixin' to eat I believe he has an eye for you Scarlett darlin'." Robin Calhoun looked out through her sunglasses it was none other than Thomas Norris Junior. Over his shoulder she saw a familiar face, she strained, looked harder and recognized *Jessy*, her heart skipped, *what in hell is that DC snoop doing down here of all places?*

The band followed Dame McKnight's dance card and segued into *'Jeanie with the Light Brown Hair'*, the floor was packed with more couples and they waltzed on.

Robin Calhoun had a terrible time stay'n in character; she had to know what that woman was do'n here at *this* party. She had seen Jessy numerous times around DC, although they'd never met, Robin was aware of her reputation as being one of the top investigative reporters in the blogosphere. She tried to look away several times but her eyes came back to her, she needed to find out exactly the purpose for her being here, and this could spoil everything if she recognized her.

The band completed the tune and went into another Stephen Foster selection this time it was the lively *'Camp Town Races'*, everyone joined in sing'n over the music, *'Doo-dah! Doo-dah...*, *'Oh, doo-dah day'*. Everyone sang except Robin. She sat there peeved, she just had to know what was happening here, this was not going according to her script, and this woman could ruin her party. *'Gwine run all night! Gwine run all day! I'll bet my money de bob-tailed nag, somebody bet on the bay,'* the ladies sang on and Robin Calhoun fumed on.

She couldn't take it anymore, rose, hoist the front of her skirt and threaded across the dance floor avoid'n couples as they skipped long to *'Doo-dah! Doo-dah...*, *'Oh, doo-dah day'*. Skeeter told Jessy, "Hey I'm hungry here boss how about a lunch break Simon Legree," and grinned at her, she came back: "Don't get carried away with this throw back stuff there buster. I'm somewhat famished myself, let's take a break and grab something to eat, everything smells so delicious."

"Now you're talking," he turned off the camera and they stepped into the serving line, selected their choices, sauntered over to a table and settled down next to Thomas Norris Junior. Robin Calhoun arrived a moment later and said to him, "Hi darlin', may I have a seat suh?" he was happy to oblige and said, "Why of course ma'am," rose slightly and she sat down to his left, with him in between her and Jessy whose back was turned, "Marvelous party, your daddy sure knows how to throw a soiree," she said, keep'n an eye on Jessy, he told her, "Well he's had enough practice at it, this is the thirty second one I've attended and my grandfather sponsored parties well before my father took over, actually it's Dame McKnight who's the driving force behind everything, she spends the entire year preparing for this event."

Jessy heard Dame McKnight's name mentioned, turned and momentarily looked Robin in the eyes; she didn't recognize her and turned back to eat'n her fried chicken. Robin Calhoun sat there engaged in idle banter with Thomas Norris and strained to hear what they talked about. After they had finished, Skeeter cleared their plates, disposed them into a trash barrel, came back, sat down, Jessy had opened her laptop to check her emails.

Robin Calhoun had gone through the service line, returned with plate of bar b q and fix'n', removed her gloves and started in. Thomas was busy work'n his way through his second plate, no words passed between them so she was able to hear clearly what was being said by Jessy, who had checked her inbox, nothing of import was waiting so she said to Skeeter: "You know Fred Harris don't you? He works part time for the Sentinel?"

He said: "Yeah, yeah I remember meeting him at one of your office parties, what about him? She responded: "Well he called one evening last week when you were with your partners and told me the strangest tale about some secret organization called the SOS...," Robin dropped a rib into her lap, bar b q sauce slid all over the front of her bright yellow spring dress and her eyes went wide, "...they are according to him behind a long series of murders and supposed accidents over the last sixty years."

Skeeter Macklin looked up from his plate and said, "What?" and she plunged on: "Well I thought it was preposterous until I opened his emails and read the file he has complied on them...," - Robin Calhoun was petrified - "...here take a look at all the deaths that have happened under mysterious circumstances, car accidents, airplane crashes, sniper incidents some of them date back to the early sixties, what's so strange is they are all prominent black people, you know high profile individuals, entertainers, athletes, politicians what are the odds of the that?"

Skeeter Macklin said, "Astronomical I'd guess."

Jessy told him: "Correct, you just won the prize," he smiled and she carried on: "Once I've file this story, I'm going to get into this SOS matter and see what I can dig up on this group, organization or whatever it is and help Fred get to the bottom of this."

Robin Calhoun felt sick, she couldn't believe this was happen'n, not here, not now, not ever, what to do, Thomas Junior finished his second plate wiped his mouth and asked: "My I have your hand for the next dance Scarlett?" *Dance*. That was the last thing on her mind. This was all wrong, not in the plan. What to do, what to do? She said nothing, he waited and waited finally he asked: "Scarlett are you okay, you look a little peaked, it isn't the food is it?" She finally heard him and said. "No, no, the food is delicious darlin' I just had a momentary thought, nothing else sweetie."

Meanwhile the festivities were in full swing the band played a series of polkas, quadrilles, galops, redowas, and jigs displaying their full repertoire and musicianship. The dance master kept the party mov'n, it was near'n sundown, the tempo picked up with *'The Old Folks at Home'* again the ladies waited and sang over the chorus, *'Still longing for de old plantation, And for de old folks at home'.*

Robin Calhoun was out of it, she had to excuse herself, now she stood in front of the mirror in an upstairs bathroom, tears shone in her eyes and they began to leak. *How could this be*? She stared into the mirror she was bent out of shape. She had to get a grip and think it through. If this woman started investigating the past of activities of the SOS that could hinder things on the war front, something she couldn't allow to happen, this woman had to be neutralized and soon. Then it hit her, she would have Billy Bob eliminate her when she returned to Washington, *that's it*, "I'll have this bitch killed along with this Fred Harris bastard, that will do it, problem solved," she said aloud, smiled, wiped away the smeared mascara, reapplied her make up and left to rejoin the party.

When she returned Thomas Norris Senior was at the mic where he addressed the party goers, he hoped everyone was enjoying themselves and they were invited to next year's event, he left the stage and the band started play'n what everyone waited for, the Confederate anthem, *'I Wish I Was In Dixie'.*

The first note sounded, they jumped up, formed lines with the men on one side and the women on the other, and they were ready to do the Virginia reel, wait'n for the caller's commands. The couples took three steps forward and bow to their partners, then they swung their elbows, returned to their original positions, did a do-si-do and the head couple joined hands, sashayed down the line and back. The head couple then reeled down the line, interlocking elbows doing full turns with each person until they reached the foot of the line raised their hands, joined them forming an arch, and the next couple repeated the process and reeled back to the front. Robin Calhoun had joined the group, reeled her way along with the rest and was definitely enjoy'n herself, her bar b q smeared hooped skirt twirled as she went through the line. Skeeter Macklin had turned on the camera and caught the entire dance on tape, Jessy said, "This is so good, honey, what a way to end the show, Horace is going to simply love this."

Everyone joined in on the chorus: *'Look away! Look away! Look away! Dixie Land'.* Robin Calhoun was happy as she could be this was the ultimate liv'n a long dreamt dream, being Scarlett O'Hara do'n the Virginia reel on a fine plantation.

Jessy said: "Honey I'm fatigued I think we should call it a rap," Skeeter Macklin said: "Fine by me love," they packed up and left the Thomas ranch with strands of "*...hooray*! *...hooray*! *Away, away, away down South in Dixie*," ringing in their ears.

THE FOLLOWING MONDAY the president sat at his desk which was cluttered with files, his Codex sounded he picked up and said, "So nothing of any import has come to the surface?" Mad Sam told him: "No sir, things have slow a bit, but we are still on the hunt for the rest of these people, Captain Wong's on watch for this Billy Bob Broussard."

Jasper Bohannon asked him: "Do you think he's still in the area?" The general told the POTUS, "We believe so sir, he's probably hiding somewhere in the metro, but the worse case scenario is he could have escaped to parts unknown in a car."

"That would be unfortunate if he got out into the hinterlands secreted away among fellow sympathizers that wouldn't be good." Mad Sam said, "In the affirmative sir, but I have a gut feeling he's here somewhere local." The president told him, "Let's assume that's the case, he'll make a mistake and when he does, nab him or switch him off."

"I prefer the latter, sir, but apprehending him would be the best solution, we have ways to make him reveal what he knows, seems he's the one who could lead us to the ringleader of this SOS crowd." The POTUS told his general, "Agreed that would be best, but a vicious and mindless killer such as he would go down swinging, I would think, he's shown a willingness to kill indiscriminately so sacrificing his own life wouldn't be out of the question, these terrorists are maniacal like that, no respect for life including their own."

"If memory serves sir, they have a propensity to be cowards when it's their lives on the line in some cases, I believe he's just that, a bone fide coward, and we'll see if that's so." Jasper Bohannon told Mad Sam Falk, "I've spoken to the Director this morning, he said they are still waiting for Max Bedford to slip up and reveal the name of this woman who appears to be the head evil doer, he has a team of agents on his backside 24/7 eventually he'll make the fatal mistake that will lead us to her front door."

"I have total confidence in the Bureau sir; if Bedford does stumble they'll know it." The president looked at the clock over the fireplace, and said; "Well general I have a important meet scheduled shortly, so we'll touch bases later in the day," Mad Sam said, "Very well sir, I'll tend to things on my end, if Broussard comes up for air, we'll get him one way or the other, have a good day, Mister President," Jasper Bohannon said, "Thanks General, the same to you and your people."

SUPERB WORK JESSY, a masterful job," Horace Hackett told her, she said, "Why thank you it was a very wonderful trip we enjoyed it ever so much." They were on the phone, he had just opened the file she sent and called her right away to congratulate her, he was most satisfied with her work, he said: "Your husband is an excellent cameraman, if he needs something to do in that regard have him give me a buzz." Jessy told him: "That's a kind offer but he has plans," and her boss was somewhat let down, "You can't win them all, so you take your maternity leave and we'll see you went you return, oh by the way be sure to email me photos of you and your new baby, that's an order," she laughed and said, "Will do, but I've another story I'm going to pursue while I'm on leave," his curiosity was piqued, "What story is this?" Jessy went secretive, "Now, now Horace, you'll just have to wait until I've submitted it, it's something that might be the story of the last fifty years, one Fred's been working on and I'm going to assist him, the story is his, but I want to help out, that's all I'm going to say presently, and do not quiz him about it either, you'll be very pleased when it's in your lap, okay?"

"You know how much I despise secrets Jessy, but I'll respect your request," and she said, "Great, now I have some errands to do, so it's good bye for a while, I'll be sure to send you those pictures, bye."

ON THE FLIGHT back all Robin Calhoun could think about was that little snoopy bitch who somehow had stumbled onto the secret doings of the SOS. She had to be dealt with immediately and harshly. If she got her nose into things and was allowed to reveal what she found that would be tragic to everyone in the organization. How did this bastard Fred Harris stitch this together they had covered their tracks with the greatest of care. Yes there were some setbacks during the 60's when they first started their assassination campaign against blacks, a few of their hit men were caught but most were acquitted by all white juries who'd been paid off, but most of the cases went unsolved, especially the instances where things were made to look accidental.

Her father CC was the architect behind these clandestine operations, after the big ceremony at Stone Mountain in 61, he approached the leader of the White Citizens Council and presented his plan to systematically killed high profile blacks who were mak'n waves on the civil rights front. Cody Calhoun was given the blessing of the leader and went ahead with his plan, targeting anyone perceived as a threat to the status quo in the south.

CC had his hand in most of the kill'n and bomb'n in Mississippi, Alabama and Georgia. He financed those murders with money extracted from the Sumter Fund, paying off local and sympathizing law enforcement officials, most of who were devoted Klansmen anyway. It was a diabolical scheme that proved to be very successful, now these two were investigating things and they couldn't be allowed to continue. If it came to light that the staged plane crashes, car accidents, supposed random murders of prominent entertainers, athletes, other well known celebrities and their children were not accidents but vicious murders perpetrated at the behest of her father that would devastated the Calhoun family and have a ripple effect that would wash over others like the Blounts, especially Moses who had plenty of blood on his hands.

When she landed at Dulles she rushed home, used a disposal cell and rang Billy Bob at her condo in Georgetown. Billy Bob picked up, "Hello there Chief, how was your trip?" she said, "No time for small talk, I have an urgent matter to discuss," he said, "Shoot," and she told him: "That's precisely what I need you to do, there are two individuals that need taken care of right away, they are snooping around about our past activities and must be silenced." He asked who they were and she told him.

"It shouldn't be hard to locate them, find out where they live or what their movements are and take care of things expeditiously," Robin Calhoun ordered. Billy Bob Broussard said, "With pleasure, they'll be cold by tomorrow night, I'll have Harry assist me."

"Whatever. Do what you have to do. Have you been staying put like I instructed, you know you are hot and should not come out in the daylight. They obviously know of you they have photos I am sure and those Big Brother cameras are stationed all over the metro."

"I haven't left once since we arrived, Harry goes out and gets us our supplies, no need to worry there, when we move on this woman and her black buddy we'll do it under the cover of darkness let the cameras try and pick us up when it's dark."

"Alright, be careful and make sure not to leave any tracks, as usual you will be compensated," Billy Bob said: "At this point it's not a matter of cash Chief, this is for the cause and my brother," she told him: "I understand I have a personal stake in this also, they must be stamped out."

"I understand fully, but we're going to need transportation and weapons, we're naked over here," She said, "I will rent a car and place what you will need in the trunk, but when you make your move be sure to remove the plates and put them back on once you have cleared the area, understood?"

"Yes I do, you're very cautious Chief, I admire that," she told him: "That has been the hallmark of my survival, vigilance is the key to longevity in this business, I learned that from my father, who never was suspected of any wrong doings, because he was super careful about whatever he did, he said 'it should remain unknown to others'," he said: "Sounds like a wise man your dad," and she told him: "That he was, now be about this and I would like results as quick as possible," he told Robin Calhoun: "Consider it done.

11

2 For 1 Sale

Belize; Metro DC; Boston; Washington

AS FAR AS Karl K. Kussman was concerned the situation in America was ripe for his plans to usurp Robin Calhoun if she succeeded in her attempt to gain independence for the South. He intended to use her for his own agenda, to establish a fascist style government with him as the Der Fuhrer, in place of the democratic one she was proposing, the complete autonomy for each state to govern them as they saw fit without the interference of the central government of the Confederate States of America.

His plan was to cross her as soon as things were settled, he'd muscle in with his men, stage of putsch, seize control with his bio weapons mak'n everyone subjugated to him. He planned to intimidate the United States into becoming a satellite by threatening to release his weapons in the North, grabbed control of America's nuclear arsenal, frighten the rest of the world by set'n an example nuk'n some innocent country. Making a statement right out the box, Karl K. Kussman would succeed where Hitler had failed, total domination of the world it was a brilliant plan, one that couldn't miss, now he was ready to take the queen off the board. Robin Calhoun was the rung to the top of world.

He sat in his private quarters and put the final touches of make up on, he was preparing for a private party with a group of his fellow travelers, finished, he slipped into a chartreuse gown, put on magenta high heels and wrapped a black boa around his neck, Karl K. Kussman was a cross dresser, he was torn between being Heinrich Himmler in the light and Ernst Röhm at night.

He's enjoyed dress'n up as a woman ever since he was a young boy, who'd slip into his mother's closet, put her clothes on, strut around and pretend to be her, whenever his parents were off rid'n around the plantation. It was kept secret until his mother caught him, surprisingly Harriet accepted his strange behavior and they'd sit together pretending to be mother and daughter. If she approved then the hell with the rest of the world, but he never let it be known outside his circle of likeminded freaks. Before he got ready for the get together he sat in his office and told Obergruppenfuhrer Schell about his deal with Robin Calhoun, they were going to supply several men to assist in the attack on Boston. He kept the objective from Schell; he didn't want anyone to know until Billy Bob Broussard told them what the mission was.

"You have selected the best men we have, those who are trained in seize and control, our highest trained soldiers, and your choices are excellent."

Schell was in full uniform that denoted his rank, "Reichfuhrer I submitted them for your approval, Hauptsturmführer Müller will lead the team consisting of Hauptscharführer Krause, and Sturmscharführers Schröder, König and Schmitt, sir."

"Superb Schell, they are the most prepared men we have, all dedicated and loyal, I applauded you once again Obergruppenfuhrer you didn't disappoint."

Obergruppenfuhrer Schell enjoyed every compliment Kussman gave him it reaffirmed his position as the second in command. He willingly followed the doctor's orders, he knew to disobey or disappoint him would begin down the wrath of hell, he'd been with Karl K. Kussman since they were school mates in Belize City and had observed firsthand the anger he could muster when someone made him cross. Kussman was a big man, stood just over six foot four and weighed in at around two hundred thirty five. He was the biggest kid in school, he threw his weight around the yard, commanded the high ground at all times and other boys always cowered, so it was to this day.

The doctor said: "Have them prepared to leave for the States within eighteen hours, here..., he reached across his desk, "...are their tickets to Boston, if you'll notice..., Obergruppenfuhrer Schell look at them, "... they will be departing from different locations here in Central America although they destination is the same. This is to ensure they wouldn't be detained as group should anything go awry, which I don't anticipate, but we must remain cautious about each and every move we make, this is the end game."

"I understand fully sir," Obergruppenfuhrer Schell said and stood there and waited for further instructions from the doctor, he seldom spoke without following the lead of Kussman, always the follower even in casual conversations, wait'n for the doctor to make a comment or ask a question then he'd play to that. The doctor stood up, flung his boa over his shoulder and said: "Well Obergruppenfuhrer, I have things to attend to, I do not wish to be disturbed tonight, and you are in full command."

"Yes Reichfuhrer, I will oversee things sir," he said and Karl K. Kussman told him: "Be off and inform the men that I wish them great success and look forward to greeting them upon their triumphant return."

Obergruppenfuhrer Schell brought his heels together in front of Kussman's desk, thrust his arm out and gave the Nazi salute, "Heil Hitler!" turned smartly and left the doctor as he put his party hat on and padded to his bungalow for the soiree.

OVER THE NEXT two days that followed, Billy Bob found the whereabouts of Fred Harris, it wasn't that difficult, he was listed in the phone book, so Billy Bob simply called him and acted mysterious, speaking in hushed tones, he told him he knew some important information about the SOS. Fred Harris was so excited he didn't bother to ask how Billy Bob knew he was investigating the group. That was a fatal oversight. They set an appointment to meet at Fred's home late that night. Harry Reynolds had gone to pick up the rental car from a downtown park'n lot; Robin Calhoun called Billy Bob and told him the key was in a magnetic case stuck under the right front wheel well.

Harry Reynolds drove back to Georgetown, parked two blocks away, opened the trunk, found handguns in a canvas bag, reached in, grabbed it, closed the trunk and walked to the condo. There they loaded the weapons, sat about the house and waited for their ten o'clock appointment with Fred Harris.

"It was easy finding this noisy coon, he'll be a history come one minute after ten this evening," Billy Bob said. They were watch'n a movie on cable, drink'n Bud Lights and snack'n on pizza. Harry Reynolds said, "Taking him out only makes up for one of the guys we lost, we need to drive though northwest DC, a staged a drive by and shot us bunch of those nappy headed bastards until we even the score," and took a long pull on his brew, belched and bit into a slice of pizza.

Billy Bob told him the only thing that would satisfy his revenge was to find out somehow who the son of a bitch was that offed his brother. "That will quench my desire for personal vendettas, until then I'm going to be a murdering motherfuck'n machine, and I don't give a shit if I live or die, that's how it is with me man."

Harry Reynolds looked over the top of his beer can, paused, set it down on the coffee table and told him: "Yeah man, I can identify with that, none of those guys were related to me but they were like brothers so I can get behind what your say'n dude."

Billy Bob snapped, "It ain't the same, that was my flesh and blood we were split from the same egg that's a big, big difference dude, so don't compare those guys as equals in pain as my brother okay, I lost part of my soul."

Harry Reynolds went silent and let it drop he knew he was right there wasn't anything he could say that would ease the pain. They sat in the silence and finally, Billy Bob said, "Hey it's gotten dark now let's roll toward Silver Springs, take this black bastard out, stop by a pool hall and shoot some stick, I've been cooped up in this place for too long, I getting stir crazy," Harry Reynolds told him, "Yeah sure why not," and downed the rest of his brewski and belched.

THE MOON WAS ripe, in full bloom that evening as they drove to Silver Springs, past by Fred Harris' home, where light shone through the windows, they continue on about a two blocks farther Harry Reynolds put into a park'n space, Billy Bob said: "Stay here and removed the plate, in case someone sees me leaving and tails me," Harry said: "Okay," opened his tool kit, took out a screw driver, climbed out and proceeded to remove the plate as Billy Bob stepped off toward Fred Harris' home. He arrived about three minutes later, went the steps, checked the Beretta, slammed a seventeen round magazine in, racked the slide, put it in his jacket pocket and knock on the door.

It swung open, Fred Harris said, "I see you're punctual Mister Watts, come in," he stepped aside, Billy Bob entered, the door closed, he looked around and said, "Are we alone?"

Fred Harris told him, "No one's here just my two cats and I...," he stopped mid sentence when he saw Billy Bob pull the Beretta out of his jacket pocket, he said to Fred Harris, "Too bad I wanted to off as many of you coons as possible, oh well you'll just have to do for now," he pointed the Beretta and shot him point blank in the chest, he fell to the floor and Billy Bob squeezed off five more, said, "That should do it," as Fred Harris died there in the foyer, Billy Bob picked up the casings put them in his pant pocket, placed the gun back inside his jacket, took a handkerchief and placed it over the door knob, opened the door, closed it and he casually went the steps and strode back to the car.

"How'd it go?" asked Harry Reynolds, Billy Bob said: "We won't be having any more trouble out of that one, he's departed for the great beyond, let's go to a pool hall maybe we'll find some chicks there to bang, I could use some twat what about you?"

"Yeah, my nuts are smok'n and I ain't jok'n," he put the car in gear; they drew away from the curb and headed out to find some fun and games at the nearest billiard parlor.

IT WAS TEN THIRTY when Robin Calhoun's smartphone peeped, it was Billy Bob on the air, "Yes," she said, he told her, "One down and one to go, that coon's history. You won't be having any more trouble out of him, that's for certain."

"Great, but that little bitch has his files she has to be taken care of immediately."

Billy Bob: "We found out where she lives, but she always with her husband, I'm waiting for the right moment when she's alone, we'll tail them maybe they'll slip up and separated so I can take care of business, you know no witnesses and all that."

Robin Calhoun: "It has to go down no later than tomorrow night I need you to get to Boston, our cousins from Belize are waiting at the safe house there, so try and make it happen no later than that."

"Well if he gets in the way he's a goner too, fuck him," Billy Bob said with distain, she replied, "Fine by me just to it, I have a chartered plane waiting for you at Dulles that will fly you to Boston."

"Cool, Harry and I will go straight there after we've knocked her off," she asked, "Are you heading back to the condo?" He told her: "We're going to stop, grab a bite to eat and then head in," he didn't mention their little detour he knew she'd blow a gasket and he didn't want to hear any lip from her, he needed some chick's lips kiss'n all over him.

"Just be extra careful do not hang around, get it and go back to the condo and stay put, until you set out tomorrow to take care of the rest of this problem, understood?" Billy Bob looked over at Harry Reynolds, smiled and said, "Yes ma'am," Robin told him, "Alright I'll get back to you later," and switched off. Billy Bob said: "Shit she doesn't have to worry about any twat she's already got one," and they drove on yuk'n it up.

AFTERWARDS SHE WENT into the kitchen to hook up something to munch on and her smartphone peeped again, "Shit, who is this now?" she padded into the living room and picked up, "Yes," and the voice said: "They're searching feverishly for you," Robin Calhoun sat down: "What?" The voice said, "They know a woman is behind the SOS and they're trying to identify who she is, you need to be extra careful they're tailing Max Bedford and have his phones tapped."

Robin Calhoun blanched, "How do they know about him and a woman being involved?" she asked. The voice said: "Are you kidding, this is the US government we're talking about here, they can find out most anything if there are slip ups, your people have made blunders and left trails that could lead to your front door."

Robin Calhoun: "Who's behind this hunt for me?"

The voice: "The president, who else?" The voice told her like she asked the dumbest question in the history of questions.

Robin Calhoun: "That bastard, well he can keep looking he will not locate me that is for sure," she said confidently.

The voice: "Well you're paying me to keep you informed if you choose to ignore what I'm telling you, then that's on you, not me."

Robin chewed on it and told the voice, "I appreciate you supplying me with inside information, but I doubt they will find out before we attack next."

The voice asked: "Are you referring to something going down in Boston?" Robin Calhoun gulped and said, "Boston who said anything about Boston," trying to throw the voice of the scent.

"Well that's where they are concentrating their efforts, if it's not your next target, you needn't worry, but if it is you'd better be extra careful, they have some serious people trying to hunt you down and take whoever's involved out of the game with extreme prejudice."

Robin Calhoun tried to maintain her cool, she told the voice: "Trust me they are barking up the wrong tree, Boston, that is a good one," but she was shaken by this news, and needed to alert Max Bedford, so she said, "I have to go now, but thanks, keep your ear to the ground and let me know what that bastard Bohannon is up to, okay?" The voice told her he'd try to keep the info com'n but it was get'n risky now that the government was wise to the SOS planning something spectacular and she had better be super watchful of her activities, and switched off. Robin Calhoun stared at the phone, for the first time she actually showed panic, she grabbed one of her disposals and called Boston.

MAX BEDFORD WAS enjoying a nice cognac at his home kick'n back after a extremely charged show, he ranted against the president and his administration's incompetency trying to find out who was responsible for the Washington attack, and everyone knew it was al-Qaeda or a splinter group, Jasper Bohannon was drag'n his feet about retaliating against one of the terror sponsored states in the Middle East. He laid his smoke screen down he was hav'n big fun with his deception.

Max had Bose bump'n the greatest shit kick'n hits and was quite happy about things but that was about to change, he's smartphone twittered, he stood up, crossed over to a hallway table where he had laid his keys and phone, he thumbed on, "Hello," and heard Robin Calhoun say, "We have a major problem," he said, "How are you tonight...," she rolled over him: "No names, just listen, I just received a call from my main contact and was told the FBI is tailing you...," his mouth dropped open, "...and they have your phones tapped." Max Bedford swore he was hav'n a bowel movement.

Outside Adam Segal's ears perked up, he reached over and shook the SAC awake, "Sir, she's back on the phone," Dennis McMorris opened his eyes and said, "Are you getting this?" The SA told him, "Why of course sir, that's what I'm here for," the SAC ignored that, "Hopefully she'll stay on the line long enough so we can run a trace on this mysterious woman. Have you contacted the office to have them do that?"

Adam Segal said, "They're under instructions to automatically start a trace upon hearing a woman's voice sir, I'm sure they are all over it as we speak."

"Good enough, turn it up a little so I can hear what's being said," the SA did as told and they heard Robin Calhoun's voice as it came out through the amp, "The packages have arrived but do not go near the store, stay as far away as possible and do not try to contact me under any circumstances I will get in touch with you, understand?" Max Bedford was shaken to the core, this was not a good development, he tried to rally himself and said, "I understand totally and will comply with your wishes."

"I'll be in touch," and she was gone. Max Bedford realized the game had taken a sudden turn and his team was in serious jeopardy if the government was this close, *too close* for his liking. How did they latch onto him? He'd been extremely prudent in his activities. *Tailing me*? He went around the penthouse, turned off the lights, shifted over to the window, looked out down at the street try'n to see if anyone was lurk'n in the shadows, he eyes toured up and down the block and he couldn't see anyone. He stayed at the window for a full five minutes, turned and stepped to the sofa settled down and in the glow of the fireplace Max Bedford started to worry, seriously worry.

Outside the FBI agents noticed the lights douse and Adam Segal said, "This guy's probably having a shit fit about now sir," the SAC told him: "Defecation is the least of his concerns treason rates the death penalty."

"Death would be too good for him, all the destruction they caused down in DC, several rounds hit Headquarters, you know the Director wants us to get this guy and bring him in." Dennis McMorris said: "In due time Segal, we needed him to lead us to everyone who's involved, but she's pulled his coat, we may have to reach out and touch him, it depends on what the Director says."

As they sat in the car, all was quite in Max Bedford's flat as he sat in the dark and wondered what to do, he knew what she meant about the packages; the team from Belize had arrived. One of his operative picked them up from Logan International and transported them to the safe house, they'd have to wait until Billy Bob came up from DC and then they'd make their move, things were on schedule, but that didn't do Max Bedford any good. He thought he was off the skyline, and now the light was on him. He had to make plans for a getaway if things got any hairier for him. But how could he shake the FBI? That was the burn'n question. He was in a bind trapped between a rock and a hard place, Max Bedford had to figure out a way, a way out of this predicament and fast. Presently no solution came to mind; he worked his cognac considered his lot and thought *what a revolting development* this was turn'n out to be.

BACK DOWN IN Washington President Bohannon was on the Codex with the Director of the FBI, he informed the president about the latest from Boston. Jasper Bohannon listened then asked: "Were your men able to trace the call?" the Director said: "No sir, she hung up before we could lock in, but we do know the call originated from here in the Metro. She's a cagey one. She didn't stay on the line more than twenty seconds, but the question is who told her about our surveillance and us knowing about Boston?"

The president said, "That would suggest we have a major leak somewhere, whoever this mole is he knows a lot about our doings, we've been tight lipped as possible on this." The Director said, "This could be a hindrance for us if they're privy to our every move sir." Jasper Bohannon said back: "Agreed. We have to find this person before he does the country great harm. Have you considered arresting Bedford?"

"Yes sir, but as of now all we have is implied innuendo, with his money his attorney would have it thrown out in arrangement, although we know he's in this up to his eyeballs, we should wait until we have more concrete evidence, then we'll roll him up tight and there will be no wiggle room for a slick attorney to get him off the hook." The president chewed on it and commented, "I see your point Director every keen of you, let him sweat, like you said there's no way for him to make a move without our knowing it."

"He's probably thinking of ways to get out of this jam he's in, her alerting him will make him super cautious about what he says on the phone and he knows we're on his tail so I can say he's in a quite a pickle, let's wait it out, although I don't believe she'll contact him any time soon."

The president told him: "Well Director thanks for keeping me up to date, let us called it a day and we'll speak on it tomorrow." The Director said, "As you wish sir."

ON THE FOLLOWING afternoon Jessy and Skeeter were shop'n for baby clothes and other items for the expected one, they were spend'n big and enjoying it to the max, buying this and that, it was a day of bliss, but that was about to be shattered, Jessy's smartphone peeped, she thumbed on: "Hi there Horace," he said, "I wish this was a social call but something tragic has occurred," she braced herself, "*What is it??*" He paused and then told her the news, "I'm sorry to be the one who to tell you this, but Fred Harris is dead...," Jessy let out a scream, Skeeter Macklin looked at her and said, "What's wrong?" before she could answer she heard Horace Hackett say, "Someone shot him in his home last night, a cousin stop by and found him lying in the foyer, he'd been shot several times."

Jessy went weak and started to collapse; Skeeter caught her, still not knowing what was being said, "What's going *on*." He guided her to a seat and settled her down, "Fred Harris was killed last night in his home," she told him, her boss went on, "I hate to bring this up now, the police are investigating all angles, do you think this might be related to that story you and Fred are working on," she was too distraught to reply, handed the smartphone to Skeeter who said: "Horace this is Jessy's husband she's too upset to talk right now, could we get back to you?" Horace Hackett: "Of course, I'm sorry if the news has caused her any stress, but I thought she should know, I'll get back later when she has time to gather herself," Skeeter: "Thanks Horace, good bye."

Skeeter Macklin sat down beside his wife, wrapped his arms around her as she sobbed, trying to comfort her, his thoughts were, *could Fred's murder have something to do with this SOS affair? Things are too coincidental to ignore, maybe she's in danger also,* he knew something wasn't right about this, his protective instincts kicked in he had to react as if it was so and protect Jessy, until the facts came to light.

They left the store, drove home, Jessy laid down and quietly wept, Skeeter sat beside the bed rub'n her forehead, he knew his wife was in pain, he had to be there for her, she was deeply affect by this and it would be sometime before she'd get over it.

TEN HOURS LATER Billy Bob and Harry Reynolds sat in the rental parked a block away from the Macklin residence. Harry was at the wheel, they had their eyes peeled on the house and waited for Skeeter and Jessy to emerge. Harry Reynolds said: "I have a feel'n tonight's the night we switch this bitch's lights off", Billy Bob looked over at him and said, "So now you're in the predicting business?" and laughed, Harry Reynolds shot him a look, "We've been at this for two days, let's end this nonsense and just rush 'em when they come out, ice 'em both."

"They'll be out soon like they did last night and go to a restaurant, that's where we'll hit them, when they come out. Did you remove the plates yet?" Billy Bob asked. "No I wanted to make sure we're go'n to do it here before I did that," Harry told him.

"Good thinking we can't be tooling around with no plates on and get pulled over on a lark by some stupid lawdawg - hey the garage door just opened, I think it's time for some more pay back."

Skeeter Macklin backed out on the street, turned and gunned off in the split window Vette, Harry Reynolds said: "That's one baaad ass ride he's push'n, too bad we can't take the car, man I love to have that sumbitch." Billy Bob nodded and said back, "You're right about that man, candy apple red with gold metal flakes, that's a one sweet ride right there

- okay now pull out and let's get this over with, we're due in Boston." Harry Reynolds drew away from the curb and set out after the Macklins.

The red Vette zipped in and out of traffic; they were head'n to the Georgia Brown's restaurant in Georgetown for some low country cuisine. It was one of Jessy's favorite spots in the city, he looked at her, "I'll drop you off and pick you up in about an hour is that enough time for you to eat?" She told him: "It should be, they should've slow down a bit, so service should be quick, are you sure you won't join me?" Skeeter Macklin told her, "Sweet's got this buy over in McLean, an old guy has a 57 Bonneville convertible and he's hurting for cash, Sweet said we could pick it up for about fifteen, do a ground up restoration and move it for about seventy five, nice piece of change, I'll just check it out and swoop right back, it shouldn't take too long." She faked a pout and said, "You know I hate to eat alone." Skeeter pat her baby bump and said: "You won't be eating alone." She laughed, looked down and said, "Hey in there did you hear your daddy, cracking wise?"

Skeeter said; "I have a feeling that kid's going have a smart mouth like its mom," Jessy said back, "That way we can tag team you and give you the big smack down." Skeeter told his wife: "Jessy you're too much. Here we go," he said as he pulled up in front of Georgia Brown's, he got out, trotted around, opened the door, handed her out and said, "I won't be long love," she reached up, kissed him and said: "We're off to eat alone, bye," turned and entered the restaurant. Skeeter Macklin waited until she was inside and got back in the Vette and dashed off.

"Hey there's a space just up ahead on the right, pull in, we can watch the door and wait for her." Billy Bob told Harry Reynolds, he did as ordered, kill the engine, and they sat and waited.

Inside the waiter appeared, "Are you ready to place your order, ma'am?" and Jessy looked at the menu, "How's the poached salmon?" he told her: "Simply sumptuous if I dare to say so," and she said, "Yes you may, I'll have that along with the low country spinach salad and iced tea," the waiter said, "Excellent choices, I'll be back momentarily with your tea," he collected the menu, spun on his heels and disappeared.

Jessy looked around the restaurant to see if anyone was there she recognized, not seeing anyone, her thoughts went to Fred Harris then it hit her, he was the one who first recommend Georgia Brown's to her. She became melancholy and fought back the tears as the waiter approached,

"Here you are, ma'am", he looked at her and asked, "Is everything all right you appear to be preoccupied with something, is it stressing you?" Jessy righted herself and lied, "I'm fine, thanks for asking," with that he left her with her thoughts.

Soon after she turned to her meal and began to eat, savoring it, but her mind drifted to Fred Harris and she had to ask herself, *is Horace is right, could this be about Fred's investigation of the SOS,* a cold chill swept over her and she felt ill.

She finished eating, looked at her watch, she had been here for about fifty minutes, Skeeter should be returning shortly, she sat there wait'n for his call. She didn't have to wait long her cell went and it was him, "Hi love, I'll be there within five, be outside," she waved the waiter over paid her bill, suddenly feel'n queasy she got up and made for the restroom. Inside she threw up, thinking about Fred had clearly upset her, and outside Skeeter Macklin pulled up, not see'n her he had to park, drew into a space and waited.

Up the street Billy Bob and Harry Reynolds saw this and Billy Bob said, "Get ready she should being coming out anytime now," Harry ignited the engine and they waited.

After a couple of minutes, Skeeter Macklin began to wonder what was taking her so long, he waited a little longer, then decided to go inside and collect her. He got out, started up the sidewalk about a block away, he saw her come out and waved, she saw him, smiled and padded in his direction. Billy Bob shouted, *"Hit it,"* and Harry Reynolds gunned out of the space, raced up to the entrance, the car braked hard. Billy Bob leapt out with the Beretta raised, ready to squeeze the trigger, Skeeter saw him, and yelled, "Jessy," she had a questioned look on her face, a couple came out of Georgia Brown's, the lady screamed see'n Billy Bob hold'n the gun, as he pulled the trigger she screamed again which threw his aim off, he popped two quick shots hit'n Jessy in the shoulder and the chest, she fell to the ground, Billy Bob jumped back in the car, Skeeter Macklin arrived as it pulled away, he heard Billy Bob holler out the window, "That's a two for one sale, motherfucker," and he and Harry Reynolds laughed as the car squealed off.

Skeeter knelt down, he knew she was severely injured, he cradled her in his arms, looked around: "Someone call the rescue squad, *please,*" He begged. The lady who screamed was already on the phone doing just that, and Skeeter spoke to his wife, "Jessy, stay with me, stay with me," and knew from his experiences she was in deep trouble. He pinched her cheeks, try'n to make sure she didn't slip into shock; he kept repeating, "Jessy, Jessy hang in there the ambulance in on its way." Within minutes the rescue squad arrived, the paramedics piled out, unloaded a gurney, lifted her on to it, loaded it in the back, Skeeter leapt in and they raced away to a hospital.

SCRATCH ANOTHER ONE off the list," Billy Bob said, Robin Calhoun told him, "Well done, now you need to head to Dulles, get on the plane and fly to Boston, our cousins from Belize are waiting for you." Billy Bob and Harry Reynolds rode away from the shoot'n, about a mile away they stopped, and Harry got out and replaced the license plate. They continued on, Billy Bob phoned Robin Calhoun; she was waiting and picked up on the first ring.

Robin Calhoun told him: "We are going to step up our timetable, seems the government is snooping too close, they are aware of Max Bedford, they are tailing him and have his phones tapped, so do not make contact with him, understood?"

Billy Bob said, "How did they get on his trail?" Robin Calhoun said back: "I have no idea my source said they are aware the something might happen in Boston, so you have to be extra cautious when moving around up there. Make sure our friends understand they are under your command and that they follow your orders to the letter."

"Don't worry about that I'll keep them on short leash at all times, we should arrive at Dulles within twenty minutes I'll call you when we get there." Robin Calhoun said: "Alright, one more thing, I should have the schedule of the surprise sometime within the next forty eight hours, so be prepared to move on that info, Max has stored all the necessary weapons and such at the safe house, so everything is in place all we are waiting on is the schedule and then it is post time." Billy Bob told her: "I'm the jockey etching to ride this pony." Robin Calhoun allowed herself a laugh and then said, "Well call me when you are airborne." Billy Bob said, "Will do," and switched off.

Robin Calhoun sat back, sip at her Jack, they eliminated both threats, her daddy's secret was safe, she had done what was necessary to preserve that, she smiled and knew CC would be proud of his little girl, and prouder still of what's to come. She needed to hear from Cole Harper soon, they needed the information from him now, she hadn't spoken to him since Stone Mountain, and she'd chance a call tomorrow to see what was up.

Robin Calhoun had to call Jake Carlisle, she wanted to relax, and take her mind off things for a while, a nice romp would do her good, she hadn't spread her legs since she returned from Americana, she was overdue, so she reached for the phone.

AT THE SAME time the ambulance with its lights flash'n and siren on full blast raced through the streets toward the nearest hospital, inside the paramedics worked feverishly trying to stabilize Jessy, she had an oxygen mask over her mouth and nose, plasma dripped, and Skeeter Macklin distraught sat hold'n her hand.

They were only a minute away, the driver craved in and out of traffic, finally they arrived, the vehicle come to a stop, a paramedic jumped out, swung open the back doors, Skeeter got out, stood out of the way as they unloaded the gurney, hospital personal were there, they rolled her through the emergency entrance. The hospital had been alerted en route, they were prepared to perform surgery, the gurney turned down a hallway Skeeter trotted along behind, they went through a set of double doors straight into an operating room, a doctor stepped in front of Skeeter and said: "Sir you'll have to remain outside, the attendant will direct you a waiting lounge," Skeeter looked over his shoulder as the gurney transporting his wife turned in and disappeared, "Is she going to be alright?" The doctor heard this question thousands of times, he told him: "We'll let you know what happens shortly, now go with the attendant and wait in the lounge, please." Skeeter Macklin reluctantly turned, stepped off with a nurse at his shoulder.

He paced back and forth, and replayed the incident in his mind, *what if* abound. Could he have *done something* to prevent this? Maybe he should've gone with her to dine instead of going to McLean maybe he could have stepped in the way and took the bullets. His mind was racked with questions, *who did this, why was she a target, was this related to Fred Harris' murder*, and the most frightening question of all sprung to the fore, *what if* she doesn't survive ? He felt himself being consumed with intense grief and biting anger, she had to pull through, he would get the persons responsible, *will the baby survive*, would his beautiful and sweet Jessy, and the most painful thought of all dominated the others, *what if* he lost one or both of them?

Skeeter collapsed onto a sofa, hung his head between his legs, tears puddled at his feet. Skeeter Macklin the hard core warrior, Skeeter Macklin the loving husband, Skeeter Macklin expectant father wept uncontrollably tortured and vexed about *what happened* to his beloved Jessy. He agonized as he waited for some word from hospital officials he needed to know *what's happening* to her and their baby. Skeeter Macklin found himself pray'n something he hadn't done since he was young, now he needed these prayers answered. He never felt this helpless. Hanging on to hope, fretting, worries eat'n away at his heart. Anger boiled over, fear his only companion. He needed answers, and he needed them now, not knowing was unbearable.

He went frequently to the nurse station and asked what was going on, any word about how the surgery had progressed, when will they know something, the nurse told him several times they would let him know soon, please have a seat was the answers he received to his questions, answers that didn't satisfy or dampen the pain he felt.

AFTER TWO HOURS of this Skeeter approached the nurse's station prepared to quiz her again, she had no answers to his myriad of questions always the same and always the same replies. She looked up from her work, started to speak, as a doctor emerged through the doors, stepped up and said: "Mister Macklin, come with me sir," Skeeter Macklin tried to read him as they went back into the lounge, but his face was stoic, so he waited, his heart and mind thirsted for answers, the doctor said: "Have a seat," Skeeter looked at him and braced for the worse, he said, "I don't need to sit down, tell me about my wife, now," it came out as an order, the doctor paused before he said, "I've good news and not so good news," Skeeter Macklin fraught with anxiety said, "Tell me doctor, I can't take this," he told him, "The baby is fine she's in the ward, she's two months premature so she'll be looked after constantly, and now the other news, your wife survived also, but she's in a coma."

A thousand emotions washed over Skeeter, relief eased the pain and joy gladdened his heart. "When can I see her, my wife, I mean?" the doctor said, "You'll have to waited for awhile before you can go in to see her, but you can go to the maternity ward and view your new daughter." Skeeter asked: "Doctor what are her chances of pulling through this?" he asked with uneasiness in his voice, he was told, "At this time I'd say fifty fifty, but that could improve we'll just have to wait and see, why don't you venture to the baby unit and see your daughter," Skeeter Macklin nodded, went to the nurse and asked for directions to pediatrics.

When he got to the maternity ward there seemed to be a silence even more profound than what would be typical given the time. The nurse led him to a room where a tiny baby laid in a clear plastic crib. Skeeter Macklin looked through the window at his new baby girl, smiled, he was overjoyed to see her, and thought about the conversation he had with Mickey aboard the USS *Key West* about wanting a girl and there she was. He stared at her taking in all her essence a product of him and Jessy, his ladylove and there another little lady to love too.

Skeeter Macklin stood at the window for another half hour, two emotions ran riot, bliss and worry, he was happy about the little person on the other side of the glass and unhinged about Jessy lying alone in room in the ICU, he couldn't be two places at once, so he choose to leave the little one and head to her mother's side, he back pedaled away and held this gaze on window, behind it laid the future, he had to go to Jessy and help her in any way he could to maintain the present, she had to pull through, he finally turned and bi pedaled down the hall.

IT WAS JUST after eleven thirty when Billy Bob Broussard and Harry Reynolds climbed out of the rental, stepped off to the chartered jet, it was parked away from Dulles proper, where the big mucks store their toys. The captain saw them approach, they ran the ladder and he said: "I'm Captain Davis we can lift off right away, welcome aboard," they nodded, walked into the cabin, the door closed, the plane taxied down the runway, three minutes later the Gulfstream when wheels up into the night sky.

As DC receded to the south, Billy Bob stared out the porthole leaving this battleground, he had ignited a war, and that war produced causalities, one of them Billy Ray, was it worth it to lose him, was he a martyr who died for the cause, it was bigger than just one individual he had accepted his death like the ones he produced, the war and Billy Broussard headed north to Boston the birthplace of American democracy, he had hit its heart in Washington now he was out to destroy its soul. The US would never be the same after the event went off, he was prepared to kill or perhaps die, it mattered not, this is what soldiers do they fight and try not to die, but death was a warrior's shadow ever lurk'n to collect as many souls as possible. Death showed no favor, it mattered not who the victims were, Billy Bob was primed to take on death, he was prepared to do the ultimate, die for the cause and join Billy Ray.

So be it.

He was immune to fear, he had conquered it, now fear had a name, Billy Bob.

He closed his eyes and sleep took him and he was at ease fly'n to Boston, to bake Bean Town.

12

1 Bitch 2 Many

Washington; Boston

THE PHONE RANG on the end table, a hand fumbled, then flipped on the light and picked up, it was Captain Stovall on the line, "Sorry to wake you sir, but something tragic has happened," he told General Falk, who said, "No frills, give to me straight no chaser," Mickey Stovall paused and said, "It's Jessy Macklin sir, she's been injured, I'm here at Georgetown University Hospital with Skeeter." The general shot up from the pillow, swung his feet on the floor, "This is horrible news, Captain, and how'd it occur?"

Mickey Stovall proceeded to tell him, when finished Mad Sam said, "I'm on my way tell the Major I'll be there shortly," he heard Mickey Stovall, "Yes sir," and rang off. Mad Sam called Top Cooper, ordered his car, started to dress, he was beyond angry he was truly Mad Sam Falk, this was family on a lot of levels, now in his civvies he made for the door, outside Top had the back door open ready to receive the general, who rushed past, "Head to Georgetown University Hospital, double time," he said as he climbed in, Top closed the door, raced around, got in behind the wheel and the limo drew away.

IN THE BARN'S communication center Andrew Wong was on post where he watched for Billy Bob Broussard. The computer ran through all the streets cameras, his photo had been programmed in, face recognition software sorted through thousands of images per hour, he had been at this for the last four days, Billy Bob was not to be found, he had been careful up until tonight, when his image triggered the sensors, there he was hold'n a gun outside Georgia Brown's restaurant, further photos showed the entire shooting and he's escape, Andrew Wong zoomed in on rear of the car and expected a license plate, there wasn't one, *crafty birds* the captain said in silence as he printed the images. *But not wily enough* he clicked on the high speed satellite cameras and found the car on the expressway, other footage showed it in a park'n lot at Dulles International, then he brought up the airport security cameras and there he was, he tightened the image, it showed the plane's serial number *gotcha* he called the control tower at Dulles and got the destination of the plane, Boston, he knew this was telling, now to inform the general.

IN THE LOUNGE at the hospital Mad Sam and Mickey Stovall sat on a sofa, Skeeter Macklin in a chair, the general said, "Captain Wong's on his way, he'll be here momentarily," they had been sitting here for the last forty five minutes, when the general's car pulled up to the emergency entrance, before it came to a complete stop, Mad Sam opened the door, jumped out, raced inside, he walked up to the nurse station: "I'm General Sam Falk..., showed his ID..., "direct me to Jessy Macklin's room," and the nurse came to full attention: "I'm sorry sir, but she's in ICU, her husband's in the lounge outside the ICU, just follow the...," Mad Sam left before she completed her instructions, he was a mission, he came into the lounge area, Mickey Stovall and Skeeter Macklin rose their feet, the general said, "As you were, no need for protocol, how is she, Major?"

"She's in a coma, the doctor said the odds stood at fifty fifty, sir, but Jessy is tough as nails," Mad Sam said, "That she is, tell me Major the circumstances behind this tragic event."

When he finished the general looked at Mickey, "Captain have to two men from the Barn brought here without delay, in civvies to stand guard outside Jessy's door, I want men post there 24/7 until further orders...,"

Mickey Stovall thumbed on his smartphone hit speed dial, rose and stepped away..., "Who's ever responsible for this may want to finish the job if they find out she's alive."

"I appreciate that sir," Skeeter told the general who replied: "Major your wife must be protected she was a direct threat to someone, was she investigating anything of magnitude that would provoke a reaction such as this against her?"

Skeeter Macklin told him: "Maybe sir, we returned from Brazil Monday and she allied with another reporter, colleague, and friend named Fred Harris he was murdered in his home two nights ago...," the general listened intently, "...and he'd emailed her a file on a secret organization calling themselves the SOS...," Mad Sam stepped in, "That's it, Major I'm going fill you in what's has happened since the attack on Washington," he brought him up to scratch, even through Skeeter was no longer a member of the Eradicators or the military, he still had a ultra secret clearance, the general never canceled it, so the info he revealed was allowable. Mickey Stovall walked back over, the general looked up, "Sir the men are en route, twelve on, twelve off until further notice, Finch and Forte will stand guard on the first shift, they'll be armed with hand guns until further orders."

Mad Sam: "Mighty fine. This SOS is a sick herd, diseased bovine, we will cull the herd completely, the only one I want alive is the bell cow, and all others are to be eradicated with impunity, take no prisoners, no one lives to moo about this affair."

Mickey Stovall: "Yes sir, we are prepared to do just that sir, with rigor, no survivors."

Mad Sam: "Captain Wong's on his way with the...," he paused and looked at Skeeter, "...photos of the entire sequences of the event outside the restaurant, Major I hope you won't be disturbed?"

Skeeter Macklin: "No sir, I'll be okay, I want to see who did this so I...," he stopped mid sentence but the general knew the conclusion, he said, "Major this Billy Bob Broussard bayou bastard is nasty piece of work, he's rabid dog who must be hunted down and put out of its misery for the nation's sake, he's what they called back in the day public enemies, well this crud is Public Enemy Number One through Ten that's how danger he is."

Andrew Wong entered the lounge: "General," and looked at Skeeter: "I'm terribly sorry to hear about your wife Major," Skeeter: "I appreciate that, thank you very much," the general stepped in, "Show us what you have," Andrew Wong opened the packet, took out the photos, handed them to him, Mad Sam examine each one, passed them to Skeeter Macklin, he fought back his emotions, looking through them triggered the scene to replay in his mind, he wretched, and handed them to Mickey Stovall, Mickey said, "That's definitely Billy Bob, he and his brother were spitting images of each other, I can't wait to meet up with this one we have a conversation to conclude."

General Falk: "And when you do put a period on this bastard, as the expression goes bring me his head," just then a doctor strode in, "Excuse me gentlemen, Mister Macklin you can see your wife...," Skeeter sprang to his feet, "Take me to her," they left the general and the captains, going to see Jessy, that's where he needed to be.

"Eliminating the SOS was business, now it's personal, the major and his wife are family, Captain Wong return to the Barn, work the phones, cameras and everything we have at your disposal, find Billy Bob Broussard and when he does Captain Stovall I want you to make a dash to wherever that is and make it your business to kill this bastard, he's number one on my hit list, I'll remain here with the major, I need to update the president about this development now off you go." They rose as one, "Aye, aye sir," and took their leave and left Mad Sam with his thoughts, his painful, painful thoughts.

AFTERWARD THE GENERAL hit the president on his Codex and told him the latest, when through, Jasper Bohannon said: "Indeed tragic General please convey my sincerest sympathy to Mister Macklin, and tell him I'll put his wife in the center of my prayers."

"Will do sir, that will be most appreciated by the major, now on to the root of all this, Captain Wong searched for this Broussard duck, he's now focusing his attention on Boston, that's where this story will end, I have a feeling closure is nigh."

The president said, "Sounds good to me, we have a tall task in front of us General, we must stop whatever they intend to inflict on Boston, which remains unknown, we have to accelerate our efforts finding out what it is and prevent it from happening, priority one."

Mad Sam said, "Agreed sir, I will step up our efforts, and concentrate my forces on Boston, as soon as the whereabouts of this gang is found, they will be in there in a New York heartbeat and turn the city upside down to see what drops out. Sir, if you don't mind, I'd like to go and see what the disposition is with Jessy Macklin," Jasper Bohannon said: "By all means, please let me know what that is when you can, good night to you."

THE SMALL HOSPTIAL room was painted a drab gray, park'n lot light shone at the window, Skeeter sat on a chair and looked at his wife, she was unconscious, tubes were inserted into her nose and mouth, plasma and medication dripped continuously, she looked so small and helpless, he stared, torn between love and hate, her, his ladylove, the nearest to his heart and animosity for the man responsible for this scene.

He whispered to her, "I'm right here love, we have a beautiful little daughter she has your eyes and nose, wait until you see her, she's everything we expected and more, so tiny and precious. Jessy I know you can hear me, listen I pledge to you I will get the man who did this to you, us and the baby," tears gathered in his eyes and began to leak, Skeeter Macklin the warrior, now the grieving husband and father wept silently at his beloved's bedside, General Falk entered, walked over and placed his hand on his shoulder and said, "She'll make it through this Major, her will is too strong for otherwise, this will have a happy ending I'm positive of that." Skeeter replied not and sat there and sobbed away, the general told him, "Let it flow son, let it flow, I'll be in the lounge if needed," turned and left them alone, Jessy the patient and Skeeter her guardian.

THE GULFSTREAM ABOUT twenty minutes out from Logan International, started its descent, there was shock of turbulence it shook Billy Bob awake with a start, he looked across the aisle, Harry Reynolds was in deep sleep, both men were exhausted and needed any rest they could steal, the work ahead will demand their most. He suddenly remembered he hadn't called Robin Calhoun as instructed, he pulled his cell out and punched her digits, her phone sounded, she pick up on the third chime, "Well it is about time, where are you?"

"Sorry about that, I was done in as was Harry, we should be landing soon."

Robin Calhoun lay next to a sleeping Jake Carlisle, after danc'n between the sheets, he passed out as usual, and she waited for the phone to ring but fell asleep tuckered out, she rose, grabbed her robe and climbed into it on her way to the living room, where the conversation would go unheard in case Jake Carlisle woke up. This was not for his ears, she said: "Well okay...," accepting his explanation, she didn't blow a gasket her normal MO when she was disobeyed, "...once you have arrived, there is car waiting in the name of Barry Coleman, at Mass Auto Rentals, get it and go directly to the safe house, remain put until you hear from me, which should be sometime this afternoon. I am calling my contact demanding that info, we are up against clock here."

"Understood, if Max's not accessible, who do we rely on in case there's any hiccups?" Robin Calhoun told him: "I will direct things from down here, just stay focused and there will be no chances for any snafus, make sure you watch those guys from Belize, not that I do not trust them, I do not know them, so keep an eye on them, I am out."

Billy Bob reached over and shook Harry Reynolds, "We're here, now it's on to the big show, no more pussy footin' around, let's burn this town down, bake beans anyone?" He sported a most hideous grin, the sign of a madman, laugh'n uncontrollably and lov'n it. Billy Bob Broussard was insane with hate, a total nut job.

LATER IN THE lounge at Georgetown University Hospital Skeeter Macklin and Mad Sam Falk waited for word on any improvement in Jessy's condition, they sat and sipped coffee when Skeeter said, "General, I know I'm retired but I have to get into this for Jessy's sake, I have to find this Billy Bob A-hole and take him out personally," the general looked over the rim of his cup, "I've been waiting to discuss that with you Major, but I wanted you to broach the subject, well here's my thoughts...," he paused and worked his coffee and went on: "...as you've said you're retired so there's only one way I can legally use your services and that's to employ you as an independent contractor, that should cover our backsides."

Skeeter Macklin smiled for only the second time since he walked up the street headed toward Jessy before she was shot and the other when he first saw their little girl. He knew Mad Sam would come up with a way for him to get involved and he wasn't disappointed he beamed on and the general continued: "I will of course run this passed the president but I don't anticipate any problem there."

"Thanks sir," Skeeter said. General Falk told him, "Major do not let you personal feelings clouded your judgments when you take on this task, I know it will be hard not to insert that into the equation but you must remain professional in your approach, understood?"

"Totally sir," he replied and Mad Sam said: "Mighty fine, now how about some breakfast, I could use a tune up what about you?"

Skeeter realized he hadn't eaten for a while and said, "Yes sir, I could do with a bite to eat, but not this hospital chow, let's find somewhere within strolling distance, I'll ask one of the nurses they should know," he rose went to the nurse's station, returned and told the general, "She said there's an IHOP about three blocks away, so if you're ready we can go sir, I left my cell number in case anything happens while we're gone," Mad Sam stood up, "This is on me, let's hop on down to IHOP and see what they can do for us. They should be able to hook us up." Skeeter Macklin smiled at hip Mad Sam Falk.

ROBIN CALHOUN SLEPT until noon and when she awakened she was ill, she awoke with a dull headache and foul taste in her mouth, she rose up, looked over expect'n to see Jake Carlisle there but he'd left earlier and he had chosen not to wake her. She was relieved that he had left she had an important phone call to make. Robin Calhoun stood up, stretched, headed to the rain room and took a shower, felt so much better when she finally stepped out, toweled off, headed for the kitchen, prepared coffee and now sat on the sofa where she nursed it. Robin had to clear her mind for the call she had to make, it was critical to her plans. Robin Calhoun had to put on her general's cap; she was calling the shots out on the battlefield, hands on leader who tactics would prove to be decisive in the days to come. Her confidence was at an all time high but she needed that info to win.

After three cups she finally had the cobwebs cleared out of her head, it was time to make that call straightaway, the most crucial one of all in this scenario, she had waited, but the expected call never came, it was time for her to push some buttons. She needed to know one thing and she need to know it now.

Robin Calhoun picked up one of her disposal cells, she only used them once, then she'd destroyed them she was cautious on all fronts, mistake prone she wasn't, but things were about to tamper with that string of luck she was enjoying.

Robin Calhoun waited for the call to be connected finally someone said, "Hello," with a question in his voice, that someone was Cole Harper, she said, "Hi Cole, it is me how are things?," Robin was trying to be a pleasant as possible, this was the first time they'd spoken since she rudely yanked on his private parts, now she needed to sound as if everything was okay and forgotten, but that wasn't the case, not even close, Cole Harper said, "By me, do you mean the wicked witch of the south, lose my number bitch."

The cell went dark Robin Calhoun sat there and chewed on what happened, she flung the phone into the fireplace and watched the fire consume it, while it burned she fumed, this was not good, not good at all, Cole Harper obviously was still smart'n from their last encounter, she had to come up with a solution, a new sense of touch and employ another tact to get that much needed info from him.

She let five minutes elapse and then picked up another cell from the stack, punched Cole Harper's number again, this time when he answered she jumped straight into it, "Cole please do not hang up, this is important you know that, let us not dwell in the past, I am sorry..." she heard noise in the background it sounded like restaurant activity, then the cell went dark again, she screamed, "*That son of bitch*," and threw that phone into the fire. She had to react, Robin Calhoun knew what was required she'd to have a face to face to smooth this out.

Robin Calhoun the frustrated and pissed leader of the SOS had to quash this rebellion in the ranks, she stepped into the bedroom reached in the closet grabbed a pair of slacks, shimmied into them, donned a sweater, slipped on a pair of Ferragamo pumps, located her car keys, struggled in to her mink and left the townhouse to catch Cole Harper at the restaurant, hoping he'd still be there when she arrived. Robin Calhoun was determined to get that information, one way or another she was dialed in now, the general had to make an example of one of her troopers, if necessary she'd have him snatched and tortured to gain what she needed, there were no two ways about that, Robin Calhoun was on a mission to try to salvage things and continue her war, Cole Harper was the key and if she had to kiss his ass, so be it.

Robin Calhoun glanced at her watch, she lived fifteen minutes away from Mendocino Grille & Wine Bar, Cole Harper's favorite water'n hole, if she was quick enough she'd arrive before he departed. She knew his habits after a torrid fling two years ago and was aware of how he felt about her, she was confident she'd win him over once he saw her, so she stepped on it and the Maybach responded.

She drew up outside the restaurant, doubled parked, she didn't wait for the valet, and climbed out, tossed him the keys and made for the restaurant door. Inside she spotted Cole Harper where he sat alone in a booth along the far wall, Robin Calhoun floated across the room, and he looked up, his jaw dropped as he watched her thread through the tables, she sauntered over, settled down and said, "I hope I am not too late dear, my apologies, I got caught in traffic - have you ordered yet?" And flashed her patent smile which she knew he was weak for.

"You have a lot of nerve after what you did to me, in front of everyone no less," he was visibly agitated at her being here, he still had stitches in his forehead from crash'n head first onto the pavement down on Stone Mountain. She drove right past that: "Darling, I would like to order, I am famished, what is the day's special?" Cole Harper couldn't believe this woman, "You have a lot of gall to come here and torment me with your presence, you psycho bitch." Now Robin Calhoun had to tact in another direction the sweetness approach hadn't gone over too well.

"First off let me apologize for the little...," Cole Harper rode over her: "Little? Do these twenty stitches look little to you? I'm tempted to slam your pretty face on this table and give you dose of what you did to me."

Robin Calhoun sat back out of range and said: "Once again I am sorry about our misunderstanding, I was not feeling well that night and my thinking was affect by it, I am truly sorry Cole," she reached across the table and touched his hand, he immediately pulled away, "You're not going to lay that crap on me, you think I'm stupid or something, you are one nasty little bitch, no matter what façade you present, you are a sick bitch." That was *one* bitch *too* many, Robin Calhoun bit back, "Look you pompous bastard, we can trade insults and call each other names, but what is the point? So let us cut to the chase, you know why I am here."

"Yeah, yeah, I know why, you need me and what I can provide you," he snapped.

"That is a correct statement, so what is the problem, we had an agreement, which you have failed to keep...," Cole Harper jumped in, "The key word is had, that was before you humiliated and caused me bodily harm, since then the situation has turned dramatically as you can tell."

Robin Calhoun knew this was going to be more difficult than she had anticipated so she said, "What will it take to get past this impasse Cole?" He told her: "Well it will take a lot more than a bullshit apology that's for certain," *Aha,* she said in silence *now we are getting somewhere* and told him: "Okay what will it take to get the information from you?" Cole Harper knew she was primed, but he intend to make this smart ass bitch squirm some more, so he said, "I'm having second thoughts about this whole affair, you've bitten off more than you can chew, you greedy, power hungry cunt." Robin Calhoun winced, "Again with the name calling can we be adults here?"

"If you don't like being called a bitch or a cunt stop acting like 'em," Cole Harper relished tell'n her that. Robin Calhoun was not use to someone talk'n to her in this fashion, it was she who dealt out the smart remarks and biting japes but she had to endure, so she smiled and replied, "Perhaps you are right I can be supercilious at times...," he leaped in, "That's a big word for a fucking snot isn't it," and grinned he was enjoy'n this to the max, she the great unflappable Robin Calhoun *wiggling like the worm she is,* he said in silence and he wasn't about to let her off the hook, "You keep forgetting you need me, I don't need you," and feign like he was prepared to leave and started to stand up, she reached across the table again, touched his arm hoping he'd stay put, he brushed her hand away and remained seated. Robin Calhoun had never experienced anyone treating her so condescendingly. This was new and it definitely threw her off her game, she was lost as how to deal with this *pig head.*

Cole Harper fired hard balls and Robin Calhoun had a hard time catch'n them, she had to do something else; threats were out of the question. She knew what time it was, reached in her purse, came out with a pen and paper, proceeded to scribble something, she turned it over, slid it across the table and kept her hand over it and said, "This is what I am prepared to pay you," and removed her hand, Cole Harper picked up the piece of paper, turned it over and looked insulted, "What's this, the signing bonus?"

Robin Calhoun was taken aback, she knew what she wrote down was a lot of money, she started to sweat this was becoming a serious challenge deal'n with this guy, she had grossly underestimated Cole Harper, "That is a very generous offer Cole, above and beyond what we agree too."

"That was then this is now and from my calculations you're a few zeros shy of what it will take to get what you need, you fuck'n trollop, oh I'm sorry that's what trollops do they fuck a lot," the man was deeply hurt and it showed, he was unrelenting, he was going to get paid and tell her what he really thought about her at the same time. Robin Calhoun said, "I need a drink," and waved for the waiter. Who trotted over, "What do you require, ma'am?"

Robin Calhoun told him the obvious, "A triple shot of Jack Daniel's straight," the waiter raised a brow ever so slightly and said to Cole, "And the gentleman?" Cole Harper told him, "I'm fine thanks," he was getting drunk off see'n this woman fall apart. The waiter said, "Okedoke," and left the adversaries staring at one another.

A mood hung over the table, Cole glared at her said in silence *at last someone has shaved this cunt down to size,* he spoke into the quiet, "Well Robin are you ready to discuss some real money and not insult me with this meager offering," she looked at him, "Two hundred and fifty thousand dollars is not what one would call meager."

"That might be intoxicating to an idiot, but to someone who knows what it will do for you its peanuts, now are you going to talk real money or continue to sit there thinking I'm that idiot." Cole Harper knew he had her over the barrel, and it felt *oh so good.*

The waiter returned with her drink, sat it down, "Here you are ma'am, will there be any else?" Robin Calhoun told him, "Bring me another, please," grabbed the glass, and chugged it down in one turn up and handed the glass to the waiter, he was amazed, but kept quiet, spun on his heels and zipped off. Cole Harper reared back in his seat and savored as he watched the great Robin Calhoun go to pieces right before him.

This was indeed good.

Robin collected herself and caved in, "Alright Cole you have me by the balls now, so what is your bottom line and be realistic."

Cole Harper: "Well I'm thinking something in the range of let's say a cool million for starters."

Robin Calhoun: "One million dollars, for *starters*?"

Cole Harper: "I don't remember stuttering, that's six zeros with a one in front of it, and I want another ten when you succeed in your raise to power in your glorious country down south."

Robin Calhoun: "This is extortion...," he stepped in, "Now that's a ugly word, let's call it my nest egg, a 401K or something to that effect, I'm sure you get my drift."

Robin was floored, this was nowhere near what she expected, she thought she'd be the one doing the dealing but suddenly he was hold'n all the cards and dealing off the bottom of the deck. She had gambled and lost so she conceded, "Very well, done," he was sport'n a shit eat'n grin and said, "I'm so glad you see things my way," just then the waiter returned with her second drink, and asked with a twinge of sarcasm, "Will there be anything else?" Cole Harper said, "Yes, would you please call the lady a taxi," the waiter looked at him as if understanding his intent, "That's a good suggestion I'll tend to it, sir," and once again turned and left them alone.

Robin Calhoun said: "I can drive, I do not need a taxi," Cole Harper told her, "Why Robin I am concerned about your wellbeing, I want to make sure I get paid and to relieve you of that car you drive, you know the one you reached out and crushed my nuts from, I think I'll take that as a down payment, what'd you think?"

She was stupefied, this man had worked her over, she'd been outflanked by the one she thought she'd have eat'n out of her hand, now that hand was going to hand over the keys to her Maybach, she was clearly the loser, that move on Stone Mountain had proven to be very costly, very costly indeed. She said, "You win, now when will I get that information I need?" he told her: "Just as soon as I check my account and the money's been deposited, not a moment sooner, how's that for an answer?"

Robin Calhoun said, "It will be there by close of business tomorrow is that soon enough?" He said back, "I think I can suffer until then with anticipation knowing twenty something hours from now my financial status will have been upgraded considerably. Yes that's satisfactory." He stood up, wormed his way into his coat, put his cap down on his head and pulled his gloves on while tell'n her, "Well Robin I can genuinely say it's been a blast watching you crumble before my eyes, the great one cut off at the knees, truly a wonderful event to witness. And by the way, pick up my tab." Fully suited up for the weather outside, he turned and bi pedaled away and left Robin Calhoun to mull over what just happened. Cole Harper walked out and told the valet to fetch the gold Maybach, his date was too intoxicated to drive and she'd take a taxi home.

INSIDE THE MENDOCINO Grille & Wine Bar Robin Calhoun pondered what just happened, lost in thought, she was despondent to say the least, Cole Harper proved to be one cold hearted man, who left in her ride, and this was not the scenario she expected when she first strutted into the restaurant, full of confidence now she'd been had and had good, what to do, what to do? The waiter stepped up: "Ma'am the taxi will be here shortly, do you require anything else?" Robin snapped out of her reverie and told him, "Bring me another triple while I wait," he offered, "Are you sure, you've had two...," Robin Calhoun asked him, "What, so you are suddenly my accountant?" And then said: "Just bring me the drink and keep your thoughts to yourself," the waiter was admonished and felt about two feet tall, he grimaced at the prospect her down'n another, but that was not his job to be her adviser and left again and thought what a *nasty bitch.*

She sat there and waited for Jack and the taxi that would carry her home with her tail tucked between her legs, Robin Calhoun was in a stupor, not from the alcohol, but from that ass whup'n she just received, she sat there, licked her wounds and started to plot out what to do about this unexpected turn of events.

Yeah, Cole Harper raked her over the coals, but she intended to have the last laugh in this episode, he may now have her ride and the money deposited into his account later but after he gave her what she needed and he wouldn't spend a dime of it, he had marked himself of death. She might be sit'n down but she wasn't tak'n it, not her, not Robin Calhoun, not CC's daughter, if her daddy knew she'd accept this he'd raise from the grave and give her spank'n. Cole Harper was going get paid alright, paid with a bullet in the head, *yeah that's what to do about that cheeky bastard.*

She smiled as the waiter returned who thought the grin was for him, he sat the glass down, Robin Calhoun said, "Sorry about our last exchange of words, I am having a bad day, but I am quite over it now," she reached for her purse and came out with a wad, looked at the tab, put forty dollars on the tray, "That's for the bill," and handed him a crisp Ben Franklin, "And this is for you," the waiter's eyes blew up as she down the Jack, stood up, pulled her mink on, stepped off to get into the taxi and to get revenge for the humiliation she had received from that Cole Harper, he would be cold by sundown tomorrow, that's for sure. You don't treat Robin Calhoun like that *not me, not ever.*

DRIVING THE GOLD Maybach, Cole Harper enjoyed his new ride it was a serious upgrade compared to the Jag he was push'n, he knew he couldn't drive to work in this, eyes and question marks would be all over him, everyone would asking *how did he rate on a government salary?* He'd have to keep it hidden from pry'n eyes and jealous hearted snoops, he'd park it in his garage until he made a getaway soon after the money hit his bank account then he quit his job on the spot and head out from parts unknown. He knew he couldn't trust Robin Calhoun, not *that conniving bitch*, he was sure she was at the very moment plot'n to take him out, like he told her at the table, he was *no idiot* and intended to enjoy this windfall gallivanting around the globe hav'n big fun and enjoy'n the high life, that's the plan. Cole Harper intended to stay two steps ahead of Robin Calhoun, he was fully aware the she was out to get him, but she made a misstep he wouldn't tell her what she desperately needed know until he was safely abroad somewhere *let that smart cunt figure that one out.* Cole Harper, smiled as he looked out the window, this would be his next to last day in DC, he planned to get out of Dodge by sundown tomorrow, *yeah that's the ticket.*

LATER IN THE day Billy Bob and Harry Reynolds were safely ensconced in the safe house in Boston, actually just outside the city in Everett where they hooked up with Kussman's men. The house was quite large, seven bedrooms in fact, with a couple of outlining buildings where their weapons and explosives were stored. Billy Bob and Harry Reynolds examined the ordnance and found it more than suitable to do the job they had over twenty five pounds of Semtex and the time pencils to denote it.

Satisfied they instructed the Nazis on how to set the explosives in place and to activate the delay switches, everything depended on timing, and they had to have the charges in position within five minutes after they seized the target, to keep the authorities at bay. Timing was the most crucial component of the operation, everything was predicated on precision.

But Harry Reynolds had a severe problem deal'n with Kussman's men he told Billy Bob he was not comfortable work'n with them, Billy Bob asked what was the problem and Harry Reynolds told him, "They're fuck'n Nazis man, that's the problem." Billy Bob said, "So what, we need every swinging dick we can get, our guys were dead, we don't have time to train anyone else, those other SOS folks are talkers not doers, you think Max Bedford, Reverend Blount and those types can handle this kind of shit, hell no, they freeze up in a heartbeat or break camp."

"It's personal man, I can't get behind these assholes," Billy Bob asked him, "What do you mean personal, you just met them you don't know these guys from a can of paint and you're talking personal, what in the hell are you flapping away about here?" Harry Reynolds went solemn and told Billy Bob, "Those Nazi bastards, killed my grandfather and two of his brothers in WW2 man, that's what I'm flap'n about, they killed my dad's dad."

"That was a long time ago, you got to get over it and move on...," Harry chopped him off, "If that's your logic then why did we start a war with the United States about some shit that happened over a hundred and some odd years ago, answer that if you can."

That caught Billy Bob off guard he thought on it for a moment and finally said: "You have a point there, but this is about the future not the past, we're fighting this war to gain something." Harry Reynolds: "Gain what exactly, Billy Bob?" he was very serious about his objections. Billy Bob said: "Freedom that's what and if these Nazis are willing to help us gain that freedom I'm down with using them that's what Harry." Harry wasn't hav'n it but he kept his thoughts to himself and said, "I still don't like it, but I guess I'm willing to go along to get along," Billy Bob: "Now you're talking the right shit," and pat him on the shoulder and they left the storage area on the way back to the house.

13

Please, Please, Please

Washington; Greenville, SC

IN WASHINGTON THE following morning Skeeter sat in Jessy's hospital room, he had been here for two days, he needed to go home and freshen up. Jessy's situation improved a lot, she was in stable condition the doctors were encouraged by the fact she hadn't digressed any since the operation to remove the bullets. They checked her vitals, temperature, blood pressure, pulse, respiratory and oxygen saturation every hour since she emerged from the operating room, they told him the prognosis was she'd fully recover from her injuries and they have to wait for her to emerge from the coma.

Emboldened, Skeeter Macklin decided to dash home, hit the rain room, change clothes and come back to her side, first he'd go visit the baby, the hospital had asked him what the little girl's name was he told them that would be Jessy's call and to wait.

The nurses like that.

He reluctantly left her room and willingly went to the maternity ward.

AT NINE THE previous evening Robin Calhoun was on a disposal and she spoke with Moses Blount in Charleston, she had emailed him and told him to call her from a pay phone because his might be monitored. The reverend left his antebellum home and drove to the nearest 7/11.

"Robin that's a lot of money to give him," he said, they discussed Cole Harper's demand for a million dollars and future millions. She said, "What could I do other than agree, he left me with no choices, we need that info, so we will just have to give it to him, but I have a surprise in store, he will not enjoy any fruits of his extortion, that is for sure, trust me on that."

He glanced up, saw a couple approach, waited until they'd past and then said: "I hope you have a way to dispose of the body, we don't need any trails that lead to us," she laughed and said back: "There will not be a trace of Cole Harper after he is taken care of. You remember what happened to Janet Miller when she tried to blackmail us, well that is the same way we will get rid of Cole Harper."

"Yes I do, that was very ingenuous of you, no body no crime, I think you said at the time." She laughed, "A little trick daddy taught me back in the day, it is still foolproof and always will be. You know that bastard made me pay for his lunch. Well slick Cole Harper will be lunch this time tomorrow that you can bank on."

"Speaking of banks, if we give him the money and he's eliminated how will we be able to retrieve the money from his account?"

Which was a *very* good question, Robin Calhoun told him: "His offshore account believe it or not is in Belize, the good doctor's cousin is the bank president, and I am sure for a hundred grand he will play along with us especially when the money came from the doctor."

The reverend asked: "And you know this how?"

She was delighted to tell him, "When we were intimate he told me all his business, I am sure he has forgotten that, since he told me when he was smashed trying to out drink me one night," he told her, "Robin you are one of a kind always thinking ahead, the mistress of the double cross," she had to consider whether she like that and then said, "I prefer beguile it sounds softer don't you think?"

"Yes it does, I'll make the transfer in the morning, is there anything else?" Robin Calhoun said, "I'm glad you asked, we need to make sure once we get the info, we are careful in revealing it, the only one who needs to know is Billy Bob, so make sure you stay tight lipped about the schedule and the attack, understood?"

Moses Blount told Robin Calhoun: "No other ears will hear of it, I know I have a tendency to be over zealous in my sermons, but I promise there will be no mention of the impending doom, I'll save the fire and brimstone hyperbolic talk until it's over, then I'll crow," Robin Calhoun told the reverend: "Fine, I'll call you in the evening, Moses, good night now."

IN THE COMMUNICATIONS room back at the Barn, Andrew Wong woke up his computer as he stood over the console with his eyes peeled for the whereabouts of Billy Bob Broussard, the trail had gone cold since he boarded the Gulfstream at Dulles, before he could track him at Logan International he disappeared in the unknown.

The search for the pair had intensified, Andrew Wong notified the Massachusetts State Police and all law enforcement agencies in the area were on the lookout for Billy Bob and Harry Reynolds, per the general's orders they were declared wanted dead not alive. All law enforcement officers were ordered to kill them on sight, no questions were to be asked, instant liquidation was the standing order issued to all parties involved in the search. Mad Sam Falk meant it when he said: "Take no prisoners."

COLE HARPER WAS in his cubicle at the DOT and checked the schedules, he knew the information was constantly updated and he wanted the latest to give to Robin Calhoun.

The thought of becoming an instant millionaire was eye pop'n he'd packed one suitcase last night and was ready to leave everything behind once the money was wired to his account. He had checked it five times since he arrived and was quite anxious, could he trust Robin Calhoun to fulfill her end of the bargain, he knew he'd never receive the other money from her, but that was alright, he told her that to watch her squirm on pins and needles in the restaurant, *I loved sticking it to the bitch.*

Although at one time he was in love with her, that love turned to distain when he learned she used him because of his position at the DOT. That heartless bitch didn't love anything but power, and this confederacy nonsense. That was the extent of her affections, oh yes, she worshiped the memory of her parents the ones responsible for creating this monster, he said in silence as he looked around the office.

It was now twelve thirty, most of the staff was at lunch, he was invited to go with them but begged off, he had to catch up on some back work. Cole Harper wanted to hit the door as soon as the money hit his account, he plan to drive in his new to him Maybach to Atlanta and catch a flight to Europe, he'd called a shipping company to have the Mercedes transported to Monte Carlo, where he intended to set up shop, live the high life, a man of private means, who would devoted himself to the pleasures of nightclubs, expensive holiday resorts, female company and play the role of an international playboy. That was the plan and it was a good one. Cole Harper had his future mapped out he liked the road he was get'n ready to travel.

But unbeknown to him his adversary had plans for him also, and they didn't include any exotic lifestyle in his future, in fact she planned to cancel his future with an exotic demise in mind. What really lurked in her heart was Robin Calhoun wasn't going to be taken by a small time hustler, *not me, not now, not ever.*

He checked his account again and his heart skipped, there it was, a cool million had been transferred into his account, Cole Harper was now a bone fide millionaire, hot damn, he was all smiles and so nervous he couldn't control his happiness. Cole shut down his computer, grabbed his coat off the rack, climb into it donned his cap, and looked around the office for the last time and moved for the elevator. This was it his circumstances had changed in an instant, now it was time to change his environment.

The lift opened, he stepped lively across the lobby and out the door, he'd call his boss later to inform him he had quit and apologize for not giving a two weeks' notice. He was in a hurry, he parked the Maybach in a garage six blocks away and quick stepped in that direction. Cole Harper millionaire, it had a ring to it, it kept ring'n in his head. *Wow*, he said in silence *I brought it off*, now to make his getaway.

And two hours later he tooled on eye 85 through the Virginia countryside on to Atlanta, when his smartphone trilled, he looked at the caller ID, it was *the bitch*, and he ignored it and kept on motor'n south. He wanted to put as much distance between him and Robin Calhoun as possible before he spoke to her. Just before he got on the plane, he'd ring her, and give up the info, not a moment sooner. He knew his life depended on it, she'll be after him the instant she got what she needed.

Robin Calhoun was ruthless, he was well aware of that, so every second he gained meant the longer he would live if he stayed in the States, his only option to continue living was to get out of here as fast as possible nothing short of that would do. He was run'n scared he had reason to be Robin Calhoun was after him with cruel intentions in her heart.

The smartphone trilled again he paid it no mind and kept his foot on the gas.

The phone chirped over and over, Cole Harper was not going to answer she'd have to wait until he was safe inside Atlanta International, then, and only then would he speak with her. This went on for ten minutes finally he shut the phone off and laughed.

Let her steam while he made for the border.

INSIDE ROBIN CALHOUN'S townhouse she fumed, she heard herself say, "This bastard is trying to renege, failing to carry out his end of the agreement," she had just completed her tenth call try'n to reach him, she returned from Capitol Hill about five minutes ago, where she put in an appearance and called him several times from the Senate floor, now his phone was say'n the customer was not receiving calls at this time and to try later.

What to do, what to do?

She was super pissed, she called his office and was told no one had seen Mister Harper since noon, again she was stymied.

How could he, cross the double crosser?

This was not play'n out right, she had to come up with a solution to this nightmare, but what was the answer, if Cole Harper made off with the money and didn't reveal what she needed to know all was lost. She had to find a way to get that info and quickly, Billy Bob was hyped, if she didn't come up with it, she knew he was a loaded gun and he would go off the leash and do something rash that would jeopardize everything, he was a time bomb.

What to do, what to do?

COLE HARPER HAD been on eye 85 for seven hours travel'n at a steady seventy five, the Maybach was on the outskirts of Greenville, South Carolina, he was hungry and hadn't eaten since this morning, he stopped twice to refuel, the car's twelve cylinders needed constant feed'n, but that was alright he loved this machine and he'd look good tool'n along the French Rivera in it, the Mercedes would be a babe magnet, what a life ahead, just then red lights appear in his rearview. "Oh shit," he said as he pulled over to the shoulder, halted, killed the engine and waited for the officer to give him *a ticket* and he'd be *back underway*.

He sat there and watched in the side view as the highway patrolman exit his car, stepped his way, tapped on the window, Cole lowered it and the officer said, "I thought you were Senator Calhoun, this is her car isn't it?

Cole Harper said smoothly, "Yes it is officer she lent it to me a make a quick trip to Atlanta on some official business for her, wonderful automobile, how fast was I travelling?" The cop said, "I clocked you doing seventy eight, eight over the limit - you say she lent you her car to make a trip?" Cole Harper said, "Yes sir, that's correct, I have to be back in Washington tomorrow afternoon, that's why I was perhaps a little heavy footed," he was trying to ease his way out of this, suggesting he had close ties with the junior Senator from South Carolina, hopefully the cop would go for it, give him *a warning* and send him on his way.

The officer looked down into the interior and said, "Could you show me your driver's license sir," Cole Harper said, "Why of course," reached into his inside jacket pocket, took his wallet out, opened it, took out his license and handed it to the cop. He looked at it and said, "I'll be right back Mister Harper," and shifted back to the patrol car Cole Harper watched in the side view and waited. And he waited.

He waited some more, the tension was kill'n him, *what's tak'n this cop so long to run my license, get out, handover the damn ticket and let me continue*, Cole Harper said in silence, at that moment, he noticed the officer approach with his hand on the butt of his gun, *what's this*?

The cop walked up and away from the car and said: "Please get out of the car," Cole looked up in shock: "What's seems to be the problem officer?" He asked as he opened the door, stepped out into the glare of the highway patrol car's headlights, "Come around to the back, place your hands on the trunk, and spread your legs," the cop demanded, Cole Harper said, "Come on officer is all this necessary for a speeding violation, I happen to work for the Department of Transportation and I know the law."

The officer pat him down and said, "Well if that's the case you should know the law about stealing an automobile," Cole Harper's whole body went slack, he stumbled, the officer had to catch him, he helped him up and told him to put his hands behind his back, he complied and was cuffed.

"Look sir, there must be some mistake...," the cop cut him off: "Yeah I'd say so, stealing the senator's car was a big mistake and driving through her state was an even greater one, Mister Harper you are indeed an idiot," as he led him back to his vehicle, he opened the door and did the ceremonial thing all cops do, he placed his hand on Cole Harper's head, guided him into the car, so he wouldn't bump it as he slid into the backseat and the door closed.

It closed on a lot of things, his dreams and his life.

The officer went to the Maybach, let the window up, took the keys out of the ignition, closed the door, locked it, and walked back to the patrol car, got in and drew away from behind the Benz into the traffic headed to Greenville, to book Cole Harper for grand theft auto, speeding and possibly one or two federal violations.

IN WASHINGTON AT that precise moment Robin Calhoun was on the horn chartering a jet to Greenville, she had received a call from the South Carolina Highway Patrol's office, her car had been found, one Cole Harper was driving it, and said she had given him permission to drive it to Atlanta, she said that was *preposterous,* to arrest him and transport her car to the Greenville Highway Patrol offices.

Robin Calhoun after she hadn't heard from Cole Harper and wasn't able to reach him called and reported her car stolen, she knew he'd be driving it somewhere, but *this idiot* drove through her home state trying to make his getaway, *what a clown* she said in silence as she left her townhouse climbed into a taxi tak'n her to Dulles International.

AN HOUR AND fifteen minutes later Robin Calhoun got out of another taxi, paid the driver off and noticed the Maybach parked outside, smiled and strode into the South Carolina Highway Patrol office in Greenville. The cops saw her step through the door and everyone snapped to. The duty sergeant said: "Good evening Senator," Robin Calhoun said back, "And the same to you, I understand you are holding one Cole Harper here."

The duty sergeant said, "Yes ma'am he was brought in about two hours ago," and waited, she looked around the room and asked, "Is the Deputy Commander available?"

He told her: "Presently he's not in Senator is there anything we can do for you?"

"Yes I wish to speak with the prisoner privately I know him and want to find why he took my car?" She said with so much authority in her voice it came out as a demand and not a request.

The duty sergeant was intimidated and said, "Why of course, Senator, I'll have the jailer bring him to a private room where you can speak with him, just follow this officer...," he pointed to a female hover'n over by her desk sip'n ice coffee; "...she'll take you there." Robin Calhoun thanked him, told him to contact the Deputy Commander and have him come there immediately and followed the officer down a series of hallways, finally they came to a private interrogation room, the cop pushed on the door and Robin stepped in, there was the standard table with chairs on each side of it.

Robin Calhoun stepped around to the ones that faced the door, drew her gloves off, climbed out of her mink, laid it on the table, pull a chair out, settled down, removed her sunglasses, smiled and waited for Cole Harper to be brought to her. She thumbed her smartphone, called a local farmer she knew, told him to come with two men and meet her at Bubba's Truck Stop within thirty minutes and thumbed off.

The door swung open, a shackled and clearly frighten Cole Harper stumbled in, "Ah there you are," she said with a grin; he was shocked and terrified to see Robin Calhoun sit'n there grin'n away at him. He shuffled over with the assistance of the jailer and sat down, the jailer asked Robin, "Do you want me to remove the cuffs and shackles?" She considered for a moment and said, "No, now please leave us," the officer turned on his heels and did just that.

"Well, well, what have we here, a car thief, shame on you Cole, running off with my Mercedes, why oh why did you do something like that?" Cole Harper didn't answer he was too petrified.

Robin Calhoun sat there grin'n away, finally she broke the silence, "Let see where we are here, as you can see I am free to walked out of here anytime I choose, and you dear Cole can be buried here for, oh, say six months before you are brought to trial and then sentenced to ten years for grand theft auto from the junior Senator from South Carolina no less, that is it in a nutshell, what do you think about your predicament?"

He opened his mouth and this tumbled out, "Robin...why...have...you, you done this to me?" She said, "That is your answer?" Cole Harper in total fear said back, "You agreed to let me have the car as part of our deal, remember?"

"Unfortunately for you I do not recall any such thing, as I remember it, you coerced your way into it, and I never agreed to give you that car." He felt his stomach sink, Cole Harper hung his head and sat there, he couldn't think of anything to say.

"All you had to do was give me what I paid for and we would not be here under these or any other circumstances but no, you had to run away with my car and my money."

He told her: "I wasn't running away with the money I was going to call you when I got to Atlanta, I was on my way to Houston to visit my folks, that's all."

Robin: "A likely story."

Cole: "It's the truth why else would I be way down here?"

Robin: "My guess is you were making some kind of break for it, trying to abscond with my money and my car that is probably the better answer."

Cole: "Abscond?"

Robin gave him a look of displeasure, "Is that too big of a word for you? Try one of these, flee, get away, bolt, disappear, skip, run off, slip away, clear out, departing in a sudden and secret manner trying to escape with my cash and the car I love so." She was into her torture mode he sat there and stared at the wall over her shoulder.

Robin Calhoun knew she had him and had him good, now was the time to scare the liv'n daylights out of him, "So what we have here is a petty car thief and grand larcenous idiot who thought he could do the above without any possibility of him being caught, well here is what is going to happen, I'm getting ready to leave, you are going back to your cell and then you will transported to the most notorious prison in the state to wait for your trial sometime in the distant future," she stood, picked up her coat, struggled into it and carried on, "I will be leaving now, it was so good to see you in this fashion you pompous bastard, you do not feel so vainglorious now do you?" and smiled.

Cole Harper was frightened and desperate so he asked her: "What about the information I have for you?" Robin replied, "Oh so now you want to make nice, is that it?"

And sat back down, she went into her coat pocket, came out with the same pen and notepad she had with her yesterday at the restaurant, slid it over to him and told him, "Now it is your turn to write something down, here is the deal, if you give me the correct information without any hesitation I will drop the charges and you walk out of here with me a free man to continue your journey to Houston, but not in my car, how is that?"

Cole Harper grabbed at the chance with both hands and wrote feverishly, finished, he pushed the pad back to her, Robin Calhoun lifted it up, looked it over and said snidely, "Now that was not so hard now was it."

He went tense and asked the most important question from his point of view, "Do I get to keep the money," she told him, "Why of course, Cole a deal is a deal is it not?"

He sighed and a slight grin creased his face. The door swung open behind him and in stepped the Deputy Commander, "Good evening Senator, you summoned me?"

"Yes I did, I have had an opportunity to discuss this matter with Mister Harper and it appears, I made a terrible mistake here."

The Deputy Commander: "Ma'am?"

Robin Calhoun: "It seems I *did* give him permission to take my car, last night he was over to my house and we were enjoying some drinks, obviously I had too many, this morning when I went to get into my car, I had forgotten that I had told him to go on an earn for me in Atlanta, after discussing things with Mister Harper, he reminded me of that."

The Deputy Commander was lost for words, he had to accept her explanation and said, "What does the Senator want done in this regard, ma'am?"

Robin Calhoun sounded remorseful and told him, "Because of my lapse in memory I have cause this man a great injustice and I am seriously regretful of that, I think the best way to resolve this is to release him, I will take him in my car and we will continue onto Atlanta, my sincere apologizes to you and your department for reacting to my lack of memory, this man has committed no crime."

Cole Harper was overwhelmed by her speech and looked at the officer with a glint in his eye, the Deputy Commander opened the door, told the jailer to step in, he did, he unlocked the cuffs and shackles, and Cole Harper rubbed his wrists and stood up.

Robin Calhoun did the same and shook the top cop's hand, "Thank you so very much I will certainly remember you for your understanding and make sure there will be money earmark for the department in my bill that I will introduce next week, you know how things go sir." The Deputy Commander beamed, "Why thank you Senator, the department could use an infusion of money to meet our current budget target."

The Deputy Commander escorted them out of the building. They stepped up to the Maybach, Cole Harper was elated to have been released and he had a new found respect for his *angel of mercy* Robin Calhoun, so he thought. They got in, drew away from the curb, he watched his nightmare in the rearview recede, the cell that would have been his home, now he rode on with his *angel of death.*

INSIDE THE MERCEDES Cole Harper sat there and thought it over, *to hell with the car,* the main thing was he'd be in Monte Carlo this time tomorrow liv'n it up, he looked over at Robin Calhoun maybe he had her wrong all this time, she saved his behind and he felt a tinge of that old feeling he had for her, but quickly moved past it and moved his eyes back to the highway and kept them there.

She had other thoughts, Robin Calhoun sat at the wheel and thought about how much she would enjoy getting rid of *this asshole* that'd caused her a day full of stress and spoke to her like she was a commoner and not the brilliant person she was, this was biting at her ego, Cole Harper's *going to pay for that* and pay with his life.

Robin Calhoun was not to be trifled with, not by him, not by anyone, that was the moral of this story.

She saw Bubba's Truck Stop blink sign on and off in the distance, turned to him, "Are you hungry, I am, how about it if we stop up ahead and grab a bite to eat?" Cole Harper hadn't eaten since he lunched at Mendocino Grille & Wine Bar yesterday where this nightmare began, so he said, "Yes that would be great," she told him: "Bubba's food is a lot better than what you would have had back in that old stinky jail," she looked over at him and flashed that Robin Calhoun smile.

They drove into Bubba's, parked in a space, got out and strode to the front door, entered, it was your typical highway stop, the joint was full of the usual suspects, truckers, farmers and travelers all grub'n down, some looked up at the woman in the gorgeous mink, a man at her shoulders and went back to feed'n their faces.

The waitress recognized her, "Hi there Senator, so good to see ya, love what y'all are doing up there in Washington, given 'em hell, that's why we keep voting ya in office," Robin Calhoun said, "Thank you, Sally Mae, how are the kids?' the waitress told her, "Growing like weeds, turning my hair grey, you know the usual things chilwren do to their folks."

Robin Calhoun forced a laugh and said, "Some things never change, been that way since the dawn of time." She hated chat'n small talk, but it came with the territory all part of be'n the people's choice.

The waitress said, "Ain't that the true - come I have a nice window booth over here," and led them there, it had a commanding view of the lot, that showed a string of semis parked where the big rigs idled, they settled down and waitress said, "Coffee while y'all look over the menu?" Robin Calhoun told her, "That would be just fine, Sally Mae," and she left.

Cole Harper said, "You know Robin you can be sweet when you choose to be, that was what attracted me to you," she said in silence *this fool is not going to go there is he?* And said to him, "I have my moments Cole, what do you have a taste for?" Chang'n the direction he was headed, she knew *this idiot* still had a soft spot for her, but he didn't know this was the condemned's last meal, so he had better enjoy it.

Sally Mae returned with coffee, filled their cups and asked, "Ready?" They placed orders, him, bacon, eggs, toast and jam, her, ham, hash browns, grits and side of grandma's biscuits and gravy, the waitress went off to fill them.

Robin Calhoun looked over Cole Harper's shoulder noticed a farmer in the standard red and black plaid shirt, with the requisite tooth pick in place, seated at the counter, she nodded and he did the same. Sally Mae returned within five minutes, laid the plates before them and said, "Enjoy," and left.

Fifteen minutes later, Robin Calhoun wiped her mouth, put the napkin on the table and looked at the plaid shirted farmer, nodded again he rose from the seat, passed their table and went out the door. Robin said to Cole, "Did you enjoy your meal?"

"Quite delicious," and she said, "Told you they had good food here, I know all of the best spots in the state," smiled and went on: "Cole could you be a dear and go out to the car and get me my purse," he came back, "That's okay, I'll pay for it, after what you did back there, it's the least I can do," Robin Calhoun told him, "I will not hear of it, besides I kind of enjoy paying for your meals," threw her head back and laughed, he got the joke and said, "Okay, I'll be right back," and smiled all the way to the door, she watched him pass the window, she waved at him as he stepped toward the car, went to the driver's side, opened the door, searched around for her purse, not locating it, he withdrew and looked toward the window held his arms out as if to say *I can't find it*, just then the plaid shirted farmer slipped up behind him and slugged him over the head with a sap, Cole Harper collapsed on the ground the farmer closed the door, two other similarly clad men ran over, lift him up by the armpits, drug him over to a van, toss him in the side door, jumped in and drove off tak'n Cole Harper on the last ride.

Robin Calhoun watched the show, and chuckled, *what an idiot,* stood up, reached in her coat pocket, took out her wad, dropped two tens and a five on the table, made for the door and said to the waitress on her way out, "Thanks Sally Mae, delicious as always," push the door open and heard over her shoulder, "Thanks Senator, y'all be sure to come back ya hear," she stepped to the Maybach, and took out after the van.

IN DIDN'T TAKE long for the Maybach's twelve cylinders to catch up, she slowed down, and followed. Soon after, they turned off the highway onto a country road that led straight to a chicken farm. The vehicles halted at the entrance to the enclosure that housed tens of thousands, Robin Calhoun climbed out of the Maybach and strode up to the van as the men pulled Cole Harper out, he saw Robin Calhoun's slender shape silhouetted in the headlights, his eyes were wide with fear, he looked at her and demanded, "What's going on here?" there was tremendous fright in his voice.

She stared at him for a long moment and casually told him, "Well Cole as they say, this is the end of the line," she let him absorbed that and carried on: "Here's the sequence of events, these gentlemen here are going to take you over to...," she pointed, "...those trees where there is a mulching machine standing by...," she let that sink in, "..., then turn the machine on and shoot you, stuff you in head first, you will be ground into a fine pulp, funneled into a bag, hauled to the barnyard, spread all over it and you will be what they call chicken feed."

Cole Harper yelped, felt to his knees, looked up at her and hollered, "Robin please don't do this, *please, please, please.*" He sound just like James Brown, she bend down, looked him in the eyes and said, "Did you say something, I thought I heard you say something," tears began to stream down his face, he pleaded, "Don't do this, Robin," and grabbed her leg, held on to it, look'n up into her eyes he saw the corridors to hell, Cole Harper, screamed, "I'll give you the money back, just don't do *this*."

She tried to separate her leg from him, but he desperately clung to it, one of the men jerked him away, he remained on his knees with his hands in the prayer position, "You can have the money just let me go, *please*."

Robin Calhoun leaned in close and stared coldly into his face, "Again with the please noise, well Cole I have to run now, but you are not going anywhere but through a bunch of chicken's assholes, you wanted to play chicken shit with me, so now you are going to become chicken shit, bye," with that she turned and stepped off to her Maybach, Cole Harper's body slouched, he babbled incoherent sounds as the men drug him toward the trees, Robin Calhoun stop at the car door, the mulcher roar to life, a gunshot was heard above the din, then the sound of high pitched grinding followed, she smiled, swung the door open, climbed in, put the Maybach in gear, made a U turn headed home and left Cole Harper with a new destination, he won't make it to Monte Carlo because his chickens had come home to roost.

And he had counted them before they hatched.

THREE HOURS LATER in the dawn light Robin Calhoun was tool'n up eye 85 back to Washington, she had Sirius on, the Bose was kick'n, Carol King's, '*You're So Vain*', she waited for the chorus and sang along, '*Don't you?, Don't you?*' And thought about Cole Harper and his vanity that led to his demise, she grinned, turned down the music, thumbed her smartphone, and called Billy Bob. After five six rings he picked up, "It is me, get a pen, write this down," and she gave him the news. Billy Bob said, "Excellent, three more days and it's on," she told him she'd be in touch, thumbed off, and returned to, '*Don't you? Don't you?*' Robin had a good time tool'n up the highway, she was so, so happy.

14

Evil 2 the Bone

Washington

SKEETER WENT BACK to check on Jessy. The split window Vette pulled into the lot, Skeeter saw a space, parked, switched off the engine got out and stepped through the entrance, rode the lift to the tenth floor, walked past the nurse's station, went down the hall, made a right turn, stepped up to Jessy's door, swung it open and he heard a weak, "Hi honey," Skeeter stop for a moment, then ran to the bed, "Jessy, Jessy," she said, "Yes it's me..." he cut in, "Don't try talk right now, just listen, this is so good, words elude me at this moment, but...," he had the hardest time express'n himself, so he stopped try'n, Jessy laid there, Skeeter stroked her hair and kissed her forehead.

She came out of the coma about an hour ago while he was away and she waited for his return, she told the doctor not to call him, she wanted it to be a surprise, Skeeter and Jessy inhaled each other, love and happiness filled the room. The sun shone through the window casting the light of life, the room was bright with joy.

Mister and Missus Macklin remain quiet and let the moment speak for itself.

IT WAS JUST after four went Robin Calhoun came through the door, she closed it, kicked off her Ferragamos, climbed out of the mink and threw it over a chair on her way to the bar. She hadn't had a drink to celebrate her victory over Cole Harper and the pending one over the United States she grabbed the bottle, walked around and settled down on the sofa, put her feet on the coffee table, crossed her ankles and hit Jack hard.

She enjoyed the drive back she was on her all time high.

Robin Calhoun thought about the end game, she believed she'd made all the correct moves on the board to end the game in her favor, victory was within reach, once the event went down, *checkmate* United States, her belief in self had her delusional to point of blindness, all she could see was her as the paladin of a lost cause.

Her plan to resurrect an idea whose time had long passed, was delirium, Robin Calhoun failed to recognize her insanity. Her mind was warped early in her childhood that young mind absorbed all the poison her parents fed it, and now she was that poison personified, the culmination of years that caused ruin, injury, and pain without shame, she was the end result, evil, that created misfortune and destruction on small and grand scales. Her repugnance had no bounds she was the epitome of vile, evil to the bone.

When all else fails there's delusion and Robin Calhoun was sick with it.

She put the bottle down for the third time, thought about the night ahead, she had to get off and release her desire to be carnal and lewd, after she ordered Cole Harper's death, Robin was as they say, *horny*, the excitement of know'n she had the power to summon the reaper, and could decide who died was sensual to the extreme.

What to do about this urge that needed scratch'n she threw her head back, closed her eyes and fantasized being Aphrodite, her name at the playpen in Virginia, her secret getaway where she resided over the bacchanalia, in fact she called it *The Bacchanal*, she had three faces, Robin, Scarlett and Aphrodite, three ladies of extreme. She could see herself in the Girdle, smok'n hot, orchestrating things, the maestro who led the debauchery, a symphony of lust was on her menu tonight, Robin

Calhoun, reached for her cell, someone picked up, "Yes," she said, "The party deluxe is on, call all the players have them at the spot by eleven," she heard that someone say, "Yes Aphrodite, it shall be as you wish, wine, women and wrong," she chuckled, "Delicious," and then said, "I arrive at midnight straight up, so have things under way when I get there," and rang off.

Robin Calhoun stood up, and stepped into the bathroom, ran water in the tub, stared at herself in the mirror, she saw the face of pure evil there, but of course it mattered not, she loved what she'd become, everyone wants to be the hero in their own story.

SKEETER COULD HARDLY get the words out, "Jessy it's so wonderful to have you back," she told him, "Being able to come back is a good thing honey," and he said, "It's a miracle, an absolute miracle that you and the baby survived, the doctor told me in most cases like this, either the mother or the baby generally don't make it, the odds of both coming through something like this are astronomical."

"You know me, I always beat the odds, and what were they against me landing the perfect husband?" she said and smiled up from her bed. They stared at one another for the last hour, the doctor came in a couple of times to check on her progress, satisfied it was going well, he told them to go easy at first, so they just sat there, no words past between them, but they communicated nonetheless.

"You know I could actually hear you talking to me, but I couldn't respond, but I clearly heard you telling me about the baby, I think you said she has my eyes and nose, and something about going after the person responsible for this, am I right?"

Skeeter Macklin told her, "Yes and I knew you could hear, me, I knew it." She hadn't seen the baby as of yet and was anxious about that, the nurse told her they might be able to bring her little girl to her sometime soon for a brief visit.

"Wait until you see her, Jessy, she's so beautiful and precious, I have two ladies to love and look after, I am so happy, I really can't put it into words right now." She said, "I know honey, we'll be one happy family, you me and...," she stopped mid sentence *the baby has been named yet* so she went on: "What do you want to name her?" Skeeter said, "I want you to decide that, have you chosen one yet?" Jessy said: "I had a couple of names in mind, I'll wait until I actually see her, then I'll make a choice." He said back, "I like surprises, I'm sure it will be the right name for our little girl." In walked the nurse and she asked, "We brought the baby to you, are you ready?"

Jessy rose up, looked at door as the nurse rolled the bassinet, a special transport incubator into the room and Jessy saw her baby girl for the first time and began to cry. She looked at her and said to Skeeter, "She's indeed beautiful if do I say so myself, she just a little miracle...," she stopped, looked at him and said, "That's *it*," Skeeter: "What's it?" Jessy: "That's her name, Miracle, *Miracle Macklin*."

He beamed and the nurse nodded in agreement, "I love that, should we record it, now?" Jessy told her, "Yes please, no other name fits, she's definitely a miracle, and her middle name is...," she paused and then said, "Macayla, Miracle Macayla Macklin, that's perfect." Skeeter, "If I know my Irish, Macayla means a gift from God," and Jessy told him, "Precisely, she a miracle and a wonderful gift to us, honey."

Shamus Macklin smiled at his two ladies and he was a happy man indeed.

THEY'RE ACTIVELY LOOKING for you and Billy Bob Broussard," the voice told Robin Calhoun.

"What do they know?" she asked, and the voice told her, "A lot, they've concentrated their search in Boston and they that know he and Harry Reynolds are somewhere in the vicinity, they've alerted all the law enforcement agencies in greater Boston to be on the lookout for them, and orders to kill on sight have been issued."

Robin Calhoun was in her Maybach return'n from her Virginia romp and she felt relieved and was quite happy about things then her smartphone sounded. Now that euphoria evaporated by the news the voice was telling her, Robin said, "Kill on sight?"

"Yes, they have a secret unit called the Eradicators hunting for them to kill with impunity."

"The Eradicators, what in the hell is that," she asked.

"It's an ultra secret unit that's at the president's disposal to do away with anyone who's deemed enemies of the State they have the green light to kill at his command."

"What is this, some James Bond bullshit?"

"No, it's real shit, and they're not bullshitt'n about finalizing everyone involved, the axiom is, take no prisoners." She asked the voice. "How long has this been whispered?" The voice told her, "It's beyond whispers, it's a hot and heavy discussion that has been going on since the attack on Washington, in fact the Eradicators are the ones who stormed your compound in Virginia and attacked the caravan on the highway, and I'd say that's well beyond the whispering stage."

"I need to know their every move, to stay ahead of them, we are two days out from creating the most devastating event in American history," the voice told her: "I don't need to know the details, just pay me my money," Robin Calhoun said, "It is always the money, with you, do not you have a sense of loyalty to the cause?"

The voice said emphatically: "I have certain sympathy for it, but it's strictly business with me, and I need the money before any more info will be forthcoming from my end."

Robin: "The next payment will be given after we meet face to face, not before."

The voice: "Why do you insist on face time?"

Robin: "I do not trust any more transfers of money into accounts, I just had an episode concerning that and I will only handed the money over face to face."

The voice was reluctant to agree but the money was the issue, so the voice said, "Very well, when do you want to meet and where?" Robin Calhoun: "Tonight at the Jefferson Memorial at eleven thirty after the Park Rangers have left," the voice: "All right, I'll be there and bring the money in cash."

Robin Calhoun told the voice, “I will have it with me, but I need pertinent information about what this bastard Bohannon is up to.” The voice told her, “I’ll try to make you happy, later,” and the voice was gone. She turned into her townhouse driveway, killed the engine and sat there, thought about the pace of things, the situation was on a *short fuse* the day after *tomorrow* was D Day for the SOS. She believed once the event happened and devastated Boston, the United States would sue for peace under the threat of other attacks. She’d deploy Kussman’s bio weapons if they didn’t submit to her demands.

She was exhausted from frolick’n at the playpen the party was over about nine this morning, now she needed some rest. Then Robin Calhoun would get back into her Commander in Chief role and bring this to a quick close. She climbed out of the car, padded to the door, opened it, and stepped inside. Robin needed to soak, she walked across the living room, taking off a garment here and there, she went past the bar straight into the bathroom, ran water, stepped into the tub, she put her head back, submerged up to her neck, closed her eyes and let things flow past her mind’s eye.

Robin Calhoun had a range of concerns, time was run’n quickly through the hour glass, she had bet and bet big, on things falling into her column, there had been a few hiccups, but all in all things were on track. All that needed to be accomplished was Billy Bob Broussard seizing the target and being prepared to destroy the intercity of Boston with a massive terror attack on her orders. She felt confident they’d bring it off before the US could prevent the event from happening. She had planned this with such precision it had only a five percent chance of failure. *So what* if FBI tailed Max Bedford, he was a pawn to be sacrificed in the name of the cause. The only thing that mattered was the final objective, the reestablishment of the Confederacy, everyone was dispensable except her of course, and she was the one, who had the plan to set the South onto greatness, surpassing its former glory, she would be remembered as the true Savior of the South, not these sacrificial lambs who were means to an end, *so what if they died* she thought as she soaked in the tub. Robin Calhoun only cared about her wellbeing and the southern way of life that existed over a hundred and fifty years ago, it was her birthright, she was the chosen one, as Cody Calhoun had told her over and over in her childhood, *yes*, Robin was convinced of *this*.

IT WAS JUST after noon when Skeeter told Jessy he had to see General Falk, she said: "Do you have to do this, I mean the baby and I are alright...," he cut in: "Yes I know and I'm elated about that, but this is something I have to do, this man almost killed you and her, I can't let him think he gotten away with it." She said: "Why not let the general handled it, he has other assets at his disposal, Mickey's more than capable of dealing with the situation."

"That's true, but it's my family, this bastard almost destroyed, I'm the one who must avenge that, not Mickey, it's a personal issue with me, and I will get this guy so help me." She knew Skeeter well, once he made his mind up, there was no way to dissuade him, so she said, "Okay, but please be extra careful, Miracle and I survived one incident and I need you here with me to raise her, she needs her daddy just as much as she needs me." Skeeter Macklin looked at his wife and told her, "Believe me, I will take of care of this and nothing is going to happen to me, I promise you that, now I have to go and see General Falk, get caught up on what's going on, join up with Mickey to bring this to a close."

Jessy looked at him, "Alright go, do what you have to do, we'll be right here when you get back," Skeeter bent over, kissed her and said: "I'll return after I've spoken with the general, I shouldn't be gone more than a couple of hours," and stood up, looked at her, smiled, turned on his heels and headed back to the Eradicators to kill Billy Bob Broussard who almost killed everything dear to him, Skeeter Macklin was on a mission.

GENERAL SAM FALK sat at his desk when Skeeter stepped into his office he had just left Jessy at the hospital and raced to the Barn to meet with him.

"Ah there you are Major, come have a seat," Mad Sam said as he entered, "How're the wife and baby getting along?" Skeeter got him up to speed, the general said, "Miracle, hmm, very apropos Major, I like it, I like it a lot, quite fitting."

Skeeter Macklin took a seat opposite him, "Yes sir, I'm very fortunate to have had them both survive this incident, now I'm here to find his guy and do what's necessary to neutralize him and this so called SOS, what's to be done, sir?" Mad Sam reached for a set of documents and handed them to Skeeter, "Here's your independent contractor agreement, just sign it, and of course it's in triplicate, the government's way of doing thing, always in excess." Skeeter took the papers, he didn't read them, just signed on the lines, and handed them back to the general, who said, "Now to the business at hand, we have it on solid information that this Billy Broussard and his sidekick are holed up somewhere in the Boston area, we haven't pinpointed their location as of yet, but like all crime players they'll make that fatal mistake and we'll take them out of the game."

Skeeter Macklin asked, "Sir would it be alright if I led the search for them? I know Captain Stovall is the lead dog on this, but I liked to spearhead it if possible."

The general looked up from his desk, "I don't envision a problem with that, I'm sure the captain will understand and gladly subordinate himself to you on this mission, you and Captain Stovall are a formidable team as I recall." Skeeter told him, "Yes sir, General, Mickey and I have had quite a successful run together he's one hell of a marine, sir." Mad Sam said, "That's a consensus Major - speaking of rank I intend to promote the captain at the conclusion of this affair, your thoughts?" He answered: "Sir, I think that's an excellent decision, one that's long overdue, the captain has been in graded for I think five years now, in my opinion he deserves a promotion."

Mad Sam: "You know your opinion weights well with me, Major, considered it done, now on these SOS bastards and bitch."

Skeeter: "Bitch, sir?"

Mad Sam: "From what we've able to glean, there's a female mastermind behind this whole affair, who that is hasn't been determined as of yet, she's the one calling the shots according to the FBI."

Skeeter: "A woman is the leader of this organization? That's a new one, sir."

Mad Sam: "From what the FBI told the president they overheard two conversations with a major player in this, up in Boston, one Max Bedford, you may have heard of him, he's this over the top right wing kook who's lives a handsome life hawking fear and hate on the radio."

Skeeter: "Yes I'm aware of him sir, I listened to him once and once was enough, the fact free paranoia and poison that comes out of his mouth is beyond comprehension, I don't know what's goes on in a bigot's head sir, but it must be a sick, sick, world."

Mad Sam: "My sentiments exactly. He knows the FBI's on his tail, so we'll have to wait until she makes a mistake and this affair will be brought to a swift and successful conclusion."

Skeeter: "Wasn't the Bureau able to trace the calls, sir?"

Mad Sam: "She's cagey that one, she only stayed on the wire for a few seconds and was gone before they could get a bead on her, but like I said she'll make a slip up and we'll root her out and roll this wacko up, end of story."

The conversation continued in this vain for another ten minutes or so, then Mad Sam said: "Well that about sums things up, check with Captain Wong and see if he's made any progress as of late," Skeeter rose, "I'm headed that way sir," and withdrew.

CAUGHT UP IN the whirlpool of war, Robin Calhoun was in attack mode, with her fantasies fulfilled, she got back in the saddle ready to ride across the finish line, when the event went down the race was over, she was the filly going to take it to the boys and show them her behind.

Robin Calhoun was ready to govern, she needed to start her selection process, deciding who was going to assist her, only true blue, die hard southerners like Moses Blount and his ilk, unwavering in their loyalty need to apply. She'd pick someone who was staunch, smart and articulate as her vice president, someone she knew and could manipulate, the only person who met that criteria was Senator Jake Carlisle, her lover, *yeah yeah that* Jake Carlisle, her love toy, *perfect* she thought and reach for the phone.

AT 1600 PENNSYLVANIA Ave Jasper Bohannon wound down his day, he had a lot of balls in the air, several crises needed his attention, but the SOS issue was big ball number one, the others were important but none could bring the country to its knees like the SOS, they were a definite threat to existence of the United States, a spark that could ignite into something that could get out of control. Whatever they planned for Boston had to be stopped at all cost there was no margin for error, President Bohannon was confident, he knew, Mad Sam and his Eradicators were up to the task.

He was in the Oval Office where he sat with Taylor Jackson, as they critiqued the day's events and went over tomorrow's schedule, the Chief of Staff asked, "Do you still want to meet with the Ambassador of Afghanistan at eleven?"

Cold wind blew at the windows, the fireplace was a glow, and they sat on the sofas seated over the oval rug, President Bohannon answered, "Yes, there's much to discuss, multiple problems that have to be addressed by his government, I will be emphatic about the area of concerns that are undermining our objectives there, so yes I will see him at the appointed time, what else is burning besides the usual daily issues?"

Taylor Jackson side stepped that and asked, "Any developments on the SOS front?"

Jasper Bohannon told him the latest, "We narrow our search down to Boston, General Falk has concentrated his efforts there, and all indicators tell us that's where they plan something catastrophic. But we are prepared for them, I ordered the Massachusetts National Guard on alert, they're ready to move out at a moment's notice, we have the entire city and surrounding environs clocked. All our technologies are in place if they come into the light they will be spotted, then it's the end of the SOS." Taylor Jackson said, "Good riddance too bad rubbish is what I say sir," the president looked at him, "That about sums it up, Taylor, good bye to an evil ideology and its adherents, the country needs unity not disintegration to meet the times ahead in this century and beyond, we have to maintain that closed fist, not fingers splayed there's no strength in that. These criminals can't win at the ballot box so they resort to the cartridge box."

Once again Taylor Jackson was awestruck and mulled that over, he finally came to his senses and said: "Mister President each and every day you never seize amaze me with your take on things, believe me, sir, you are an original thinker, par excellence, I'm duly impressed," Jasper Bohannon look over at his friend, "But not to any great extent, I presume," and laughed at his own wit, it did him good to hear laughter emit from him, this was the first time he had any hints of enjoyment since the Inaugural Party and the meet with General Falk here in the Oval Office. The SOS was front and center, there was no room for levity, not now, maybe later but this was a serious matter that called for focus, lasered in on these traitors, who want to impose their will on the people, terrorizing them first, then dictate to them how life was going to be, not free just listen to me. All voices muted but one, the Orwellian voice reigning supreme over the masses.

The Chief of Staff said, "No sir, I truly am a believer in what you perceive for the country, once we put the stamp on this SOS crowd, you'll be able implement your vision for the country." Jasper Bohannon nodded and said back, "When do you intend to leave?" Taylor Jackson looked at his watch it told him it was ten forty, he said, "Well sir, if you don't need me for anything further I would like to leave and meet Sally for a bite to eat," the president: "Fine by me, I'll just go over my thoughts for my meeting with the Afghan Ambassador and retire, see you in the morning." Taylor Jackson stood up, adjusted his tie and said, "Goodnight Mister President," and sidled to door.

AT ELEVEN THIRTY all was quite as Robin Calhoun stood on the Jefferson Memorial marble steps, a cold wind drove across the Potomac, white clouds driven by the wind sailed across Washington as she huddled inside her mink wait'n for the voice to appear, her eyes made the circuit. From behind, she heard, "I see you've made it," Robin Calhoun turned around, not seeing anyone, she said, "I have no time for games, show yourself," the voice said back, "Let's not get impatient here, I'm making sure we are alone, you know we can't be seen together," Robin looked over her shoulder trying to locate the origin of the voice. She walked around the monument, the moon peeked through the clouds, a finger of light pointed him out in the darkness and she saw amid the shadows of the evergreens, the voice. Robin Calhoun crossed into the dark and in those shadows stood one *Taylor Jackson.*

"What news do you bring?" asked Robin Calhoun right off the top, Taylor Jackson told her: 'We'll get to that, where's the money, I don't see it." She looked at him and said: "Do you really think I would be standing out here with a briefcase full of money do you?" he thought about it and said, "I guess you're right, but where *is* the money?" Robin Calhoun wasn't here for games, "In my car, okay, now start talking."

So he did and sketched in the events.

When his story ended she asked, "Shamus Macklin is a member of these so-called Eradicators?" Taylor Jackson said, "No, he's the former leader of them, the most feared man in the unit, Billy Bob shot his wife and they almost lost their baby, happy he's not."

This part of the story she didn't believe, Billy Bob had assured her he had killed Jessy, she choose not to address that and stayed on point about the here and now.

"I recall seeing them together in Brazil he did not strike me as being dangerous...," Taylor Jackson jumped in: "That's another mistake you've made don't underestimate these people they're totally without mercy, the unforgiving as it were."

"I am not taking anyone lightly Taylor, I guess you cannot judge a book...," she let him complete the thought in his head. He told her: "Well the worm has turned it's very personal with him, and I'd beware if I were you," she spat: "Well you are not, so save the scary stories for the kiddies," and she looked him hard in the eyes, "How can I get to them before they can attempt to foil things?"

He broke the news to her, "You can't, the genie is out of the bottle, and he not granting wishes, he's kick'n ass and tak'n names but he's not bring'n a pencil, he's bring'n grief." She looked at him and saw a hint of humor in his eyes when he told her what she was up against.

"You are kidding me?" He told her, "You ever know me to kid?"

The whirlwind was about to descend.

Taylor Jackson told Robin Calhoun, "This is where I get off," her head jerked back like she heard a shot, "What do you mean, get off?" and he told her: "To be blunt, you're on your own, I've done all I'm going to do, this is the last time we'll speak I have to protect myself, and right now I don't have any faith in your success with this madness." That tore it, "Madness you say, that is what you think is going on here, madness?"

He said, "Well if it isn't sanity, therefore it must be insane," he paused and carried on: "Now take me to my money and let's forget we ever knew each other."

Robin Calhoun felt he was run'n scared so she tried to tact in this direction, "You need to man up, I am paying you a ton of money, I expect you to...," he rode over her: "Don't try to challenge my masculinity with that drivel, now enough chatter take me to the money," and he led her by the elbow to the Maybach.

Robin Calhoun and Taylor Jackson two traitors of a feather stepped off together into a dire future, as they passed in front of the Jefferson Memorial they failed to notice the inscription that adorned the frieze, *"I have sworn upon the altar of God eternal hostility against every form of tyranny over the mind of man."*

AT ROBIN CALHOUN'S townhouse just after one in the morning, Jake Carlisle sat look'n at his heart's desire, man, how he loved this woman, she was the essence of femininity and her sensuality was off the charts. She stared at him and invited him into her sphere of inference, the spell and the die was casted.

Robin Calhoun was on a tight schedule every moment was spent with reason, all roads led to Boston, she had no time to waste, Robin told Jake to be at her place by twelve fifty-two, and he was there on the dot.

After she left Taylor Jackson she drove home with vengeance in her heart, *no one* runs out of the SOS, and lives to tell about it. Taylor Jackson was the fast track to his appointment with the reaper. Just as soon as she assumed power he would knock on hell's door sent by Robin Calhoun's own hand. Taylor Jackson was a double traitor, he'd betray twice before, he would betray again.

"So you are probably wondering why I called earlier wanting to see you," Robin said," as they sat on the sofa, Jake Carlisle laid his arm across the back and said, "I hoped you'd call,..," he went romantic not prepared for the real intent behind her question, "...it seems when I am away from you all I do is long to be back with you." She like that, it played into her plans perfectly, *this love struck puppy* would follow her anywhere, so she rolled with it, "Jake I have something to tell you,..." she reached for her glass, worked it and carried on, "I never love any man other than my father until now, I found myself suffering from missing you, I realized it when I was in Brazil, I am in love, madly in love with Jake Carlisle, and it felt so good," she smiled at him and Jake fell apart.

Robin Calhoun opened her negligee, her arms and legs went wide, and Jake Carlisle felt into those arms and legs and went wild. When it was over she rubbed his hair, "Jake I love you, honest I do," she smiled at her own deception, her intent for it was not far away, staying in her l love you mode Robin Calhoun told Jake Carlisle, "I think it's time I got married, and the man I want to marry is you," he rose up and said, "Is that a proposal?" and smiled, she returned hers and told him, "Yes it is, I want to get married today, first thing in the morning," that stopped him cold like a deer caught in the lights.

"What, in the *morning*." His voice rent the air and he found the thought appealing.

"Yes, this something I decided when I returned...," that was a lie, but she knew it would hit his sweet spot, "...I want this more than anything else in the world, I want to be the wife of Jake Carlisle, please do not disappoint me," that did it, he was ready to wake up the Justice of Peace, his hopes, dreams and prayers had been delivered, fulfilled and answered. He didn't take time to think it through, his love for this woman was so genuine it blinded him to what he loved, a person who loved nothing but her own madness. Robin Calhoun the mistress of manipulation needed him as her husband so she could reveal to him her SOS plans knowing he could never testify against her in court if things went south, so to speak. Robin Calhoun had to cover all bases, Jake Carlisle, her husband the Vice President of the New Confederacy was the goal.

He was so smitten he led the way and Robin Calhoun happily followed tak'n her where she needed to be, "Let's do it, like as soon as the office opens up, we can probably be married by twelve, this is going to catch the entire city, no, the world off guard, the cable news channels with be frenzying I can hear them now calling it the Power Marriage," and laughed, this was exactly what Robin Calhoun had in mind, she told her husband to be, "That sounds so wonderful," and ran her tongue in his mouth light'n a fuse and the explosions went on into the early morn, by nine they had a marriage license in hand and by eleven twenty they were man and wife, the CC's had gotten married, Robin Calhoun and Jake Carlisle the power couple of Washington.

LIKE HE PREDICTED the city erupt about their marriage, the vultures fed on it for hours, the story appeared above the fold, it was the talk, spoken about at great length, sliced and diced by the pundits and the commentators, it was none stop word noise.

Robin Calhoun had made a coup of epic portions she was rid'n high, they were in the honeymoon suite at the Hay-Adams Hotel, and from here they could see Lafayette Park and the White House, Robin Calhoun, the new Missus Jake Carlisle was ready to spring another surprise on husband, she eased into it say'n, "Now that we are married there can be no secrets between us, right?"

Jake Carlisle rose on an elbow, looked at his wife with puppy love in his eyes, "Of course, we must be honest with each other from this day forward," his new wife anticipated his answer and told him: "Well I have a major secret to reveal," she paused and made him wait for the bombshell, "You know who was behind the attack on Washington?" He told her: "I've heard your theory several times now, has it changed from al-Qaeda?"

Robin Calhoun studied his face in the pause and then detonated her bomb, "No, it was me and my people," this was met without warning, he was blown away, Jake Carlisle's jaw dropped, he fought to find words to response, but they eluded him, he laid there in disbelief, surely his wife was kid'n in some morbid way to test his sense of humor, what he saw in her eyes wasn't funny, tragedy dwelled there instead of comedy.

Jake Carlisle caught himself and tried to control the volume of his voice he told her: "Surely you jest," she told him with coolness that sent bolts of cold thunder down his backside, "No, I am serious the SOS was responsible for the attack, not any foreign entities."

Jake: "SOS?"

Robin: "Saviors of the South, a secret organization started by my father years ago, we have been plotting to resume the Civil War and the mortar attack was done under my instructions." His face changed as if the sun had slipped behind a cloud.

The astonishment on his face was something to see.

Jake: "I don't believe a word of this," he fought hard against the truth he heard.

Robin: "Believe it, every word is true, I will tell you the entire story," and so she did, when the story was completed he was thrown by it, and at the point of tears. The woman he loves and now his wife was a murder, an unremorseful mass murder, no less, a cold nausea seeped through him, and he had a bad, bad feeling in the pit of his stomach.

She told him, "Being a southerner, I sure you understand, why this had to be done."

He looked hunted and said: "I understand a lot of things, but this is not one of them."

Robin Calhoun pushed a tendril of hair back from her forehead, her voice was flat and colorless when she told him, "Well I intend to see this through to the end without reservation, and we will set off a WMD that will deliver us to victory in this war."

Jake Carlisle, at this moment realized this woman was certifiably insane. He gave her a long look, saw unholy joy on her face and it frightened him so.

What to do, what to do?

He swung his feet onto the floor, lowered his head between his legs, *where's this conversation go'n*? Robin Calhoun told him: "And I want you to serve as my vice president," his face clouded, an expression of gloom settled over it, he didn't like this; he didn't like it at all. For a while there was silence between them, a minute sloth past, then two, finally she spoke into the quite, "With you at my side, we will be able to govern like no other tandem in history, the President and Vice President of the New Confederacy."

There was an edge there he hadn't notice before, bars of afternoon light cut through the Venetian blinds' slats and anger was beginning to break though now, he walked about the suite, his anger overflowed like white hot lava, "You are totally off your rocker Robin, this is lunacy, there will never ever be a New Confederacy, that's a long dead experiment, a bad one at that and may it rest in peace. You've got to stop whatever it is you intend to do, how could you dream this up and then follow through on it? *Tell* me."

The conversation moved from uncomfortable to excruciating for her. This was not the reaction she expected, not even close, she had anticipated him receiving the news with glee and would gladly participate in her scheme, but he sounded like somebody who didn't get it. Had she made a mistake in tell'n him, in marrying him, in trust'n him with her secret, Robin Calhoun realized she had to make adjustments and quickly, so she said, "That was my wedding present to you, I gave the man I love, what I love, and how is that for loving you?" Damn. She hit him straight in the heart with that, it momentarily buckled his mind, he shook it off and told her, "You lay this on me on the happiest day of my life, our wedding day and this is where I open the box and out jumps Jack the maniac and I'm supposed to be happy, well I'm not." He exploded and came apart at the seams, Robin Calhoun rose from the bed, stepped up to him, placed her hand around his neck, stuck her serpent into his mouth and kissed him passionately, Jake Carlisle pushed her away, for once the little head didn't overrule the big one, his voice tightened, "Your seduction will not win the day for you, I have to go to clear my head and think, I can't do that right now here with you," he put his clothes on, while he told her the news.

The silence was a heavy one. The room was wrapped in quite.

She let the silence ride and then her answer came boil'n out of her, hot with rage, "Today is my wedding day, I shall have my cake and eat it too, if you dare to tell anyone what was told to you on this our wedding day, this day will be your last day, you do not want to know what I am capable of, so heed those words wisely."

The words washed over him like Niagara Falls, an atmosphere of brooding quietly hung over the scene, he struggled into his coat as he made for the door and at his back heard, "I want you at the house by seven, do not be late, we have to plan our strategy for running the government of the New Confederate States of America," Jake Carlisle, the broken hearted groom, stepped out of the room and the door closed.

15

Judas Kissed

Washington

DARKNESS WAS BEGINNING to fall as Jake Carlisle rode the streets of the nation's capital going over what happened at the Hay-Adams with Robin Calhoun, his wife, the bride from hell. He wrestled with the fact that he was married to a supreme criminal one beyond the borders of dementia, a raving lunatic was his wife, this, hurt so.

She had a host of illusions. And the danger lies in her believing them and she had convinced others to believe in them too. His new bride, was criminally insane, she had to be stopped that was the only solution, he could never be a party to what she'd conceived and executed, Jake Carlisle was devastated this day, his wedding day, he heard himself say: "My wedding day has turned out to be the ugliest day of my life."

How could this be?

He told himself this when he stepped out of the room: *I'm stepping out of her life too.*

Jake Carlisle knew what he had to do there was no debate about that, he'd notify President Bohannon right away and tell him what he knew, that was the only solution, he had to shelve his pain and try to prevent greater pain from being inflicted on Boston, suppress any personal anguish he was suffering through. Jake Carlisle the senior Senator from Virginia knew he had to stop his wife, how that hurt, from doing the unthinkable; he drew into the curb, grabbed his smartphone and thumbed the digits for the White House, straight away.

GINNY CRAWFORD THE president's private secretary came into the Oval Office on the run, "Excuse me Mister President but Senator Jake Carlisle's on line two, and he says it's urgent that he speaks with you," Jasper Bohannon was behind the Resolute Desk working a pile of papers, Taylor Jackson sat on the sofa, his ears perked up at the mention of the senator's name, his marriage raised brows and start tongues wag'n, and here was the groom want'n to speak to the president on his wedding night, this was *not good* he told himself, Taylor the traitor Jackson heard the president ask, "What could he possibly want," Ginny Crawford shrugged and Taylor Jackson's heart rate went warp, the president said when he punched Jake Carlisle in, "Good evening Senator, and congratulations on your wedding."

"Good evening to you sir...," he drove right past the congrats, paying it no mind, swallowed hard and plunged straight in, "...I have something of the utmost importance to discuss with you, it's a matter of national security."

Jasper Bohannon: "National security did you say?" Taylor Jackson fidgeted on sofa, his radar went hot, and he listened in closely.

Jake Carlisle: "Sir I have vital information that you need to hear as soon as possible."

Jasper Bohannon: "Vital information pertaining to what exactly Senator?"

Jake Carlisle: "I'd rather not get into specifics on the phone, but one word should suffice for now."

Jasper Bohannon: "And what word might that be?"

Jake Carlisle: "Boston."

Jasper Bohannon: "Stay on the line, Senator," he put him on hold and said to Ms. Crawford, "Clear my calendar for the remainder of the evening," she walked back into her office and closed the door, the president looked at Taylor Jackson, "The Senator just said the magic word, I need him here right away," Taylor Jackson felt his stomach sink, everyone knew about Jake Carlisle and Robin Calhoun marriage this morning and now he wants to see the president on this night of all nights, *something's very, very wrong here* he said in silence as the president punched Jake Carlisle back in, "How soon could you be here Senator?"

Jake Carlisle: "I can be there in ten minutes or less Mister President."

Jasper Bohannon: "Good, I'll see you went you arrive."

The president switched off, and looked at Taylor Jackson, "Seems the good senator has information about Boston that couldn't wait until tomorrow, quite odd that, don't you think, this being his wedding night and all?"

Taylor Jackson was taken aback by the call also, but in a totally different way than his boss, this had blow back written all over it, not good, not good at all, he said: "This is his first call to you since election night, he's your moral enemy on the political front, I'd say this is strange indeed sir, do you mind if I sit in?"

"Of course not, that's what you're here for Taylor, helping me at this pivotal time. We're a team, remember?" Jasper Bohannon smiled at his friend.

Taylor Jackson's face dropped, the president's question sliced through him like a hot knife through butter, there was a reluctant smile on his face, "Yes sir, that's me ever ready to assist in any fashion I can," but his thoughts were on the pending visit of Senator Carlisle. He had to know what was going to be said, was Jake Carlisle aware of his wife's past and present plans? More important did he know of *his* involvement?

The president stood up, "Quite curious this, what information could he possibly have about Boston?" He walked over to the sofa, settled down opposite his Chief of Staff, "Your thoughts on this surprise visit," Taylor Jackson forced a grin: "It's rather strange to me that he'd take timeout from his wedding night to request an urgent meeting, it must be of the extremely important, sir." Jasper Bohannon stretched his legs, crossed his ankles and said: "This is very intriguing my main political opponent is giving me a heads up about something that has been kept close to the vest, what could he possibly know about Boston in this regard?"

Some inner caution prompted Taylor Jackson to say, "Well sir we'll hear shortly, I don't wish to speculate on his pending appearance."

"I agree, speculation never pans out anyway, so you're right, let's wait and see what the good senator brings with him." Before the conversation could be taken any further, Taylor Jackson asked, "Could you excuse me for a moment there's something I must attend to on the personal front," the president said, "Why of course, we have a few minutes before the senator arrives." Taylor rose, shifted across the room, opened the door and went into the corridor that personal matter was a phone call to *Robin Calhoun*.

Which he made, the smartphone went at her townhouse and rang insistently but she failed to pick up, seems she had reached her limit of Jack and passed out on the sofa. "Damn it," he yelped, looked up and saw her husband approach, headed his way.

Taylor Jackson outstretched out his hand as he stepped up, "Good evening Senator, the president waits just inside," Jake Carlisle shook his hand, "Good to see you Mister Jackson," who read him to see if he could detect anything in his eyes or voice that he should be immediately concerned about, satisfied there weren't any telltale signs, he smiled, swung the door open and shepherd him into the Oval Office.

Jasper Bohannon looked over his shoulder, "Ah there you are Jake," he said amiably, "Welcome to the Oval Office, a room you would be occupying if the election had went in your favor," as his eyes toured the room the senator wasn't sure what to say, so he didn't say anything and extended his hand, the president stood up, shook it and gestured for the senator to be seated, they settled down and Jasper Bohannon got right down to business, "So what is so pressing that you needed to see me Senator?"

He said with a pained look and element of strain in his voice, "Sir I have some damaging information to convey," the president: "So tell me," which he did in the finest detail, so great the shock, he had their rapt attention, he rolled on relentlessly, relief seemed to ooze out of him like dirty water, and then there was not a sound in the Oval Office for another full minute, then Jake Carlisle tried hard to smile but failed miserably.

There was a heavy and awkward silence, finally Jasper Bohannon said, "Senator Robin Calhoun is the leader of the SOS, quite incredible to grasp, and I'm lost as to what to say other than this is a most unhappy revelation, this is painful, and it must be excruciating for you on a several levels, Senator."

Taylor Jackson tried to put real regret in his voice, "Senator I echo what the president said, I'm deeply sorry for this agony you must be experiencing but it was the correct thing to do coming here telling the president, a mark of a true patriot, you put country above your personally feelings, Senator, we thank you for this, the country thanks you," not hearing any possibilities that the senator knew of his involvement he was taking the lead to keep them off his trail, so he sailed on: "Senator, there will be difficult times ahead for you personally, but the world will know what heroic thing you've done, saving the country further anguish, did she happen to mention the actual target?"

This was a smooth segue into the crisis. Jake Carlisle made a brave show but a shadow passed over his face, "No she never mentioned the actual target, the last thing she said was she'd reveal her plans to me this evening she expects me home at seven."

The president listened raptly, assembled his words he had to make the tough call, it was no struggle, Senator Robin Calhoun must be apprehended tonight, by his clock tomorrow was the day she scheduled to played the terror card, but this was hearsay she had to be caught red handed nothing short of that would do, Taylor Jackson spoke again: "I understand a lot of things I understand why people rob banks, but this is beyond comprehension, I can't fathom the rationale in this regard...," he made a show look'n at his watch.., "Mister President I have an appointment with the Budget Office at six, about the numbers they've crunched to insert in the press conference in the morning concerning the new job creation bill you submitted to Congress, I shan't be gone long, an hour," he stood up, the president said, "Of course, get back as soon as you can," with that Taylor Jackson stepped off getting himself out of the room, he had to see his crime partn'a let her know what the hell was *go'n down* and cover his ass *now*.

IT WAS JUST after five thirty, sharp knocks went at Robin Calhoun's door, followed by insistent chirp'n of the door bell, she was stretched out on the sofa, where she passed out after she returned from the hotel, after two minutes of this she snapped to, rose up, thinking it was Jake she shuffled to the door, opened it and there stood Taylor Jackson.

He shouldered his way in and stepped through the doorway, she watched his back with her face gone slack, he walked to the sofa, seated himself, and he plunged in spill'n the news. Robin Calhoun tried to gather her thoughts while she listened to this tale of betrayal, but Jack still had a hold of her and wasn't letting go, she struggled to focus as he plowed on, when he concluded his narrative he looked at Robin Calhoun.

She bridled.

The silence hung heavy in the room, finally from over by the fireplace her voice went.

"This is the most horrible news I could ever receive, brought to me by the one who had ducked out yesterday and then drug himself into my home with his hat in his hand, now sits there and mopes."

Robin Calhoun was having a bad, bad day, it was blatantly obvious things weren't going to plan her husband had blown the whistle, turn informer, committed treason, and stabbed his wife in the back.

When she spoke next her voice was cold and hard and utterly ruthless: "We need to silence this traitor, who Judas kissed me on my wedding day, not only has he broken his vows, he has turned his back on his country, and this man cannot continue to live."

Taylor Jackson knew she was right Jake Carlisle had to be dealt with severely and soon, before the trail led to his doorstep he had to join in, the demise of Jake Carlisle, was the only option on the table, nothing could save him, but his death and then Taylor Jackson realized the real threat stood only feet away, Robin Calhoun.

Taylor Jackson took stock of the situation, he was in deep doo doo and he knew it.

So he manufactured agreement, "You're right Robin, he has to be silenced, you don't have much time to do what's necessary, I need to return to the White House and see what's going on, I been away a little too long."

Something moved in her eyes, but her face betrayed no emotion, there was a moment of silence as if darkness had stepped into the room, Robin Calhoun said into the stillness, "You do just that, let me know the moment he leaves and what they are up to, I will handle it from there."

He was relieved he didn't have to participate in the actual kill'n and being here gave him the creeps, he knew at this moment he was in the presence of raw evil. He stood up, "Well I should be getting back," and made for the door, swung it opened and he was gone.

Robin Calhoun stood at the fireplace, hostility prevalent in her eyes, there were hot tears in them, the rage in her was a living thing, she had to step it up and call Billy Bob to implement the plan as soon as possible that was her only way out or so she thought.

ABOUT TWO MILES away Taylor Jackson raced to the Budget Office to fetch the numbers to get back to the White House, on the way over to Robin Calhoun's house, he ran all the possibilities of how this scenario would play out, he went over all of it in his mind, none provided any assurances, and he was up the creek without a paddle.

Taylor Jackson was in a pickle of epic proportions, his stupidity had led him to this point in time, accented with money, and money was the lure that caused him to turn on the president, shit this was a big time problem, the only solution was to lay it on thick to Robin Calhoun so she'd boil and kill the immediate threat, Jake Carlisle and then something had to been done to neutralize her. *Robin Calhoun* had to *die* too and *soon.*

HE RUSHED INTO the Oval Office and heard the president say: "Ah the man in question...," hearing that his heart fluttered with fear it almost made Taylor Jackson turn on his heels and dash for his life, "...where've you been?" Jasper Bohannon demanded as he looked at his watch, Taylor Jackson eyes toured the room, *where's Jake Carlisle*?

He said, "Sorry Mister President, I stopped to grab a bite, ran into an old friend and lost track of time," it sounded lame but that's all he could come up with at the moment, he was shook to hear he was being discussed, the president sat with the Oscar Valdez, Head of Homeland Security when he crossed the room.

"Good evening, Oscar," he said as they shook hands and he sat down, "What did it I miss?" Taylor Jackson's inquiring mind wanted to know what was said in his absence and *where in the hell is Jake Carlisle*?" Jasper Bohannon told him, "We were just discussing the imminent arrest of Robin Calhoun...," Taylor Jackson stepped in: "Arrest, sir?" That caught him off guard it was Oscar Valdez who put in. "Yes the FBI will excuse a presidential arrest warrant for her as soon we get the evidence."

The Chief of Staff pulled a face, his mouth went dry: "How's that intended, sir".

There was silence.

And it was Oscar Valdez who spoke again with a certain pity in his voice: "Taylor we have to be extra careful, Robin Calhoun is after all a United States Senator and we have to hermetically seal her where the evidence against her is beyond question and silences the naysayers before they can get off a word."

Taylor Jackson was on the edge, "And how to we propose to do that, Oscar?"

Oscar Valdez looked at Jasper Bohannon, who nodded: "Senator Carlisle agreed to set her up this evening she told him she'd would tell him about her plans and hopefully she'll tell him the SOS moves as they relate to Boston," Taylor Jackson processed this and kept his voice neutral and said with hope: "Once she admits her involvement with the green light apply?"

It was the president who answered, "No we need her alive to extract information from her about their past activities, if we eliminate her it dies with her." Taylor Jackson said, "As always you're correct sir...," he was in a box, a small box with nowhere to turn. How could he get out of the Oval Office to warn her? No excuse came to the rescue, he carried on in a quiet voice, "...just how do we, as you say Oscar hermetically seal her?"

"The FBI will be outside listening to and recording every syllable said, when she admits her crimes on tape, she's sealed up airtight, no debate, it's over, ball game."

For Taylor Jackson, this was horrible he needed her dead, *not talking* her head off.

Taylor Jackson's head was on the anvil and a big, big hammer was about to drop.

He thought he was under attack from everywhere including his own shadow.

AND AT SEVEN THIRTY that evening Jake Carlisle car's pulled into the driveway he sat and sighed, climbed out, sighed again, his footfalls took him to his wife's front door.

Across the street FBI Special Agents Tomas Aguilar and Brenda Henry sat in an unmarked car, they were posted here per the Director's orders, the orders were to record the conversation that was about to take place in Robin Calhoun's home and when she admitted explicitly her participation in the mortar attack they would move in and arrest her. Metro Police had two unies parked around the corner, the trap was set.

EARLIER IN THE Oval Office after Taylor Jackson left on his mission to see Robin Calhoun, the president and Jake Carlisle continued the conversation, "Senator, here's what I propose we do, would you be averse to wearing a wire to record your pending conversation with your wi...," he switched gears, "...the senator when you return?"

The senator told the president: "I'd rather not, sir, is there any other way to capture it, other than me wearing a wire, she's ever clever?" Jasper Bohannon rose up, stepped to Resolute Desk, picked up the phone, "Ms. Crawford, I need to speak with the Director, right way," she replied in the affirmative and he said, "Thank you," turned and looked at the senator, his distraught was a heavy thing, hang'n in the air above him like a dark cloud, Jasper Bohannon told him, "Senator, there are no words one could say that will soothe what you are experiencing so I won't attempt to pretend to know what it feels like, so I'll confine our comments to matters of state and not your personal anguish," the senator replied: "Thank you sir, we have to prevent the senator from doing more hurt to the nation, that reigns supreme, my personal situation painful as it may be at this moment, is nothing in comparison what another attack would do if it were to happen so soon after the first one, the nation could fracture, preventing that is priority number one."

Two men from opposite ends of the political spectrum who now sat in the Oval Office knew they were on the same side, protecting the nation, as Jake Carlisle said, it was the only thing that was important, all else mattered not.

This was huge business.

Just then the phone twittered, the president rose, stepped to the desk, picked up, "Director, there's been a major break in the SOS case," and in the fewest sentences he brought him up to snuff. The Director listened and told the president they'd use a laser microphone, no problem there. And Jasper Bohannon told him, "I'll have the senator come to your office to fill in pertinent details, and I need real time updates," and he heard the Director say, "Not a problem, send the senator over, sir," and they clicked off. Jake Carlisle left the Oval Office and headed for the J. Edgar Hoover Building.

Duty bound.

WHEN TAYLOR JACKSON left her with the bombshell, Robin Calhoun came to her senses, picked up a disposal and said to someone who answered, "Sent cleaners to my home within the next..," she looked at the grandfather clock, "...at eight o'clock," and rang off, into the fireplace the phone went, she'd need a cleanup crew to remove Jake Carlisle's body after she killed him. She grabbed another cell and called Billy Bob Broussard, he answered on the first ring, "Yes Chief," and Robin Calhoun told him the latest, when she finished he replied, "Sounds like you severely misread him, this is a major bump, we have to accelerate matters," he took the thought right out of her head.

Robin Calhoun told him now, "Yes, we must do this by two thirty tomorrow morning, the target will be available at that time, I'll tend to matters down here, you are under orders to seize the objective and hold it until you hear from me, understood?"

Billy Bob told her, "Loud and clear," and she told him this, "You are a true southern patriot, worthy of the same respect as our glorious warriors of the past, your name will be mentioned in the same breath with Lee, Jackson, Longstreet, Hood, Forrest, you are my Beauregard," and he said, "That's high praise, release me to do what I came here for," she told him, "The world waits to hear from you, long live the New Confederacy."

THE DOOR SWUNG open to his touch, Jake Carlisle entered the foyer and he saw Robin Calhoun at the fireplace, she gave him a sharp look, she was not happy and it showed, with ice on her tongue she said: "Look what the cat drug in, my brand new husband has come home to his lovelorn bride to consummate their marriage."

He advanced into the room, positioned himself near the front window as instructed by the FBI so they could plainly hear, she stepped away from the fireplace, settled on the sofa and looked up at him, "You have been a busy little bee, buzzing around spreading secrets have you not?" She said with a hard note of disappointment in her voice.

Jake Carlisle's face on the instant turned deathly pale, *how did she know* about his conversation? He quickly assessed things *Taylor Jackson* quick stepped across his mind; this was a serious, if she knew all. Her silence served as his answer.

Staring directly into his eyes she asked with a cutting edge to her voice, "How could you betray me, my love?" Jake Carlisle asked, "What are you talking about?" Robin Calhoun her voice dripped in scorn told him: "I know about your meeting with that bastard Bohannon after you left the hotel you scurried over to the White House like the rat you are." She was on the verge of telling him how she knew but hesitated and drew back: "I have spies everywhere, did you really think you could actually get away with this treachery?" She told him with a mocking smile hooked firmly in place.

Jake Carlisle felt like he'd been electrocuted, before he could take the conversation any further, a mirthless chuckled and a dry sob bubbled up from her throat and with her face set into a steel grimace she asked him: "I thought you loved the South?"

He told her the news, "Robin you didn't do your homework. My family stayed loyal to the Union, we loved the South, but we loved the United States more."

He let his declaration hang in space.

She left it there for a moment, mak'n him wait, and then she said, "You said you loved me," and he told her, "Oh I love you, yes I do, but I love my country more and I would never betray that love for any personal feelings I may have for you."

His voice contained an edge that wasn't there before.

The look on her face was terrible to see, she told herself, *this little shit, acting tough* and told him: "You seemed to be confused, when one is prepared to die for their country, that is love dear," there was a terrible threat in her voice, Jake Carlisle gave back, "That's the first thing you've said that makes sense in all the word exchanges we've had today, Robin you've done a terrible thing and yet you sit there without remorse, soulless, face it Robin you're no patriot, that only exist in your head, out here in reality you're a *hatriot*, a coldblooded one at that."

"That is your opinion and one that I do not share," her expressions blink and changed like a fiber optic sign, like he just told her some kind of perverse joke, something stirred in him, filling him with white hot rage he spat out a laugh but it contained no happiness. "That's nonsense on stilts, Robin you're truly insane to believe you're not a wanton killer who has caused so much pain to an entire country, to its people and to think it's not, is the Mount Everest of arrogance."

She looked at him as if the statement was an insult, her stature was taller than that, "Call it what you will, my confidence seems to have you confused, but the thing is my love, you will not be around to find out. You have tried to spoil my plans, but here is the news, things will proceed but you are doomed not to know how they turn out, why..." she reached under a sofa pillow and her hand swung up with a *huge* 9mm Ruger.

Jake Carlisle's eyes grew wide his mouth opened in shock, "*PUT THAT GUN DOWN*," his eyes took in the pistol, she pointed the 9 at him, and smiled, her smile resembled a shark's grin, it was terrible to see but a shark's eyes couldn't have been colder then hers.

The Special Agents listened in, when they heard Jake Carlisle holler something about a gun, Tomas Aguilar and Brenda Henry, flung the doors open, drew their guns and raced across the street.

Inside the 9 spoke, the slug churned from the barrel and whapped into the wall above his head, Jake Carlisle with a fearful look in his eyes couldn't believe it, *she actually pulled trigger* and then she pulled it again, the 9 spoke again and again, more rounds issued from the 9, stitching bullets across his chest, he was punched back against the wall and burgundy pedals were in full flower on his tan overcoat, a hollow pop went from the barrel, he clapped his eyes and Jake Carlisle's head exploded, a red mist filled the air, Robin Calhoun let the Ruger speak for her and he got the point.

The silence that followed might as well have been a nuclear bomb.

The phone purred.

This was where the other shoe dropped, the FBI ran the steps guns at the ready, Tomas Aguilar push on the unlocked door, they rush in, and saw Robin Calhoun holding the 9, squeez'n the trigger, requesting more rounds from an empty magazine, the phone purred, it was Special Agent Brenda Henry who ordered, "Drop the gun, I'm only going to tell you once," and took aim, Robin Calhoun looked to her left, then back down at Jake Carlisle, there was a moment of dead air and she let the Ruger slide out of her hand, the agents rushed over, through the open door, in the middle distance a siren lifted on the night air, outside two cop cars arrived at speed.

Back inside, the phone purred, as Brenda Henry searched and cuffed Robin Calhoun, she said to Tomas Aguilar, "Maybe you should answer the phone, it's rang about ten times now," he holstered his piece, stepped across to the bar, picked up, the line was dead. Frustrated Taylor Jackson hung up he was call'n to tell Robin Calhoun that the FBI was outside listen'n; he finally had an opportunity to excuse himself from the Oval Office and ducked into the nearest restroom and made the unanswered call.

The Special Agents Brenda Henry and Tomas Aguilar tried hard not to let their emotions leak in, but the sight of the two senators, one seated on sofa and the other lying dead up against the wall was enough to fracture even the most granite of hearts.

Senator Jake Carlisle the true patriot in the room, had died for his country like other soldiers on the battlefield, a real hero, whose love of country far exceeded his love for the woman who shot him, like she told him, when one dies for their country that was true love, and now Jake Carlisle the late Senator from Virginia had proven her point.

Outside a siren howled to a stop, inside the cops and the suspect knew this was bad.

It was a ten minutes to twelve situation. Five alarm headlines throughout the media.

16

Unknown Quantity

Metro DC; Boston

RED WHITE AND blue lights winked outside the townhouse, the vultures were here in full force, their vans clogged the streets, forensic techs sifted the scene, a meat wagon stood at the ready, and it was pure catnip for the media. A throng waited in the cold as they watched and whispered about the biggest thing to ever happen in their hood.

The news percolated through to the crowd, among them, were the two cleaners Robin Calhoun had ordered to her home at eight o'clock, but this situation was beyond their abilities, no amount of scrubbing could clean this up. No way. No how.

The FBI tried to put a lid on it, but too many of her neighbor's cells went ballistic and the word hit the Blog at the speed of life, this story was way, way too big to contain.

After the Special Agents secured the crime scene, Brenda Henry phoned the Director seeking instructions on what to do with the suspect, she heard the Director say on the other end of the line, "Get her out of there now, do not let the media ask her any questions, transport her to

Quantico." The agents quickly bundled a shackled Robin Calhoun into a van and zipped off before the vultures could flock and begin to feed.

Jake Carlisle, the late Senator from Virginia was bagged and tagged then loaded onto a gurney. The paramedics rolled him out of the townhouse, the gurney was lifted into the ambulance and it silently drew away with the groom who died on his wedding day, he was right when told himself earlier, this was truly the ugliest day of his life.

TAYLOR JACKSON WAS nearly out of his mind, he sat listen'n to the president's conversation with the Director, they were on speaker, what he heard was traumatic, Robin Calhoun was *alive* and in the FBI's *custody*. He listened intently and heard the president say, "It's most disquieting to hear of the senator's death, this has really evolved into a story only a mad man could write, or should I say a mad woman. Senator Carlisle was an American of the first magnitude. The nation has lost a great man and a real patriot." Jasper Bohannon was suffer'n a personal guilt for suggesting to Jake Carlisle to return and trapped Robin Calhoun, if only there had been another way.

The POTUS: "He gave his life so his country could live."

The Director: "It is truly a sad day sir the nation lost one of its finest servants, now what to do with the perpetrator of these hideous crimes."

The POTUS: "She'll be prosecuted to the fullest extent of the law, and in this case I shall ask the Attorney General to seek the death penalty."

The Director: "I agree Mister President, but first we need to extract that information from her tonight, I fear we have no time to waste on that front."

Jasper Bohannon knew things were tight, they had to get Robin Calhoun to talk by any means necessary, and nothing was off the table in that regard, she had to be broken and quickly, her threat to Jake Carlisle about going forward with her plan was ominous indeed, she had to be dealt with severely to make her tell them what they needed to know and without delay. It was a no holds barred situation this was total war.

The president had said take all threats seriously.

Jasper Bohannon, the POTUS assumed the lead.

He told the Director: "I will instruct the general to use any and every resource at his disposal to get her to tell us what we need to know, before sun up we'll have that information and the names of all of her accomplices in this treasonous affair."

Taylor Jackson eyes went wide, *I'm on the list* and somehow he had to make sure his name was not revealed, but how could he prevent that?

What to do, what to do? The Director's voice floated out of the speaker and Taylor the traitor Jackson heard this.

"In the annuals of our nation's history this is the most tragic example of betrayal, Robin Calhoun certainly ranks above any of the traitors of the past, sir."

The president told him, "My thoughts coincide with yours Director, in the league of traitors I'd say she's at the head of the class and everyone associated with this treachery will be drawn and quartered to use an old English term when dealing with those who betray their country."

Taylor Jackson was petrified, a distressed look occupied his face, his involvement was crucial to Robin Calhoun's plans, his betrayal was on par with Cole Harper's, and he knew there was considerable dirt under his fingernails, dirty dirt.

The Director told the president, "This is a most unthinkable thing I've ever heard."

The POTUS said, "It's unthinkable until you think about it."

Taylor Jackson was think'n hard about what to do.

He was in a jam he had to think things though.

He was jammed up between a rock and a hard place.

Taylor Jackson had painted himself into a corner and he had just run out of space.

ROBIN CALHOUN SAT nude in a dark room with a bag over her head, sequestered somewhere at the Barn, she was placed here after the FBI dropped her off, her legs were shackled to the chair's and she was cuffed to its arms. Excruciating electronic noises thundered from the speakers, it was loud as the interior of a jet engine.

She sat on the floor in the van as they crossed Washington DC, the capital she served and wanted to destroy, Special Agents Tomas Aguilar and Brenda Henry rode in silence, she didn't know where they were tak'n her surprisingly Robin Calhoun was not frightened. She realized the moment Taylor Jackson told her about her husband's betrayal, she was caught and there was no escape. Whether she killed Jake Carlisle, they were com'n to get her, so Robin Calhoun made the sacrifice, herself, to the cause. The woman practiced what she preached, no doubt about that. No matter how ill she was, Robin Calhoun was a diehard fanatic willing to martyr herself for the South.

Inside the bag Robin Calhoun's mind was warp'n and became unhinged, the distortion from the speakers was eat'n into her sanity, she could hear faint voices in her head wail in pain and they put up a howl beg'n for relief from the insufferable noise. She recognized the voices that gave utterances of fear and agony. She tried to quiet the conversation between them, the voices paid her no heed, and they vented their displeasure at having to endure the situation Robin Calhoun had placed them in.

She'd been in this position for the last twenty minutes, her tolerance was ebbing, and she tried to muster the inner strength to resist crack'n up, but she was losing that struggle. Robin Calhoun was a verge of los'n her mind. The noise continued for another ten minutes and suddenly things went eerily quiet. She grappled to regain her mental balance she had been subject to tremendous mental stress. Her clothes were removed to further humiliate her and to strip her of all esteem, reducing her to silly putty.

The door swung open smoothly before him with light fall'n into the room, the door closed and Skeeter Macklin shifted up to Robin Calhoun snatched the bag off her head, she winched, her eyes tried to search the darkness. He stepped back, stood behind a bank of flood lamps and hit a switch the room was instantly bathed in blaz'n light. She fluttered her eyelids trying to bring them into focus the glare so intense it seem to burn.

She heard a voice say: "Robin Calhoun you are now in the custody of the United States government, we shall begin a Q&A session, if you don't provide the correct answers you will be put through an arduous process until you give us the info we seek."

Robin Calhoun stormed at him, "Go fuck yourself, whoever you are, I will not tell you a thing," Skeeter Macklin told her: "Talking tough will not benefit you in the least, many a person has expressed your sentiments before and they always succumbed, no question about that, so you can make it easy on yourself or I will make your life a living hell."

Robin Calhoun eyes looked cold, in a defiant voice she said: "Whatever you do it will not make me give you one iota of information, so do what you will, I await it with pleasure." Skeeter stepped in front of the lights she took his face in and said, "So it's you Shamus Macklin." He was thrown that she knew his name and said, "How do you know who I am?" She told him: "I remember seeing you in Brazil at the festival you and that noisy wife of yours, how did you take her death, badly I hope," and smiled. The smile was quite mad, and she obviously meant it. That needled, he wanted to step over, pull his gun and shoot her in the head, but he pushed the thought away from him, his mind was focused on other matters, he schooled his thoughts to focus on the task ahead: "Obviously you haven't heard my wife survived Billy Bob Broussard's attempt to kill her." Her smile faltered for a moment, her smile returned, she glared at him defiantly, "That's bullshit, the bitch is dead you cannot fool me with that," her eyes glittered with hate. With polished arrogance she said: "No way, she lived, her and that baby of yours."

Skeeter Macklin ignored his irritations and told Robin Calhoun: "Believe what you will, the facts are the facts...," Robin Calhoun was not pleased and it showed, "...now back to you and this SOS gang you head, we need to know what your plans are in regard to Boston."

Her eyes settled on him, she braced herself for the obvious question which came in an instant, "Enough chit chat, tell me what are your intentions?" he asked her. Something stirred in her eyes, hate looked at Skeeter Macklin and she told him; "Give it time your answer will be delivered shortly." Nothing seemed to disturb her composure.

He raised a brow at that one, felt his jaw clinch as anger crept into his voice, he said as cold as ice: "During the last administration you were a vocal advocate of water boarding. You stated on the Senate Floor that water boarding was a necessary tool to extract information from the enemies of the United States. Isn't that accurate?" Her eyes widen in fear, he went on: "Being you're a certified enemy of the state water torture is my next option if you don't tell me all you know and reveal the names of everyone involved in this SOS conspiracy now."

After a brief show of thought, she said: "You cannot do that, it's against the law...," Skeeter Macklin bowled her over: "*Law*. You have the audacity to invoke the law when you're guilty of murder, high crimes and treason and shamed the office you held, and you dare to hide behind the very laws you have so blatantly violated against your country."

For the first time her composure broke, "So where is the good cop?" she asked and he told her: "I'm afraid there's no good cop, I'm it, the bad cop and the worse cop."

And with that he stepped back and made a vast show rotating a lamp to reveal a large glass tub filled with water off to the left, above was a robotic hoist, with a smile on his face, not a nice smile he said: "Are you refusing to tell me what we need to know?" She tried to maneuver around the question: "I will not be intimidate by your threats or your deeds, you will not get one scintilla of information for me, but you will know everything you are seeking, up close and personal like, come soon before sunup." Her head snapped at the sound of the hoist mov'n, Skeeter had hit the button operating the hand held switch box, he guided it over to Robin Calhoun, she looked up at the jaws as it approached, her eyes went big a worried look occupied her face and she said: "So I'm going surfing?"

Skeeter Macklin told her, "No, you're going ducking," as he lower the jaws down and guided them into place, they opened and closed on the ring on back of the chair, as Robin Calhoun started to rise, he told her now, "Back in the day ducking was the method used on those thought to be witches and common scolds it was called punishment of women, what we have here is Robin Calhoun a combination of both, a bitch," as the hoist lifted her high in the air. She said, "Don't think you are scaring me with that medieval bullshit, I am ready to die, so dunk me, I will gladly drown myself, you are not getting anything out of me," and smiled.

Skeeter Macklin turned on his cold voice.

"That's all right by me, because you're going to tell me now or tell me later." As the hoist positioned her above the seven foot tank filled with icy water she spat: "You will not get any answers from a corpse," it doesn't get any truer than that, but Skeeter Macklin told Robin Calhoun, "I guess we'll both find out huh," as if to prove his words the robotics eased her toward the waiting water, will suicide or murder be committed, she heard him say into his shoulder mic, "Stand by," Robin Calhoun was lowered into the water, she immediately opened her mouth, she was ready to accept the dark she tried to speed things along, but just as she reached the point of death, the robotics yanked her up out of the tank, she gasped and spit, coughed and caught her breath, her eyes were lit with fear. She panted and coughed, panted and coughed until she was almost breathing normally and in she went again, Robin Calhoun repeated her desire to die and tried to drown herself, but she out came with a yank, she spit and gagged.

The voices returned.

Inside her head they screamed wanting to live, they told her she had no right to kill them, the voices kept at it, and demanded that Robin Calhoun cease trying to kill herself thereby kill'n them, she had no right to make that decision without putting it to a vote.

In the door came three technicians with an internal manual defibrillator, Robin Calhoun met the water for a third time, again she persisted and tried to kill herself, she almost made it. The hoist shot her up out of the water and she went through the routine, cough'n and gag'n, Skeeter Macklin's dark eyes stared into her soul, and he knew she was ready for the final plunge. She hollered, "*WAIT...*," but Skeeter didn't wait and he dunked her for the fourth time, Robin Calhoun's natural instincts to live kicked in overriding her desire to die and she tried to hold her breath. The voices in her head cried: *we want to live! We want to live!* But it was a futile plea, Skeeter Macklin kept her submerged until the dark settled in, she ceased movement, Robin Calhoun was *dead.*

THE HOIST LIFTED her out of the water, the robotic arm swung the chair over and lowered it to the floor, the techs removed the shackles and cuffs, Robin Calhoun's lifeless body was placed on a table, they applied solid gel adhesive pads to her skin, one paddle was placed on the upper right of her chest and the other was placed on her left side, slightly below and left of the chest muscle, then a biphasic shock was applied, trying to reset her heart's normal rhythm sending an electric shock to the heart muscle.

Robin Calhoun jumped with each shock, they were up against the clock, she had been dead three minutes now, and Skeeter Macklin looked on and watched them work feverishly trying to bring her back. More shocks were applied no positive sign was seen, was this a huge mistake and did the information they need die with her?

The shocks were applied every five seconds without any results, the situation was becoming dire, they continued for another minute or so and they were about to abandon their efforts when her body convulsed violently. Her eyes opened and water poured out of her mouth, she coughed and coughed until all of the water was expelled. Robin Calhoun looked up at the bright lights and blinked repeatedly trying to grasp what had happened. The room was wrapped in silence, Skeeter Macklin was relieved to see her breathing again, his gamble had paid off, now he believed Robin Calhoun would tell all.

Skeeter Macklin said, "Did you enjoy your trip to the other side, meet any other evil souls there?" When she opened her mouth it wasn't Robin Calhoun who spoke it was *Scarlett O'Hara*, "Why suh, it was the most frightful thing you could imagine," her accent was a throwback to the nineteenth century, then she hid her breasts behind her arms, looked at him say'n, "Why have you done this to me, suh?" Her question was genuine.

Here he frowned and thought was this some kind of stunt, his eyes searched her face: "So who are you supposed to be?" He asked and she told him: "Why I'm Scarlett O'Hara don't y'all remember?"

He gave her a long level look, "Remember? Remember what?"

"Seeing me at Thomas Norris cotillion two weeks ago?" Skeeter was stunned, he stared back into the past, his mind reversed gears to Americana, the festival at the Norris ranch, and he stopped and zoomed in on the woman in the yellow spring dress sit'n three people away from him. *That was Robin Calhoun.* Strange that, very strange.

Her voice brought him back to the present, "How's your lovely little wife faring, suh, I must sincerely apologize for Robin's actions, I thought it was absolutely despicable." Skeeter Macklin continued to look shocked,

"Robin?" he asked, "Yes, she ordered Billy Bob Broussard to kill her, no account southern trailer trash that one."

Skeeter Macklin hooked a thumb over his shoulder it meant leave, the technicians went out. He watched them go and returned his gaze to Robin Calhoun, whose alter ego told him, "I'm glad she's dead, a horrid woman, the things she's done, I being an eye witness, can tell you she was an insufferable hussy and that Aphrodite, what a slut that one, she died too. I never really liked her anyway, what a tramp."

He asked, "Aphrodite?" And she told him, "Yes she was Robin's best friend, they had so much in common, and did things I can't repeat in polite company, suh." She shivered in distaste then asked in a melodious voice: "Would it be permissible to allow me to put some clothes on? I'm as naked as a jaybird here suh," he was thrown by what transpired before his eyes, it might have been comical under different circumstances, he couldn't think of a thing to say, so he stepped over to retrieved her clothing, walked back and handed them to her. "Why thank you kind suh," she flashed a delightful smile.

She stood, put her undergarments on and shimmied into her dress and waited.

The silence hung between them and he left it there probably to gather his thoughts on how to proceed, if this was an act, it was a damn good one. He decided what the hell and to play along. He'd see where this charade would lead perhaps to a good place, so he said, "Now Scarlett tell me what you know about Robin's activities," with a suspicious tone in his voice. She looked at him, "Gladly suh, she was a wicked, wicked person, I'm ashamed to have known her and she was a disgrace to all that's holy." Skeeter said, "Well tell me what you know." Her voice was flat and she began fill'n him in on what Robin Calhoun had done over the last few weeks, he was all ears and took in everything she said. She went through the details and when she finished he looked at her with new interest, "So what were her plans concerning Boston?" And Scarlett O'Hara revealed the much sought after info. Skeeter Macklin listened to her voice for false notes, her eyes were hot, and the tears came when she concluded her tale, for a moment, time had no meaning...no meaning at all, he fell silent for that moment his eyes lost in thought then some kind of understanding dawned and *he knew* she was telling *the truth*.

THIS IS THE most incredible story I've ever heard, Major," Mad Sam told Skeeter Macklin after he informed the general about what had transpired with Robin Calhoun.

"Do you believe this twaddle?" Mad Sam asked and Skeeter Macklin told him, "Sir, I'm convinced she's telling the truth and that Robin Calhoun is a genuine schizophrenic I believe the medical term is dissociative identity disorder a condition in which a person displays multiple distinct identities or personalities."

"Well I rather be safe than sorry, so let's run with it as if it were true, we can't afford to ignore what this Scarlett O'Hara...," the general shook his head at that, "...has told you, we'll proceed in the affirmative, I'll notify the president and you prepare to leave at once for Boston, we must stop this Billy Bob Broussard bastard from executing her plan. You will be leading the blue team and I'll dispatch the red team to Belize to kill this Nazi prick, Karl K. Kussman, I'm gonna sic Mickey on him."

Skeeter told him, "As you wish sir," he rose from the chair, strode to the door and went out to assemble his team to take down Billy Bob Broussard and his Nazi cohorts.

Mad Sam reached for his Codex, rang for the president the thought of Nazis and Confederates in cahoots, what a nightmarish scenario, this was beyond comprehension. Even Stephen King couldn't pen a horror story such as this he thought. Only a truly sick individual could think this up and have the daring to execute it. Mad Sam believed this was the ultimate in fiction, he also knew it was a true story. This had to be reacted upon with great speed to prevent a most horrific story from coming true.

IN THE OVAL office, Jasper Bohannon sat with his Chief of Staff, he had ordered all hands on deck awaiting the outcome of the interrogation of one Robin Calhoun. The president was aware that the hour hand was moving rapidly and they had to stop whatever she has planned. Taylor Jackson was uncharacteristically quiet since he listened in to the Director's and Jasper Bohannon's conversation. His anxiety was at an all-time high, he had reason to be on edge, she could expose his participation in her plot and he'd be doomed to incarceration or worse, execution for treason. This weighted heavily on his psyche, his head was on the block and the ax would fall very soon.

The Codex trilled its unique sound and the president picked up, "General Falk, what have we learned," Taylor Jackson's blood pressure went off the charts, he tried to control his emotions but they ran amok. He had to get a grip and he hoped she didn't give him up. The general got straight to it, "Well sir, the interrogation went well but I'm afraid the Robin Calhoun we knew is no more," the president swung his chair around to face the window and said, "Robin Calhoun is expired, did I hear you correctly General?" Taylor Jackson relaxed at once, this was good news to hear, but Mad Sam made that a short lived relief when he said, "Not in the conventional sense, it's rather complicated...," Jasper Bohannon broke in, "I'm confused here, General, unpack that for me, please," the general carried on: "It seems sir, she has a split personality, perhaps multiple ones and the Robin Calhoun entity was suppressed during the interrogation, and what emerged was this person calling herself, are you ready?" The president replied, "As ready as I'll ever be, give it to me gently," and heard the name, "Scarlett O'Hara," the president said, "As in Gone with the Wind?" The general said, "The same but in the flesh sir, she emerged as the dominant personality and told all."

Jasper Bohannon: "Tell me everything," so he did and when the telling was done the president said: "This is both wonderful and depressing news, is it possible for them to share the same space on this topic, General."

Mad Sam: "Quite a unique situation we have here sir, but I'm pleased with the outcome of the interrogation, we learned the target and the names of all of her co-conspirators in this affair."

Jasper Bohannon: "I'll inform the Director to execute warrants for all parties involved tonight we have to roll up all of these traitors with the quickness."

Mad Sam: "I've ordered Mister Macklin to lead to team to intercept Billy Bob Broussard and his Nazi assistances. Captain Stovall will be en route to Belize to eliminate this Kussman character who was a major player in this whole scenario, sir."

Jasper Bohannon: "Well done, what are the prospects of Mister Macklin arriving in time to prevent the seizure of their intended target?"

"It's going to be close sir, but if I know the major, he'll try his hardest to prevent that from happening, although this Scarlett O'Hara told him the time and place they may have stepped up their timetable, let's rely on his abilities to get it done before they execute their intentions, sir."

"We couldn't keep the lid on the murder of Senator Carlisle and Robin Calhoun's arrest, the media wanted to cooperate but once it hit the blogosphere there was nothing they could do about sitting on the story, so these criminals most likely are aware of this."

The general replied, "We have to assume they are sir, and they've taken the initiative, this Billy Bob character was trained well in the Army, so we'll operate under the assumption he's proactive in his thinking and will take matters in his own hands."

The POTUS said, "We're so close to the end of this horror story, we need a taste of luck here to bring it to a successful conclusion by corralling these monsters tonight."

Mad Sam told him, "Luck is an unknown quantity but it still counts."

Taylor Jackson sat on the sofa tak'n the president's side of the conversation in, he hadn't heard anything that should worry him, seems the bitch kept her mouth shut concerning his involvement and he felt the tension ebbing, so he relaxed and smiled.

While Taylor Jackson settled into a new comfort zone, Mad Sam said to Jasper Bohannon, "Now comes the worse part of this story, are you sitting down, sir?" The president said, "Yes...," and braced himself, "...what could possibly be worse than what has transpired thus far?"

"I hate to be the one who bears the bad news, but I know it's my duty...," here the general paused to assemble his words so the impact would be less damaging, "...to inform you of something that will hurt, but it must be said."

The president rose and stepped to the window in its reflection he could see the entire Oval Office and Taylor Jackson seated on the sofa work'n a stack of papers, he said, "Tell what you will General."

Mad Sam hesitated before he revealed the bombshell, the president waited, and finally he told him: "According to this Scarlett O'Hara, Robin

Calhoun had a deep mole in the White House who kept her informed of our activities, and to my regret sir, I have to tell you that person is your Chief of Staff, Taylor Jackson," the president's mind went blank at this revelation, he stood at the window looking back into the room and saw his lifelong friend there in the reflection. Jasper Bohannon stepped back and settled down in his chair, so complete was the shock there was a gap in the conversation and General Falk waited for the president to respond. This hurt ran deep, a myriad of scenes flashed before him, his college roommate, his teammate, his campaign manager, and his Chief of Staff and more important, his friend had betrayed him.

The devastation was total.

Mad Sam's words cut into the president's thoughts, "Sir, I know this must be one of the most excruciating things you ever been told and it pains me to have been the one who told you."

The POTUS seemed to awaken from a kind of daze; he put his personal heartache aside though it chafed he had to do his duty to the nation and said to the general, "I appreciate your words, stay on the line," Jasper Bohannon swiveled his chair and smiled when he said, "Excuse me, Taylor but could you ask Agent Marshall to step in there's something urgent I need to convey to him?" His Chief of Staff said, "Not a problem sir," he rose from the sofa ambled to the door, went out and returned with Kenny Marshall Head of White House Security, they stepped in the Oval Office and closed the door, the president's smile resembled a grimace, the pain plain in his eyes when he said, "Agent Marshall, I want you to place his man, Taylor Jackson under immediate arrest," the agent looked bewildered and failed to comprehend the president's order, Taylor Jackson slack jawed it, Jasper Bohannon said, "Agent Marshall do I have to repeat myself? If so I will, place this traitor under arrest, *now*." With that Kenny Marshall drew his handcuffs from his belt, turned the ex-Chief of Staff around and put the bracelets on him.

Taylor Jackson knew the jig was up and remained quiet, the cuffs had sealed his fate.

Jasper Bohannon stared at his betrayer and said to SSA Kenny Marshall, "Get this person out of my sight and transport him to Quantico," he swung his chair back to face the window and saw in the reflection the agent escort his longtime friend out the door and out of his life.

TWO HOURS BEFORE General Falk called the president, Billy Bob Broussard and Harry Reynolds went over their plan of attack, they were in the safe house garage preparing the Semtex explosives, and Kussman's men were outside loading their weapons into the van they stole from the Massachusetts Department of Transportation.

Harry Reynolds was still at odds with the mission if it involved partner'n with the Nazis, his reluctance was based on his hatred of them for what happened to his relatives during WWII, though this was decades ago he still harbored ill feelings toward anything German, he even hated their bratwurst, their sauerkraut and their cars. Since he first broached the subject with Billy Bob he had hidden thoughts of not participating in the attack on Boston. Those hard feelings overrode his disdain for the United States.

Finally it came to a head and he had to express his principles.

Harry Reynolds looked at Billy Bob and said, "I'm having serious reservations about this, I don't feel comfortable deal'n with these fuck'n Nazis, I'm don't want to be involved with this any longer."

Billy Bob cocked a brow, gave him a sharp look and said, "What'd you say?"

"You heard. I'm not going through with this if these Nazis bastards are a part of it. I didn't sign on to be partners with these fucks."

"We're way too far into the game to tell me you're quitting because of some shit that happened before you were born." That rang hard with him.

And Harry Reynolds couldn't let it pass, he stepped up and got into his grill, "What do you call this confederacy bullshit that happened way back in the day, but here we are, so your point is bullshit." He was physical larger than Billy Bob so his intimidation worked to a degree, Billy Bob backed up and tried to reason with him, "Come on Harry, we took a blood oath to see this through, remember, now is not the time to quit, not now when we are on our way to complete the mission. We have to see it though."

Harry Reynolds burned him with his glare. "Fuck the mission and fuck those German bastards outside too, count me out," he said and went on, "I'd rather shot them than go through with this, that's how serious I'm about it."

This was atrocious mutiny in the ranks, Billy Bob had to do something to quell it, so he said, “The chief will up the ante, she willing to pay more money if that’s the issue,” not know’n what had happened back down in Washington, seems Max Bedford was a frugal millionaire he didn’t include a TV when he rented the farm house, so they had no knowledge of Robin Calhoun’s arrest. Max Bedford had explicit orders not to phone them, besides he was under surveillance, so he couldn’t shake the FBI to place a call to warn them about her arrest. They were on their own.

“Did you hear me say anything about more dough?” Harry Reynolds demanded.

Billy Bob knew at this moment there wasn’t any way to dissuade him if money couldn’t do the trick, so he had to take another avenue of approach, a more violent one.

He told him: “Well if that’s your final decision, there’s really nothing I can do about it.”

“You got that right. My convictions are set in stone, I’m out of here.”

Billy Bob Broussard had lost his twin brother in this affair, martyred for the cause and here was his main lieutenant tell’n him he was cut’n out, this couldn’t stand, he had to set an example here and now, he told him, “Okay, then be on your way, we’ll see it though,” Harry Reynolds outstretched his hand and they shook on it. He turned to leave and Billy Bob Broussard drew his Glock and pop, pop, popped him in the back.

Kussman’s men heard the shots, raced to the garage and saw Harry Reynolds there on the floor, they stop in their tracks and stood aghast at Billy Bob Broussard hold’n his Glock on them, his eyes were smok’n now and there was a dreamy quality to his voice, in words that would brook no argument, he said, “If anyone else has ideas about bugging out or show signs of cowardice, this is the fate that awaits, understood?”

His face was hard and his words carried a definite threat the Nazis had the look of naked fear on their faces. Billy Bob let the moment sink in and then told them, “Now that we understand one another load this coward into the van and we’ll dump him somewhere.”

Two men reached down, lifted the corpse up and struggled it out the door.

They loaded Harry Reynolds into the van. Billy Bob holstered his gun, grabbed the satchels containing the Semtex charges and followed the Nazis. Once inside the van they moved away to the Bunker Hill Bridge to do their dirty work. Game on.

BILLY BOB BROUSSARD and his men drove across the cable stayed bridge until they reached the center and stopped. Five Nazis dressed in Massachusetts Department of Transportation overalls climbed out, placed men at work signs and cones behind the van whose hazard lights winked. A few cars, a truck or two stole past. Billy Bob remained inside raised his field glasses and looked down the Charles River he could see the objective approach slowly up the channel. It was enormous in size.

Clouds obscured the moon as a massive one thousand foot tanker crept toward the bridge. The LNG ship contained thirty three million gallons of liquefied natural gas. Two helicopters circled overhead, the surface flotilla included marine patrol, firefighting tugs, environmental police, city police boats and Coast Guard vessels. The huge hulk advanced at four knots toward the unloading facility in Everett.

The moon came out from behind a cloud and the ship's four storage tanks loomed, this was the target. Billy Bob exited the van, opened the side door, reached in and came out with the Semtex satchels and weapons. He set them on the ground, looked at the oncoming vessel about a half a mile away and grabbed the rappelling gear and said, "Krause attached the anchors to the railings and we'll descend on my command." Krause stepped up, secured five static ropes and attached the descenders. Billy Bob could see the tanker now about a hundred yards away from the bridge, he ordered his men into their harnesses, they put on their gloves, shouldered their MP5's, scaled over the rail and waited for Billy Bob's orders.

He paused as the clouds slid in front of the moon and in the darkness he said, "Krause once we started down lower the satchels and when we're on board, gather the gear, get the hell out of here and take the van back to the farm on the way find a spot to dump that coward, and wait there until you hear from me." They hung over the side of the Bunker Hill Bridge as the ship's bow approached, Billy Bob Broussard yelled, "Now," and the team started down, the descenders allow them to control their rate of fall.

The bow of the ship slipped under the bridge, they propelled downward, the hundred foot distance was closed within seconds and they quietly landed on the ship's deck.

Above Krause released the anchors and the ropes, they dropped onto the ship, he gathered the signs and cones, when he looked up he saw two Massachusetts Highway Patrol cars approach at speed, their red lights flashed, he tried to run to the van, but a patrol car cut in front block'n his escape, Krause knew he was caught, reached inside his jacket, drew his Glock, racked the slide and started shoot'n. The bullets hit the second car's windows, shattering it, the highway patrolman stood on the brakes, threw the door open, leapt out and returned fire, several rounds slammed into the Nazi and he dropped to the ground. The cops cautiously stepped up and one of them kicked the Glock away, reached down and turned Krause over, lying on the pavement he said in pain, "You're too late, assholes," and died there on the Bunker Hill Bridge.

On board the tanker, they collected the satchels. Billy Bob and his team climbed the ladder that led to the bridge, raced to the front end of the superstructure opened the door, a shaft of yellow light sliced into the night and they stepped into the conning tower. The helmsman's head snapped around when he heard the door open and his jaw dropped; there was complete horror on his face when he saw five men hold'n their submachine guns on him. Billy Bob told him, "Easy, and no one gets hurt," and walked up to the console and put the point of the MP5 in his back, "Follow my instructions and you live, if you don't, you die understand?" The helmsman nodded *OK* and stared straight ahead. Billy Bob turned to Müller, "Take three men with you, round up the crew and secure the rest of the ship. Lock them up in their quarters and make sure you disable any form of communications, and don't forget to seize all cell phones and throw them over board, now go." Müller and three others turned on their heels and went out the wheelhouse to execute his orders.

Billy Bob told the man at the helm to order the crewmen in the engine room to stop the tanker, he grabbed the ship's intercom, repeated the order and they could hear the engines shut down. It took the tanker close to three minutes to coast to a stop. It finally came to a halt in the middle of the Charles River between downtown Boston and Cambridge. Now Billy Bob and his Nazis were in absolute command of the LNG tanker and they set about placing the Semtex charges around the liquefied gas holding tanks. Billy Bob and his men had completed the first phase, now to set the final one in motion.

17

Johnny Lawdawgs

Metro DC; Boston; Toledo, Belize

WHEN THE HEAD of White House Security escorted Taylor Jackson out of the Oval Office to his rendezvous with Mad Sam, the POTUS said to the general, "Now that that's been resolved, the pressure at hand has to be dealt with expeditiously, there is no margin for error here General, pull out all the stops, end this affair with a positive conclusion, a negative one will not do," and Mad Sam replied, "Well understood Mister President, I have supreme confidence in Captain Stovall and Mister Macklin and I will personally deal with Taylor Jackson," the name cut deep, in Jasper Bohannon's eyes tears started to gather and he fought back let'n them flow, he righted himself and said with no emotion, "Do what you will, Mad Sam, no one is above the law or the nation, no personal persuasions can be factored into this equation, I repeat, do whatever's necessary and more important, stop this Billy Bob Broussard."

With that Mad Sam rang off and prepared to receive Taylor Jackson, he said aloud, "This traitorous son of a bitch's mother should have choked him at birth," he knew at that moment what it was that made his lads react with such ferocity toward Taylor Jackson in the Oval Office, they could smell the rat in him, Smedley Butler and Chesty Puller knew Taylor

Jackson was the fox in the hen house. He smiled a cold smile and let his thoughts cook on how to dispose of this traitor, he wasn't lik'n this not one little bit, Taylor Jackson was about to meet the head Eradicator face to face, it's going to get ugly, Taylor Jackson fucked up, and Mad Sam was really, really pissed.

AT THAT MOMENT two things happened, in Boston Dennis McMorris and Adam Segal sat outside radio station WBMA where they waited for Max Bedford to come out and get into his limo, his show was over at twelve this particular night, and then the SAC's smartphone beckoned, he thumbed it on: "McMorris arrest the subject now, without delay," it was the Director speak'n, the SAC replied, "Understood, sir," and thumbed off, he looked over at Adam Segal, "Now you get to do what you've been dying to do, let's go get this clown, we're taking him down," the SA flashed his grill, "Let's do this." They left the interior, adjusted their coats against the wind and stepped off to do just that.

AS THEY HEADED for the WBMA entrance, down in Charleston, two FBI agents accompanied by local unies followed the road to the antebellum home they switched off their engines, climbed out and stepped up the steps to Moses Blount's front door. Inside he was hold'n court with several of his parishioners, a hard rap came at the door, he excused himself and sauntered through the foyer, when he opened that door, there were five law enforcement officers in front of him. His eyes widen, Special Agent Lloyd Packard asked, "Reverend Moses Blount?" He replied cautiously, "Yes." His answer sealed his fate and he was arrested in full view of his house guests, Lloyd Packard told him: "We're executing a presidential warrant for your arrest the charges are terrorist activities and treason against the United States of America." And read him his rights.

MCMORRIS AND SEGAL padded across the lobby stepped into the lift and rode up to the tenth floor and stepped out and there they followed directions to the radio station; they rounded a corner, saw the entrance and strode inside with their guns and badges exposed. The receptionist stood up and immediately leaned back against the wall, her eyes followed them down the hall, the on the air sign was hot, but that concerned them not. They entered the studio, Max Bedford looked up while speak'n, "... and this administration has neglected...," he stopped mid sentence, his eyes popped as the FBI agents approach the console with their service pistols pointed straight at him and they read him his rights.

AT FIRST LIGHT a pall hung over Boston, the city was under a duet threat, nature was lurk'n with a nor'easter in mind, and Billy Bob was in control of the tanker. After the LGN tanker halted, he told the ship's captain to notify the safety armada to pull back or he'd denote the Semtex. Everyone complied, the tugboats, the Coast Guard, marine patrol escorts, the underwater divers and the police retreated five miles away from the bomb.

The helicopters flew to safe distances and hovered.

The stage was set.

WHEN THEY SEIZED the tanker, Billy Bob ordered his team to set the charges. The red bricks of Semtex 1A were perfect for destruction and blasting through the storage tank thick metal casings and its insulation, they were placed at the base of the tanks where they met the ship's deck, and the number ten delay switches were set to twenty four hours and were accurate to within plus or minus two three minutes. The Nazis crushed the ends of the thin copper tubes that contained the cupric chloride, the pliers dent them sufficiently to break the glass vials and released the liquid contained within, then the countdown started and the brass safety strips that held back the strikers, were removed and discarded. Finally the ends of the time pencils, the actual detonators were fitted into the explosives and all was ready.

Once detonated the Semtex would slam through the tanks' hardened casings and released the liquefied natural gas that had been cooled to minus 260 degrees, spill'n over the water, a vapor cloud would seep into streets then its ignition would cause a catastrophic, searing white hot fire that would burn people and buildings two and half miles away, producing a force equivalent to a small nuclear explosion that would instantly incinerate everything in its path and then it's baked Bean Town.

AN HOUR EARLIER, Skeeter Macklin arrived on scene but he was too late. He met with the commanders and opened to view an executive order to follow his lead, everyone subordinated to him. He assessed the situation and he knew the only way to board the ship had to be an underwater approach. They would have to wait until dark to retake the tanker, ten hours of daylight and tension loomed ahead, between now and then was the critical time frame, it allowed Billy Bob Broussard to dictate things, his way, and his way only. Skeeter Macklin had to buy time and invent a scenario to stall things.

WHICH HE DID, he phoned Andrew Wong at the Barn and told him to prepare Scarlett O'Hara to speak to Billy Bob. Andrew Wong knew what was required to bring off the deception, the difference in Robin Calhoun's tone and phraseology was considerable from those of Scarlett O'Hara who spoke in contractions and with a pronounced accent. Robin Calhoun's speech was more formal as opposed to Scarlett's informality. He would employ a new voice transformer a sophisticated technology to add certain distinctive traits to Scarlett's voice. The voice simulator will compare their voices in terms of pitch, timbre, and intonation. Based on this information, Andrew Wong would adjust the pitch, timbre, frequency levels, and apply effects, to make Scarlett's voice sound exactly like Robin's targeted one. This voice morphing will transition Scarlett O'Hara's speech signal into Robin Calhoun's, to fool Billy Bob into believ'n he spoke with Robin and not Scarlett. This bluff was crucial to prevent him from doing someth'n rash without explicit orders from Robin Calhoun. It had to work or things could spin way out of control, downtown Boston and Cambridge could be incinerated.

IT WAS JUST after six thirty and there was a school of thought that things were teetering on extreme danger and possible disaster, in a word things were, desperate.

Billy Bob Broussard contacted the command center and requested to speak to the man in charge, and spoke to Skeeter Macklin, he didn't know he was speak'n with the husband of the woman he shot down on the streets of Georgetown, Billy Bob told Skeeter, "I want the entire area cleared of military and Johnny lawdawgs, if I can see them, they're too close and I will set this motherfucker off, think I'm bullshit'n let me see any types in my field of vision and I'll roast this fucking town."

Skeeter Macklin knew, for the moment, Billy Bob was call'n the shots so he said smoothly, "We'll comply with your wishes, is there any others you'd like to submit?" Billy Bob was thrown for a second, and then he said, "Yes if I see any kind of evacuation underway, I will set it off." Skeeter had to agree to everything for the time being, Billy Bob was do'n the deal'n he had to play the hand he held until the final cards were exposed, so he said, "No problem there. There will be no evacuation just the normal flow of city traffic, that'd be best to eliminate any possibilities of panic setting in, we don't want that now do we?" Billy Bob had a hard time putting his arms around what he heard, no counter demands, no belligerence, just compliance, so he demanded, "Who am I speaking too?"

Skeeter Macklin: "You requested to speak with the man in charge, and you got me."

Billy Bob: "Does the man in charge have a name?"

Skeeter Macklin: "We want to get personal here? I didn't ask you your name so what's with the familiarity talk we have to find a way to resolve this without any fireworks."

Billy Bob: "You sound like a reasonable guy, so expect to hear from me with a list of demands, which are non negotiable, comply or die." There was a note of finality there. Billy Bob plunged on: "I'm sure you understand that things are not in your favor, right?"

Skeeter Macklin: "So it would appear. We certainly grasp the magnitude of your intent, a result no one wants to see transpire."

He had to play around Billy Bob's aggression for the moment. He lulled him to believe things were go according to his lik'n, Skeeter knew he had to fake Billy Bob out so he played the role and he knew also how this story would end, come sundown, Skeeter Macklin would kick things gear, and retake the tanker, but for now, he asked him: "When will your list be made available, so it can be discussed in Washington?"

He heard Billy Bob say: "I'll get back to you by ten and remember what I told you, any kind of lawdawg or military activity it's KABOOM," and the line went dead, Billy Bob had made his point and Skeeter Macklin gained valuable time and Billy Bob just lost some of his. The quicker the daylight burns, the better, come dark it's Skeeter bit'n time.

AT THE BARN Andrew Wong had the electronics set up, he waited along with Scarlett O'Hara for Skeeter Macklin's call, it came after he hung up with Billy Bob, he told Andrew Wong: "We need her to phone Broussard and give him orders not to make a move until she says so." The captain said, "Understood sir, she's prepared to say what Robin Calhoun would say, and her voice will be totally masked, she kept his number in her smartphone, so here goes."

On board the tanker Billy Bob stood in the wheelhouse and watched the ship's radar as it swept for any hint of activity on the river or in the air. All was quiet on that front so when his cell spoke he was at ease, he heard Scarlett O'Hara say: "Job well done Billy Bob, you have delivered us the upper hand, I have submitted our formal demands to the White House...," here he smiled, "...and we have their undivided attention." Billy Bob Broussard was enraptured, "Are they willing to give us what we want?" He permitted himself a mild chuckle, he had finally struck back at the United States with a hate so profound and it felt oh so good to hear they had brought the US government to its knees, he heard Scarlett O'Hara say, "I am scheduled to have a table top with Bohannon, first thing in the morning to start the process of our secession, Billy Bob you have done it, you have set the South free." Scarlett O'Hara played her part well, there was tremendous enthusiasm in her voice, she enjoyed pull'n the wool over Billy Bob eyes, she had always harbored ill feelings toward him, he was so beneath her station, she'd never associate with such trash, she hated Robin Calhoun when she brought him into her life and if Scarlett O'Hara could do Robin Calhoun in, she was ready to do it.

Billy Bob rose to the bait, "What if they don't cave in and what then?" Scarlett O'Hara told him now: "Then turn the lights out in Boston on my orders, but I'm certain things will not get to that point, we have totally subdued the great United States, this will be a moment in time that will changed the world and you Billy Bob are greater than all the Confederate soldiers of the past, one name stands above all, Billy Bob Broussard", stroking his ego. Scarlett O'Hara went heavy on the conviction to convince Billy Bob he was speak'n with Robin Calhoun, and he came back: "Chief you are the architect of this moment, that's the historical significance of this endeavor, your unrelenting belief has led us here, and I am honored to have served under your command." That did it, he was locked in, Skeeter Macklin had staged a time coup, it suck the life out Billy Bob's plan, time had just ran out for him and his Nazis, point, set, the match was nigh.

IT WAS VERY quiet in the Oval Office and Jasper Bohannon stood at the window and peered out, but he stared back into the past three weeks, his worse thought was confirmed, the dirty bomb had arrived, that thought first came to him here at this very window, and now that thought had manifested itself into reality. The president knew they had come a long way fast, but the conclusion was in doubt. He was counting on the abilities of his forces to fight the good fight and for right to triumph over evil. Billy Bob Broussard and his cohorts had to be neutralized before they went suicidal, if they realized their situation was hopeless, its known that desperate men have the capacity to do dangerous things, they would more than likely set off the bomb kill'n them and ten thousand others, the situation was not over by any stretch. The final grains of sand poured to the bottom of the hour glass, time was the enemy and time was run'n out.

The light at the end of the tunnel was bright enough to read by, the end to this nightmare was so near, victory within sight yes they were close, but still so far away.

The President of the United States, turned away from the window and sat down behind the Resolute Desk, an apropos name, this is where others had sat before him determined to see their crises through, Jasper Bohannon now had to carry that mantle and bring his to a positive end, no more innocent lives must be given to this affair.

AT THAT SAME moment six hours back in time Taylor Jackson sat shackled to a chair somewhere in the Barn's complex. The requisite black bag covered his head and his ears strained for the slightest sound. He was picked up at the White House by a trio of Eradicators who transported him to this location. As he sat there he put Taylor Jackson on trial, he was guilty as charged, he couldn't lie to Taylor Jackson, not seated here in this unknown location. Having been privy to Eradicators' modus operandi, he knew as their name implied, they were ready to rain down pure hell on his head. He was committed to his fate, there was no way out, he purchased a ticket to ride, but he rode the wrong horse, now the race was over, all he had was a worthless stub, torn in two.

Taylor Jackson's guilt was complete he had betrayed everything, his country, his friend and himself. He sat there and thought about what he'll leave in his wake, his wife, his folks and everyone who had respected and liked him will forever remember him as the ultimate traitor, the one who had the president's ear, the most trusted person in the administration and that person turned out to be the lowest of the low. At that moment Taylor Jackson felt lower than whale shit and that's at the bottom of the ocean.

MICKEY STOVALL RODE in Falcon E1 headed to Gitmo, he and his red team were one hundred and fifty miles out; they'd been in the air since just after eleven when Scarlett O'Hara named Karl K. Kussman as Robin Calhoun's main accomplice. After Skeeter Macklin past the word to Mad Sam, he phone Mickey and told him the news, the doctor was declared a high value target and Mad Sam ordered Mickey Stovall to eradicate Karl K. Kussman and his followers. This was a no prisoners' mission.

The Falcon touch down at Gitmo four hours later, there was a taste of fog in the air as the plane taxi to a hanger, the door swung open and Mickey Stovall bound down the ladder followed by his twelve man team. At the bottom Lieutenant Tim Locke threw up a salute and Mickey Stovall saluted back and he told Mickey, "Sir the Osprey is standing by to transport you and your men to the USS *Iwo Jima* she currently on station in the Bay of Honduras." Mickey Stovall demanded: "Have the weapons and equipment been loaded?" as they climbed into the Humvee and drew away from the hanger.

"Yes sir."

"Excellent, what's the flight time to the *Iwo*?"

"Approximately two and a half hours, sir, there's a tail wind, so I say you'll arrive around sunrise." Mickey Stovall, replied, "Perfect," and looked out the window as the Humvee raced across the base, two others in line hot on its bumper. He was focused and mapped out the attack plan in his mind; this was the a deep penetration mission, Kussman's ranch was twenty five miles inland from the Caribbean coast, they had to approach the compound by Zodiacs up the Rio Grande River north of Punta Gorda in Toledo and then trek through the rainforest to reach the ranch near Big Fall. This was their environs, Mickey Stovall and his team was at their best in the jungle, a Force Recon's dream, it may be Karl K. Kussman's home field but it's the Eradicators' playground, this is where they go beyond others in a contest of quality and ability, to put it simply, this is the place where they excel.

Like Skeeter Macklin, Mickey Stovall will launch his attack under the cover of darkness, night their ally, night their weapon.

IN THE SHOCKED silence it was Taylor Jackson who spoke, he voice dry, when he heard the door open, "Who's there? Where am I?" The only reply was toenails that tapped across the floor. He heard the taps sound their way up to him and then silence returned. His mind processed this and it came to him, those were dog toenails, his heart collapsed, Taylor Jackson knew there were two bulldogs parked right in front of him.

Low growls gurgle up from their throats; inside the bag he turned a ghastly pale color.

Suddenly he heard slow steps approach and then stop, the bag was yanked off, an explosion of eye searing glare met his eyes, the shock of light blinded him momentarily and then his eyes leveled on the bulldogs of his nightmares sit'n on their haunches, Smedley Butler and Chesty Puller stared at him, with sardonic grins in place, he avoided eye contact and he eyes looked up into those of Mad Sam Falk, the image that dwelled in his, was twice as fierce as the ones contained in the dogs'.

The general made a striking figure in his camies starched to a cardboard like stiffness, with razor sharp creases down his pant legs, the image of the squared away jarhead. He paced behind the dogs with his swagger stick tucked under his armpit, his face twisted with rage: "Ah so here we are, just the four of us, three against one, the odds don't look too good for you Jackson." Now there was a confident smile on his face and he heard Taylor Jackson say, "General, I know the fate that awaits me, and I deserve whatever you intend to do," Mad Sam told him, "I don't intend to do anything, it's out of my hands, you have to convince my lads here not to rip you apart." He led that hang for a moment then laughed but it wasn't a pleasant one and carried on in a low dangerous voice: "When they first saw you they knew you were a traitor, you had a rotten scent about you, and being gung ho about the red, white and blue my lads could smell the fink in you, you latter day Benedict Arnold." Taylor Jackson didn't look down at Smedley Butler and Chesty Puller but he felt them feed'n on him with their eyes.

Every time Mad Sam said *you*, utter contempt drip from it he was not in the mood for any small talk so he said, "Remember the game show *Let's Make a Deal*?" He didn't wait for any response and went on staring directly into his eyes: "Well that's exactly what we're going to play here you'll have a choice between door number one and door number two. Behind one of the doors will be my lads waiting to tear you to shreds...," Taylor Jackson's eyes flashed in alarm, "...and behind the other one will be a loaded gun sitting on a table, if you open that door you will go in alone and do the right thing." Then the general said with just the right amount of steel in his voice: "So choose your door very carefully, you won't get a second opportunity, one and done, understand?"

Taylor Jackson's face was damp with sweat and something caught at the back of his throat bile rose there threaten'n to choke him, finally he spoke with a pained look, the words falling over themselves in his eagerness to get them out: "I'll take the door with the gun," he sat there, looked up at the ceiling with the dogs' icy glares locked on him.

Mad Sam noted the fear in his eyes, he took the swagger stick out from under his armpit, slapped his left palm with it as he paced back and forth, his tone had grown much darker, "Only if it was that easy Jackson, there's no game in that. The contest is whether you open the right door or the left one, either way you're a dead man."

Taylor Jackson looked down and pulled a frown, he was on the verge of asking why but then thought better of it, he said tightly, "I see," with a particular interest in not pick'n the wrong door, although death lurked behind both, the dog option was too frighten'n to consider. He had suffered that outcome many nights since their encounter in the Oval Office. Death by mauling and mutilation was not the choice of choices. There was a long pause and the general allowed the silence to linger between them. Finally Mad Sam said, "I'm going to place the bag back over your head, then lead my lads into one of the rooms and you'll have fifteen minutes to make a choice." With that he stepped up, put the bag in place and Taylor Jackson heard the taps and footfalls move away. He sat in the dark and thought he had minutes to live but his infamy will live forever.

It was the fastest fifteen minutes in the history of time, the door opened and he heard footsteps approach, the bag came off and Mad Sam said to him, "It's decision time." The lights were on and Taylor Jackson saw two doors to his left marked one and two. He was uncuffed and led forward, vicious barks and growls emitted from behind them; here he paused to make his choice. Would it be death at his own hand or the horror of being chewed to pieces, what was the doom that awaited Taylor the traitor Jackson? He selected door number two, turned the knob and shifted inside to accept his fate.

IT WAS LATE in the afternoon and evening was just getting started as darkness tinged the sky on the eastern horizon, Karl K. Kussman was in his office where he paced the floor he stopped and said to Obergruppenfuhrer Schell, "There's been an unfortunate event in America, and Robin Calhoun has been arrested for murder." The Obergruppenfuhrer stood at attention and replied, "Murder, Reichfuhrer?"

"Yes, she let her emotions overrule her common sense, seems she shot one of her lovers, Senator Jake Carlisle no less, and she's in the custody of the US government."

Obergruppenfuhrer Schell: "What of the plan, does it still move forward sir?"

The Reichfuhrer: "Yes, fortunately Mister Broussard was able to commandeer the target and is in control of the tanker." Kussman K. Kussman turned and looked out the window as evening fell.

Obergruppenfuhrer Schell: "If she's in their custody, she might reveal our involvement, they have methods to make her talk, Reichfuhrer."

The Reichfuhrer: "Yes they have Schell, but Robin Calhoun is a dedicated fanatic who'd rather die than reveal what she knows, I don't envision her exposing us, but as a precaution, post sentries on the perimeter of the compound, just in case. We don't want any surprises, understood?" He said that over his shoulder and remained at the window as the night settled in.

Obergruppenfuhrer Schell: "Clearly sir, I'll double the detail and make sure the entire compound is patrolled until further orders from you."

The Reichfuhrer: "Very good Obergruppenfuhrer now carry out your orders."

Obergruppenfuhrer Schell brought his heels together and thrust his arm out in the Nazi salute: "*Heil Hitler*," pivoted and went out. Doctor Kussman turned away from the window settled down behind his desk and considered the situation, Robin Calhoun's arrest was a good thing and it could be very beneficial to his scheme. Now she was out of the way, he was in charge and would implement his plan to seize control of matters. He would call Billy Bob tell him that he was now in command and to standby for his order to detonate the bomb if the US government didn't capitulate within the next sixteen hours.

Karl K. Kussman wondered whether Billy Bob Broussard was aware of her arrest. *Surely he knows*. It was all over the satellite news channels. He'd give him a call after his evening meal, he was pleased at the sudden turn of events and this was good, very, very good. He heard laughter erupted from his mouth, he was one happy man, and things were now in his favor, but his delay in mak'n that call could prove fatal.

ON THE EVENING of the same hour in the gathering darkness a bone white moon hung low in the sky over Boston as Skeeter Macklin prepared the blue team's mission profile to retake the LNG tanker. He chose to approach the vessel from underwater; his men were trained water borne warriors, so this was not something foreign to them. He selected his best swimmers. He ordered them not to fire their weapons unless it was positively unavoidable, they had to eliminate the terrorists using special weapons due the volatile nature of the liquefied gas.

Skeeter Macklin said to Frank Nye, "Corporal we'll swim to the tanker and use our grappling hooks to scale the side of a ship, once we're on board, take four men, look for any charges and disarm them," he looked around at his team to make sure he had their undivided attention, all eyes were riveted on their leader as he carried on: "I'll advance with two men to the stern and we'll proceed to the wheelhouse, your orders are to eliminate anyone you see who's a terrorist, no ifs ands or buts understood?"

Corporal Nye replied: "Perfectly sir."

Skeeter Macklin told him, "We have to secure the ship with a minimum of gunfire, only shoot if you can't get a clean shot with your blowguns, and use knives for close quarter work. This liquid gas stuff's very sensitive, so only fire when it's absolutely necessary."

The seven man team nodded as one.

There was nothing else to be said but the obvious, "It's an absolute must that we secure the vessel and kill everyone involved, under the strict orders from the general, no one is to survive, is that clear?"

There was a chorus, "Aye, aye sir."

"Alright, now be prepared to dive within twenty minutes, any questions?"

There were none, anyone understood the water borne operation and their roles in it.

Skeeter rifled through the closets of his own mind and searched for a mission similar to this one, he recalled an incident in the Gulf of Aden back in oh five when he and Mickey led a team to recapture an oil tanker seized by Somali pirates. This was conducted under the cover of darkness, but in tropical waters, the frigid Charles River presented a unique set of challenges. He knew to dive in near freez'n water would be hazardous and his awareness of environmental conditions, water depth, temperature, wind velocity, current, visibility, and light conditions was vital to success of the mission and the blue team's safety. He had to make special preparations for this circumstance.

Soon after the team assembled on the deck of the USS Coast Guard *Tiger Shark* stationed out of Newport, Rhode Island. The cutter was anchored five miles down river the team went over their pre dive ritual. Skeeter made sure they'd eaten a good meal to stay warm and had fuel to burn during the twenty five minute swim in the thirty seven degree waters of the Charles River. Before the Eradicators donned their wetsuits they wrapped cummerbunds that contained sodium acetate heat packs around their backs and kidneys to help keep them warm and their blood circulating. Each man made sure their wetsuit fit well, everyone wore neoprene boots and heavy insulation socks and titanium gauntlet dive gloves. Skeeter Macklin ordered them to poured warm water into their socks and boots before zip'n up so the water would enter their suits, fill'n the gaps with warm water before the icy cold water flooded in, then they poured more water down the neck and swayed side to side so the water ran down their arms to the wrists, getting the warm water in there before the cold stuff could enter and to make sure they wouldn't be thermally depleted and had the stamina to make the journey to the tanker. Once their suits were primed it would make entering the frigid water hardly noticeable.

Now the special warfare commandos added their gear, GPS, TAC boards that included a timer, compass and depth gauge. Finally they placed re-breathers over their front underwater breathing apparatus. The re-breathers would deliver high concentrated oxygen and the expelled breaths would be recycled into the closed circuit where it was filtered for carbon dioxide. Expelled air would leave the divers' mouths and enter a tube that led to the apparatus that re-oxygenated the used air, circulating the new air back to the divers. The result was the complete elimination of expelled bubbles as they swam at a depth of twenty to twenty five feet below the surface and those on board the tanker wouldn't see a trail of bubbles which would make the underwater team susceptible to fire from the tanker. The Eradicators could infiltrate the water bound to the enemy's position undetected from above.

Everything was set.

Skeeter Macklin told his team to recheck their equipment and weapons, satisfied, he stepped down the gangway and plunged into the water followed closely by his men.

Now the game was *really* on.

BACK AT THE BARN Andrew Wong's fingers danced across the keyboard as he programmed a Predator from Hanscom Air Force Base to military satellites linked to his computer. Its entire flight would be controlled by satellite from the Barn's command center. The aircraft was equipped with a color nose camera, a variable aperture day TV camera, and a variable aperture infrared camera allowing the radar to look through smoke, clouds or haze and low light. The Predator's infrared camera with digitally enhanced zoom had the capability of identifying the heat signature of a human body from an altitude of ten thousand feet, making the aircraft an ideal search platform to notify Skeeter Macklin of the actual positions of the terrorists, allowing him and the blue team to pinpoint Billy Bob Broussard and his Nazis without a prolonged search.

BILLIONS OF STARS burned like candles as two Zodiacs from the USS *Iwo Jima* plied the dark waters of the Rio Grande River and screams from howler monkeys echoed throughout the rainforest. Mickey Stovall was in the lead boat. His red team was twenty miles up river near landfall. They left the helicopter carrier lying twelve miles east of the barrier reef an hour and half ago headed toward Kussman's ranch.

The team was clad in ghille suits, the enlisted men were armed with Mini-Uzis but Mickey Stovall was tot'n a SAW light machine gun along with a M9 pistol, everyone had fragmentation, concussion and incendiary grenades.

They were prepared for some serious warfare.

So in the darkness at eight thirty, the coxswains shut down the engines and the Zodiacs coasted to the riverbank. The team disembarked and Mickey Stovall told the coxswains to wait until they returned, he anticipated it would take four hours to make it to the ranch and back. The sailors acknowledge his orders. The night wind blew in from the

Caribbean, it was warm and salty, gardenias heavy clunk on the damp air as the team melted into the shadows of the rainforest, there they'd became one with the night, once inside, the ghillies suits were customized with twigs, leaves, and other elements of the local foliage as much as possible and then they were swallowed by the night like ghosts. The undergrowth was thicker than expected so the going was tough to say the least. Mickey Stovall wanted to arrive at Kussman's compound around ten o'clock then slip in without firing their weapons, once inside the perimeter they would unleash the full fury of their firepower.

The Eradicators were out for blood, Nazi blood.

FIFTEEN HOURS BEFORE Taylor Jackson took a deep breath, the barks ceased when he turned the knob, he stepped in with Mad Sam at his back, the door closed, his eyes toured the room he was ready for death. To his relief he saw a loaded 45 on a table he quickly stepped over, put it to his temple and pulled the trigger. He didn't know there weren't any dogs wait'n for him, both rooms contained pistols. The trick was on him. Mad Sam smiled when the 45 barked, *so long asshole.*

Taylor the traitor was *dead*

18

Ribbons of Fire

Toledo, Belize; Boston

A **SHAFT OF** moonlight pieced the trees and fell upon the face of Mickey Stovall stay'n well in the shadows. He stood behind one and peered out at the Kussman compound. Through his night vision monocular he found several Nazis on patrol, but their attitude was lax, they didn't really feel threatened this was to satisfy the Reichfuhrer's whim. Just another night under the stars that shimmered like diamonds spread over a black cloth; the sentries were at ease. Mickey Stovall smiled and said, "Finch, take two men and approach at the crawl, eliminate the guards," the corporal replied, "Aye, aye sir," hooked his thump twice and two men fell in behind him as he crawled out in to the open, Mickey Stovall watched them creep forward, death was on the hunt as clouds moved across the night sky and a swath of darkness spread over the compound.

Night birds called to each other as the trio crept closer.

Thunder banged in the distance.

And the darkness swallowed them up.

Ten minutes later Corporal Finch laid behind a Nazi in a box of blackness, the clouds were thunderheads that moved west from the sea. An ominous bang exploded above the compound, the Nazi cowered for a moment, another bang rocked the scene, and that's when Finch stood up he caught him by the collar, a knife in his hand pulled his head back and drew the blade from left to right across his throat. He sagged, life oozed out of him as Finch laid him on the ground and the clouds dropped their load.

The rain came in a sudden rush fill'n the air with its voice.

The others repeated his act. Three Nazis lay dead as Mickey Stovall and the rest raced across the open through the rain prepared to do maximum damage, eradicate all inside and gather Karl K. Kussman's research papers.

So let the carnage begin.

Finch raised his rifle with a M203 grenade launcher underneath, held the magazine, fired at the compound doors and blew them off their hinges the blasts were muffled by the peals of thunder that racked the night. To those inside it was nothing out of the ordinary, just the tropical sky do'n the damn thang. But what was to come would prove to be the Eradicators liv'n up to their name. They raced through the opening headed toward the barracks, for a visit, but death the uninvited guest was here to stay.

The night sky lit up like Broadway, lightning blinked on and off with great intensity. Thunder skipped across the sky and muffled the fire that spat from the Uzis' as the Eradicators kicked in doors, and caught the Nazis snooz'n and sent them into the permanent sleep. Mickey Stovall led the charge as he searched for Karl K. Kussman. With malice in his heart Mickey was on a mission to finally put this Nazi bullshit to bed.

Seems the leap into the Cuba and float'n through the storm that night steeled the Eradicators who displayed no fear as the sky clowned above. They were the tip of the lightning whips, light'n up those unfortunate to be inside the compound, if it breathes, killed it was the order of the day. And they executed their orders to the fullest. Their Uzis' spat their tongues of fire. The rain fell in silver strands; the guns spewed a torrent of lethal rounds, rain drove down like the Eradicators' bullets.

Ribbons of fire from lightning and from Mickey Stovall's SAW rent the night.

While his men died in their racks, Karl K. Kussman stood at the mirror in his office where he put on the final touches of rouge. He had his full blown freak getup on: four inch open toe stilettos, a lavender lace mini dress, with a pink boa wrapped around his neck and the fire engine wig matched his red cheeks all aglow and he had a smile on his face. The storm outside was the farthest thing from his mind as he stood there drown'n in the stew of his own madness. He planned to party and revel into the night.

Finally the dy'n died, the stench of cordite was everywhere, Mickey Stovall held his SAW at the port as smoke leaked out the barrel and said, "Finch incinerate the place, give these assholes a taste of the oven. Burn the joint to the ground, kill everything growing," he had a cold grin on his face, Finch noticed the look in the captain's eyes and knew that he was serious, erase the memory of these fucks, with malice and prejudice.

Karl K. Kussman saw off in the distance a glow as the barracks burned, it got his attention too, he grabbed his phone but it rang to no avail.

The Reichsführer reached for his gold plated Luger, as he racked the slide the bedroom door blew open, the concussion flung Karl K. Kussman up against the wall. Overhead a photo of the Fuhrer was peppered with SAW rounds. Mickey Stovall stood behind his weapon as red fire crisscrossed the room. He had a shit eat'n grin on his face as he stepped on the gas and lit the joint up. Intense pleasure coursed through him as more rounds shivered from the SAW and swastikas were sliced and diced as the torrent of tracers set Nazi shit ablaze. Portraits of Adolph, Herman, Joseph, Heinrich and the rest were consumed by the flames, an apropos ending to these bastards.

Finally things went eerily silent.

Karl K. Kussman stared at Mickey Stovall and death stared at him from the barrel of the SAW. The doctor eyes contained disbelief at the black marine stand'n before him, this couldn't be, but here he was at the mercy of an inferior human being. He struggled to his feet and stagger stepped across the room. Mickey Stovall kept the SAW trained on him, silence filled the void. Only the crackles of burn'n wood filtered into the quiet, and finally Mickey Stovall spoke: "So this is Karl K. Kussman, the sick fuck who thought he could wage war on *my* country."

The doctor wasn't sure what to say, so he didn't say anything and just stared at the SAW's black hole staring back at him. The silence settled upon them with weightless pressure, the doomed Nazi and his executioner ready to finalize him. With a firm wall between them, Kussman matched Mickey's silence with silence of his own. Mickey said into the quiet his voice had a taken a menacing edge, "I'm here to send you to other side to join up with those other Nazi turds," the doctor accepted the situation without any utterance, Mickey Stovall carried on in his best Conrad Veidt voice: "Show me your papers," as the fire and the smoke increased. Karl K. Kussman coughed and fell back up against the mantle, and regarded him with a frown, "What papers??"

"Your research papers, *asshole*," Mickey Stovall stormed at him; the doctor's eyes went wide as he watched him unsling his SAW, let it drop to the floor and then he charged the M9, gave a bark of laughter and demanded, "On your knees."

Karl K. Kussman dropped to the floor as fire climb the walls, it crept across the ceil'n and backlit Mickey tower'n over him. He stepped up, shoved the barrel into his mouth and cocked the hammer, "Start sucking you big freak, try not to make it come," Mickey Stovall flashed his grill, pushed the M9 into his throat and laughed, his laughter had an ugly ring to it and again in his Conrad Veidt voice said, "Show me your papers," he pulled the M9 out, Kussman gagged, fought back the urge to hurl and this stumbled out: "They are...in my lab...ora...tory on the...far...far...end of the com...pound," seems the super freak was a super punk he didn't have the nuts to die like Robin Calhoun did. He yak'd all that high powered Nazi shittiness, but went it came time to check out with his mouth shut, he went diarrheic and told all he knew fill'n in the gaps.

Mickey Stovall stood there and listened as he poured it all out, he was a babbl'n machine, when the doctor stopped snitch'n Mickey said, "Well that tidies things up," Karl K. Kussman asked, "What do you intend to do with me?" the question was as lame as it gets, Mickey leaned in close, smiled darkly and told him: "You've seen this movie before, the Nazi always dies at the end, ain't nothing changed," he placed the gun between his eyes, the M9 coughed and Kussman's head explode like a melon, blood and gray matter spewed all over the wall and hissed when it met the flames. The blow back spattered blood all over Mickey's cammies.

Karl K. Kussman never heard the M9 go off, never felt anything except the jolt of the muzzle against his head as Mickey pulled the trigger and the heavy slug ripped through his skull, blow'n out a large chuck of the back of his head. As he lay on the floor, his eyes were frozen in shock. Mickey Stovall aimed the M9 downward and coughed more rounds into his face.

It was so thrill'n, kill'n Karl K. Kussman he failed notice the fire had engulfed him. He surveyed the situation, the fire had started in on the doctor and lapped at his feet, he reached down grabbed the SAW, the only way out was to leap through the window, and that's exactly what he did. He crashed through and landed on the patio as the roof collapsed in on the evil doctor. Mickey Stovall smiled as he put out the fire on his pant legs and headed out rac'n back to his men cough'n all along the way.

Everyone shed their gullie suits, exposing their rucksacks and Mickey Stovall sent Finch along with seven others to collect whatever was of value in the laboratory, and his final order was, "Give the last rites to the Fourth Reich." They returned minutes later with their rucksacks crammed with papers including those given to Karl K. Kussman by Josef Mengele and they humped off to the Rio Grande with the compound ablaze.

AT THAT EXACT moment, Skeeter Macklin's head eased out of the moonlit water, the blue team was about five meters off the bow, the massive tanker loomed eighty-five feet above. He signaled to Gunnery Sergeant David Sinclair and Corporal Harlan Jenkins to fire their aluminum grappling guns, moving quickly, they unhooks the air hoses from their scuba gear and attached them to the pieces of equipment crucial to their mission, aimed and fired. With a sharp poof of compressed air, the three-pronged titanium hooks tow'n Kevlar ropes lugged their ladders upward and grabbed onto the bow's railing, the pair scurried up the lines and dropped the ladders down to the others.

Once on board Gunny Sinclair and Corporal Jenkins made a quick exploration of the area and signaled down to Skeeter, all clear. The rest of the blue team removed their fins and equipment, secured them to the ladders and lashed the ladders to the anchor chain to prevent the river's current from pull'n the ladders into view. Skeeter Macklin and the rest started their ascent. After they were on board, Skeeter whispered to the gunny, "Fan out and do what we've came here for," David Sinclair nodded *OK*, pointed at five men to follow him, they set out to kill Nazis and release the crew.

In the wheelhouse Billy Bob spoke with Oskar König: "We'll know in about four hours whether we set this town on fire or not." The Nazi replied, "The Reichführer will be most please if it happens." Billy Bob shot him a stare and said back: "Don't get things twisted, Kraut..., Oskar König looked at him, "... this is an SOS operation, you and your kraut buddies are here as side players and don't think there's going to be any crosses going on. I had to pop my best friend because of you Nazi fucks." Billy Bob had a twinge of remorse for having plugged Harry Reynolds and he wasn't in the mood for any bullshit. The Nazi flashed back to Harry lying on the floor and quickly decided he'd spoke out of turn about Karl K. Kussman's true intentions and he hoped he hadn't revealed too much with his comment, so he adjusted his statement: "I meant nothing on that order, it will be a glorious event that's all, and we are most aware whose operation this is, sir," he added the *sir* to give the impression he was a subordinate in this affair. Did it work?

Billy Bob regarded him for a moment and said, "As long as you and yours stick to the script things are cool, but try to flip it and it's going get ugly, so paid heed," and looked out the starboard window, the Boston skyline was on full blast. The city's streets glowed red and white as folks went about their lives going here and there all was as it should be. But the Bostonians had no clue of the lurking doom that sat innoxiously in middle of the Charles River; liquefied death was wait'n to announce itself in a mega kind of way. Cold LNG would become hellishly hot in a nanosecond, and then the skyline and all below it would be roast and broast.

The only force that could prevent the unthinkable was the Eradicators.

The Predator's laser cameras went hot and displayed the exact locations of the terrorists, sending their radar signatures to the blue team. Real time data was passed to them telling the whereabouts of the hostiles by Andrew Wong from the Barn providing eyes on info vital to the operation and mission success. He punched in the Predator as it loitered above the scene, even though the clouds had ganged up on one another and now hid the moon, the eye in the sky clearly saw through the overcast the thermal signatures of two Nazis glow'n red on the screen and he said in to his shoulder mic, "Two targets at your one o'clock," Gunny Sinclair and Corporal Jenkins with their backs against a storage tank crept forward and round the corner, the Nazis saw them, before they could raise their MP5's two darts from the jarheads' Amazon Commando .50 cal blow guns pieced their necks and they died instantly, the tips were laced with toxicants from poison dart frogs.

Sinclair and Jenkins quickly stepped up and pulled the bodies out of view stack'n them against storage tank one, and then they shifted to tank two; with their backs flat against it they moved aft seeking more targets.

Meanwhile to port Skeeter Macklin along with four others worked their way toward the stern ready to finalize any SOS or Nazis, no ifs, buts or however.

The shadows were closing in on Billy Bob.

In the wheelhouse he told Oskar König to take a tour of the ship to make sure all was well, he brought his heels together, raised his arm, "*Seil Heil*," before he could take that shit any further Billy Bob on the instant grabbed his MP5, pointed it at him say'n: "Didn't I just warn you about that Nazi *bullshit?* I guess you didn't hear me. Maybe you can hear *this*," pulled the trigger and stitched him with ten quick shots, Billy Bob's eyes were lit with the danc'n flames of hell, and he wore a shit eat'n grin say'n in silence: *Can you hear me now? I bet you didn't hear a thing, deaf son of bitch*, and kept on grin'n.

A few moments before Skeeter and his men had reached the fourth tank, he halted, his eyes toured the final approach to the wheelhouse just then flashes of gun fire went behind its windows. He said to the grunt nearest him: "Weaver you and Smith continue the search, I'll head to the bridge and take care of matters," the sergeant nodded, *OK*.

Skeeter Macklin hunched over and moved off to the steps that led to Billy Bob.

Who looked down at Oskar König and thought about all the death that came from his hand, it bothered him not, Billy Bob, the reaper himself stood there loving it up.

Skeeter reached the stairs, looked around and slowly started up heading for the one who attack his country and shot his ladylove. This was business on a personal tip.

Billy Boy looked out the port window and said in silence *fuck everybody, Robin Calhoun, Boston, the whole damn thing; I'm going out on top of the world.* Was he think'n about a hav'n '*White Heat*' moment? And bow out like Cagey did? Oh shit. *Not that.*

From his location at the Barn Andrew Wong told Gunny Sinclair: "Two hostiles at your eleven o'clock," the gunny X stepped up to the curve of the last tank, peered around the edge, his eyes made a complete circuit of the stern, looking up, down and all around he spied the remaining Nazis perched on the catwalk fifty feet above his position, he said to Corporal Jenkins: "Targets at our eleven, it's too far for a dart shot, bow shoot them," Jenkins from his shoulder removed his Excalibur Matrix crossbow, which he'd primed prior to their dive, the tips were coated with poison dart frog juice, he removed the point's tip protector and loaded the crossbow.

Following in their wake team members had started defusing the Semtex charges rendering them harmless.

Jenkins stepped about a half a foot to his left, just enough so he could see through the bow's scope two Nazis stand'n at the railing with their eyes parked on the skyline taking in the view, and they'd better enjoy it, for it's the last thing they will ever see.

He sighted in, squeezed the trigger a bolt shot from the bow, its flight was fast and furious it slammed into one Nazi's back, before he could scream out the poison instantly kick in and he slumped over the rail, the man to his left looked over, "You, OK?," and then shook him, when he bend down to examine his mate, Jenkins had reloaded, and now fired, the second bolt smacked into his partn'a and he too died there on the catwalk.

Many players in this drama now lay dead across a wide stage from here to Belize the only one left was the most dangerous, Billy Bob, the psycho who didn't give a fuck.

THE CLOUDS MOVED on and left pools of moonlight glimmer'n on the Charles River as Skeeter Macklin made it to the landing that led to the conclusion of this nightmare, his adrenaline was pump'n, he was revved up in severe kill mode, high on know'n the one responsible for so much grief was just inside the wheelhouse. He left his shooting iron on the deck armed only with a K-bar he was bring'n a knife to a gunfight.

This was going to be an up close and personal execution.

Billy Bob glanced out the window look'n out over the storage tanks, his eyes trawled to make sure the Nazis were on post, he panned here and there not seeing anyone, he grabbed his weapon and stepped to the door, *these assholes have disobeyed my orders.*

Skeeter now midway up the last set of steps froze when he heard footfalls head'n to the wheelhouse door, just before it open he swung over the side of the ladder and dangled underneath like an orangutan hang'n from a limp. There was a rattle of bolts at the stout door. It opened and yellow light sliced the darkness in two. The MP5's barrel eased out across the threshold with Billy Bob emerging behind it. The door closed, the dark return, his night vision hadn't kick in as he searched for the Nazis, he started down the ladder as Skeeter listened to him advance toward him five steps below. He waited until his right foot landed on the one at eye level then he outstretched his left hand and through the gap grabbed Billy Bob's ankle yanked it backwards causing him to trip and tumbled down, he yelped: "*WHAT THE FU...,*" as his weapon flew out of his hands over the side into the river.

Billy Bob fell head over heels, bounced off the landing and continued downward. Skeeter went after him on the underside of the ladder grab'n the steps as he went like a kid work'n a set of monkey bars.

Billy Bob came to a stop on the ship's deck he was dazed from the blows to his head. Skeeter Macklin reached the landing, swung himself up and casually stepped down the steps toward a clearly stunned Billy Bob. He reached up, grab the railing, struggled to his feet, looked up and saw Skeeter advancing toward him, "*WHO ARE YOU,*" he cried out as Skeeter clanged the K-bar against the railing. As he passed in front of the throw from the lamp that hung from the bulkhead, Billy Bob took in his face, his eyes went wide: "*MACKLIN.*" Skeeter remained silent the sound of approaching death echoed off the bulkhead. Billy Boy stumbled back into the wall and froze.

After neutralizing the Nazis Sinclair's team headed down into the tanker's interior to release the crew he told them to remain below deck until the ship was secured.

Then the team went top side.

A sliver of moonlight lit the corridor between tank four and the bridge, Billy Bob stagger stepped into the passageway seeking an exit. Skeeter arrived at the bottom of the ladder and kept com'n toward him. Just then Sinclair and his men appeared at his back any hope of escape was abandon. He stopped, looking around at his circumstance he knew the end was nigh. Skeeter Macklin halted about ten feet way and eyed him like a buzzard sizing up road kill. "Well if it isn't Billy Bob Broussard, we spoke earlier on the horn, I'm the man in charge..." he slacked jawed it, "... who's going to give you a two for one sale," Billy Bob's thoughts raced back to Georgia Brown's and him hollering the same out the window as he and Harry Reynolds roared off.

Now all of the Eradicators were on deck, they circled Billy Bob like Masai warriors surrounding a lion, in the middle distance car horns blared, play'n a street contralto as Boston went about its business; all was as it should be.

But things on board the tanker were still without a final resolution.

Skeeter Macklin flipped the K-bar over and over in his hand; he stepped inside the circle, the adversaries' face off resembled Danny Glover standing amid the Predators. Skeeter continued mov'n toward the one who almost took everything from him now he was going to mete out the final solution. Silence hung over the scene everyone waited for Skeeter to speak, finally with ice on his tongue he said. "You planned to destroy my hometown, you betrayed your country and you shot what I love most, happy I'm not," the glare that went from his eyes was as cold as an Arctic blast.

Billy Bob's head moved like a swivel search'n for an out. Skeeter kept flip'n the knife, "I'm going to kill you twice." Billy Bob: "Not if I kill you first," Skeeter: "Be original you fucking fuck - let's even things out, here," he threw the K-bar to him but his reflects weren't quick enough, he tried to catch it but missed and it clanked on the deck, as he reached for it, Skeeter Macklin said, "On guard," and kicked him in the face. The blow sent him onto his back he rolled over, pushed himself up, spat out a tooth and wiped blood off this chin. Skeeter moved back two steps to allow him to grab the knife; he did and crouched over in attack mode. Skeeter went defensive when he charged; he slid smoothly to his left, stepped outside his right arm, grabbed it and kneed him in the gut. Billy Bob let out a grunt; Skeeter slammed his elbow into his face. The sound of break'n bones rent the passageway, still holding his arm he turned into him, threw him over his shoulder and he crashed onto the deck, the K-bar fell out of his hand. As he laid there Skeeter stomped him in the chest, the air gushed out of his lungs. While he heaved trying to breath, Skeeter stomped him again, then bend down, straddled him, place his hands around his neck and squeezed. Billy Bob reached up try'n to break his hold, Skeeter increased the pressure staring into his eyes he told him: "You're turning blue you redneck motherfucker," and choked him until the light went out in his eyes.

Billy Bob Broussard was *dead.*

Skeeter Macklin used his fingers to feel for a pulse, none registered; he then did something astonishing, he started applying CPR to *REVIVE* him. He placed the heel of his hand in the middle of his chest, put his other hand on top of the first and interlaced his fingers. He compressed his chest, allowed it to recoil and repeated the process several times. He opened his mouth, tilted his head, lifted his chin, pinched his nose and sealed his mouth with his own and blew repeatedly. Billy Bob's chest rose and fell with each intake of air. After two minutes he gasped and the light returned.

When he regained consciousness Skeeter Macklin smiled at him. Billy Bob looked up the shock shone prominent in his eyes Skeeter waited a beat or two and said, "That's once," then picked up the K-bar, "This is twice," and plunged the knife into his chest. Billy Bob died again that night, like Skeeter told him it was a two for one sale. Skeeter wiped the knife on his shirt; stood up, grabbed him by the collar, drugged him to the side of the tanker, lifted him up onto the railing and then shoved him over the side. The body fell some eighty feet; there was a splash, then silence. Billy Bob wanted to go out with a bang but the noise he made was a splosh and sank to the bottom of the river.

Epilogue
Just Plain Dad

Washington

DAWN SEEPED INTO the sky as Jasper Bohannon's Codex went, he picked up and heard Mad Sam say, "Sir, mission accomplished, all the players are dead or accounted for." Relief washed over him the president said back, "Well done, General, well done."

THE SUN WAS well up now; it was Saturday and inside the Oval Office the POTUS stood at the window that overlooked the Rose Garden, where he reflected on the past month's events. It was here the night of his inauguration that smoke boiled over his nation's capital. His first day as president was one of anxiety, sadness and anger. Now those emotions were placed with happiness and satisfaction. He was content with the outcome of the SOS affair and elated that the country was safe and secure.

In the midst of all that happened, the president became the father of a new son, an event he couldn't fully enjoy because the county's worse crisis in over a hundred years needed his undivided attention. A rap went at the door, "Come in," it swung open and Carmen entered carrying little Randy Bohannon, the president turned, walked over to his wife, outstretched his arms and she handed him their son. He glowed with fatherly love as he crossed the oval rug and settled down on the sofa. He looked at his baby boy, reached for his bottle and began feeding him.

Jasper Bohannon was just plain dad.

THE NIGHT BEFORE as Skeeter Macklin and his team retook the tanker Scarlett O'Hara was whisked away from the Barn and transported to an insane asylum in the Virginia countryside where she was examined deemed to be criminally insane and incompetent to stand trial. She now sat in a Spartan cell, a far cry from the digs she was accustom to. Here in this lonely room, she was not upset or shocked, she was happy because she was free of Robin Calhoun and her evil ways.

Even though she was being held hostage in this concrete box, she was at peace knowing she'd never again be bottled up inside her body sharing space with that wretched Robin. She smiled as she twirled her hair around her fingers thinking how relieved she was no longer a prisoner of her evil sister.

Free at last. I'm free at last.

IT WAS LATE afternoon as the sun slid down the western sky. Mickey Stovall and the full contingent of Eradicators were outside the hospital waiting for Skeeter, Jessy and their baby to emerge. The men in their winter greens stood at ease but Mickey was decked out in full blues with a sword dangling at his side. Jessy along with the baby were due to be discharge any minute now. Skeeter after securing the tanker flew back to Dulles, jumped into his Vette and raced to the Barn to give Mad Sam a detailed report about the mission. When his narrative was finished the general burst into laughter and said, "Major I like your style, I like it a lot," and grinned. Skeeter told him: "If that's all sir I need to see Jessy and the baby," Mad Sam: "By all means, away you go."

A touch after four-thirty Mickey Stovall saw Skeeter Macklin and his family heading toward the door. Jessy sat in a wheelchair holding their baby as Skeeter pushed them down the hall, Mickey said: "Detail...," the men went tense, "...*Tent Hut,*" they snapped to, Gunny Sinclair stepped out of the ranks, right faced and smartly marched up to the door, swung it open as they came out with an entourage of nurses drafting in their wake. Mickey Stovall drew his sword out of its scabbard raised it to his chin and whipped it down to his side and the Eradicators threw up their salutes as they moved past heading to the waiting Vette. Finch opened the car door as Skeeter helped Jessy and Miracle in. Finch closed the door. Skeeter Macklin ran around, opened his door, looked over the top of the car saluted back and climbed in. Inside he looked at his wife and their child, smiled, put the car in gear, turn the key as they drew away Jessy said to him, "Honey, we need a bigger car," Skeeter said back, 'You're right boss," Jessy said right back, "Aren't I always," and they moved on.

IT WAS TUESDAY midday clouds wrapped the city in its shroud and an official silence settled over Washington concerning the SOS matter. But rumors have a thousand tongues; nothing started them wagging like the death of Jake Carlisle, the arrest of Robin Calhoun and the tragic suicide of Taylor Jackson. The headlines said one thing but in the small text things were masked in double talk. To simmer down the funk and quell the word noise the Justice Department issued an official statement debunking any talk of deeper meaning to what happened. Robin Calhoun the known Jack freak was so intoxicated celebrating their wedding night she accidently shot him upon his return seems she mistook him for an intruder. After she sobered up and realized what she had done, she wigged out and became a raving lunatic now confined at an undisclosed psychiatric unit for observation. Taylor Jackson had some unknown demons, such a pity he'll be sorely missed it was truly a dismal day in DC. Those were stories the public could swallow if the truth be known it would choke them to death. The truth would be too much to consume whereas the lies would satisfy and go down easy.

They couldn't handle the truth know'n a few good men kept the torch of freedom lit.

Jasper Bohannon sat in the Oval Office after holding his press conference; where the questions came fast and furious, *what about this* and *what about that* the president parried them with the ease of a musketeer. The attack on Washington was the work of hatriots whose motivate was unclear due to the fact they committed mass suicide by blow'n up their compound before the FBI could move in and arrest them. The cover up was less damning to the American psyche than the facts would have been, much less.

The sun finally came out and it was quite warm for February so two hours later Jasper Bohannon along with Mad Sam sat in the Rose Garden having finished lunch they now worked their beers. Chesty Puller and Smedley Butler were camped out on the lawn. The general said, "I have a gift for you,' the president said: "*Gift.*" He told him: "Something was missing here at the White House sir and I took the liberty to remedy that,"

Jasper Bohannon brows quirked, "What might that be?" Before he replied the general spoke into his smartphone: "Top bring him here," moments later the first sergeant came toward them carrying a puppy in his arms. He stepped up handed it to the general and took his leave.

The president smiled as he handed him his new bulldog, which immediately licked Jasper Bohannon's face. He said, "You're absolutely correct and you must have been reading my thoughts, I was considering getting a puppy now I have one, thank you very much, it's deeply appreciated." The general said: "You're most welcome sir." Just then the puppy spied Chesty and Smedley, he twisted in the president's arms, squirmed his way free, tumbled to the ground righted himself ran up and started *WOLF'N* at them. The president laughed and said, "He's a feisty one isn't it?" Mad Sam said: "He's got a lot of fire in him," Jasper Bohannon: "Now for a name," Mad Sam: "Can I suggest one?" The president said: "Why of course," Mad Sam said: "Howling Smith Mister President he was another tough Corps general."

Quoting Mad Sam Jasper Bohannon said: "I like it, I like it a lot."

Printed in the United States
By Bookmasters